ELTHEA'S PARADOX

BOOK THREE IN THE STORY OF ELTHEA'S REALM

JOHN MURZYCKI

WARNER TRAIL PRESS

COPYRIGHT

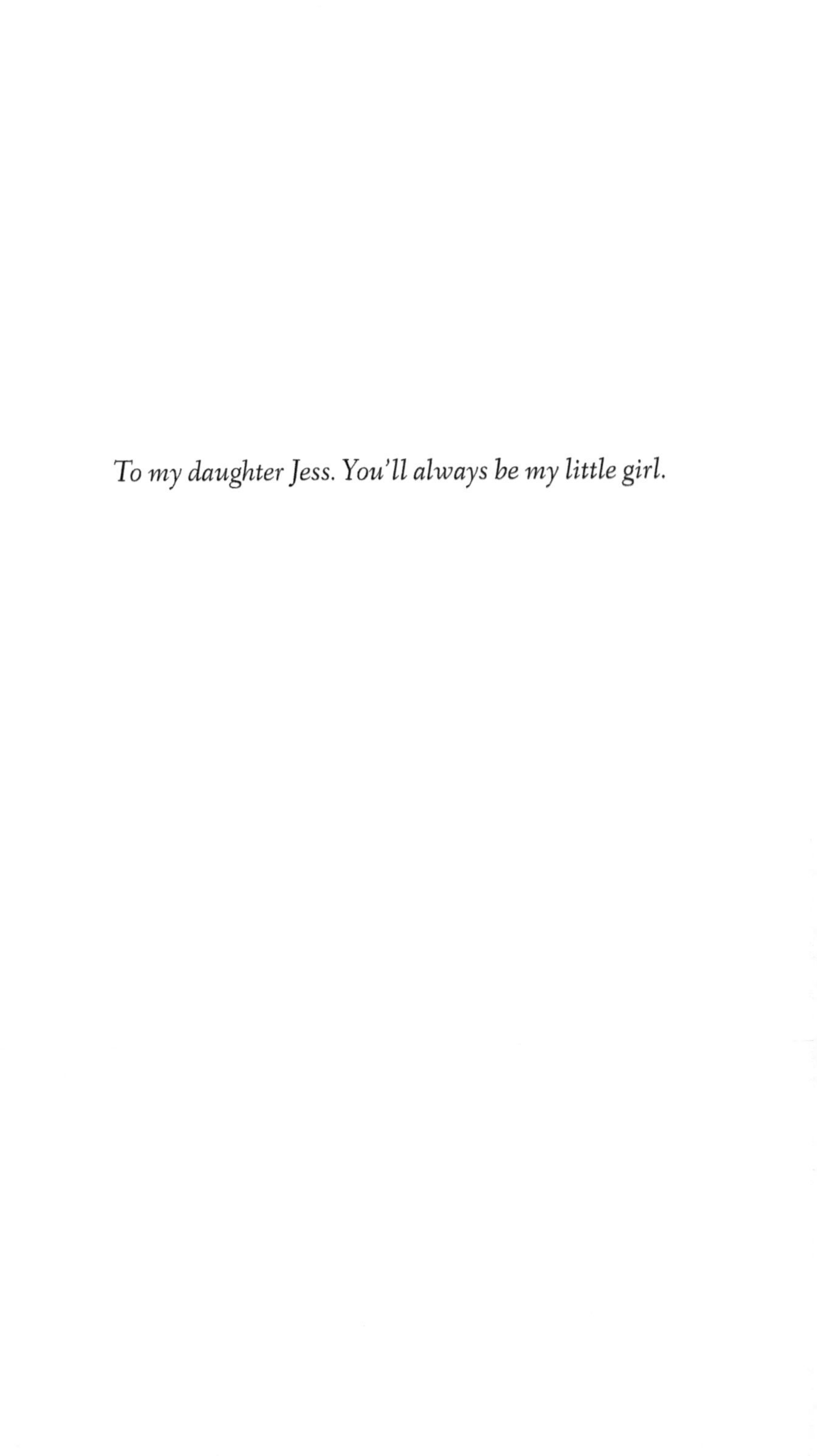

To my daughter Jess. You'll always be my little girl.

CONTENTS

FRIENDS IN PERIL

I opened my eyes, and just like that, all I had been trying to accomplish in the last hour fell apart, dissipating in the breeze like a puff of smoke. Why was I finding this so difficult? The meditative state I had been so eager to maintain slipped away.

The simple trill of a songbird had captured my attention. Was it the artificial bird sent by the Draas race? I had to find out.

Seeking the source of the melody, I gazed at the surrounding trees, which stood sentinel over my progress, or lack of it. A yellow songbird flittered from branch to branch. The feathered critter was a common variety in this area, not some fabricated replica of an actual bird. Its chirping became louder as if mocking me for my weakness.

Ignoring its taunts, I tried to clear my mind and once again focus on the life force of Elthea, as others called it. Like most days, I now spent my time trying to latch onto the mystical powers inherent in this land. My singular success had been to save the Valnorian race, an achievement I was beginning to think might have been a fluke. For me, Elthea's energies remained an enigma, as baffling as a language I didn't understand.

"You give up too easily, Earthfriend Philip," said Bevon, somehow sensing that my mind had wandered. Like me, he had been meditating with his eyes closed. "You must control your thoughts before you can hope to control the weave of energy that Elthea provides."

I grimaced, even though I knew he was only trying to help. But at times like this, his admonishment sounded more like hocus-pocus than anything helpful. By now, Quintia, Riyaad, and Ja'Krill had stopped their practice. At least I could be thankful nobody cast a disparaging comment. They wanted me to succeed as much as I did.

"You have it within you," Quintia said evenly. She was the most sympathetic, even when I was down on myself. "We witnessed your remarkable strength at the Ethwood tree when you foiled the Bot attack. None of us could have accomplished what you did."

And there was the crux of the problem. They felt I should be able to replicate my feat, even surpass it. All I needed was the proper training. But ever since that ill-fated day in the Sacred Forest, I still hadn't been able to achieve even the most rudimentary control over this power of Elthea. "Maybe what happened was a once in a lifetime gift," I offered, not for the first time.

Ja'Krill frowned. The Valnorians surpassed even the Astari at this supernatural craft. "It is not something that comes and goes like the weather. Once achieved, you only need to find the strength within you."

His race might be adept at calling forth Elthea's tonic, but he was even worse than the Astari when describing the divine energy rooted in this land. This training was becoming intolerable. "I keep telling you, I don't know how I did it before. I was in a rage at the time; I couldn't think straight. Hell, I was so angry I barely remember doing anything."

Ja'Krill and Bevon exchanged a glance. I waited for the discussion I knew was coming. They had already explained how important it would be to control this power when another Bot attack came. I mentally braced myself, expecting to hear it once again.

Surprisingly, it was the normally quiet Riyaad who spoke first. "If this was easy, we would have defeated the Bots long ago. You, Philip Matherson, alone among your human counterparts, have the ability." His eyes became unfocused. Almost as if speaking to himself, he softly added, "When the challenge becomes too onerous, remember Damek's last words. 'Keep alive your utopia.' That will only happen when the Bots are no longer a threat."

My eyes began to water, and I looked away, embarrassed that I had played a part in the death of my Astari friend. No one ever blamed me, except for myself. I would probably always feel the pain of his loss, a wound that would never heal.

"I can barely keep myself alive," I said bitterly. "Too many have died, good friends like Damek and our teammate Eric. How did words on a college term paper utterly dominate my life?"

The others shifted uneasily. They became uncomfortable when I fell into a melancholy mood. Bevon came to my rescue. "Events have a way of pulling us along, my friend. We can either do nothing but hang on for dear life, or seek to improve our plight. I know you well enough to understand that you will not remain idle while vile forces threaten us."

I turned my attention to the village of Haven in the distance. Inside its walls of thick stone lived the sole outpost of humanity in this distant world. I had never felt more at home than here. I couldn't help but wonder if we stood far enough away from it during these sessions, especially considering what happened during the battle against the Bots in the Sacred Forest. What if I unleashed that power again? But considering my lack of progress, I didn't think there was much likelihood that I could inflict that much damage again.

My eyes continued to scan the parapet on the walls surrounding the village, hoping to glimpse the two members of The Guard who had become my companions. Although everyone in the town treated me as if I belonged, I felt closest to Rae and Bryson. They seemed to understand me better than everyone except for the members of the utopia team. But Cassie, Matt, and Diane had returned to Earth. They were safe there while I remained here to figure out my capacity to wield this land's powers.

Bevon studied me as I gazed at the village. "The people of Haven have begun to depend upon you. I can see it in their eyes when they look at you."

I winced. "Great, another reason to rue my failure."

"You are not a failure as long as you continue trying," said Ja'Krill.

I glared at him, wondering if he was trying to provoke me, but he smiled innocently. Ja'Krill was one of the most kind-hearted people I knew. He had accepted me when other Valnorians considered me tainted by the Bots.

"If anyone can handle the burden, it is you," said Bevon. He stared at me with a fondness I remembered from our days on the Raised Isles. "So let us continue. Shall we, Earthfriend?"

He paused a moment to reflect. "Although..." He let the word hang as I began to think he might abandon this tedious exercise. "We could switch to training with a sword. You recall the sessions we had before departing Loralee. You learned much during those drills."

"I remember the bruises more than anything. You showed no mercy when we practiced with those damn wooden swords. No, we should definitely continue this. I'll try harder."

He rubbed his chin thoughtfully, as if I had made an important decision. We both knew he was putting on a show. It harkened to the days when my Astari companions were as much practical jokers as guardians. "Perhaps you are correct," he said gravely. "I must admit, you often make wise choices." He gazed at the sky. "We have many hours left until the sun sets. If you are sure about this, we can continue."

A sly smile formed on his lips. He had goaded me into giving the answer he wanted. "Try again, Earthfriend. Reach out with your thoughts and lightly tap into the arc of life that surrounds us. It is here for you to see and to use. Push all other considerations out of your head. Think only about reaching for the energy within you. Once you have achieved this step, we will practice how you can use it."

I silently groaned, knowing this was a waste of time. But I gritted my teeth and did as he instructed. Without the ability to harness the energy around us, I would never be able to protect the people I loved the most from the monsters who would destroy us.

THE AFTERNOON ENDED AS THE MORNING HAD BEGUN, with me no closer to controlling this land's energy, let alone learning how to use it as a weapon. I was tired and irritated, more with myself than my friends. "This isn't helping," I complained. "You must have some other practice we can try."

A twig snapped behind me, and Bevon turned his head. In a blur, he grabbed the collapsible lance at his waist, extended it with a snap of his wrist, and pointed it in that direction. The other Astari and Ja'Krill reacted at the same speed. I spun around to see a Bot standing a dozen paces away.

My muscles froze, unable to move. At nearly eight feet tall, the thing was enormous. It must weigh three hundred pounds, and all of it muscle. Its size alone would be enough to frighten anyone. But the hint of a face made it worse. It was more of a mask with no eyes or mouth, only the trace of where they should be, as if the creature was a reincarnation from an unfinished painting.

My stomach did a flip, realizing too late that I hadn't bothered to bring a weapon with me today. And now, I faced the cause of all the pain and suffering during the past two years. The Bots were responsible for killing Damek, for causing the deaths of Elderphino and Eric, and for brutally murdering so many Astari during the Midsummer Celebration. My friends fanned out protectively around me, each of them armed.

Even on a face without discernible eyes, I had the impression the Bot focused its attention on me alone. I wasn't prepared for the pounding in my head as the creature began forcing its words into my brain, whether or not I wanted to listen. I winced at the violation.

—*You are incapable of harming us, Philip Matherson. The time for the end of humanity is near. The final extinction of the human race has begun.*

I forced myself to remain standing against the hammering blow of words. Whatever happened, I would never give it the satisfaction of seeing me grovel at its feet. What was it saying? This reference to the final extinction sounded ominous. Before I could frame a response, the pounding continued.

—*We have your friends. You will join our cause and do as we say. Or else...*

The bottom fell out of my world. They had Cassie, Matt, and Diane? One reason I wanted them back on Earth was for them to be safe while I tried to puzzle out my capabilities. It seemed every decision I made was wrong.

"You're lying," I said, hoping my words carried a shred of truth.

—*We have important plans for you, Philip Matherson. It would be better if you came to our side willingly, but detaining your college companions ensures that you will comply. We have a new strategy to supplant your race. At one time, we needed you to convince humans they should yield to our superior intelligence. But humanity is already ours.*

It was bluffing; it had to be. My pulse quickened as I felt the bile rise in my throat. I would rather be dead than help these creatures. But I needed to remain alive long enough to free my friends.

Bevon's voice rang out. "You will never succeed! The Astari have stopped you before, and we will do so again. You think yourself invincible, but you are not."

If Bevon's intention was to anger the Bot, he succeeded. The creature moved toward him without hesitation and pulled out a blade holstered on its back.

Riyaad shielded me by positioning himself in front of me. "Stay behind, Earthfriend."

Bevon decided not to wait for the Bot. He rushed toward it with his lance held straight ahead. Bevon had the advantage of a longer blade, but the Bots had the speed and strength of a dozen Astari. At the last moment, before they crashed into each other, Bevon angled his lance to the left, intending to swing it rather than stab.

The Bot easily countered the feint, meeting Bevon's blade with its own and forcing the tip into the ground. The Bot twisted around and lifted its leg to stomp on the lance. The blow ripped the weapon from Bevon's hands.

I knew what would happen next. With Bevon momentarily defenseless, the Bot would stab him. I had only one chance to stop it. Using my anger and hatred, I reached for the weave of energy as I had at the home of the Valnorians. Maybe I needed to use my emotions as fuel to call upon the life force. Was that the secret? I needed to destroy this monster before it killed another of my friends.

I saw the scene unfold in slow motion. Bevon's face registered surprise that the Bot had jarred his lance free. The Bot swept its blade forward toward the defenseless Astari. I focused all my thoughts on killing the creature. The deadly energy would spill from my outstretched hands as it had once before. Bevon's life depended on me.

Nothing happened—no blast of energy, no superhuman force to stop the beast from murdering him. I watched in horror as the scene developed.

A buzz like the sound of bees split the air. An arrow appeared in the Bot's neck. The creature jerked its head up in shock. In quick succession, another shaft thumped into its chest. Both Quintia and Ja'Krill were reloading their bows. Riyaad took advantage of the opening and bounded toward the beast, plunging his lance into its mid-section. Green liquid flowed from the wounds as the Bot slumped to its knees. In another moment, it fell face forward on the ground.

I felt myself shaking. All that remained of the nightmare was the dead Bot's body with its dire warning. *We have your friends.*

2

AS GOOD AS DEAD

I felt a shortness of breath as I gazed at the dead Bot. *We have your friends.* How was I going to live with myself? I forced air into my lungs, hoping it would calm me as I tore my eyes away from the body.

Someone was ringing the town bell, three sharp peals, a long pause, and three more, the alarm belatedly warning of danger. We were still at the far end of the field that surrounded the town. Bevon had sent Riyaad ahead of us to alert the villagers about the Bot, and even now we could see members of The Guard scurrying out of the open gate to protect the workers in the fields just in case more Bots lurked nearby.

My stomach roiled as I thought about what happened. *We have your friends.* I couldn't stop replaying the words in my head. Could the Bot be telling the truth, or was it a bluff? "Bevon, what are we going to do?"

Misinterpreting my question, he answered, "In time, you

will harness the ability to draw upon Elthea's power. You need to continue your practice."

I shook my head. "No, I mean, what if it's true that they have Cassie, Diane, and Matt? How are we going to save them? I'm responsible for them."

He gazed back in the direction of the body. "We have to hope it was trying to deceive you. The other Earthfriends should be safe on Earth, at least safer than here." He gazed at me as if concerned about my health. "I am worried also, but we can do nothing right now. I do not trust the word of a Bot. They are devious and dangerous. He may have told you this as a ploy to capture you."

"But what if my friends have been taken? I have to save them. I have this power. That is, I had this power. I told them to go back to Earth without me. I should be able to do something." My voice rose to a squeak.

"Calm down, Earthfriend. Nothing will be solved by acting recklessly. We will do what we've always done and strike when the time is right." He thought about it for a moment and added, "I will not allow the Bots to inflict more harm."

I took another calming breath. I owed my life to Bevon. He saved me more than once. My trust in him was the only thing that helped steady me.

Ja'Krill was on my other side. "I understand your concern, Earthfriend. Honestly, I am more troubled by the Bot's assertion that the final extinction has begun. Any idea what it meant?"

I shrugged, glad to be thinking of something other than

my companions and what they might be going through at this very moment. "It's the first I heard of it."

He held my gaze. "The Bots may be devious, but they always have a purpose. This talk of a final extinction might be the beginning of a new scheme on their part. I wish I knew more about it. As for claiming they have your brethren, I side with Bevon. They may well be attempting to deceive you. Don't be so ready to believe what it said."

His words gave me a small ray of hope. It would be just like the Bots to capture me by having me surrender willingly. I chewed on this as we began walking toward the open gate of the settlement.

The villagers working in the fields had already begun making their way toward the safety of their fortress. The people here were fully aware of the dangers posed by the Bots. There hadn't been a full-fledged attack against Haven since it was built several decades ago. That didn't stop the village from maintaining a well-oiled militia they had named The Guard. Many of the residents still remembered the terrible destruction caused during the great war when the races united to fight against the Bots.

I was still lost in thought, my head bent low as we reached the gate, not watching where I was going when I nearly collided with Rae. She was storming out to reinforce The Guard out in the fields. A small knot of other guardsmen followed her. She carried a bow, adding to the collection of blades holstered at her waist and legs. Her shock of red hair, one of her most endearing qualities, was tied back on her head.

Her face softened as she looked at us, although it seemed

her eyes lingered mostly on me, though I couldn't be sure. She hesitated before telling the rest of her company to go ahead and that she would join them shortly.

"Riyaad told us what happened. Is anyone hurt?" She addressed Bevon, but her eyes took in Ja'Krill and Quintia as if to be sure.

Bevon shook his head. "Only my dignity for being unprepared. The others were forced to save me."

Her eyes widened as she shifted her gaze to me. "You used the power?"

I couldn't meet her stare. She knew how badly I wanted to recapture what I had done before. "No. I tried to, but I couldn't."

She tightened her lips but tried to put on a brave face. "I guess we'll fight them the old-fashioned way." She put her hand to the hilt of a blade at her side. Turning her attention to Bevon, she added, "The commander is on his way. I'm sure he'll want to speak with you. We're moving everyone inside the gates, at least for now."

I wanted to say it didn't matter. If the Bots were going to attack, the walls wouldn't stop them. But I didn't want to be responsible for any more deaths. It was probably best to be prudent. Besides, Russell, along with colleagues Tess Armstrong and Alan Sabrinsky, knew more about the minds of the Bots than just about anyone.

Rae lingered for a few more seconds, looking at me curiously before she moved away without saying more. How was it she could make me feel both uncomfortable and beguiled at the same time?

Once through the gates and inside the walls of Haven,

the area opened into a broad courtyard. Commander Russell Ingram stood near the steps leading up to the parapet as he spoke with a member of The Guard. When he saw us, he broke off and stepped in our direction. "Did you see more of them? I'm closing the gates as soon as everyone is back inside."

Bevon answered. "Only the single Bot confronted us. If there are more out there, we didn't see them. It is wise to be ready, but I do not believe that Bot was about to attack the village, at least not right now. It seems that he only wanted to convey a message."

As we spoke, men and women hurried in different directions across the courtyard. I imagined a similar scene was being replayed throughout the village. The greatest fear for those who lived in this outpost was that the Bots would someday attack.

"The Bot said they have my friends," I blurted. Russell knew who I meant. Cassie, Matt, and Diane had spent time with me here in Haven only a few months ago. I could see the concern in his expression. Before he could respond, I added, "And the Bot said something about a final extinction beginning."

The color drained from his face. Russell stood speechless as he processed this additional information. He shifted his attention to the fields beyond the open gate. "If that's true, we all may be as good as dead."

Russell wouldn't explain more about his terse warning. There were too many demands for his attention at the moment. "We should speak at length," was all he would say.

As I watched him leave, I decided I wanted to be alone, wishing for the quiet solitude I always sought when troubled. It was my escape, a space to ponder my situation, time to regain my purpose in life.

Everyone in the village seemed to have a task except me. Residents shuttered windows, others darted through the street as they went to one of the armories for a weapon. All of them were ordinary citizens who were typically bakers, blacksmiths, shop owners, or any other number of civilian duties. Right now, they were united against the common threat of an attack.

I knew the fortitude of these people. If necessary, they would fight to the death. Yet, it was me the Bots wanted, not them. Would they be the next to die because of me and my failure?

Bevon was at my side as we walked back to the small, three-story house with my room on the second floor. Ja'Krill, Riyaad, and Quintia had joined The Guard on the wall. I had told Bevon that he should help defend the village, but he remained adamant about accompanying me. I still had my doubts that the appearance of the lone Bot was the beginning of a plan to assail the village, but when the Bots made a decision, they didn't hesitate. The lone Bot had given me the chance to join them willingly. I knew their next step would be to take me by force. Either that or they would kill me.

A new thought clicked into place. If I weren't here,

maybe the Bots wouldn't attack the town. I made my decision and turned to Bevon. "Can you summon Arianell? I'm going back to Earth."

He let out a breath. "And you would abandon these people?"

"I can't help them," I said louder than I expected. I lowered my voice. "No matter how hard I've tried, I can't grasp the energies of this world. You know it as well as I do. I'm no good here, I can't protect anyone. And if I leave, there's no reason for the Bots to attack Haven."

As we walked, a man burst through an intersection in front of us. He ran with a blade held awkwardly in front of him. I wondered how many people would hurt themselves before inflicting any damage against a Bot. "I have to save her," I said. "Save them," I corrected.

His scowl deepened. "No matter what happens here, if they attack the village or not, these humans will only remember how you turned and ran when danger was at their door. Is that the legacy you want? Besides, I can't summon Arianell. She now answers to Elthea. I do not believe the Bots will attack us now. Never before have they done so. And finally, we do not know whether the Bots actually captured the other Earthfriends. Even if they have, you assume they are still on Earth."

I loved Bevon as a trusted friend, but in moments like this, I hated how he was always right. Without thinking, I bit off the words, "I have to do something. Don't you understand?"

"I realize you are upset, both about the Earthfriends and

your inability to master Elthea's energies. That is no reason to blunder forward without thinking."

I looked up at the white puffy clouds slowly drifting overhead. This world was much like Earth, with a sun shining down from a blue and white sky. But in other ways it was completely different, with its own laws of nature, so unlike those I had known before.

"Okay, we'll do it your way," I relented. "Just understand this, I will not let those bastards get away with holding my friends captive. Even if it means I have to sacrifice myself in the process."

Bevon looked at me, and for a moment, I didn't think he would respond. "We will find an answer," he finally said.

His voice was reassuring, but I knew him too well. The uncertainty in his eyes came through.

ALONE IN MY ROOM, I COULD FEEL THE SPECTER OF MY mistakes threaten to overwhelm me. I had thought I was so smart, able to outwit the evil that imperiled two worlds. But I had been played the fool. They were always two steps ahead of me. And now, I would pay the price, not with my life, but with the only person I ever loved.

My love had always been Cassie. From our time at Woodbery College through all our ups and downs, she was the one I cared about most. She, along with Diane and Matt, formed the foundation of my life. Nothing would ever be the same if I lost them.

I went to the small balcony that looked out toward the

town and gazed toward the wall that surrounded us. Everything looked calm. At least I didn't have the added pressure of conjuring a lightning bolt if we were under attack.

"Phil, can you hear me?"

I spun around, looking for whoever had snuck into my room.

It was empty.

I craned my head up and around to see if someone was standing on one of the other balconies or leaning out a window.

Again, nobody.

Stepping off the balcony back into my room, I inspected the small, spartan quarters to check if anything was amiss. It looked exactly the way it had when I entered.

"Great, now I hear voices," I muttered. "Can anything else go wrong?"

"I can hear you, Phil. It's me, Cass."

The voice was as clear as if someone had been standing next to me. I jerked my head to the side, half expecting to see her. She sounded sad, or maybe afraid.

My eyes darted wildly around the room. "Cass, where are you? The Bots said they have you? Are you safe?" I stopped to give her a chance to respond.

"Phil, we're scared. Matt and Di are here. I don't know where we are."

A crack of what sounded like static filled the room. "Stay calm. Tell me what happened."

Silence.

"Cass, are you still there? Can you hear me?"

No response.

I took a moment to replay the words in my head. Did I imagine this or did it really happen? I was tired from everything that happened. Maybe my desire to see her had pushed me off the deep end.

She said only a few words, but I knew from the inflection of her voice that it was Cassie. I had no doubt. *Phil, we're scared.*

My emotional morass receded as I thought about her. I would make the Bots pay for this if it was the last thing I ever did.

3

YOU CANNOT OUTRUN THEM

We gathered that evening around a large round wooden table in the corner of the public mess hall. The few candles cast dark, gloomy shadows, adding to the somber mood. Small groups of villagers lingered well past the usual dinner hour, as if taking comfort in the company of others. Typically, the massive hall would be bright with the glow of oil lamps, the rows of tables crammed with hundreds of ordinary citizens, and members of The Guard, everyone enjoying one another after a hard day of work.

Russel Ingram, Tess Armstrong, and Alan Sabrinsky—the team that had created the Astari, and inadvertently the Bots —were at the table, as well as Bevon, Quintia, Riyaad, Ja'Krill, and myself. The cook looked apologetic as he placed platters of cheese, breads, and cold meats on the table. "Sorry, my friends. With all the upheaval today, this is all we have."

Russell, always the diplomat, thanked him kindly, saying it was more than we expected. Once the server departed,

Russell furrowed his eyebrows as he regarded each of us around the table, lingering on me the longest. "This has been a difficult day," he said. "I suspect that's especially true for you, Philip. If indeed the Bots have captured your friends, well, I speak for everyone in Haven by saying we wish there was something we could do to free them."

I held my tongue about Cassie's visitation. Why give them a reason to wonder if I was going mad in addition to losing the skill to ply the powers of Elthea.

"Something else about what the Bot said today also bothers me," said Bevon. He directed his gaze at Russell. "What do you know about the Bot's plan for what it calls the *final extinction*?"

The commander hesitated, allowing Tess to respond first. "We heard them use that term once before. It was when we first came to this land." She paused to look at me. "I assume you still remember the history of our time on Elthea when we first came here?"

I considered asking her if this was a test, but I knew it wasn't a time for levity. "Of course," I nodded, hoping I did remember what Bevon had explained to me in the past. History wasn't my strong suit, but then again, what was?

"It was a confusing time for us survivors and our families," she continued. "And I do mean survivors. Left on Earth, many of us would have died within the year from a variety of diseases. Elthea gave us another chance at life. I accepted her offer, as did many others. The spirit of Elthea extended her overture to family and friends." Tess smiled, glancing between Russell and Alan. "We were told that our presence in this land would stop a conflict. Only later did we realize the Bots were puzzled by our appearance, causing them to hesitate. The pause in the fighting allowed the great races time to mount their final offensive."

I suspected she went through this brief summary for my benefit. The others at the table knew the history of what happened during that war.

"During that time, before the races launched their offensive, the Bots' curiosity got the better of them. They sent a small contingent to meet with us. That was when we first learned that the errant computer virus we had unwittingly unleashed on Earth had evolved into a physical form in this land." She glanced over at Alan. "Our good intentions had gone awry. Never would we have thought such a thing possible."

Alan shifted uncomfortably in his chair. "We understood that the code we had written on Earth was highly adaptable, but to see it evolve to a physical state was way beyond what we thought possible." He reached forward to grab the last piece of bread on the table, inspecting it as he considered his next words. "When the Bots existed as computer code, they were satisfied with unleashing havoc on Earth's networks. But then, when we saw their physical manifestation here in this land, we realized their agenda had evolved. We learned that they wanted to supplant humans on Earth and all the other races of Elthea. They truly believed they were superior to any other living race."

Bevon leaned forward in his chair. "Why did they explain that to you? What did they hope to accomplish by letting you know they wanted to become the master race?"

Russell responded. "That's a good question. I wondered

that myself many times since then. I can only presume they wanted to gloat about it. It was as if they had this secret. They needed to tell someone, and we were the people who would care most about what they said."

Alan shook his hand in front of him as if to disagree. "That implies they have human emotions, which they don't."

"What's your explanation, Alan?" I asked. "Why did they explain it to you?"

He hesitated. "I have two theories. The first is that they didn't care. It's possible that overthrowing humans was always their goal, and we never realized it before. Their psyche is hard-wired in a way that makes them determined to rule over others. It's a holdover from who they were before they became computer code. They couldn't deviate."

He remained silent, lost in thought until I asked, "And the other reason?"

Alan blinked as if coming awake. "They're overconfident. They carried that flaw since the time they first gained awareness on Earth's neural grid."

I frowned, not sure I understood. Seeing my reaction, he added, "If the Bots have a shortcoming, they believe in themselves without question. They believe in their core that their synthetic intelligence is preferable to the organic method of evolution. In their minds, reason and logic surpass all other concepts. As far as I can tell, they don't question or test their assumptions. They simply act. They have no soul to hold them back."

Alan's explanation made sense. They often acted too soon. "If they don't question themselves," I said, "maybe that's the one thing we can use against them."

I knew it wasn't much, but so far, it was the only weakness I could grasp onto.

I NEEDED TO BE ALONE ONCE I LEFT THE DINING HALL, a time to think without the company of others. Once outside, I said to Bevon, "I need to stretch my legs. I'm going to walk before turning in." Before he could respond, I added. "Don't worry, I'm fine inside the walls."

He reluctantly nodded. I knew, however, that he, or one of the other Astari, would still follow me at a discreet distance.

Tonight, the cobblestoned streets of Haven were eerily quiet, unlike most evenings when families or couples would be out. The life these villagers faced was a stark contrast to my previous existence on Earth. Before coming to Elthea, I had always taken for granted the ease of modern conveniences, as well as the benefits provided by all sorts of tech devices at my fingertips. None of that existed here.

For these people, life could be difficult. People here put in a hard day's work and never complained. Yet, there was a bond among these citizens I had observed nowhere else. If anyone could be considered an outsider, it was me. So it's strange that of all the places I've ever lived, this is where I felt most at home.

I had become familiar with my way around the town, so I had no trouble knowing exactly where I was. I also knew where I would eventually end up. Others in the village had their favorite places. For some, it was the pastry and pie shop, a preferred destination for families with their children. Many residents enjoyed visiting the public flower gardens that Tess had helped develop through the years to gaze upon their colorful displays, a pleasant contrast to the stone construction through the rest of the town. Some were partial to the Central Tower, standing five stories and the tallest structure in Haven with its unobstructed view of the entire hamlet and the fields beyond.

For me, I always spent my time on the wall. I was drawn to it like a moth to light, taking comfort in the view with the fields on the outside and the human village on the other.

Tonight, however, was different from other nights. The town was on a war footing because of the potential threat from other Bots, and a villager challenged me before I even made it to the top of the stairs. An armed sentry held his palm up. "Only members of The Guard belong here," he said gruffly. I tried to make out his face in the dim light of Halcyone, unsure if I recognized him. Judging by his clothing, which wasn't the standard dark garments worn by The Guard, he was probably an ordinary citizen pulled into duty.

"Don't worry, Sten," said another voice farther along the wall. As if to explain himself, he added, "That's Master Philip." He was one of the regulars from The Guard, although I couldn't remember his name right this moment. The first sentry seemed a little embarrassed at his error, as if he had made a grave mistake. He moved back toward his position and motioned me forward. I thanked Sten as I stepped up the final rungs of the ladder.

The watchman who had given the order turned and smiled as I approached him. He was a young man; it seemed they were all young, not nearly old enough to be defending a village from the danger of the Bots. "Rae's not on duty this evening," he said. Did he assume I was looking for her? Was I without realizing it? Maybe strangers knew me better than I did myself.

"That's all right. I just wanted to look around." I began walking along the battlement, but then I turned back to ask him, "What about Bryson? Is he standing watch tonight?"

"Aye, he's stationed on the south wall tonight."

I thanked him and began walking unhurriedly in that direction. I nodded or exchanged brief greetings as I passed those standing guard. Every one of them would give their lives to save the rest of the village. I should do the same. Bevon was right when he told me I was wrong to abandon them when all I wanted was to return to Earth to save my friends. But these were now my friends, and they were expecting more from me.

I would do what I could for them, but that didn't stop me from wanting to return to a simpler life when I wasn't responsible for an entire village. More than anything, I wished for a time when Cassie and I could look forward to the days in front of us with an existence free from the Bots. How did I ever become the person responsible for keeping everyone safe?

The answer, of course, was the stupid power of Elthea. Because I used it only once, and although I might never again, I had unwittingly become the defender of Haven. An apt epitaph for my tombstone might be: *Here lies Philip Matherson, if only he could have saved the village.*

"Hi, Phil," said someone from the shadows. I couldn't

make out the face, but I knew the voice belonged to Bryson. I moved toward him, glad to see him again. The young boy had matured considerably since I first met him many months ago when he was an awkward boy who always talked too much. Back then, he was the son of a baker who dreamed of becoming a member of The Guard. And now, although he was still officially in training, he had already surpassed the level of many other recruits.

I moved over to him and gazed out at the fields. "You managing okay?" I asked, after a brief silence, not sure how to start the conversation. In the past, I never had to think about what to say because he would always find something to talk about first. It was yet another measure of how he had matured in such a short time.

He shrugged as he continued to scan the fields outside the wall. "Mostly, it's just a lot of waiting around, standing guard, looking out at nothing. I try to tell myself it's the same as what I've done a hundred times before." He shook his head. "I know it's different now. We all realize it. With one Bot out there, chances are there're more. They've mostly left us alone during my life, except for that one storm they hit us with. But it seems they're back again." He turned his head to study me. "The real question is, how are you holding up?"

Should I give him a glib answer? During another time, I might. But now, it didn't feel right. Besides, like Rae, he had a sixth sense when it came to comprehending other people's moods. I tried to keep my voice even. "The truth is, I'm afraid. But not so much for me. I'm more worried about my friends. This morning, the Bot said he had captured the others." The voice of Cassie confirmed it, but I didn't want to explain that event right now.

He nodded knowingly. "We heard; everyone knows by now. Word travels quickly in this town. That's why I asked about you."

Of course he knew. I should have realized it. This was a tight-knit community.

I thought again about Cassie, Matt, and Diane, how they were holding up as hostages. I knew how I would feel. Bryson continued to look at me, expecting me to say more. I tried to put on a brave face, but my heart wasn't in it. My eyes watered, and my voice cracked. "I have to save them. I couldn't bear it if something happened to Cass. But I don't know how." I wiped my sleeve across my face, feeling foolish for letting my emotions betray me. He looked away, studying the landscape beyond the wall. "They're in trouble because of me," I continued.

He looked at me with a hardness in his eyes. "I don't know much about the Bots, but I know you put too much on yourself. You have a way of taking the blame, like that time you thought you tried to kill Cassie. The Bots were using you then. Maybe they're doing it now."

I blinked my tears away. "This is different. After the battle in the Valnorian Forest, the Bots know I can hurt them. They don't want me running free. And this is their way of stopping me. I can't just stand by."

He softened his voice. "Phil, none of us know what the Bots are thinking. But it may well be that they want all the members of your team, and it was easier to capture the others first. Now they're using them so you will surrender and make it easy for them to take you captive."

I wasn't sure if I believed him, but I didn't come here to debate. "What would you do? You and Rae always seem to have an endless supply of advice."

He laughed for the first time. "She's the one with the good ideas. I'm just a lackey trying to become as skilled as her."

"You're no lackey," I interjected. "You've helped me as much as anyone."

He held his head a bit higher. "We don't know each other all that well, you and me. But I believe you're a good person. In the end, you'll do what's right. You always have. That's who you are. We all understand you'll do the best you can."

He meant well, but here was yet another burden on my shoulders. This was what Bevon had said. The villagers had begun to depend on me.

How did I always manage to put myself in this position?

I took little comfort in speaking with Bryson. Most of the time, he would cheer me up by sharing a funny story or two. Tonight, a weight hung heavy on both of us. We each knew the Bots were coming. Would either of us be ready when the time came?

I left him to his task of standing watch while I walked alone through the empty streets of the town, lost in my own thoughts, wondering what I was going to do. All my life, I had been swept along by events, never able to chart my own direction. Another person might take better control of their life. But that wasn't me.

I looked down at my feet, not caring where I was going. One direction was as good as another, and I would eventually find my way back to my room for a night of tortured sleep.

"You cannot outrun them," boomed a loud voice from the shadows. "Even you must understand that."

I snapped my head up, surprised to see anyone out at this hour. What was more astonishing was the person speaking. He was attired in a gray woolen robe with a hood over his head. The garment was appropriate for the dead of winter, not a warm night such as this evening.

I hesitated, realizing I was unarmed. "Who are you?" I couldn't see his face, which remained hidden in the shadows of his hood. I looked to see if he carried a weapon, but folds of the robe covered his arms and hands.

"Who I am does not matter. What should interest you is that I can save you. The evil that spreads across the land will soon have you. Without me, you will be lost to us."

My mind raced. "What are you talking about? Save me? How? Why do you care?"

He slowly removed the hood from his head without answering. His skin was darker than mine, reminding me of a person who might have spent his life in the sun. The contours of his face resembled a human, but there were differences marking him as someone from another race. "We will meet again, Philip Matherson."

The person slowly dissolved and faded away. In moments, he was gone. I continued to stare at a blank wall for several seconds, too stunned to do anything else.

The clapping of running feet against the cobblestones came from behind. I spun around, expecting to see the stranger running at me from that direction. It was Quintia, her pink hair reflecting off the moonlight, the glint of a blade in her hand. "Who was that?" she said as she reached me, her eyes scanning the now deserted street.

"I don't know." I replayed his words in my head. *You cannot outrun them.* "He wasn't from here; he was another race. And he said he wanted to save me."

She stepped over to the spot where the stranger had stood seconds before and bent down to the cobblestones. That's when I noticed they were wet. The last of the snow left behind from his boots was quickly melting.

Quintia looked up at me with a frown on her face. "A foe or an ally?"

She wasn't expecting an answer; it was more of a question to herself. I felt sick, thinking again about what the figure had said. *The evil that spreads across the land will soon have you.*

Not for the first time, I wondered what I had ever done to deserve this.

4

THE WORLD WAITED

The spirited melody of birds chirping outside my window woke me at first light. The sound comforted me, giving me a measure of assurance that life would continue. Unlike my mood, the birds were untroubled by the demons, which continued to gain strength no matter how much I tried to stop them.

For some reason, I thought back to a time that seemed so long ago, another place, another world, far from the mythical land of Elthea and this village of Haven. The time of day was much like now, the predawn sky barely illuminating the darkened room. Cassie lay next to me, our naked bodies close to each other, the soft curves of her chest up against me. We had made love during the middle of the night, both of us feeling the first stirrings of a bond that would grow stronger. But then one day not long after, a violent and inexplicable act on my part would nearly rip us apart.

But on this particular morning, unaware of what was yet to come, we were blissful in the knowledge that we had survived an ordeal that nobody should have ever faced. Our adventure in the land of Elthea was over; we had returned safely, at least some of us had. The only comfort was that Cassie and I had found each other amid the suffering and the killing and the horror.

"Promise me," she whispered so softly I wasn't sure if she spoke the words or it was the sound of her breathing. I opened my eyes to see that she was looking at me. A soft smile came to my lips, thinking she would say something about our lovemaking. "Promise me you'll never leave me behind if they come after us again."

I came awake. "What are you talking about, hon? Nobody's coming after us."

She furrowed her eyebrows, one of her expressions I was beginning to cherish as each day passed. "You don't know that. And I'm not as strong as you are. If I falter or lose my way, swear you'll come for me. I'll do the same for you. We're in this together."

The scar of what we had endured was still fresh in our minds. I thought about telling her again that we had nothing to worry about; the Bots were gone because of Eric's sacrifice. But I knew it was a hollow wish. I slipped my arm around the small of her back, pulling her tight against me. "I have you, I always will. Don't worry ever again."

Her eyelids grew heavy, slowly closing. After a moment, I thought she had drifted off to sleep. I was about to do the same when she spoke again in a weak voice, her lips so close to me I could feel the warmth of her breath against my face. "Promise you'll come for me."

My heart went out to her. Never before had I loved

someone so strongly. "I promise I won't let anything happen to you. It's you and me, side by side forever."

Her eyes had closed, her face softening. After a moment, her breathing became more regular. I wasn't sure if she remained awake long enough to hear my answer.

We never spoke about that conversation. In the harsh light of day, the fears and insecurities discussed in the cover of darkness seemed too painful. We still worried about the Bots, even during the best of times. To dismiss them entirely would be reckless. We talked about those monsters on rare occasions, but we didn't want to tempt fate by dwelling on them too long. We had a new life to build, and we approached it as any new lovers would, with the prospect of good days yet to come.

And now her worst fear had come true. The Bots had taken Cassie, and I was powerless to help her. My promises and pledges amounted to nothing. How was I going to live with myself?

I sat on a stone bench set among the plants and flowers in a section of Haven known only as the town garden. The morning was still early, but I wasn't alone. A half-dozen villagers were already working their plots of land, tilling the soil, pulling weeds, or picking one or another vegetable that had ripened.

I had spotted Ja'Krill shadowing me from a distance, his turn to stand watch over me. He somehow knew my moods and understood I wanted to be alone right now. Otherwise, he would likely be at my side with us enjoying each other's fellowship. He realized more than the others I needed time to think, time to steel myself for more arduous days that we knew were coming.

Looking around, I noted the surrounding view, especially the similarities of the sights and sounds that resembled my time on Earth. Here, the splendor of life surrounded me, reminding me of home. I allowed my thoughts to slip into the illusion that nothing had changed from my prior existence. The buzzing of tiny insects permeated the air as they flitted from flower to flower; delicate birds in a rainbow of many colors chased one another from tree to tree; the smell of recently turned loam filled my nostrils. All of it was as life should be.

"They told me I would find you here," said Russell Ingram from behind, interrupting my reverie. He came over and sat next to me on the bench.

I was mildly annoyed at the intrusion, but also troubled that he had sought me out. "Commander, is everything all right?" I asked, wondering if there were some signs the Bots were about to attack.

He must have noticed my concern. "No, all is fine. Well... as fine as you might expect considering that you ran into a Bot yesterday." He looked down at his hands as he rubbed his thumbs against each other, a nervous habit I had seen from him more than once. "The reason I'm here is to discuss the defense of the village."

I tilted my head. "I'm no military strategist. Why ask me?"

"No, I suppose that's not your calling. But Quintia told

me what happened last night with the stranger. It's bad enough that the Bots might come at us from outside the wall, but if someone can simply appear and attack us from within, I don't know how we protect ourselves. I need to hear it from you. Do you believe this outsider is a threat or not?"

I looked at him for several seconds, not sure how to answer. "I don't know what to believe, and that's the truth. But I'll say this, I don't think he's interested in Haven. It's me he wants, and whether it's to save me or destroy me, I'm not sure."

He nodded absently, accepting my answer. However, the worry lines on his face remained, and he continued to fidget with his thumbs. Even though he must have a million responsibilities, especially now, he remained seated. I suddenly felt sorry for him. All this time, I was only preoccupied with myself and my troubles. I never considered the plight others faced. Even worse, all of this was because of me. I'm the one the Bots wanted. "I'm sorry," I said, a catch in my voice.

He cocked an eyebrow. "For what?"

I shrugged. "Everything. I'm the cause of all your problems. If I had never come here, the Bots would have left you alone, as they always have. Everyone would be safer if I never existed."

"They would never leave us alone," he spat the words, suddenly angry. "I knew it was only a matter of time until they came after us. Tess and Alan understood it. If anyone should be sorry, it's the three of us. We were so young and foolish when we unwittingly opened Pandora's box." He scrutinized me for a moment longer. "You, on the other hand, are doing what we should have done long ago. You're trying to end their reign. And for that, you have my undying gratitude."

"Don't thank me yet. So far, I've managed to mess up more than I've helped."

He smiled, and his shoulders relaxed. "I admire you, Philip. Trying to save the girl you love." He gazed at the residents working the gardens around us. "Unlike Tess and Alan, I never married. There are times I regret it, seeing how they've settled into loving relationships. The love of my life is this village, at least it has been since it was built. I owe it to the people here."

I heard the laughter of children in the street beyond these grounds. "They admire you, I can see it when they look at you. They understand what you've done for them."

"Maybe, but I never wanted this job. Tess is the one who should have the title. She was always our leader. We would follow her anywhere, even to another world. But after her sickness, she didn't want the responsibility of running a village, even after she had been cured. It's too bad. She would have made a better commander than me." He grunted. "And as for Alan, well, he's brilliant and an exceptional person, but even he recognized the last thing he should do is take on the burden of managing a village. He was never interested in the details and minutiae of running anything, let alone an entire town. Writing code was his thing, and he did it well back when we did that sort of work. So, you see, I have this job by default." He blinked, as if realizing he had rambled for too long.

At that moment, I felt as close to him as I ever had. "For what it's worth, I don't think anyone else could have done more for these people than you. I've always thought of Haven as a fledgling outpost of humanity. You've done a remarkable job keeping this settlement vibrant and alive."

He patted me on the shoulder as he stood to leave. "I appreciate your kindness. And thanks for suffering my aimless discourse."

He took a few steps away, the resolve and assurance back in his stance. Then he turned. "Get her back, Cassie and your friends. Do it for love. Don't try to do everything by destroying the Bots, at least all at once. First, act on what's in your heart."

He walked away, head high, the picture of authority, leaving me to wonder if I could ever be as confident.

THE EARLY MORNING WANED, GARDENERS HAD COME AND gone, yet I remained. Struggling with my internal demons, I wrestled with how to save my friends and how to help the people of Haven. But mostly, I wondered if I had the fortitude of Russell. He understood the part he played in the life of others. I had no idea of mine.

I was no closer to finding a solution to any of my problems. Feeling defeated, I was about to move when a sparkle of sunshine in the middle of the garden caught my attention. At first, I thought it was a reflection from one of the tools used by a villager.

The brightness lingered, expanding to the size of a large shrub. I stepped closer to see it better. Could it be the stranger who had mysteriously appeared last night? I stumbled back a few steps, reaching for my lance, which I had remembered to take with me today.

A ripple of astonished gasps and the clink of dropped tools from the others in the garden told me they could see this as well. Before I knew it, Ja'Krill was at my side, his blade already drawn. "I won't let this charlatan get away so easily this time."

We stood ready, waiting for the mysterious figure to appear once again. The indistinct ball of light gradually became the image of a person. But it wasn't the hooded stranger. I felt a catch in my breath as the likeness of Cassie formed.

For a moment, she appeared puzzled, as if not sure what was happening. Then a weak smile creased her face. "Phil, it's me. Can you see me?"

My throat felt dry, my mind a jumble of emotions. I tried to frame my words without babbling. "Yes, Cass. I see you. Where are you?"

She winced and then rushed her words. "I don't know. We were together, with Di and Matt. Someone might have slipped something into our food or drink. Either that or put a spell on us. It knocked us out, and we woke up in this place, a chamber or something."

"Stay calm, I'm going to find you. Do you have any idea where you are?"

She shook her head, her eyes frantically sweeping back and forth. "I don't know how long we can talk. It must be the Bots. It's the only thing we can figure out. But we haven't seen them, we haven't seen anyone. They slip food and water to us through an opening."

I felt a stab of frustration. "Do you know if you're on Earth?"

She looked bewildered, and my heart went out to her. She appeared to be on the verge of sobbing. "I had thought we were, but now that you ask, I don't know."

I tried to console her. "We'll figure this out." I wanted to ask her more, say something witty to bolster her spirits. But the image of her face lost its consistency as it dimmed and broke apart. "Cassie, stay with me," I shouted, hoping she could still see me. In another second, her vision was gone, leaving only a wisp of smoke carried away by a light breeze.

I made a sound that came out something between a grunt and a sob. Ja'Krill looked at me with a sadness I had seen on his face only once — the time he had lost his entire family because of the Bots. "Stay strong, my friend," he whispered. "You will win them back. I swear, if it's the last thing I do, I will help you."

My legs felt leaden as Ja'Krill helped me walk away from the town gardens. I wanted to be out of public view, to curl up in my bed in a fetal position and forget all this. I was incapable of saving my friends; everyone must realize it. Ja'Krill urged me forward, just as I had implored him to do after the loss of everyone he had loved.

The villagers in the garden who had witnessed the appearance of Cassie watched silently as we exited, sadness in their expressions over my plight. Yet, there was something else in the way they watched me. They held their heads high in a sign of respect; they trusted me, believed I would over-come whatever obstacles the Bots placed before me. They told me as clearly as if they had spoken out loud: I will rescue my friends and protect the village.

It was too much. I was cut from a different cloth. One thing I was sure of, I was no hero. The savior of worlds was never part of my hopes and dreams. Hell, I couldn't even save myself. Happiness eluded me for many years after college. How could I ever hope to succeed at protecting anyone, let alone worlds?

Just as we reached the street, the town bell rang. Three bells, the warning for danger. Ja'Krill said nothing. We both knew what the signal portended. Lives were in the balance, and I had nothing to offer to change the outcome.

We broke into a run as Ja'Krill led the way with me following on his heels. He made his way to the closest section of the wall. Everyone I passed wore an expression of panic on their faces, even as they responded to the warning by closing shops, shuttering windows, or racing to the armory.

Ja'Krill took the stairs two at a time toward the top of the rampart, urging me to keep pace. We gained the top and looked out over the battlement, my insides clutching at the sight.

Out on the horizon, miles away, the blue sky with its puffy white clouds ended. It was as if someone had taken a pencil and drawn a jagged line across the heavens and replaced the other side with a blackness darker than any storm clouds. The air around Haven became deathly still. Nothing else mattered now as the world waited to discover what would take place in this village of Haven with the only vestige of humans in the land.

A percussion of thunder rumbled from far away, a sound so low I felt it on my skin as much as heard it. I knew it was the sound of death, and it was coming for all of us. Any hope I once had fled.

5

WHAT WAS ONCE SO MIGHTY

The next day, I made my way to the spot on the wall where Rae stood watch. Outwardly, she appeared relaxed, but this was only an illusion. She was a fighter at heart, aware of the danger and ready to deal with any threat, as she scanned the horizon. I noticed she gripped the hilt of one of the blades at her side, maybe a subconscious gesture to reassure herself.

She turned as she saw me approach, resting her back against the battlement. "Ugh, this waiting is the worst part. At least if I were fighting..." She let the words trail off, not wanting to hasten what we knew was going to happen.

I thought about the Bot attack in the Valnorian forest with the layer of ice killing everyone it touched. A simple blade did little to stop it, and I knew this would be much the same. "The Bots don't play by our rules," I said. "Don't expect a fair fight. When the time comes, tell me you won't do something stupid."

She eyed me warily. "The only stupid thing I've ever

done is try to save you from yourself."

She spoke lightheartedly, but with the miasma of despair hanging over us, her words felt hollow. "You haven't always seen me at my best," I countered.

"Hmm, I should say not."

Not that long ago, I had been lost in despair after I had tried to kill Cassie. This young soldier, more than anyone, had helped me find a way out. It was her concern for me at a low point in my life that cemented our friendship. I nodded toward the horizon. "My point is, this is not something we can fight with blades or bows and arrows."

"We can kill Bots with a blade." She jerked her head at the oncoming darkness. "All this is just window dressing."

Despite her bravado, Rae's guarded emotions couldn't hide a young girl with all the insecurities and misgivings of any person her age. We were far from Earth, a place she had never seen. But her humanity came through. I wanted to protect her, but my self-doubts were always in the way. Seeing the weariness in her eyes, I asked, "How long have you been on duty? Maybe you should rest before they attack."

I might as well have asked her to join the other side. "I'm a member of The Guard," she responded coldly, as if that was answer enough.

My heart went out to her. Like everyone else in Haven, no matter what the odds, she would fight to the death to protect this community.

A dozen paces away, Bryson raised his voice as he barked instructions to the untrained citizens on the wall. Blacksmiths, bakers, cooks, and many others had armed themselves and taken their place next to The Guard. Rae observed him for a moment while I tried to read her expression. "He's come a long way in a short time," I said.

She nodded, still looking in his direction. "Yes, but he's untested and I worry about him. I'm not sure he's ready for this, but he has it in his gut that this is his calling." She grunted. "Reminds me of myself when I took the pledge. It was all I ever wanted in life."

"It must run in your blood. From what I've heard, you are much like your mom when she was your age."

Her face softened at the mention of Tess. "She blames herself for the Bots. But hearing her recount what happened back then, I don't believe anyone could have expected this."

Many years ago, Tess, Alan, and Russell developed the antivirus software that ended up becoming the Astari, while the failures became the Bots. Each faction evolved into a synthetic life, each so different. "Who could have expected that another form of life might one day threaten humans?" My eyes were drawn to the coming darkness. "And here they are, slowly putting a noose around our necks. They could have attacked quickly, but they prefer this drama, a slow torment. They might consider themselves the replacement to humans, but in this regard, they have only the worst of human attributes."

Running out of words, we watched the black sky approach as the afternoon wore on, unable to keep our eyes off it, yet knowing there was nothing we could do about it. An irrational dread pulled at me; this was something nobody could fight. The air became stifling, weighing us down with an unseen presence. The darkened sky slowly made its way toward us, and after a time, even those standing on the streets of Haven could see it without needing to climb to the top of the wall.

I remained on the rampart, hoping against hope that when the time came, I could somehow turn the tide of battle in our favor. If not, the Bots would take me and force me to do their bidding. Their only interest in me—in any of us who were members of the utopia team—was to convince the people of Earth to accept their perversion of life.

Death might be my better option.

ONCE THE DARKNESS REACHED THE SPACE OVER HAVEN, the heavens transformed from inky blackness into a roiling mass of deep red hues. It looked to me like swirling rivers of molten lava floating above us.

If Rae still considered this display window dressing, no one else in Haven did. Men and women of The Guard cast fearful glances toward the sky while they bent a little lower to the ground, as if the atmosphere itself would soon engulf them in the fire. Given all I had seen in this land, I wondered the same myself.

Out beyond the fields surrounding the village, the howling cry of new atrocities cut through the air. Misshapen figures, barely visible as they roamed farther away in the woods, waited and bided their time until the moment was right. I tried not to look there, not wanting to see what awaited us. I put my forehead against the stone, relishing its coolness and firmness.

"What the hell is he doing here?" Rae asked as she looked along the parapet. I jerked my head up and turned in the direction she was staring. Of all people, Alan Sabrinsky was walking toward us. He kept his head down, either because of the danger from the Bots beyond the battlement or because he was afraid of tripping on some unseen obstacle. His rapid pace gave him the appearance of a man on a mission, although he usually seemed that way because of his obsessive preoccupation with one or another idea.

Watching him approach, I suddenly felt sorry for him. Tess had often explained how brilliant a software programmer he was on Earth; she claimed he was much better than herself or Russell. Now, he filled his days attempting to be creative in a world with no technology. He tinkered with inventions, which I usually referred to as contraptions, although not to his face.

Rae moved to intercept him before he passed us. "Mr. Sabrinsky, it's not safe up here. You should be at one of the secure halls that Russell arranged."

He looked up and blinked, causing me to wonder if he was even aware that he had been walking along the rampart. But then his eyes shifted toward me, and a new intensity blazed. I felt my body stiffen. Alan could be comical at times, but when he spoke, his words were always relevant.

"There's something you must know. Nothing can stop them."

I felt lightheaded. "I don't understand. What do you mean?"

He waved his hands in front of him as he often did when trying to make a point. "I ran the analysis in my head. From the very beginning, even before they became code on our networks, they always evolved. They will adapt to their environment no matter what you throw at them."

"I have nothing to throw at them." I heard the hysteria rise in my voice. Like the rest of the village, he assumed I would somehow recreate what I had accomplished in the Valnorian Woods. "But even if I could, what are you suggesting? Should we stand by and let them walk in here so they can kill everyone?"

He looked as if he might cry. I had never seen him so distraught. "No, you shouldn't do that." He wrung his hands. "I am trying to provide you with information. You must understand, the more you try to destroy them, the closer they advance to the next phase in their evolution. You can win in the short-term. You did before. But that won't help you, or help us, in the long-run. They will survive. They have before, and they will continue. And all the while, they will garner other resources, as they're doing here." He shot a glance at the blood-red maelstrom above us.

My eyes were wide as I tried to grasp his meaning. I so wanted to dismiss his rantings as those of a crazy scientist. But that would be a mistake. A nugget of what he was trying to explain sank in. Maybe I had already understood. "What can I do?" I looked at my friend Bevon, who stood near as he absorbed Alan's words. My Astari friend understood his meaning.

Alan licked his lips. "Put your trust in the human capacity for ingenuity and compassion. The Bots may seem like the devil to you, but they were once alive. They existed just like you and me, not as they are now. They have both the light and darkness within them. Bring the good part back into their souls."

I began to think he was mad. Was I foolish believing he could offer anything of value? "Can't you understand? They have my friends. I don't give a damn about any of this crap."

His head slumped, and he looked down at his feet. For a second, I thought he was going to either cry or turn and walk away. Instead, he slowly lifted his head and looked me in the eye. His face hardened. "Remember this: we're perched on the edge of a blade. One direction brings something astonishing. The other leads to a horrible future for all humans. Like it or not, I fear it all comes down to the choices *you* will make. Whatever you decide, you must remember what I've told you."

Alan slowly turned to walk back in the direction he had come, his words ringing in my head. *It all comes down to the choices you must make.* I knew the stage was set. The setting for the end of all things.

WHAT HAPPENED NEXT WAS A BLUR. MY THOUGHTS were still on Alan as I tried to grasp the meaning of his words. The world around me fell away as I remained lost in my thoughts. But urgent shouts and the clang of the town bell ringing three times in warning tore me from my brooding.

I looked out over the battlements, my hands grasping the cool stone. The garish light from the burning sky cast an evil glow onto the fields around Haven. What I saw made no sense. The ground itself had transformed into a liquid, rippling in waves. It looked as though it had come alive, and like the Bots, was about to attack us.

Everyone here was going to die. I could feel it in my bones. We couldn't fight this any more than we could fend off the oceans. The Bots could throw anything at us with impunity. Humans were no match for this deity. All the human civilizations that had risen and fallen meant nothing now. We were at the end of our rule. It was over.

Deep remorse washed over me. Here I stood, alive to witness the beginning of the end. Our society would crumble, and I remained the only person with the skill to prevent humanity's downfall. At the end, when civilization needed it most, my prowess failed me. I had lost my ability to draw upon Elthea's source of power.

Regardless of Alan's warning, I longed for the power to smash this foe. It was my only hope. A voice deep inside urged me not to give up. For the millionth time, I reached for the energy, hoping that maybe this time, I would find the strength to fight back. My thoughts again drifted back to the Valnorian forest, a time and place I could freely draw upon the destructive power needed to stop the Bots and their weapons. I closed my eyes and concentrated as Bevon had trained me.

I felt nothing, no shred of energy to stop the churning ground. I knew our enemy wasn't far away, yet I felt only a barren emptiness.

"Off the wall," someone from The Guard was shouting.

I took one last look out beyond the battlement. The ground continued to swell up and down as if it were an ocean. The surges had nearly reached the base of the wall.

Only a few more feet before the swells would advance to the solid stone surrounding Haven.

Two sets of sturdy arms pulled me away from the battlement. One on each side, as they held me tight, lifting me off the ground as they rushed me toward the stairs. Rae held one arm and Bryson the other. Why were they moving me away from here? I twisted my head to see Bevon and Ja'Krill in back of us, with Quintia and Riyaad behind them. The other members of The Guard, along with the civilian reserve, were all scampering down the stairs.

I tried to gain my footing, but Rae and Bryson had a firm grip, taking the stairs down to the courtyard below. Like the others, we moved to the center of the plaza, away from the wall and the buildings surrounding the courtyard. Only then did they loosen their hold on me.

The Stonewraiths had built the wall surrounding Haven to withstand an assault from virtually any opponent. But even they could not have foreseen that the solid underpinning of the ground could someday turn to liquid.

Just as the last of the sentries stepped away from the wall, a terrible cracking, rupturing noise split the air. The base of the fortification began to undulate, leaving gaps in places between the soil and the bottom of the wall as the liquid ground rose and fell. The dreadful sound of crumbling stone continued for long moments. It was a testament to the skill of the Stonewraiths that the wall lasted as long as it did against this onslaught. Everyone in the courtyard held their breath, transfixed at the ghastly power. Never could they have prepared for an attack as intense and unexpected as this.

The splitting noise grew louder. Fissures along the face of

the wall opened. This wall was the only protection against outside danger. It had been as sturdy and as enduring as any defense.

Then, a section of the wall could not withstand the ripples at its base. It began to crumble. And once started, the rest of the wall lost its consistency. Entire portions fell into heaps of stone and dust. The enormous main gate, constructed of wood, lost its support structure. It wobbled for several heartbeats as if not sure what to do before it fell outward in one piece with a thundering impact.

Sections of the wall to my left and right fell to the ground. The echo of crashing stone continued as the entire wall encircling the town collapsed. What was once a mighty structure was now rubble.

Dense clouds of white dust wafted up from the destruction. Villagers began coughing from the irritation of fine powder. I pulled my garment up over my mouth and nose.

Everyone in the courtyard stood awestruck, unable to believe this had happened. Never could they have imagined the wall would fall so easily. Once it had finished collapsing, the liquid ground once again turned firm, as if it had accomplished its purpose.

Haven was now defenseless. The door was open, and the safety of the wall had been reduced to wreckage. I knew what would come next. They were here for me, and nothing was going to prevent them from their mission.

Another cog in the wheel of the Bots plan was about to slip into place.

6

WE ARE ALL GOING TO DIE HERE

The cry of wild animals cut through the air, dispelling the eerie silence that had settled over Haven after the wall had collapsed. Dust slowly cleared, and with it, a new horror became visible in the fields outside the village.

Packs of beasts scampered aimlessly in every direction. Many ran on all fours, and a few sprinted upright on two legs. Some had hair covering most of their bodies, while others were more reptilian-like creatures. Some attacked each other for no apparent reason, savagely clawing or snapping at each other in a crazed struggle. Dead bodies already scattered the ground. The blood-red sky above made the spectacle seem unreal.

This was a nightmare from hell.

As bad as it was, The Guard had trained for this purpose. The animals were dreadful, but not otherworldly to them. Soldiers began shouting commands, and troops took up new defensive positions around the rubble.

Even as the militia scrambled to prepare, hideous beasts had already crawled their way to the tops of stone piles where they lurked, looking down at us but not yet attacking. I understood why they had paused.

Another, more powerful force would soon arrive.

Bevon was on one side of me while Ja'Krill stood close on the other. Rae and Bryson positioned themselves defensively in front of me, with Quintia and Riyaad not far away. Each of them believed I was the key to saving what remained of the village. "We should move back and let The Guard do their job," Bevon urged.

He feared for my safety over his own life, but the time had passed for me to turn and run. "There's no safe place for us now," I responded.

I had crossed a line with the destruction of the wall, the principal means of protecting the village. I no longer feared what was to come. My senses felt numbed by too many horrible events. The time had come for me to be reunited with the utopia team. That was the Bots' plan all along. And then, when I was together again with Cassie, Matt, and Diane, we would help usher in a new reality where humans were no longer the dominant race. By collapsing Haven's wall, the Bots had made it clear there was no stopping them.

Rae took a sharp breath as she raised her sword higher. Somewhere during the mad rush to abandon the wall, she had lost her bow. She now focused her attention on the spot where the mighty gate had once stood. There, on the top of the smashed wooden door, a single Bot stood. Behind it, just outside the demolished wall, a tight ring of a half-dozen more waited.

I peered at the nearest figure and saw my fate in its blank face. The monster was here for me, and I knew how this was going to play out. My friends standing near my side would fight to the death to prevent the Bots from taking me. Against one, they would have a chance, if they took it by surprise, or were blessed with good luck. But not against a half-dozen or more. Who knew how many more Bots might be lurking? The creatures would not leave without me.

I remained remarkably calm. Maybe that's the way of it when one realizes the end is near.

Bevon inched closer. "Earthfriend, now would be a good time for you to reach for what you have lost. Our options are limited."

I gazed fondly at my friend, no longer even thinking about him not being human. He was always at my side, regardless of the risk. I wanted to respond with a witty remark, as he might, to dispel the smell of fear. But my heart wasn't in it. Instead, I said, "I'm afraid I lost that ability long ago. If I couldn't summon it before this attack, I don't know if I'll ever be able to again."

His lips tightened. "Then we will fight with our blades. Let us make the people of Haven proud." He looked at me and smirked. "Maybe they will write a song about us one day."

I smiled weakly. "A song would be nice, wouldn't it?" Yet, I couldn't help but wonder how much more preferable it would be to grow old with Cassie by my side rather than dying now, no matter how glorious. Did every person think this same thing before death?

Another three Bots joined the one at the top of the fallen

gate. Each held short, curved blades in one hand. With the Bots' strength, the scimitars were deadly. I had seen them spin those weapons around as if they were propeller blades on an airplane.

All four Bots stepped forward, moving with inhuman precision, navigating over the broken gate and crushed piles of stone without bothering to watch their footing. They reached the undamaged courtyard just as Tess Armstrong pushed her way past the sentries to stand before the towering figures. She hadn't bothered to arm herself.

Rae shouted, "Mom, what are you doing?"

Tess turned, a wild expression in her eyes. "Stay where you are. I mean it. He needs your protection." Her eyes flicked toward me before she faced the Bots. She raised her hands high over her head, and shouted, "Stop. Leave this place. Remember who you once were." Her voice resounded forcefully across the shattered courtyard, yet it held a hint of fear. "There is good within you. I saw it long ago." She paused a moment, studying their lack of response. "Everyone here is under my charge. You have no right—"

The pounding, piercing voice cut her off.

—We have every authority. Do not presume to tell us what to do when you do not understand who we have become. You played a part in who we have become. That is the only reason we spare your life. At least this time.

Without waiting for a response, the knot of Bots moved forward, toward me. Tess shifted to stand in their way. "Mom, don't," Rae shouted.

She stood there, a lone figure with a storm about to crash upon her. Her deed was reminiscent of a famous scene from

Earth's history when a Chinese dissident had once stood unarmed in front of a line of tanks advancing against the protesters in Tiananmen Square. The soldier driving the first tank stopped, unsure of what to do.

There was no such hesitancy with the Bots. The first Bot swatted at Tess as if she was a fly. She flew a few feet through the air, falling to the ground, her face full of anguish, either from the pain of the blow or because her bid had failed. Words were not enough to cause the creatures to rethink their purpose, no matter who spoke them.

Bevon and Ja'Krill inched closer to me while Rae and Bryson tensed for the assault. Quintia and Riyaad advanced toward the Bots to intercept them.

My fate was sealed. I had run out of options. Without the ability to grab hold of the powers of Elthea, I was helpless. Others would die because of my failure. My companions were too damn bull-headed to allow the Bots to take me.

I gritted my teeth, knowing this would not end well. The specter of all my fears approached. Quintia and Riyaad gripped their spears tightly as they moved toward the attackers. The blood drained from my face, realizing this was likely the last thing they would ever do and that I was about to face a lifetime of imprisonment.

A booming voice startled me, freezing everyone. "Enough!"

Twenty yards to my left stood a hooded figure. I quickly realized it was the same person who had appeared to me last evening. The image of the person wavered in the air, insubstantial as morning fog. I knew it was a projection, much like a hologram.

A moment later, the Bots reacted. They began charging forward, but not toward the intruder. They rushed directly at me.

I felt lightheaded, and my vision blurred. I felt as if I was going to faint. I blinked to clear my head, thinking this was no time to pass out. But then my senses went numb as the world fell into darkness.

MY EYES FLUTTERED OPEN. I WAS ON MY BACK, LOOKING up. Gone was the nightmarish image of swirling black and red clouds. I now saw a familiar blue sky with puffy white clouds. Had we defeated the Bots and dispelled their darkness?

I jerked my head up. Nothing I saw made sense. For a second, I wondered if I was losing my mind. Seconds ago, I had been in the mangled village of Haven. Now, all I could see were immense, snow-covered mountains with a sun setting behind them.

How could this be?

A blast of frigid air ripped through me. It was the sort of cold that could cause frostbite. Staggering to my knees, I saw the most inexplicable image of all. A dozen or more Bots hung in midair thirty paces away. They appeared frozen in time, the closest ones stopped dead in their tracks in the motion of rushing toward me. All the Bots had their weapons raised. A sparkling haze surrounded them.

Comprehension dawned on me. The Bots had captured me, and they had me now. But a twinge in the back of my head told me this wasn't right. Why were they dangling in the air like that? And why weren't they moving? They stood suspended as if paralyzed in midair.

My eyes remained focused on the Bots as I ignored everything else. They were the only threat that required my attention. The haze surrounding them dissipated, blowing away in swirling eddies by the brisk wind. Before I could frame another thought, a gust of wind blew the remaining fog away, and the Bots dropped toward the ground as if released from some unseen barrier.

I watched them for a few seconds until the rough edge of granite upon which I stood—or kneeled, as I now realized—blocked their view. I flattened onto my stomach and scrambled closer to the rim, searching for the Bots. I wondered if this was a ploy, but I couldn't imagine its purpose.

As I came closer to the edge of the landing, I realized it ended in a sheer drop of thousands of feet. Without a barrier or guardrail to grab onto, nothing prevented me from slipping off the side and plummeting to my death. I pushed back from the perimeter but stayed close enough to keep the Bots in sight. They were still falling and now appeared as specks against the leaden background of snow and stone mixed with bits of scrawny trees. I kept staring, transfixed, needing to confirm that they were dead. I still had it in my head that they might sprout wings and fly back. They might yet perform some other trick.

After what seemed an inordinately long time, they finally smashed against the ground. The color of a Bots' blood is green, and I could see traces of it, even from this distance. They were dead.

Remaining on my belly, I squirmed back from the precipice, my heart beating faster. Once a safe distance, I turned my head to look around. There he stood: the hooded stranger, about a dozen feet away. He was dangerously close to the edge of the outcropping. His hands were raised, and eyes closed as if in a trance. This was no projection. He was as solid as the face of the mountain rising behind him. Then he opened his eyes and looked at me, displaying no emotion.

Rae and Bryson stood at the center of this platform, looking bewildered at what they saw. Not far away were Bevon and Ja'Krill. They each held their weapons ready to fight off an attacker as if they were still in Haven.

This place couldn't be any more different. Jagged, snow-covered peaks surrounded us. The place was desolate, forbidding, and cold. I could already feel the ice creeping into my body.

Bevon was the first of my friends to recover. He lowered his blade and took several steps toward the stranger who regarded us with interest, the stare of a lab technician examining rats. "State your purpose," Bevon called out. "Why have you abducted us?"

"You are in no position to question me," the hooded person replied menacingly. "The only reason you are here at all is because you were too close to The Gifted One."

Was he talking about me? He abducted us? I stood, moving next to my friends near the side of the mountain, away from the open edge. I stole a glance above my head. The mountaintop was lost in the clouds.

I could see that Bevon wanted to argue, but the hooded

figure was right. We were in no position to quarrel about anything.

A sudden thought came into my head. "He has no intention of killing us," I whispered to my friends, trying to sound sure of myself. "He could have let the Bots finish us." Never taking my eyes off him, I spoke loud enough for him to hear. "You said you could save me when you appeared the other night." A sudden gust of wind ripped through me. Snow began swirling around us, obstructing my vision. "If we remain out here any longer, we will die from exposure. You must have a shelter. Can we go somewhere warmer before we freeze?"

He pulled the hood away from his head, exposing his face. The subtle differences showed he wasn't human. "Follow me. This is the only way inside. I needed to bring you to this larger platform first so I could perform my task." He walked away from the outcropping upon which we were standing and climbed onto a smaller ledge that was only a three-foot protrusion of rock jutting out from the mountain-side. This overhang jutted out from the mountain's face until I lost sight of it around a bend. He turned after taking a few steps. "I cannot carry you. This is safe." He paused a long moment as if considering something before adding in a dry voice, "As long as you don't fall. So please don't. I don't want to have to save you again."

I wondered if he was joking, but he didn't crack a smile. He must actually be serious.

"No way," Bryson asserted. "I'd rather freeze to death." I looked at Rae, hoping she would calm him or give him an order since she was a senior member of The Guard. She was a fighter to the core, and I would expect her to be ready for any situation, even this. But her eyes were wild, and her breathing came in rapid gasps. She was out of her element here. She had nobody to fight, and nobody was sure if this stranger was a friend or an enemy.

"I'm not walking on that," Bryson reiterated as if we hadn't heard him the first time.

I agreed with him, but it seemed that freezing to death was our only other choice. I looked at the narrow ledge, wondering how difficult it could be. The stranger navigated the trail effortlessly and had already passed the point where it followed the face of the mountain away from our view. I continued to stare, hoping he might return and offer something else. The wind and pelting ice intensified.

"It does not look that difficult," shouted Ja'Krill to make himself heard over the swirling gusts. As a Valnorian, he was born to roam with ease through limbs of the highest trees I had ever seen. But this was an entirely different magnitude of height. And there were no branches to clutch on our way. I couldn't even see handholds on the face of the rock. He moved to the edge of our broader platform and surveyed the slender ledge. He licked his lips, and I realized he was frightened. This was beyond his skill. He was only trying to ease our distress.

"No," said Bevon before Ja'Krill could move further. Every word had to be shouted over the din of the blasting winds. "I will sail over to confirm there is a shelter. If so, I will carry each of you, one at a time, on a sail."

"Thank goodness," Bryson mumbled through chattering teeth.

I had forgotten about the sail. It was a bit of Astari magic, which they used to travel from one Raised Isle to another. Because the sail folded into the size of a small napkin, Bevon must have always carried it, in the same way he carried the retractable Astari-forged blades.

He tugged the small clump of linen from a pocket, and without waiting for a response, flicked his wrist several times to unfurl the sail over his head. With practiced ease, he stepped off the platform, and in the same motion, slid onto the crossbar to support his midsection. Once airborne, he slipped his feet into bands to hold them in place. He barely began his flight when a gust of wind pushed him dangerously close to the mountainside. Even after he regained control, Bevon continued to wrestle with the sail. In moments, I soon lost sight of him as he soared around the bend of the mountainside.

The rest of us shivered, waiting, as the biting gale howled around us. Maybe it was my imagination, but the bone-chilling cold and the intensity of the tempest seemed to increase. I wasn't sure how long we could hold out in these conditions.

Seconds seemed to take forever. If only we could start a fire. "Ja'Krill, you don't happen to have any of that fireroot on you, do you?"

His lips were a thin line. The cold was probably worse on him because he had spent most of his life in the warm, humid forest. Ja'Krill had left the Valnorian forest because of me and because he had nothing left there once the Bots killed his family. Along the way, he had developed an equally close fellowship with Bevon and the other Astari, as well as the people of Haven. He shook his head. "I'm afraid I did not come as prepared as my friend, Bevon."

I tried to smile but wondered if my face was freezing solid.

"What the hell is taking him so long?" Rae grumbled.

An unbidden thought came to me. What if Bevon wasn't coming back? What if the stranger captured him? Or killed him? What if a gust of wind smashed him against the rocks? I stared at the spot I had last seen him, willing him to appear.

At that moment, I felt sure we were all going to die here.

7

THE NARROW LEDGE

The frigid air was already draining the life from me. In such an unlikely place as this, the image of Cassie appeared to me once again. Was she here to say farewell, our last goodbye? Her face warmed my heart, if not my body.

Bryson was the first to react. Through chattering teeth, he said, "Master Philip, I see Cassie." He rubbed his eyes, not realizing everyone could see her. "I think I'm hallucinating."

Cassie's lips were tight. "Phil ... all of you, there's little time. You must decide; you have no other choice. The narrow path leads to safety. Take it and live."

A blast of wind blew her likeness to tatters. She was gone before I could even respond.

Seconds later, Bevon's sail, with him under it, appeared from around the bend in the mountainside. He veered up and down and side to side, a mad, reckless flight. I had never seen any Astari have this much difficulty controlling a sail. Once he landed, the wind threatened to rip the sail from his hand before folding it into a compact pouch.

I spied another hooded figure who strode calmly toward us along the narrow path. He, or she—I couldn't tell which—unraveled a rope with one end held in place out of sight beyond the curve of the wall.

Bevon wasted no time explaining. "The only recourse is to reach the shelter on the other side of the ledge. They agreed to suspend a rope as a guide."

"They? Who's they?" I blurted.

I peered closely at the hooded person holding one end of the cord. Up close, I could see she was female, a girl who appeared younger than Rae. She eyed each of us without expression as she pulled the line until it was taut.

Bevon responded quickly. "No time to discuss." He hesitated a second longer before adding, "They agreed to string this rope from here to another platform on the other side where they will shelter us from this cold. But we cannot attach the cord to anything on either end. We have nothing to secure it and no time to hammer something into the rock to affix the line. This girl and someone at the other end will hold it as securely as they can. But it is only a guide."

"N—no, I can't do this," Bryson stammered, echoing his earlier objection. He appeared to be on the verge of having a fit. "No. Hell, no. Absolutely not. I'm not as brave as the rest of you. Leave me here, I—"

I didn't have to ask Rae to deal with him. She grabbed him by the shoulders. "Bry, get a grip on yourself. You've trained to be a soldier in The Guard. This is another test. Do it or die."

Cassie had used nearly the same words moments ago. Rae's admonishment appeared to calm Bryson. He took deep, gulping breaths and finally nodded an uncertain agreement.

I wasn't sure I could feel my toes or fingers. The cold and wind were ever present, a foe that could kill as surely as could an enemy wielding a blade. Ja'Krill took charge and was the first to step onto the narrow outcrop. "Back against the wall," he said. "Shuffle your feet from side-to-side one at a time."

My breathing came rapidly as I inched closer to the ledge. All I could see was a drop of thousands of feet. I had never been so scared in my life. I understood Bryson's terror. If not for Cassie's appeal to spur me forward, I might curl up on the frozen ground and die.

I was second in line, next to Ja'Krill, while Bevon took a position to my right. Rae followed next, with Bryson at the end.

With my back against the rock and my front holding onto the rope for dear life, I crab-walked inch-by-inch, never lifting a foot off the surface. I tried not to look down, but every view reminded me I was thousands of feet in the air, only a slip away from a terrible plunge to my death. I tried not to think about how high we were or how long it had taken for the Bots to fall before they hit the ground.

Closing my eyes was no better; it was worse. I was afraid I might lose my balance by leaning too far forward. I clenched my jaw, my body in agony, knowing I had no choice but to inch along. The panoramic sight of a vast chasm of open space, with the mountains nearly a mile away, consumed my every thought.

The rope glided through my fingers as I clenched and

unclenched my grip just enough to keep pace with the shuffle of my feet. The tether did little to prevent any of us from falling, but at least it gave an illusion of safety. I squeezed my fingers so tightly around the braided cord I wasn't sure I would ever be able to relax them again.

The wind battered against me as if it had a mind of its own, trying its best to knock me off balance and send me hurtling over the edge. I swayed backward as a powerful gust hit me, and I bumped hard against the wall behind. A pointed stone jabbed me in the back. *Don't lean forward*, I repeated to myself, again and again, a mantra that filled my thoughts as if words could keep me alive.

Snow pellets stung my face. Every inch was agony. It seemed as if we had been on this precipice forever. I stole a glance to see our progress.

We hadn't gone far at all. I didn't know if we would make it. The ledge continued, seemingly going on forever. Every second, every shuffle of one foot and then the next, was torture.

The empty air in front of and below me filled my every thought. The view burned into my brain until it was all that existed.

I somehow moved an inch at a time, not even aware of making any movements. My heart hammered in my chest, and my breathing came in shallow gasps.

With every shift of the blasting wind, my heart beat faster. If I lost my balance, if I leaned too far forward, or if a blast of wind pushed me in the wrong direction, then I was dead. A small sliver of ledge, amounting to only inches in front of my boots, was all that separated me from a vertical drop lasting thousands of feet.

I sensed, more than saw, that I was rounding the bend in the ledge's angle. Please God, let this be the end. I didn't know how much longer I could do this. I was on the verge of panic, a feeling so fierce my insides trembled uncontrollably. I pictured myself slipping off the edge, nothing but the air around me, falling, falling, falling, without end.

I kept my head angled to the left, watching Ja'Krill take one step at a time. His body remained relaxed, and he moved slowly, as if for my benefit. I gained comfort from him, knowing he could do this. At the least, it stopped me from seizing up with fear.

Somewhere along the torturous crossing, I had lost all feeling in my body. Whether because of the cold or the fear, I wasn't sure.

After what felt like ages, I saw another outcropping at the end of this thin ledge. I kept my eyes focused on it. All other thoughts fell away. My only hope in life at this moment was making it that far. I pushed away the terrible notion that I might fall within sight of safety.

My vision blurred as icy pellets continued hitting my face and eyes. I didn't dare rub them for fear of falling. I wasn't even sure if I was still moving. I urged my legs to move, hoping they would obey.

And then Ja'Krill's firm hands grabbed my arm and shoulder. I sagged with relief and lowered myself to the ground of the landing once I was safely off the ledge. I felt sure I would be sick, but somehow I avoided it.

Bevon was by my side a second later. "You did well, Earthfriend."

I turned to see Rae reach the safety of the outcrop. Her face was ashen as Bevon and Ja'Krill half carried her a safe distance from the edge, then turned to help Bryson.

The boy from Haven was five paces away from safety when he made a false step. I wasn't sure whether it was because of his haste to reach the platform or for some other reason. He stumbled and teetered forward for a second. He overcompensated by trying to regain his balance and smacked into the wall behind him. The motion sent him forward again.

For an awful second, he recognized what was going to happen. His face contorted in a silent shriek. At the last second, he pulled the tether close to him, gripping it with all his strength, hoping it would be enough to regain his balance. But the rope didn't offer enough support.

He slipped over the edge and plunged down. Everyone on the platform screamed.

As soon as he fell, my mind registered two events. The first was Bevon diving off the cliff after him. The sail materialized over his head a split-second after he jumped.

The other event was that the rope remained taut on this end, even though it had come loose from the person holding it at our point of origin. I turned to see why. The figure holding the cord had turned to stone, solid and gray as the surrounding rock.

I dashed to the side of the platform with Rae and Ja'Krill, expecting to see the worst. I again pictured the Bots falling and falling. I didn't know if I could watch a repeat of that scene with Bryson.

I poked my head over the edge of the platform. Bevon's sail was fully extended and remained stationary in one spot rather than sailing. He had positioned himself about fifty-feet below with the tether up against him. The rope was taut, but his sail blocked the view from above, so it was impossible for us to see if Bryson still held on. I knew Bevon's sail couldn't support both him and Bryson, so I had to believe he had a hold of the young man to prevent him from slipping off the rope. "Pull!" I urged the others.

We began heaving on the rope as if in a game of tug-of-war with only one side playing. But this was no game.

"Hold on," Rae shouted frantically. We stayed away from the edge as we pulled so we would gain some leverage with our feet. We couldn't see over the side to observe what was happening on the other end. From the tension on the rope, it seemed to me that we had both Bryson and the lighter-weight, Bevon. At least I hoped that was true.

From the corner of my vision, I saw the female who had held the rope on the other end come back toward us. I wanted to yell at her, berate her for letting go of the line. But she probably had no choice. There was nothing to prevent her from being pulled over the edge with Bryson. I thought she would join us to help pull him to safety, but she merely stood, watching. Her disregard for Bryson's life was appalling. I put my anger to good use by pulling even harder on the rope.

Ja'Krill was the closest to the edge as we all pulled

together. He would be the first one dragged over the side if we couldn't tug the rope toward us, or be forced to give up.

As I grasped the line, I noticed pieces of it had frayed and became dangerously thin in places. I saw the reason. The rope rubbed against the sharp rock at the edge of the platform. There was nothing to do now but pray it would hold. With each heave, the wear became more severe. What a cruel joke, to have come this far only to lose the battle for Bryson's life.

Just then, I caught sight of the top of the Astari sail.

"Almost here," Ja'Krill shouted.

I pulled harder, wanting this nightmare to be over, still keeping one eye on the rope as it caught on the edge of the platform. Inches more of the sail appeared over the edge until I finally saw two hands clutching the cord. A second later, Bryson's face, twisted and red from exertion or fear, cleared the edge. Bevon was holding him tightly around the chest.

After another pull of the rope, Ja'Krill grabbed Bryson by the shoulder and guided him onto the landing. The young boy continued to clutch the line even after he was safely on solid ground.

Bevon floated up and circled around to land a few paces away as Rae continued to hug Bryson, tears in her eyes. "It's okay, Bry. You're safe." His breath came in quick, sucking sobs as he began to cry.

Rae tried to soothe him as I looked on. I soon turned away, giving him the privacy I was sure he wanted. My gaze settled on the figure who had transformed himself to rock, the same one who had brought us here. Ja'Krill and Bevon had already focused their attention on him. The gray stone that was his body gained color as his blood began to pump within him again. In another moment, he took a deep breath, and his eyes snapped open. His body was as it was before, from stone back to flesh and blood. Did he turn himself into stone to hold the rope?

Bevon frowned. Without waiting to be asked, the figure answered, "It was the quickest and easiest charm to prevent your fool friend from killing himself." He shifted his gaze to Bryson. "Thankfully, he had the wits to hang on."

Should we thank him for saving Bryson or be angry with him for bringing us to this place? Bevon remained calm, as was typical of the Astari. "I demand you tell us who you are. We have a right to know."

The figure nodded his head in agreement. "Among my people, I am called The Herald of Life. My birth name is Teivel. That is all you need to know right now."

That sealed it. I didn't like this person. My anger burned within me, but my body was slowly turning to ice. Already, my thoughts were leaden, a terrible sluggishness gaining control over me. After the terror of walking the narrow ledge, and then rescuing Bryson, I had pushed the biting cold to the back of my mind. But now it returned with deadly force. We would freeze to death if we haggled out here in the open much longer.

As if reading my mind, Teivel motioned us to follow. He didn't bother to explain more about who he was or what we were doing here. My mind was too foggy from the cold to object or ask. The others also had a bewildered look in their eyes. I wanted nothing more but to lie down and sleep.

Teivel took a few steps to the rock wall and pushed on a

section of granite. An opening appeared, and part of the wall slid silently to the side, revealing a light source within.

As he placed a foot on the threshold, he hesitated and turned back toward us. "Once inside, you must adhere to my rules. If you don't agree, you are free to remain here."

I didn't like his demand, but neither did I care to bicker with him. Besides, I wasn't thinking clearly.

Bevon spoke for all of us. "We accept your terms." He paused before adding, "As long as no harm comes to us."

A voice inside my head told me not to agree. Something here wasn't right. But the others were already moving toward the promised shelter beyond the door. I reluctantly forced my legs to follow. Whatever this place and these people were, it didn't matter. We would be out of the cold and away from certain death.

We would be safe at last. At least, I fervently hoped.

THE GIFTED ONE

The door shut with an ominous thud, like the sealing of a crypt. I couldn't help but wonder if any of us would ever see the light of day again.

Heated air surrounded me, a welcomed sensation. I had forgotten how good it felt to be warm. Rubbing my arms vigorously, I tried to force the numbness out and coax the blood in my limbs to circulate.

My mind, muddled from the cold, caused me to gape at the sight before me. When Bevon had said there was a shelter here, I had imagined a cave, maybe even a fire.

This place was nothing like that.

The walls and floors were polished to an impeccable sheen, looking like buffed marble or precious gemstone that sparkled as if lighted from within. The actual source of light came from sections of the ceiling and walls and even the floor, which glowed with a soft luminescence, reminding me of the Valnorian fireroot—a specific wood that glowed and threw off heat without burning. Was the light here also the origin of the heat?

We stood in a vestibule large enough to fit all of us with room to spare. The stranger named Teivel regarded us without expression. Bevon and Ja'Krill gripped the hilts of their blades. Each of them had strategically positioned themselves next to me, while Rae and Bryson appeared lost and confused.

I carefully studied our new host, trying to glean any information that might be helpful. He resembled a human, but with slight differences in the contours of his face. His frame was willowy and thin, his movements graceful, as if well-practiced.

Bevon spoke first. "Thank you for taking us in, and also for the rope." He paused a moment, his voice turning more forceful. "But, I must ask you again, why did you bring us here? Please state your purpose."

"Let us begin at the beginning," Teivel replied evenly. "You asked before why I had abducted you. The Bots were about to kill The Gifted One. That is why I brought you here."

This was the second time he used this honorific. "Why do you call me that?" I asked.

He raised an eyebrow. "Surely, even you must realize Elthea has bestowed an unusual strength upon you."

I blinked, not sure how to respond. I would have believed him after the battle in the Valnorian Forest, but not now. "I'm unable to do anything," I said, feeling the anger that came with the words.

He smiled as if hiding a secret. "And so you believe. But it is the reason you are here. I am not about to let the Bots destroy you. They must pay the price for what they have done."

I had a feeling he was holding something back.

Teivel removed his woolen coat and handed it to a boy who had come forward. A few other residents lingered farther along the hallway. Ja'Krill noticed them and asked the stranger, "What is the name of your race?"

"We are the Nizaem, a simple people. I suspect you have never heard of us. We played no part in the shaping of the land."

"A simple people, yet you wield great skill," Bevon said as if accusing him of being untruthful. "How have you gained such a talent yet remain isolated in this remote location?"

Teivel responded without emotion. "We have our reasons."

Whatever his motive, I wanted no part of him or his people. Yet once again, I was drawn into events out of my control. My biggest question, still unanswered, was whether I had become a prisoner or an honored guest.

I intended to find out, and soon.

A YOUNG GIRL, BARELY OUT OF ADOLESCENCE, LED US TO our quarters. She was the same person who had clutched one end of the rope on the outside platform as we walked along the narrow ledge. We saw many other Nizaem men, women, and children in the hallways as she navigated the many intersections. None of them appeared surprised to see us, which felt odd.

How many visitors could they possibly encounter in this remote location? More puzzling was the silence. Nobody talked to each other. Even the children walked noiselessly. Everyone passed in near silence, their forearms folded within their robes as if they might be praying. The place reminded me of a monastery.

The girl brought us to a sparsely furnished room that contained a few wooden cabinets, rugs and cushions on the floor, and subdued tapestries on the walls. The most remarkable feature of the room was the view. One side opened to a dazzling sight of the towering mountains. No glass shielded the opening. A toe-wall of stone came up to about my knees, helping to mitigate the danger of slipping out, a feature that hadn't been available to us as we traversed the ledge outside.

As I stepped further into the room, I expected to feel the blast of cold air from the outside, causing me to wonder if we were being placed into a dungeon to freeze to death. But the chamber was temperate, like the rest of the residence. Some magical force prevented the biting cold from seeping through the window. I tested the opening by pushing my hand through an invisible barrier, feeling a slight restraining pressure, which gave way as my arm broke through. Sure enough, my fingers tingled from the cold.

Clutching the side of the wall for support, I stuck my head outside and peered over the edge. The distance to the bottom was dizzying, and I quickly stepped back. "I'm going to hate high places for the rest of my life," I mumbled to no one in particular.

The rest of the room offered less magical artifacts. Cloth tapestries hung on two walls with green foliage woven into the patterns, reminding me of the lush vegetation of the Valnorian Woods. The room contained no door out to the hallway. I wondered if this was deliberate, a way to prevent private conversations. Anyone could easily eavesdrop on us by standing next to the opening and hear everything except whispers. But then I remembered that during our short trek to these quarters, we had passed many other chambers, none of them with a door.

No chairs or other furniture graced the accommodations. Pillows and thick blankets offered a comfortable seating area, except it was on the floor. It took us a long time to figure out that the pliable areas built into the floor in one section of the room were the Nizaem answer to beds.

As I explored the room, I noticed Rae and Bryson standing together. They looked lost, unable to believe we were here. I remembered my initial transition to the Raised Isles, the confusion and fear racing through my head. During those first moments, I had longed to return to the world I had known my entire life. They must feel this way now. I wanted to hug them but knew it wasn't a solution. They had been ripped from their home without warning or reasonable explanation. "We're going to be okay," I said softly, hoping my words sounded more reassuring than how I felt. "We're together, and we'll figure this out."

Bryson screeched, "Why did he bring us here? He had no right."

My heart went out to him. Rae put a hand on his shoulder to calm him. Before she could speak, I said, "I'm wondering the same thing, Bry. I wish I could make sense of it. All I can tell you is that we'll find a way out of here. At least, we're safe for the moment. And he stopped the Bots from killing everyone in Haven. That's something to be thankful for."

His face softened into a brittle smile. "Now there's a switch. Master Philip trying to console me."

I almost laughed out loud at his jab. He had always tried to cheer me up whenever I had been down. "I have many talents."

Before anyone could say more, a male and female Nizaem entered the room carrying trays laden with food and bottles of liquid. They barely looked at us, and again, I had to wonder at their lack of curiosity. They placed the trays on the floor with surprising grace. The girl's voice carried a stilted cadence. "The Herald of Life offers you sustenance from your journey. Eat, drink, and enjoy."

Once the girls left, I wondered who would be the first to test the food to be sure it was safe. Curiosity and hunger quickly won out as others began sampling the fare on the tray. I gave in as well, although I still wondered if these people might try to drug us for some nefarious purpose. The food, however, was quite good, and no one suffered any ill effects.

"Where do you think this came from?" Rae asked as she sampled a piece of meat wrapped in a green leaf. "I can't imagine growing anything here or keeping a herd as we do at Haven."

"What puzzles me more is why anyone would want to live in a forsaken, desolate place like this," said Ja'Krill. "Bevon, do you know anything about this Nizaem race?"

He shook his head. "I'm not exactly the authority on the various cultures of Elthea. I should have paid more attention to my studies. Damek had more knowledge of diverse cultures and anthropology." His name brought another pang to my chest. Perhaps it always would. "I want to find out more about these people," Bevon continued. "Remember, our mission is to seek allies who will help us oppose the Bots. Maybe they can help."

While I had my doubts, I kept my silence. From what I had seen so far, the Nizaem had not yet earned my trust. Teivel had abducted us without explanation, asserting that the Bots were about to kill us. His motives might be honorable, but I still didn't understand him, and that bothered me.

As we continued eating, Ja'Krill motioned with a piece of food. "Earthfriend, we should discuss these appearances from your friend, Cassie. Outside on the ledge was the second visitation that I've seen."

After the episode in the community gardens at Haven, everyone in the village must know about the occurrences, including Bevon. But he had kept his silence. I knew someone would question me eventually, but I still wasn't ready to talk about it. I looked down at my hands. "I'm not sure what to say. I don't know why it's happening, and I don't understand how."

Bevon spoke quietly, almost hesitantly. "You may want to consider that the Bots are orchestrating her visits."

"You mean controlling her," I said, my words sounding more defensive than I had intended.

"Not necessarily. They may have a purpose in allowing Earthfriend Cassie to speak with you."

"I don't care about their intentions. As long as I can see her, and she can speak to me, it doesn't matter. They've taken everything else from me." I tried to keep the pleading out of my voice. "As long as she continues to appear, I know she's alive. It's the only hope I have."

I was afraid to discuss my biggest fear, which was that time was running out, both for her and for all of us.

Several hours later, Teivel quietly entered the room. His arms remained folded together under a brown robe, one hand against the other forearm in a fashion that I was beginning to realize was a common trait of the Nizaem people. Our host paused, making sure he had our attention. He spoke without inflection. "Now that you are here, I must explain our rules."

Bryson erupted. "We don't care about your stupid rules. Return us to Haven."

Teivel cocked his head. "A curious response, young man. Do not forget that I saved your life, albeit inadvertently. If I had not intervened, you would be dead right now. Nevertheless, you are here and part of our community. I require everyone who lives here to follow my mandates."

"Why did you bring us here?" Bevon asked, repeating his earlier question.

Teivel blinked. "I have already told you. I wanted to save The Gifted One. The rest of you were collateral."

His response was infuriating. Was he trying to be evasive, or was this his nature?

"This is my domain, my rules," he continued calmly, unruffled by the outburst from Bevon and Bryson. "Now that you are here, you are one of us. I will treat no differently, provide no extra rewards, and will expect no more or less from you than our fellow clan members. You will work at tasks for the good of all and do no harm to others. Do you agree?"

"We don't anticipate staying here very long," I said in a deadpan voice.

Bevon added, "We thank you, but we do not want to become a member of your community, however pleasant it may be." He put an extra emphasis on the word pleasant, and I wasn't sure if it was sarcasm. It wasn't like him, and was yet another measure of the frustration in each of us. "Will you agree to return us to Haven?"

Teivel remained stone-faced, but his eyes flamed with piercing intensity. Someone once told me I should look closely at another's eyes to understand fully their thoughts or feelings. Judging by what I saw, a fire burned within his wooden emotions.

He angled his head to gaze outside at the mountaintops in the distance. "It would not be wise to return you so soon. Your enemy will not readily abandon their mission." He stared at me. "You will be lost, and my efforts will be to no avail. No, you will remain here. For now."

Rae had been silent throughout the conversation, fixing Teivel with a practiced gaze. She was sizing him up, as she would any enemy. Her training as a member of The Guard had guided her for most of her life, and she wasn't about to abandon it now. "How long?" she asked.

He paid her no attention, focusing on me instead. "Those who tried to capture you are the bane of your existence, are they not? Continue on the path you are on, and they will destroy you." He shifted his gaze to Rae and added, "As for you and the rest of your people, if you try to defend him they will obliterate your home and kill you all. You are nothing to them."

I didn't want to admit it, but deep inside, I knew he was right. I was no match for the Bots. No matter how badly I wanted to, I wasn't going to stop them.

Ja'Krill motioned with his arm to the world outside the opening. "Are you hiding from the Bots? Is that the reason you live here in this isolated place?" When Teivel didn't respond, Ja'Krill continued, "You have the power of Elthea within you. This home wasn't built with tools. You easily stopped the Bots and took us away from Haven. Even with all your strength, you choose to remain this isolated."

The corners of Teivel's mouth turned upward, but it was a sad smile. "It is true. Only the Nizaem live here in the towers of the Grimtane Peaks. Isolation is our preference."

"Then how do you know so much about events in the world?" Rae asked.

He looked at her curiously, giving me the impression that he was rethinking his previous opinion of her as unimportant or unintelligent. "The land is being transformed. Old ways are being swept aside, and a new reality is coming into play. Cultures that existed for a millennium will die. New ones will take their place." His emotions flared for the first time as he raised his voice. "I will not allow the Nizaem civilization to be destroyed. It is my duty to mark events in the land." His eyes landed back on me. "And when necessary, I make adjustments." Left unsaid was whether the adjustments benefited the Nizaem to the detriment of the rest of us.

He turned and began walking away, apparently deciding to end the conversation. But after a step, he paused. "As long as you remain here, you are my guests. You may leave at any time. But I warn you, the way down the Grimtane Peaks is not an easy one. I doubt you would survive."

He glanced at Rae's collection of blades at her waist. "One more rule. We carry no weapons inside our home. Our only need for them is to hunt the beasts that roam outside, providing us with nourishment. I, for one, do not wish to be watching my back at every turn. You will not carry a weapon outside this chamber. I will banish whoever does so."

He fixed his gaze as if challenging us to disagree, or maybe he was making sure we understood the weight of his pronouncement. He strode from the room without another word, leaving me to wonder how I managed to become entangled in one disaster after another.

9

TO CHANGE THE PAST

As the day turned to dusk in the world outside our shelter, I watched the shadows of the Grimtane Peaks become more pronounced, casting a pall over many of the lower summits. The sight was spectacular, one of the most dramatic I had seen in this land, save that of the Raised Isles of Loralee.

The view could almost make me forget that we were being held against our will, a cheerless thought I tried my best to push aside. Instead, I took comfort, focusing on the panorama outside. Celeus, the larger of the two moons, hung half-full, low in the sky. It would soon set behind the tallest peaks, leaving only Halcyone to light the night sky. The unearthly image reminded me again about the improbable series of events that brought me here in this distant land, fighting a force I still couldn't understand.

Hours had passed since the Nizaem leader, Teivel, The Herald of Life, had left us alone, restricting us from carrying weapons outside this room. During this time, we had seen other Nizaem pass in the hallway outside our chamber. They didn't seem particularly curious about us, which I found odd. I asked Bevon about their lack of interest. "It is probably a cultural difference," he said. "Not all races behave the same as humans."

It seemed a hollow explanation. All intelligent beings displayed some level of curiosity.

Everything that happened during this last day remained a mystery. Teivel saved us, yet he continued to hold us here, explaining that he couldn't allow our enemy to have me. But why? What did it matter to him?

He named me The Gifted One, but he never explained what this meant, except for some vague account about Elthea choosing me for a part to play in the events of the land. His brief explanations were more like an unsolvable puzzle. The indifference shown by the rest of the Nizaem residents was also troubling. They must not see many visitors in this remote location. Why weren't they excited, or fearful, or *anything* because of our presence?

The inside of the Nizaem home was a wonder in construction, obviously accomplished by the powers of Elthea. During any other time, I would have gazed in awe at the windows containing an unseen barrier or the interior with its stone polished to a beautiful sparkling sheen. Even the communal washrooms were a marvel in architecture.

Instead, I fretted about my friends, captured and held prisoner by the Bots, while I was held captive in this place, unable to do anything to help them. If I were really The Gifted One, it seemed that my only gift was that of failure.

"You're gone again," said Rae, jolting me out of my brooding.

I hadn't heard her approach as I sat alone with my thoughts. "What?"

Her lips turned up in a droll smile. "You do it often. You become quiet, your eyes focus on something far away, and you have that sad expression on your face, like right now." Her eyes filled with laughter as if she thought something was funny. "I just thought you should know."

I stared at her blankly, only now realizing my thoughts had been somewhere else. How was it that this girl, a person I barely knew, could understand me so well? She waited expectantly for me to respond. "I was thinking," I said good-naturedly, even though it sounded sarcastic.

She didn't seem offended. "Where do you go when you're like that?"

I shrugged, not sure how to respond. I gazed again at the towering mountains in the distance. "I worry mostly." I attempted to smile, but it felt more like a grimace. "It seems I do a lot of that lately. Right now, I'm afraid of what may happen to my friends. And when I worry about them, I fret about not being able to do anything to free them." I watched her as she observed me. "I should be able to save them. I prevented Ja'Krill's race from being destroyed, but I can't lift a finger for those closest to me. It doesn't make sense, does it?"

She paused a moment, and I could almost see the gears turning in her head as she thought about it. "Lots of things in life make little sense. I try not to waste time tormenting myself about events I can't control. As far as I'm concerned, it's a good way to drive yourself crazy."

I wasn't sure I agreed with her. "It's not something I'm able to turn on or off at will. It's part of who I am."

"Maybe. But if I were you, I would agonize a little more about how we're going to get out of this place before anything else. I should be back at Haven, protecting the residents. And now, with the wall collapsed, who knows what's happening." Her voice softened as she added, "I'm scared, maybe for the first time in my life. I don't know if they're safe or even alive."

Her brow creased, and she gripped her hands together. Suddenly, she wasn't the brave soldier with nothing to fear. I saw the young girl that she was, with all the insecurities and misgivings of any person her age. Despite her armored exterior, she was no different from any young adult on Earth. I wanted to hug her, tell her we would be all right, that we would find a way back to her home. But my self-doubts stopped me. "We'll get back to Haven. I promise."

I spoke firmly, hoping she didn't catch the uncertainty I was feeling.

A SONOROUS CHIME REVERBERATED THROUGHOUT THE room, something I could feel in my bones. It sounded like a death knell, a low, mournful peal. The sound continued as we sat still, nobody daring to move or say a word. I immediately recalled Haven's bell: it would ring once for friends, twice for strangers, and three times for danger.

When it finally ended, Rae asked, "A warning?" It was exactly what I was thinking. I feared the Bots had found me again.

Bevon and Ja'Krill each gripped the hilt of their blades, but we remained where we were, waiting to hear the clamor of fighting in the halls outside our room. But everything remained silent.

As we waited, poised for the worst, a young Nizaem female casually strolled into the room. Her gray robe billowed behind her, and like all the other Nizaem, she was unarmed. I recognized her as the same girl who had held one end of the rope while we crossed the narrow ledge outside. Once safely inside, Teivel had instructed her to bring us to this room. She had not spoken to us before now.

"Evening meal is being served," she said, her words flat and toneless. Her eyes raked over us, giving me the impression that she was more than a young servant. The way she scrutinized us reminded me of Teivel, her leader. Like him, she also appeared to pay close attention to details. "Follow me. Your weapons must remain here." She stared at Rae before adding, "All of them."

Bevon fidgeted with the handle of his blade before setting it aside. "One moment, please; we will be right with you."

She frowned. Clearly, she wasn't accustomed to being disobeyed.

Bevon glanced at the rest of us, a feeling of doubt crossing his face. "I do not want to do this, but we have no choice."

"Are you serious! Leave here unarmed?" Rae grumbled. "It could be a trap, and we're simply going to walk into it?"

"If they wanted to kill us, they would have left us outside on the ledge to die," Bevon responded calmly.

He was right, but like Rae, I didn't trust these people

either. At any rate, we needed to find out more about them. "I agree with you, Rae, but he's already had two chances to kill us. He could have left us on the ledge outside, as Bevon said, or not bother to save us when the Bots attacked Haven. They were about to finish us."

Rae didn't appear convinced, but she was a soldier, and Bevon had given an order. She nodded curtly, and everyone began placing their weapons neatly on the floor. Rae took the longest to discard her collection of blades from various sheaths in her clothing. I could tell she struggled with the decision as she withdrew each weapon.

The Nizaem girl waited patiently out of earshot near the entranceway, observing our every move. Once satisfied that we had complied with her instructions, she turned to lead the way along the hallway.

I paid attention to the rest of the dwelling as we passed sleeping quarters on either side of the corridor. Each section of the hallway was indistinguishable from the other. It was as if the designer settled on a style and enforced it throughout the entire facility. Hallways were straight, with no bends, right-angles at intersections.

A steady flow of residents moved in the same direction as us. I glimpsed the insides of other rooms as I passed—apparently, doors were not something they used inside this home. Families with children occupied some chambers, while in others, I spied adults about to make their way to the evening meal. Like our room, rugs, thick blankets, and pillows were the primary furnishings. The place reminded me of a new house that someone might purchase, only to realize they had no money left to furnish it. For all the sophistication that must have gone into constructing the inside with its polished stones, glowing lights, and precise angles, the Nizaem people appeared to live an austere life.

The other citizens we came in contact with were polite but never tried to engage us in a conversation. Mostly, they simply ignored us, which only fueled my suspicions. In all my time in this land of Elthea, the other races I had met were pleasant and genial ... except for the Bots. I had begun to believe that everyone here shared this same trait.

The Nizaem were different. Not that they were hostile, their behavior felt quite the opposite. But something about them made me uneasy.

WE FOLLOWED THE NIZAEM GIRL AS SHE BROUGHT US TO a vast hall. We paused to gape at the massive room. It was filled with nearly a thousand residents streaming into the chamber from various hallways or already seated on benches at long rows of unadorned wooden tables. I had no idea so many people lived here.

The soft murmur of conversation filled the air, but it was subdued, as if people were intentionally quiet. No laughter or boisterous banter filled the air, as I would have expected with a crowd this size. The girl turned to us, indicating we should follow.

That's when it happened. I was gazing at the room, trying to figure out if the crowd remained hushed out of politeness to strangers, when the next second, I was back at Woodbery College. I stood on the edge of the school Common as I watched students stroll along the paved footpaths criss-crossing the green lawns. The crisp air gave me the impression it was early fall, although the maple trees still held onto their abundance of green leaves. A small group of students passed near me, their animated conversation filling the air as if they didn't have a care in the world.

My mind raced as I considered how this could happen. All my senses told me I was back at the college, a place I once loved. But I quickly realized I had no form. I could see everything around me, but not myself.

I set the problem aside for the moment as I took in the view. A warm feeling came over me as I observed the campus for the first time in years. The anxiety I had felt a few minutes ago left me. I felt at home here, more than anywhere else. Even though I spent only four years at this school, it was a pivotal time in my life.

I spied Smith Hall in the distance, my dorm for the entire time at Woodbery. And there to the right stood the triangle of three-story stone buildings where many of my classes were held. The library, a beautifully designed modernistic build-ing, was where I had spent many an hour cramming for finals. Nothing had changed as far as I could tell; the campus was precisely the way it was when I had graduated.

I knew, however, this wasn't real—at least I wasn't actu-ally here. Or was I?

And then all other thoughts fell away as I spied her walking by herself on one of the sidewalks that intersected the school Common, smiling at a group of other students that she passed. It was Cassie McKenzie. But not the Cassie I was in love with, at least not yet. This Cassie was younger, the age she was as a student.

My heart did a flip seeing her like this, the carefree, almost whimsical expression on her face, a time before we faced evil in the world. I wanted to run over and tell her everything that had happened to us during the last few years, tell her I loved her. Most of all, I wanted to warn her of what was to come. But I didn't have a body. How could I run to her or speak with her?

And then I was right next to her. It took me a moment to realize I had somehow willed myself to move to a different spot. Or maybe I could see what I wanted, as if I were viewing events through a camera lens with the ability to magnify the scene or change its angle.

She continued walking, oblivious to my presence as she kept her pace a few feet away. There was no way she wouldn't be able to see me. That's when I understood. I was surely disembodied. I could see her and everything else happening, but she couldn't see me. My moment of euphoria dissipated, blown away by a stiff breeze. I had so much to tell her, but that couldn't happen.

I stopped moving and watched her walk away, feeling the disappointment of knowing that I couldn't warn her or the other team members. Whatever the reason for me being here, we would still face the doom of the Bots because of The Utopia Project.

The scene darkened, and my vision faded to black,

replaced a moment later by the vast hall of the Nizaem. Bryson was supporting me with a tight grip under my arms to prevent me from falling. I was standing in the same spot before the shift occurred. Whatever just happened, I wasn't able to change history. I was fated to live the life before me, and so were my Utopia Project partners.

As I regained my balance, Rae asked, "What's wrong? It looked like you were about to faint."

I blinked, unsure of what to say. I knew she and Bryson already thought I might be somewhat unhinged. But Bevon and Ja'Krill had a better understanding of the strange events that could take place in this land. They could often sense when the power of Elthea was at work. "I had a vision," was all I could say.

They continued to stare at me as if expecting me to say more. "I saw a scene from the past. It was like a memory come to life." I gazed back at them, hoping someone would offer an explanation. When they remained silent, I added, "But it wasn't something I remember. Still, it was so real."

The view of Woodbery Common continued to run through my head. Oh, to change the past. Wouldn't that be nice? I could prevent Cassie, Diane, and Matt from being taken prisoner by the Bots. Hell, I could save Eric's life. None of us would ever be hounded by the demonic Bots. I could be back in my safe, comfortable, but mundane life.

That life would be better than this. Wouldn't it? The thought gave me pause to wonder which would be preferable. If given a choice, would I really want to go back to a time when I never knew this land existed?

I looked out again at the hall, which was quickly filling with residents. My gaze landed on the face of Teivel, The Herald of Life. He stared at me with a mysterious intensity. I couldn't be sure, but it seemed he was pleased. It was as if he realized he had prevailed.

But at what?

10

CASSIE'S GIFT

"Quickly now, we are about to begin," urged the Nizaem girl as we lingered at the hall entrance. The room was filling quickly, and she led us toward one of the few remaining long tables that had enough seats for us. Each table was the same, fitting about twenty people, and she guided us toward one in the middle of the room.

As we followed her to our seats, the assembled Nizaem remained hushed as if they were expecting something to happen. The strange stillness lent an air of expectation, as if something extraordinary was about to take place. Possibly someone was about to speak to the crowd, or maybe recite a prayer if they were religious.

But no, that wasn't the reason at all. I realized silence was part of their nature. Every word spoken was said in a whisper rather than a normal voice.

If this were the dining hall in Haven, filled with humans about to enjoy a meal, the residents would revel in hearty conversations and exchange playful banter with each other. Shrieks of laughter would often erupt as someone shared a joke or told an amusing story to their friends.

I felt alone in this room filled with other people. Except for the few friends by my side, I had no connection with this race, one that was so different from mine despite their similarities in appearance. I didn't understand their motives or their way of living. I longed to be back with my kindred spirits in Haven. Most of all, I ached to be with my closest companions, Cassie, Matt, and Diane.

Our Nizaem host seated herself on one side of the table. Ja'Krill and Bryson sat next to her, with Bevon and Rae flanking me on either side. Her complexion was smooth, somewhat darker than that of Teivel. Until now, she had said little to us. What she did say was mostly to deliver commands. Hoping to draw her out, I asked kindly, "What's your name?"

She cocked her head. "My name does not matter. We are all one." Her brusque words came as a gentle whisper. Odd that she would deliver a seemingly harsh message in such a soft tone. My voice sounded garish and loud next to hers. But with everything that had taken place, I didn't care.

Bryson chuckled at her response. "That's stupid. Everyone has a name."

I winced, thinking it might offend her. If so, she didn't show it.

"My given name is Silese, if you must know."

"Silese," I whispered, letting the word roll off my tongue. "That's a pretty name. Do you have a title or function such as Teivel?"

She shook her head. "He is The Herald of Life. There can be only one."

"That is a strange designation," said Bevon. "Can you tell us what the title means? Why the herald?" I caught Bevon's eye, knowing that like me, he was pumping her for information.

"He safeguards our way of life, and he foreshadows the advent of danger. He proclaims our right to live the life we have chosen."

It sounded as if she were talking in circles, or possibly repeating a well-used edict. Bevon persisted. "How does he safeguard your life?"

She didn't hesitate. "The Herald of Life is the strongest of all the Nizaem. Everyone knows this."

He furrowed his brow. "How is he the strongest? Do you mean in the way he uses the powers of Elthea?"

"What other strength is there? None of us can match his abilities."

Her answers explained little, even though she responded willingly. Was she cagey or naive? I decided to jump to the most pressing question. "Why did he save me and bring me here? What's so important in his mind about my life?"

Her eyes danced, and her lips turned up in a thin smile. "I believe you know that answer."

I chafed at her response. "No, I don't. And don't you dare tell me it's because I'm the Gifted One. I never want to hear that again."

She shrugged. "Very well. The Herald of Life deems you necessary for everyone's survival. He has taken you into his fold." She watched me closely, puzzled by my anger. "You should be pleased. If he had not rescued you, evil would now have you. And they would use you for their purpose. By snatching you from their hands, he not only protects you but keeps all those assembled here safe." Her smile brightened. "Now, you are one of us. He owns you, just as he owns all the Nizaem, including me. Be grateful, all is well."

Her calm, easygoing tone frightened me more than anything. I glanced at Bevon. His expression told me all I needed to know: we were in trouble.

I had no idea how we would ever find our way out of this.

ANOTHER BONE-JARRING GONG FORESTALLED FURTHER discussion with Silese. I still wanted to know what she meant by Teivel owning me, but I knew the chime must signal something important. My first thought was that it might be a command for servers to bring platters or bowls of food into the hall. For an evening meal, the room lacked anything to eat. Neither did the tables contain any plates or utensils. "A rather dramatic way to begin a meal," Rae mumbled.

The crowd fell silent, even more than before—the absolute sort of stillness, devoid of even the usual background of scraping chairs or a stray cough. Across from me, Silese closed her eyes, her arms resting gently on her lap as if she were meditating. Everyone else in the room shifted into a similar posture. Maybe they were praying. I wondered what gods they might worship. Was it the spirit of Elthea, or some other deity?

Ja'Krill moved his hand to his hip to reach for his blade

that wasn't there. Ordinarily, he remained undaunted in most situations, but this strange behavior caused even him to feel jittery. His eyes darted around the room, searching for a sign of danger.

The silence was so complete I didn't dare break it. Words now felt inappropriate. Even the sound of my breathing sounded harsh. Was this a prelude to some bizarre ritual?

And then I felt it. Even in my limited capacity to grasp the powers of Elthea, I sensed it. In fact, I could see it. Tendrils of energy flowed from each person, wisps of translucent gossamers barely seen. The energies swirled around the room until coalescing at one person near the front of the room: Teivel.

He was standing, arms outstretched, a serene smile plastered on his face as if receiving an extraordinary offering.

The demonstration lasted mere moments as the room remained eerily hushed. And then, as suddenly as it had begun, the display of energy ceased. I held my breath, waiting for something remarkable to take place. However, the assembled Nizaem resumed their hushed conversations as if nothing occurred. Silese and the other Nizaem had opened their eyes, behaving as if the last few minutes had never happened. The usual hum of background noise spread in waves across the room.

Several dozen Nizaem stood and made their way to a side passage. They returned seconds later carrying large trays that they set down at one end of each table. Others brought plates and utensils. The aromas of unfamiliar spices filled the air as those at the end dished out portions of food from the platters and passed the plates. These made their way to the far end of each long table, where the end person would step over to the adjacent table in the line and pass the food to them. Nobody took the food for themselves until the plates reached the last person at the far end. We followed their example when the time came.

"What just happened?" I asked Silese as the meal was being distributed.

She tilted her head, surprised by my question. "We merged Elthea's life force."

I shook my head. "I don't understand."

"You are not of the Nizaem tribe. I imagine it is difficult for you to comprehend our ways."

I was trying my best to avoid losing my patience with her, but her blunt answers were doing more to confuse me than help. Trying not to raise my voice, I said, "Don't make the mistake of thinking we are stupid because we are not Nizaem."

Bevon glared at me, the look he always gave when I had done something foolish. "What he is trying to say is that the way you just used Elthea's powers is puzzling. We would be grateful if you could explain the reason for what took place."

She observed him with a frown. "You are not like him." She nodded toward me to indicate I was who she meant. "He speaks without thinking, unlike you." Her gaze shifted to Ja'Krill. "You also are not the same." She scrutinized Rae and Bryson. "But you are." She turned back to Bevon. "Some of you are from different clans, yet you are together. Curious. We Nizaem do not mix with other tribes."

Bevon frowned. "You didn't answer my question, Silese."

"Yes, the powers of Elthea. For you to understand, you

must realize that the Nizaem people are bound together as a single entity. Individually, we have no need for the gift that Elthea provides. Whatever energies we can gain from Elthea, we convey to The Herald of Life. In return, he provides us with shelter and a peaceful existence safe from harm. He is the strongest amongst us, and in turn, we help keep him that way."

Teivel had taken a seat with others near the front of the hall. I craned my neck to see him better, wondering what made him so remarkable. Nothing about him stood out; he appeared like every other Nizaem. But I had already seen him accomplish feats far surpassing anything except by the Bots.

I let Silese's earlier comment run through my head. *He owns you, just as he owns me.*

I felt sick, knowing how events would unfold. Either I accepted Teivel's authority over me, or I opposed it. And all the while, those we hated the most held my closest friends, Cassie, Diane, and Matt. My greatest frustration was that I was unable to do anything to free them.

THE STRANGE EVENTS IN THE DINING HALL WEIGHED heavily on my mind as I sat brooding, gazing at the view outside our room. My mood often turned sullen when I had no response to a quandary. And this was no different. I had much to think about, but as yet, I had few answers. Night had overtaken the mountains, providing a spectacle that was as dramatic as the panorama during the day. Even lit by the smaller Halcyone, the snow-topped peaks and rugged cliffs glistened from the reflection of the nearly full moon.

When it happened, I wasn't surprised. I was looking forward to it. After seeing the apparitions of Cassie three previous times, I knew she would reveal herself once more.

Because I was facing away from everyone else, I didn't see her until I heard Rae's cry of surprise. I spun around. Cassie stood in the middle of the room as if she was always with us. Unlike the insubstantial, dreamlike image of the previous appearances, her body was now solid and firm, as if she was standing a few feet away from me. Looking more closely, I noticed the slightest translucency spoiling the illusion that she was here in the flesh. I fought to curb my impulse to fling myself into her arms.

A smile formed on her lips as she saw me. "I did it," she proudly announced.

I was bewildered, not sure what she meant. I tried to form a question, but Bevon spoke first. "Earthfriend Cassie, how are you able to appear here? Have the Bots given you this skill?"

She wrinkled her nose. "The Bots? No, why would they?" Her face brightened. "I can do it on my own. And with each attempt, I'm getting better at it."

I felt an uneasy feeling in the pit of my stomach. I had always thought of Cassie as fragile, not necessarily weak, but someone who could easily be hurt and needed to be protected. She was too independent to accept my sentiment, but I wanted to be the one to keep her safe. It was part of the allure that caused me to fall in love with her. But here she was doing something impossible. A fleeting thought came to me. The winged Astari, Arianell, had once implied that I was not the only one granted powers by Elthea.

Bevon pressed his question. "You can do this on your own with no one else?"

She nodded. "Yes, but I can do more than appear before you. I'm only now beginning to understand it fully. I can look into the past as well."

"Maybe you shouldn't do this," I blurted, my concern outweighing my happiness at seeing her.. "What you're doing could be dangerous to you, and to Matt and Diane. What do you think will happen if the Bots realize what you're doing?"

She lost her carefree grin, looking sad rather than angry. "Phil, none of us are safe any longer. That's part of what I need to show you. There's a reason the Bots are after the four of us."

"I don't want you hurt," I insisted, ignoring her plea. Fighting to keep my voice steady, I added, "When Arianell brought you back to Earth, I thought you would be safe."

"Nobody's safe. Don't you understand? Each of us has to do whatever we can, Phil. You accomplished something unbelievable in the Valnorian Forest. Maybe I can help in a small way. I don't know how this ability at seeing things in the past can help, but I know I have to try. That scene of Woodbery you saw a little while ago, it was because of me."

That frightened me even more. "You don't know what you're getting yourself into. Don't repeat my mistake. I blundered into using Elthea's powers before I understood what I was doing."

Bevon gently placed his hand on my shoulder. "The powers of Elthea are not granted to every person. Do not begrudge her this rare gift. As with you, Elthea has placed her trust in Earthfriend Cassie."

I looked from Bevon to Cassie, knowing he was right. But that made it no easier to accept. "Promise me you'll be careful, that's all I ask."

She nodded briefly, a new thought causing her to change her expression. "Tell me, did you find what you were looking for?"

My mouth felt dry, knowing what she was asking. After the battle in the Valnorian Woods, I didn't return to Earth with her, even though she had pleaded with me. I needed to understand what this power was within me and how I could harness it. I barked a mirthless laugh, mostly to cover my discomfort. "Maybe there are wonders that aren't meant to be understood. I wish I could say I know exactly how the energies of Elthea function and how I can use them, but I don't." I looked at her longingly, wishing now I had returned to Earth with her. "Maybe I'll never figure it out."

So much remained unsaid, but this wasn't the place to dwell on what might have been. Our time was short. Cassie's other visits had been much briefer.

She shifted her gaze to the others in the room, lingering on Rae the longest. Frowning, she asked, "Where's Quintia and Riyaad? Are they all right?"

My throat had tightened, so Bevon replied for me. "They are fine. We became separated when we were brought here."

"And where are you?"

"We are housed by the Nizaem race in their home high in the Grimtane Peaks." Her face remained blank, not completely understanding.

"It's too long to explain," I added. Already I could see the solidness of her figure waver.

"Be careful," she said, sounding far away. "I can sense the power of these Nizaem. They're strong."

"Do you have to leave, Cass?" I cried without thinking.

She shook her head slightly. "I don't have the strength to stay longer. Not yet."

And with that, her image melted away, leaving me to wonder if I would ever see her in the flesh again. Surrounded by my friends, I still felt more alone than I had in a long time.

11

A QUESTION OF LOYALTY

The mountain peaks outside our room grew more defined as the sky lightened, turning the summits a muddy shade of gray. When I had laid down to sleep, on this our first night in the mountain stronghold, I was bone-tired and had immediately fallen into a dreamless slumber. But now, in the wee hours of the morning, sleep eluded me. My mind raced with endless possibilities about how to escape this place. Mostly, however, I worried about Cassie's safety and what this gift by Elthea might portend for her.

I kicked away the blanket I had wrapped around me and stretched my legs. The spongy pallet fixed onto the floor gave way as I shifted my weight to reach for my socks and boots. Careful not to wake the others, I slowly stepped away from the prone forms on the floor, each on their own bedding, and made my way to the open doorway. I hoped to walk the deserted hallway alone to ponder our fate.

Bevon intercepted me before I exited the room. "You should not walk by yourself," he whispered.

Among the Astari, he was my closest friend, as beloved as any human companion. From the moment those of us from the utopia team had first transitioned to the Raised Isles, the Astari had assumed the role of bodyguard. He, especially, had saved my life more times than I could remember. "I couldn't sleep, too much to think about," I explained. "I hoped walking might help."

He poked his head outside the hallway, looking up and down the dimly lit passageway. The Nizaem glowstones that provided light had apparently been programmed to adjust to the time of day. At this early hour, they were barely lit. "I will go with you."

"Thanks, I'm grateful for the company, but remember, no weapons."

He scowled. "I already regret giving my consent." He looked at the hilt of his retracted blade as if unable to make up his mind before placing it on the floor.

Once out of earshot of our room, I said, "I'm worried about Cassie. I don't know if she understands what she's getting into by using this power of Elthea."

"None of us can portend what will help or hurt, especially with Elthea's gifts. Earthfriend Cassie is an intelligent person. I believe you worry needlessly."

I stifled a grunt. "Maybe so, but I still can't understand how her newly found power can help. At least what I did in the Valnorian Forest destroyed the Bots who were attacking us. What good does it do for her to appear to me or show me events from another time?"

He reacted with the slightest grimace. "I am no expert on the powers of Elthea. Other Astari, more knowledgeable than

I have said it defies understanding. They call it a paradox. For me, studying Elthea's life force had always been too bookish a subject to delve into. I wish now I had studied more. But I do know her power can be used for much good. You should not think of it only as a weapon."

"But we need a weapon right now."

He paused a moment. "I have learned to appreciate the complexity of Elthea's power. And so should you. It is a multifaceted gift that can be used in many ways. Who can say the good that might come from Earthfriend Cassie's gift?"

I pursed my lips. "I'm not convinced, but I suppose I should keep an open mind."

He smiled. "That may not be your strongest quality when it comes to Earthfriend Cassie."

I returned the smile, knowing it was his way of reminding me how thickheaded I could be. Changing the subject, I said, "We need to get out of here. I think this place is a trap. I don't trust their leader."

A barely perceptible nod told me he agreed. "Teivel has accomplished a great deal, both in creating this dwelling and in bringing us here. Except for the Bots, he has already accomplished more with his use of Elthea's powers than anyone else I have observed. We can't fight him, he's stronger than us."

I understood his meaning. "If only I could gain back the control I once had. It's so frustrating knowing I once was able to destroy the Bots and protect the Valnorians. Now ... "

He frowned. "I do not know why you have lost that ability. Elthea granted you the strength once. Maybe she will again."

"That doesn't help me much." Realizing I may have offended him, I added, "It's not your fault, but I feel stuck in this morass with no way of getting out. Events not of my doing have swept me along, and I can't lift a finger to help."

He smiled and patted my shoulder as we walked. "Take comfort in the positive, my friend. I know you mistrust this ruler, and I have strong misgivings about Teivel as well. But he did save us from certain death. Once here, he took us in and provided us with food and shelter. We could have ended up in worse trouble."

I stared at him, wondering if perhaps he was right. "Maybe I've judged Teivel too harshly. You don't believe he's dangerous?"

He spoke in a lower voice. "That is not what I said, Earth-friend. The threat we face from this leader is never far from my mind."

And with those words, the fragile optimism I had begun to feel vanished.

RAE AND BRYSON WERE BEGINNING TO STIR WHEN WE returned to our room. Ja'Krill was already awake and sitting on the edge of the window. The sky had brightened from the time Bevon and I had left on our walk. The sun had broken the horizon to a cloudless sky. Mornings were always the best time of day for me, a time when I felt most ready to tackle whatever problems I faced. "We need a plan," I announced to the group.

They looked at me blankly. "A plan for what?" Bryson asked.

"To figure out how to get out of here. What do you think?"

His shoulders drooped, and I immediately felt sorry for speaking so bluntly. I softened my tone. "You're always the one with great ideas, Bry. We're in a tough spot, and I bet you have some thoughts on what we should do now."

His face brightened. "Well, I'm not sure I have an answer, but as my pa always said, we should take the obvious path before tackling the weed-choked one." He rubbed his jaw with the palm of his hand. "The most obvious plan would be to leave by finding our way down the mountain. It may not be easy, but we—"

"You will never survive the descent," said a voice behind us.

I jerked around to see Teivel standing at the entrance of the room, Silese by his side. These people were so damn quiet. None of us had noticed him. Was he trying to eavesdrop?

"Maybe you could help us," Ja'Krill responded calmly. "After all, you brought us here easily enough."

Teivel remained stone-faced. "We already had this conversation. I see no need to repeat my wish to save The Gifted One."

My hands balled up into fists. "I have a problem with your answers," I snapped. "Nothing you tell us makes sense. If you saved me because the Bots wanted me, what would stop them from simply coming here?"

He smiled. "And thus, we reach the heart of the matter, don't we?"

I blinked, not sure I understood. He didn't give me the chance to question him further. "Follow me. I want to show you my favorite place in our home. We can discuss your concerns in more detail there." He glanced sideways at the others. "You may also follow, as I assume you will, but it is unnecessary." He never waited for an answer as he turned and swept from the room. Silese motioned for us to follow.

I hesitated, not wanting to give Teivel the satisfaction of knowing he could order us around, but my curiosity won out. I glanced at my friends. "Come on, let's see what he has to say." Even with Silese within earshot, I added, "I'm determined to find out what game he's playing."

By the time we exited the room, Teivel had already disappeared around a corner of the hallway. Either he didn't care, or he knew we would follow. Silese urged us to keep pace.

We followed her through a warren of passageways, and I was soon lost. The Nizaem home was more extensive than I had thought with its smooth, pristine corridors, and an endless number of rooms off the hallways. The girl led us ever upward on a series of stairs, revealing that the residence contained multi-levels. We passed other Nizaem in the halls, but, unsurprisingly, they displayed no particular interest in us.

The last flight of stairs opened onto an external platform. The floor was smooth, like the rest of those in the dwelling. It formed a semicircle on the open sides, with a wall to the left and right of the entrance. The landing had no ceiling or walls, save the one where we entered. No railing or palisade lined the edge to prevent a person from slipping off the side. My stomach churned as I wondered if the floor was suspended over open air.

I was beginning to hate heights.

Teivel stood near the far edge of the floor, facing outward. I stepped toward him, expecting to feel a blast of frigid air. However, it remained as warm as the rest of the cavern. Whatever magic was used to keep the cold at bay at the window in our room was also at work here. The only furniture consisted of a series of stone chairs arranged in a tight circle in the middle of the space.

"I call this our Hall of Potency," Teivel said, never turning around to see if we had arrived. He continued gazing at the mountains that ringed the skyline. Even though his robes covered his arms, he held them outward as if absorbing the sun's rays. "I positioned this place unencumbered by rock, so I receive the full benefit of Elthea's strength."

This was the first I had heard that location mattered when using Elthea's powers. Even though I was far from an expert on this subject, I doubted he was correct. I shot a glance at Bevon, who confirmed my assumption with a frown. I didn't think it was worth questioning him. Neither did Bevon. Instead, my friend took a different approach. "You take considerable pride in your ability to harness the powers of Elthea," he said bluntly.

Teivel turned to regard us as he grinned with obvious

arrogance. "You would also if you had my strength. The Astari of old had some of my abilities, but you have allowed your skills to decline."

A thought suddenly came to me. "If you're so powerful, help me free my friends from the Bots."

He smiled, his eyes gleaming. "Well done. I had wondered how long it would take you to ask." He considered my appeal. "It is a simple thing which you request."

My face lit up for the first time in a long while. Could my worst fear be over? "You can do this? You're willing to free my friends?" I actually laughed. "And to think, all I had to do was ask."

He smiled knowingly, and my heart beat faster as I wondered if he could accomplish it right this minute. Cassie might be back with me before the day ended. I glanced at the others, expecting to see the exhilaration I felt. Both Bevon and Ja'Krill eyed Teivel warily, almost as if he were about to attack.

Ignoring their suspicion, I asked, "When can you rescue them? Could you do it right now?"

Nodding as if agreeing, he moved to one of the stone chairs, motioning for the rest of us to sit. I felt too wound up to take a seat, but I quickly lowered myself onto the one next to him. What I had thought was solid stone conformed to my shape as I settled into it. He waited while Bevon, Ja'Krill, Rae, and Bryson sat. Silese remained standing next to the wall.

I looked at him expectantly. "You can free them without a problem, can't you? They won't be in danger?"

He shook his head slowly. "Freeing them from their

confinement by the Bots would pose no risk to your friends. But first, we must discuss the issue of your loyalty."

I wondered if I heard him correctly. "Loyalty? What?"

He smiled, his face the picture of innocence. "Yes, it is the reason I saved you from certain imprisonment by your enemy."

Still confused, I knitted my eyebrows, desperate to comprehend his meaning. "Wh—"

He cut me off, motioning with his fingers between us. "We are two of a kind, you and I. We serve a higher purpose in life. Elthea has granted us something unique. We must work to make this land a better place for our people. It is our fate to rule or be ruled. That is our only choice."

"What are you talking about? What does any of this have to do with freeing my friends?"

"I have to know we are working toward the same purpose."

A sick feeling came over me. It began to dawn on me he had a price for this favor.

His smile did not seem genuine. "Your enemy is my enemy. We shall work together. You must consent to my authority and bind yourself to me as everyone else here has done. That is all I need to know." He shrugged. "You see, it is a simple matter."

Did he realize I had lost whatever ability I once had to use Elthea's power? I decided not to bring it up right now. "Free my friends first, and we can discuss it."

He shook his head. "It doesn't work that way. I am The Herald of Life. My first responsibility is to the Nizaem living here. I must know they are shielded and kept safe."

Bile rose in my stomach. "But you just said how strong you are. You're protecting them already. You don't need me."

The smile plastered on his face was infuriating. "Oh, but I do need you. I am strong, but our enemies are also strong. With your support, I can overcome anything they throw at me." He rubbed his chin as if considering something. I gave him time to work it out in his head, hoping he might change his mind. "You saw what I did to the Bots when they attacked you. I killed them at significant risk to myself and my people. They do not tolerate those who oppose them. I have poked them, so to speak, and now you must help protect us."

I looked down at the floor, my mind racing with possibilities. Every person faces a few pivotal moments in life, a time when one decision can alter their future. This was such a moment. All I could see were Cassie, Diane, and Matt staring at me from a cell.

I was on the verge of agreeing to his proposal when Bevon interrupted. "Teivel, that will not be possible. Earthfriend Philip is under my protection, and I will not allow you to put him in danger."

A shadow passed over Teivel's face. "He is free to make his own decisions. In any case, I do not see you doing much to protect him from the Bots. He will be better served with me safeguarding him."

A sour expression formed on Bevon's face. He knew the Bots were stronger than the Astari.

Before anyone could say another word, Rae interjected, "Maybe it would help if you explained what you are asking him to do. Would he need to remain here in your stronghold?

Can he leave at any time? What if he disagrees with your decisions? How long does—"

"Enough! I will not be questioned by one so weak as you, or any others from your race. This does not concern you." He glared at each of my friends, his face turning a shade darker. "None of you are helping him. Only I can." His gaze shifted back to me, his eyes smoldering. "There are only two questions you need to answer. Are your utopia companions worth it, and what are you willing to sacrifice to free them?"

I hesitated, a host of emotions racing through me. I would do anything for Cassie and the others, but I didn't trust him. Something told me he wasn't entirely truthful. "If you're a man of honor, you will free them because it's the right thing to do. Maybe then, I will be more persuaded to come to your aid, if you needed it."

His body stiffened. With a strained voice, he said, "You are making a horrible mistake." A new thought seemed to come to him as his eyes looked out to the mountains. "But this is not over; I believe others may still convince you. Your captive friend will demonstrate. She has already tested her Farseeing ability."

I froze, my eyes wide. Was he talking about Cassie? "What do you mean?"

His arrogant smile returned, his posture relaxing. "I believe you understand. Ask her to show you how the Bots have targeted you and your utopia friends from the beginning. Maybe then you will realize you cannot outrun them. Only by joining with me can you ever hope to be free from them."

"What are you saying? What did the Bots do? When?"

His infuriating smile remained in place. "Once you learn more, we will speak again. I believe my offer will sound more palatable after you have discovered what you face."

Of everything he had said, this was the most damning. *The Bots have targeted you and your friends from the very beginning.*

Maybe we had no hope, after all.

12

WITHOUT A SOUL, YOU ARE NOTHING

I left the Hall of Potency feeling like my life had gone from bad to worse. The hallways passed as if in a dream as Silese led us back to our room. I kept thinking about Teivel. *You must consent to my authority and bind yourself to me.*

"You will find a way, Earthfriend," Bevon said kindly once Silese had left us alone in our room. "You have been in difficult straits before and have always found a way."

Not sure if I should laugh or cry, I rasped, "How can I save my friends when I can't even save us? I have no power. I'm useless."

His face remained impassive. It was an Astari trait I often found infuriating. "You saved the Valnorians," he said with a shrug.

"A fine epitaph when I die, but that still won't help my friends." My stomach churned. "What if Teivel decides I'm not worth keeping around, that I don't have any power within me?"

"It does not matter what he desires. You should ask your-self what you want. Do you prefer his offer to join forces and rule all Elthea?"

"No! You know I don't." A sudden thought came to me. "But what if I lie to him, tell him what he wants to hear? At least my friends will be free."

Bevon pursed his lips. "Trying to deceive someone is folly, especially him. If you agree to his demand, he could bind you with powerful wards. He has the strength. And if that happens, you may never be free again."

"Damn this stupid power of Elthea."

He didn't respond, but Ja'Krill cut in. "You shouldn't be so quick to condemn what you don't fully understand. The energies of Elthea have created untold wonders in this land. Some Valnorians spend their entire lives trying to master the powers. But even they cannot grasp its full potential."

Bryson and Rae were listening intently until Bryson hesi-tantly spoke. "I'm not one to talk about these powers; I know nothing about them. If you tell me to shut up, I will." Despite my dour mood, I smiled lightly. When nobody spoke, he continued, "I was thinking of something my pa might say right now. He would probably tell you that maybe you need to let it come to you rather than forcing it."

A touch of laughter colored my words. "More words of wisdom from your father?"

His face colored. "I miss him. That's all. I guess during times like this, I think about Pa even more." He grimaced. "Maybe I'm not cut out for this life and all this danger. I thought it was a simple matter when I joined The Guard of Haven. I'd become a respected person in the community.

The ladies of the town would look at me differently. Now, well, I just don't know."

He touched upon a memory of how I had once felt when I first came to this land. I spoke wistfully. "You're not alone. I always dreamed of going on a grand adventure. But then, when I found myself in a magical land, all I could think about was how I wanted to go back to my comfortable, boring life."

Rae furrowed her eyebrows. "We all think about the ones we love during times like this. I know I do. It doesn't mean you're not good enough for The Guard, Bry. Besides, you judge yourself too harshly. Nobody at Haven has ever been captured and brought to a place like this." She cut short a laugh. "Maybe you'll even return as a hero after this is over."

He smiled. "You mean if we survive."

She ignored his comment, and her eyes hardened as she shifted her gaze toward me. "As for you, stop feeling sorry for yourself. We're all tested at one time or another. How you respond says a lot about what kind of person you are."

My sullen mood dissolved at her rebuke. "I guess I deserve that." In a softer voice, I added, "You realize, Rae, that in another place and time, you could be a storyteller, able to move others with your words rather than wield a bow or blade. Of all the people I've ever known, you always say the right thing. I wish I had your talent."

She shrugged as if she didn't deserve the compliment. "They're only words. Anyone can say them." Her eyes lost their focus. "I feel there are times when the right words can change a life, hopefully for the better, while the wrong ones can dash whatever hope remains." A crooked smile came to her lips. "If I've learned anything, it's that I prefer using a knife. Its meaning is more direct."

"I'll grant you that. You're direct, if nothing else."

She looked at me smugly. "And don't you ever forget it."

CASSIE APPEARED LATER THAT DAY, AS I HOPED SHE would. I was sitting near the window in our room, with nothing to do but watch the shadows of the mountain peaks grow smaller as the sun rose higher in the sky. I couldn't help fidgeting with my hands as I wondered if the Bots had somehow discovered her capacity to appear before me and stopped her. Or perhaps something worse had happened.

When she finally emerged from empty space in the middle of the room, I had to stop myself from running into her arms. With each appearance, her vision had become more solid and less of an illusion. The only imperfection marring the sight was that her feet didn't quite touch the floor. She smiled at me.

Without realizing it, I smiled back. "I was worried," I said, knowing that Teivel had knowledge of her appearances.

Her grin shifted to a pout. "You always worry." She tried to say it seriously, but it sounded more teasing. "Although, I must say it's one of the things I love about you. But maybe this time, you have a reason to be concerned."

My throat tightened. Bevon responded before I could say anything. "What has happened, Earthfriend? Have the Bots harmed you?"

She shook her head. "No, nothing like that. Well, at least not yet. We still haven't seen any of them."

"Then what's wrong?" I said, finding my voice.

She hesitated before answering. "I discovered why the Bots will never leave us alone."

Teivel's words sounded again in my head. *The Bots have targeted each of you from the very beginning.* I fought to keep the desperation out of my voice. "Cass, what're you talking about?"

She took a deep breath. "You must understand, I'm only beginning to learn what I can accomplish with this gift. Being able to see and talk with you is only a small part of it."

"I don't like where you're going with this," I said before she could explain further. "You could be in danger if the Bots discover what you're doing. They could take it as a threat."

She made a motion with her hand as if to brush away my misgivings. Her face brightened, and she rushed her words. "Once again, you worry too much. You're not going to believe what I can do. Matt and Di didn't either at first, but then I showed them. I tried it with you. Remember?" She didn't give me a chance to reply. "Phil, I can look back and see events in the past. What you saw at Woodbery College yesterday was because of me. It's like I'm able to travel back in time and see things that happened to me—that happened to us. And I'm able to have you or Matt and Di see it."

She was so happy I almost didn't want to be negative. But I couldn't help myself. "Cass, that's not possible, nobody can go back in time."

She held her head proudly, no sign my words had dissuaded her. In the past, she would have turned despondent or angry. Ja'Krill spoke before she could say more. "Phil, it may not be as impossible as you believe." He addressed me, but he was watching Cassie curiously. "Among my people, those who were the most powerful in the arts could accomplish such a task." He glanced at me. "Elthea's powers take many forms, something you would do well to always remember."

I scowled, but before I could say more, Bevon spoke. "Earthfriend Philip, there was a time when you wouldn't have believed it was possible to shoot lightning from your fingertips, or that the ground could turn to liquid, or that—"

"I get it," I snapped. My eyes flicked from Bevon to Ja'Krill and back to Cassie. Taking a moment to calm myself, I said, "Cass, it seems unthinkable to me, but even if you can look back in time, what good is it? What's done is done, unless you can change the past."

She wrinkled her nose. "I said I can look back. I'm not able to change anything, but I can see everything that took place long ago. I can even see myself as I was back then. And I can bring others back to see it."

I rubbed the back of my neck, realizing that precious moments were passing as we talked about this nonsense. "Have you considered how dangerous this could be, especially to you?"

Her lips tightened. "Why is it you think I always need protecting? You thought it was dangerous when I first appeared before you. Now, you believe this is unsafe. We each have to do what we can. Don't you understand?"

"I'm worried for a reason. The ruler of these people knows about your ability. He called it Farseeing. If he found out, the Bots could as well. And once they do, how are they going to react? You're their prisoner."

Her eyes went unfocused for a moment. Was she finally understanding my concern? "Farseeing. I like that," she said, irritating me further that she had focused on that part of the discussion. "I didn't know what to call it before. I thought the term Farseeing meant predicting events in the future, but it works in this case. We have to see the past before we understand the future."

"Did you hear the rest of what I said?"

She brushed me off with a wave of her hand. "Yes, I get it. It's risky." She paused, gnawing absently at her lower lip. When she spoke again, her tone was more thoughtful. "Phil, we're all in trouble. You saved us once. Maybe this time, you need help. Please. Don't dismiss what I can offer."

I nodded briefly, not trusting my voice to speak without it cracking.

She smiled sadly. "I'll be back again soon. We'll explore this together. Events we never realized happened in the past. Now, they're calling out to me. We need to understand what happened to us back then. Maybe it will help you, I don't know. It might not make a difference. But I have to try. It's the only way I will know for sure."

When I spoke again, my voice felt thick with emotion. "Cass, the most important thing about the past is the time I first met you. I loved you then, and I love you still."

Her eyes brightened, but they still held a hint of sadness. Her image weakened. "Stay safe. I'll return soon."

Seconds later, her figure evaporated, leaving me with an empty feeling. My companions watched me closely, searching for how I would react. They deserved better than this. We all did. But each of them needed to believe we would survive. I met their gaze. "We'll find a way out of this. I promise."

I didn't say what was really on my mind.

Silese waited at the entrance of our room until she saw we had acknowledged her presence. Hours had passed since Cassie's appearance, and I was still thinking about everything she had said.

Silese came closer, fixing me with an icy stare as she approached. She displayed little warmth or compassion. "Evening meal will soon be served."

Bevon stood and bowed politely. I stood stiffly, wondering if she deserved such courtesy. "Welcome, Silese," he said. "Thank you again for your hospitality and the food you provide."

Her eyes flashed at his words as if he had spoken an insult. But she quickly focused on me again. "The Herald of Life provides the sustenance you need. Yet, you do not contribute to him. I do not understand."

"We are grateful for his kindness," Bevon continued. I didn't see his point in being so pleasant. "We are willing and able to do what we can."

I returned her glare. "Your leader has all the strength he needs. I have nothing to give him."

"You know nothing about him." She bit off the words, her eyes flashing. "He saved you. Now, he asks for a simple thing, yet you do not grant him what he wishes." She flexed her fingers. "He graciously consented to free your companions. Did you not understand? Do you care nothing for your friends?"

I swept my arm in front of me, cutting through the air. "I don't trust him. Maybe he has helped you and the Nizaem people survive in these frigid mountains, but he has done nothing but make demands on me."

"He saved you from certain death, or worse. Did you so quickly forget?"

My voice rose. "I don't have what he's asking. He doesn't realize it, and neither do you. See for yourself. Use your power to look inside me."

She shook her head as if suddenly afraid. "No, we do not expend our energy. It is only for The Herald of Life to use. It is blasphemy to even suggest such a thing."

Her vehemence stunned me. Into the sudden silence, Rae spoke gently. "Are you afraid of him? Has he hurt you?"

Silese looked at Rae as if seeing her for the first time. She stared for a few seconds until finally taking a deep breath and replying in a calmer voice. "I love The Herald of Life. He is the wisest and the strongest of our people. All the Nizaem feel the same. If we do not, we are free to leave."

I noticed she didn't answer the questions. Ja'Krill spoke before I could. "I am curious about this practice. What if, once you have given The Herald of Life your energy, you later don't agree with how he uses it? Do you have any recourse?"

Her body tensed as she glared at Ja'Krill. "Enough questions! We do as The Herald of Life asks." Her eyes shifted back to me. "You are The Gifted One and should respond in kind. There is no other option." She looked away. "As for the rest, you have no standing in our community. You must earn it. Accordingly, I will designate work assignments for each of you. I have the responsibility to direct your work."

At that moment, the gong sounded. Before anyone could challenge Silese further or ask about these work duties, she turned her head toward the hallway. "We serve the evening meal. Those who are late will go without food. Begin learning our rules." She looked back toward us with an unpleasant smile and added, "If you do not grasp our way of life quickly enough, you will not remain here for long." She spun around and charged toward the hallway, not waiting for a response or even to see if we followed.

We looked at each other uncertainly. Bryson was the first to move toward the entrance. "You heard the lady. If we're late, we don't eat."

Rae barked a laugh. "It figures you would focus on that bit of information from everything she said."

He shrugged as he continued toward the hallway. "You're the person who once told me to concentrate on what's most important. Seems to me, we should keep up our strength before anything else."

I smiled, once again appraising the young man. By now, I understood him well enough to realize Bryson wasn't unmindful of the danger we faced. This was just his way of lessening the tension.

Today, however, I was too deep in thought to appreciate his lighthearted efforts. I glanced at Bevon. "I'm beginning to worry we'll never leave this place. We're held captive by

Teivel much as Cassie, Matt, and Diane are prisoners of the Bots."

His smile faded. "We will find an answer. You must believe."

Something in his tone didn't sound convincing. He knew, as well as I did, that we were in trouble. Even Cassie had said it. I waited for the others to exit the room before saying, "What bothers me most is that a time may come when I'll need to sell my soul to buy our freedom."

He looked at me with an unreadable expression. "That, my Earthfriend, is something you should never consider. Without a soul, you are nothing."

I wanted to say it wasn't that simple, that I had nothing else to offer. But until the time came when I needed to decide, I tucked the thought away. Maybe I would never have to make the choice Teivel put before me.

But of course, that time would eventually arrive.

13

THE INNOCENCE OF OUR YOUTH

Teivel's gaze latched onto me the moment we entered the great hall. Power emanated from him, something I could sense more than see. Watching us enter, he turned up his lips, not quite far enough to form a smile.

As we walked between the long tables, a subdued air of expectation hung over the assembled. The silence gave me an eerie feeling, reminding me how alone I felt even surrounded by a room full of people.

We took our seats next to Silese. She made no mention of her brief flare-up in our room. Calmly, as if it had never occurred, she said, "The Herald of Life has planned something special for you tonight."

My stomach lurched. The last thing I wanted was another surprise. However, I had little time to puzzle it out as the chime rang again, transforming the hushed silence of the room to absolute stillness. It was time for Teivel to receive what I was beginning to think of as his fix.

As before, I sensed the transfer of energy taking place at the edge of my awareness. My nerves crackled even though I could see nothing amiss. Elthea's power flowed from each of the Nizaem citizens into their leader. Each person in the room willingly gave Teivel the strength he needed to maintain control over them. One of those people could be me one day if I granted Teivel his wish. An unexpected shiver came over me. Would this be my fate? He could free my closest friends, but at what cost?

Before I realized it, the transfer was complete. Teivel was a little more enriched with power, leaving the rest of the residents less able to oppose his will.

Teivel rose to address everyone. His gaze swept over the crowd with an air of superiority, his mouth bending into the smile I imagined a king might display, conveying a false sense of love for his subjects. "Fate has been kind to us," he began, his voice loud enough so that even those in the far reaches of the room heard every word. "The instrument of our salvation is now amongst us."

Rae, sitting next to me, poked me in the ribs. "I think he means you, oh Gifted One." I knew she didn't think the title was fitting, nor was our situation amusing. It was her way of injecting a touch of irreverence to Teivel's speech, and preventing me from thinking too highly of myself, although there was little chance of that happening to me.

The crowd neither smiled nor otherwise acknowledged their good fortune at Teivel's proclamation. Across the table from me, Silese fixed me with a disdainful expression. Apparently, her opinion of me hadn't changed.

"Take pleasure in knowing our future is secure," Teivel

continued. "Let us listen once again to *The Story of Our Life* and recall how far we have come since the dark days. The time is near for us to regain our rightful home."

He nodded to someone at a nearby table. A young man rose and stepped to the front of the hall as Teivel sat. The man fidgeted with his hands as if he didn't know what to do with them. He carried no notes to read from. Putting a hand to his mouth, he loudly cleared his throat. I expected him to blunder through a memorized passage. However, a deep and melodious voice rang from his lips when he spoke.

"As the telling goes, this is The Story of our Life
Although some might say it is the story of our youth
A time when we lived happily and carefree, this is the
*   truth*
No harm came to us in the enchanted village of
*   Allerholm*
Glad were we to be left alone
None to oppress us, none to leave a sullen mark on our
*   way of life.*

Glorious was the pinnacle of the Nizaem clan
Living off the fertile land
Riding the wires between East and West Allerholm
A stately community split by the ever-thundering
*   Rhaokim*
A mighty river, if ever there was one
It gave us life and sustenance.

The Grimtane Peaks rose like lofty turrets
All around did they shield us
And as for others in the land of Elthea
We cared little.

The Nizaem citizens were grounded in a code of life
That we would live, and love, and be carefree
It was the way we would always be.

Until the time when the world crashed down
    around us
It began with a well-intentioned request
To join one side in a great conflict
We will fight a great battle, said the young cadet
Join us to remain free.

No, was the reply of Iradia, our ruler
Trusting in a future that would keep us safe
Not wanting to intrude on the whims of fate
To determine the side, the Nizaem should take.

You have no choice, insisted the other
They will take what you desire most
A life worth living and a home of plenty
You will lose everything in the ultimate battle that
    even now draws nigh.

Independent did we remain
Not choosing war over peace

Yet, the other side came calling one day
Also demanding that our men should join them
To fight the war that would change our land
They said we must understand.

Iradia gave the newcomers the same response
She truly believed our fate was to remain as we had
    always been
Sheltered from the storm of change
That was seeping across this land as if preordained.

The outside world we ill-understood
As troops invaded our home
To kill the Nizaem in the once peaceful dell called
    Allerholm.

For some Nizaem, they surrendered
Begging the attackers to please remember
They were peaceful dwellers and none among them a
    warrior
To fight a war among these foreigners.

An ill wind blew that day
The killing day of what was once so fair
The troops cared little for the innocence our people
    declared
As a thriving race became no more.

A precious few did escape

And deny a wicked force what they thought was
    our fate
By scaling the lofty peaks did we demonstrate
The willpower of the Nizaem was no small weight
To so cruelly shatter on that darkest day.

Today, we live so that one day we will attain
The revenge that still burns, unfeigned
To forevermore redress the evil deed
That was committed that day upon those who once
    believed
that to be happy and carefree
Was the only life they could foresee."

THE ROOM REMAINED DEATHLY SILENT AS THE YOUNG Nizaem man shuffled back to his seat. I glanced around, seeing many with their heads bowed, others with their eyes closed as if in contemplation or perhaps in silent prayer.

The Story of our Life explained as much as it left unsaid. Was the evil force the Bots? Did these people still harbor a desire for revenge for what had once taken place? How did they expect to redress past wrongs done against them?

Mostly, the tale provided some explanation for the resolve of these people. I should be at ease with a race who had been wronged and were only trying to regain what the Bots had taken from them. Shouldn't I?

I glanced again at Teivel, unable to extinguish the apprehension in my heart. I couldn't help but feel that he was scheming to accomplish more than he let on.

WHEN WE RETURNED TO OUR ROOM, THE BREATHTAKING view of the mountain peaks outside our window was now a swirling mass of white. We all watched as specks of snow and hail bounced off the invisible barrier. I couldn't see more than a foot outside as the raging storm blocked out everything else.

"It's odd," said Rae, her eyes on the turbulence. "We can see the snowstorm but can't hear it." That was why it looked so odd, I realized. No sound penetrated from the outside.

"I'm just glad we didn't arrive outside on the ledge in this weather," Bryson remarked.

Rae turned to him with a smirk. "You're always the pragmatic one. Keep it up, and someday you'll become a captain of The Guard. Then, you'll be the one giving orders to the rest of us grunts."

I half listened to the banter. Rae was an expert at keeping spirits high, and I often admired her prowess at lifting the mood of others, which often included me. But right now, I had too much to worry about. Her life, and those of Bryson, Bevon, and Ja'Krill, depended on me. And it was wearing me down.

"Are you ready, Phil?" I spun away from the window at the question from behind me, recognizing Cassie's voice. I scanned the room, expecting to see her, but the room was empty. No vision of her appeared this time. Could she be losing her grip on Elthea's powers?

"Where are you?" I didn't bother to hide the panic in my voice. "I can't see you."

She giggled. "The same place as before. There's no need

for you to see me. I told you, I'm here to perform the—" She paused. "What did you call it again?"

"The Farseeing," Bevon answered.

"Yes, that's it. I'm going to bring you back to see events that happened in the past."

I still had serious misgivings, but knew now was not the time to argue it again. "If you believe it's important." I didn't succeed in keeping the disapproval from my voice.

"I have this gift for a reason, Phil." I could almost see her pout as she spoke. "We will only watch and observe. I'm opening this up to Matt and Di also, but you won't be able to see or speak with them. You'll only see us in the past."

It sounded like a lot of gobbledygook. I clenched my jaw, suppressing the urge to yell that we were being threatened by forces we couldn't fight or even understand. Yet, she wanted to engage in this harebrained pastime.

Ja'Krill must have noticed how tense I was. "Earthfriend Philip, take pleasure in this boon offered by Elthea. The events you witness may not solve all our troubles. But, as a wise Valnorian mage once told me, 'The more you observe and learn, the more knowledge you can apply to a problem.'"

I loved Ja'Krill, but at this moment, I wanted to throw him out the window. I forced myself to keep the rancor from my voice. "First, Bryson talks about his Pa and now words of wisdom from your mage. When does it end?" He smiled but kept silent.

"I'm sorry that the rest of you in the room won't see this," said Cassie. "It seems I can only bring a few into the ... Farseeing. It's probably a good idea for you to be seated, Phil. Or better yet, lie down."

I stepped over to the beds built into the floor, suddenly curious about what would happen. Despite my misgivings, I couldn't help but wonder what I might see. "Ready?" she asked once I had settled onto the bed. I responded and waited as my pulse quickened. Seconds later, my world upended.

THE FACE OF ERIC WEBSTER, THE FIFTH MEMBER OF our utopia team, filled my vision. His lips were set in the slightest hint of a grin, an expression I remembered so well; it was as if I had seen him only yesterday. His perpetual smile could often be infuriating, especially when he didn't take things seriously. But the passage of time and the pain of his death did much to temper my disapproval of his cavalier ways.

Seeing him again, as if alive, made me realize how much I missed the levity he brought to any situation. My episodes of despondency and self-doubt during the last year would have been greatly mitigated had he been with me. I shifted my gaze to take in younger versions of Matt, Diane, Cassie, and oddly enough, myself.

God, we were so young, so immature, a group of kids with our future ahead of us. This was the heyday of my life, the college days of The Utopia Project. It was the pivotal time in each of our lives, leading us to the land of Elthea's Realm. Blissfully unaware of what was yet to come, we had no inkling of the changes in our lives that would spring from that seemingly insignificant course. All the magic and wonder, the anguish and pain that came later, would stem from this time.

It took me another moment to understand the mechanics of adjusting the perspective of what I was seeing. Just like a camera, I could choose the view, angle, or closeup I wanted to see by merely thinking it. I quickly scanned the small room. A round conference table dominated the center. Each of us sat around it. A sizable electronic whiteboard filled one wall. Tall windows on the other side opened out toward bare maple trees and drab grass that had not yet recovered from the snows of winter.

Even after all these years, a warm sensation came over me, knowing I was back at Woodbery College. In many ways, this campus was my home, and I was back again during the days that meant the most to me. This was our favorite meeting room, where we held our team discussions, a place where we bonded as much as anywhere else.

"Is this some sort of joke?" my younger self said to Matt. My voice wasn't angry. I could tell I was more annoyed than anything else.

He frowned, unsure of how to respond. "I know it sounds crazy, but I tell you, that's what I saw. Why would I make this up?"

Eric tossed a pen onto his open notebook. "Matt, I've always said you were wrapped a bit too tight. But this? Do you have a screw loose? I can't understand how you would even suggest such a thing."

Cassie took a more sympathetic approach. "Matt, maybe you're confused. That's all."

As the scene unfolded, I realized that not until this moment did I remember it took place. But upon seeing it, I knew it had happened; it was as if my memory of this event had been locked away and only needed a whisper of recognition to bring it back. I still didn't know what anyone would say next, but the conversation up to this point was one that I knew had happened.

Matt raised his voice. "I know what we put into our Prime Theorem. Hell, I created it. I should know the purpose of the equations and the formulas they represent."

Diane had remained silent during the exchange. I had the impression she had already heard the story earlier from Matt. "I'm telling you," she said, an edge to her voice, "somehow your tablet reverted to an earlier version. That's the only explanation."

Matt exploded. "Then how did it change to that same version on everyone's tablet?" He sucked in a calming breath before continuing in a softer voice. "I know these equations. We never included them in an earlier version. If anything, the equations have become more complex."

"What's the problem?" Eric said with a smirk. "Consider it a gift from heaven. None of the professors are gonna understand that rubbish anyway."

Matt gritted his teeth. Was he going to punch Eric? I couldn't remember. Instead, he raised his voice. "You may not understand this, but if something has happened with our Prime Theorem, a major part of our utopia paper, we are screwed. *You* may think it's been a lot of trouble, but it's a major reason our paper will stand out from all the others."

The younger version of myself held up his hands as if separating Eric and Matt in a fight. "We all agreed these equations are valuable. They support everything we say in the paper." Despite what I now said, I remember having serious doubts about the equations and graphs. I believed they took too much of our time. "I don't know if I would have noticed this," I continued, "but once Matt pointed it out, I can see the difference from what we had before."

"But they can't just change on their own," Matt mumbled.

"Then let's go through the equations," Diane countered. "We can take each one and rework it through from the simplest to the most complex and figure out how they went wrong."

Eric groaned. "We have a gazillion of them in this damn paper. How the fuck do you expect to check every one of them? I vote we take them out. That would be much simpler."

"It would be simpler," said Matt, still angry. "But that wouldn't make the paper better, would it?"

The two stared, unblinking, at each other until Eric relented. He yanked a tablet from his pack. "We better get a frigging fantastic grade in this project." He glared at Matt for another second before shifting his gaze to the rest of the group, pointing a finger around the room. "And barring that, you had better nominate me for sainthood for putting up with the bunch of you."

He looked angry, but an undercurrent in his tone betrayed his genuine emotions. The others noticed it also and exchanged discreet smiles before focusing on the screens of their individual tablets. "Let's start with the individual freedoms," said Diane.

This was the moment the innocence of our youth ended. A great evil was about to enter our lives.

I blinked again, and I was back in the Nizaem room with Bevon, Ja'Krill, Rae, and Bryson, wondering once again, and not for the first time, how my life ever brought me to a place like this.

In the days ahead, I would find the answer.

14

A DRAGON'S TRIBUTE

The next morning dawned sunny and bright outside, with no sign of the snow squall of the previous afternoon. The sight of a sparkling new day buoyed my spirits. Anything was possible. Better days would come to us soon; I felt sure of it.

The vast mountain range outside the window spoke of permanence, a tribute that life would continue, and one day, for the better. I was beginning to uncover shreds of information that might help make sense of our situation. I had to hope.

Reflecting again on Cassie's Farseeing episode, I was still unsure how this glimpse into my past might help me. But I no longer felt it a waste of time. I was eager to see more. Events had taken place that I hadn't remembered. Yet, once seen, I was sure they had happened. It was as if a memory long forgotten had been restored.

Silese cleared her throat as she entered the room. "The Herald of Life has granted you a remarkable courtesy yesterday. It is not often we are treated to a recital of our most sacred ode."

The Farseeing event had overshadowed the recital of the Nizaem verse. "There's only one thing I took from it," I said. "You and Teivel have reason to hate the Bots as much as I do." The more I had thought about the story, the more I believed it was the Bots that had carried out the killing.

She glared at me. "You are an outsider and do not understand what they took from us."

"Maybe not, but that's no reason to keep us here."

Her lips tightened. "I am not here to discuss your perceived grievance." Her eyes raked across the others. "Your training in the Nizaem way of life begins today. I will oversee your first assignment."

Rae stepped forward, shoulders squared, hands on her hips as her eyes flashed. "I don't think you understand, we have no interest in your way of life. Besides, we will not be staying here long."

The two stared at each other, a battle of wills taking place in the silence that filled the room. When Silese finally spoke, her voice was calm. "In that case, you may leave now if you wish."

Rae didn't blink. When she didn't respond after another few seconds, I wondered if she might consider the offer. Rae was intelligent, but she could also be impulsive. Bevon stepped between the two. "You have been gracious by providing us with shelter and food. For as long as we are here, we will be happy to contribute to the good of the Nizaem." He glanced sideways at Rae. "Tell us how we can help."

Silese raised an eyebrow. Bevon's remarks didn't fit her

opinion of us as unproductive and insensitive. She shrugged and continued. "Today, you will forage on the upper flatland."

"Outside?" Bryson blurted.

The hint of a smile appeared on the girl's face. "Why yes, of course. While we grow most of our food in our sheltered bio-domes, we can only harvest certain edibles found in the wild. This should be an easy enough task for today. Hunting the mountain animals for food is a more advanced skill which we will save for later."

Was this her idea of a joke? If so, it wasn't very amusing. "We'll freeze outside," I said. "Besides, we barely survived the first time we were out there."

She smiled, her eyes dancing. "Do not worry. We will provide heavy clothing." She eyed the diminutive Bevon and Ja'Krill. "We can find children's coats for the two of you." She shifted her attention back to me. "As for The Gifted One, you are exempt."

I scowled. "Please stop calling me that. My name is Philip ... or Phil, if you wish. And I go with my friends."

Her face softened as she continued to stare at me. And when she spoke, her anger had dissipated. "Very well, Philip. You may stay with the others even though it is not required." She turned and walked the length of the room toward the opening, pausing at the entrance as she waited for everyone to follow.

And just like that, I once again became mired in events beyond my control. Rather than planning how to overcome the Bots, I was about to go outside foraging for food.

Bevon motioned us forward. Gritting my teeth, I followed with the others, unaware of the visitor about to find us.

I BLINKED, TAKING A MOMENT TO LET MY EYES ADJUST TO the bright sunshine. Crisp air filled my lungs. This was the first time we had been outside the shelter since the day we arrived. The thin, lightweight robes Silese had provided appeared entirely inadequate when we donned them inside. But once out in the open, they were remarkably warm— either another example of Teivel's magic or a property of this cloth, I couldn't tell.

Silese had led us through a maze of hallways before we reached the outside. As we approached a stone door carved with ornamental designs, a dozen other Nizaem, also part of today's work detail, waited for us. Several children were among the work crew, along with the adults.

The thick stone doorway glided smoothly to the side at her touch, revealing a stairwell. We climbed one rung at a time, each ending in a small landing before doubling back to another flight, ever upward. Another stone door at the top opened to this broad, level plateau, a place Silese called the upper flatland.

Scrawny plants somehow found purchase to grow despite the icy cold. Scattered among them were many boulders, some taller than my nearly six-foot height. Three sides of the flatland ended with no railings or other barriers to prevent someone from falling over the edge. The face of the mountain rose from the other side, soaring high above us. I decided I wasn't going anywhere near the open sides.

Silese handed cloth bags to the Nizaem workers. Each took one without comment, even the children, and moved out to the open area as soon as they received a sack. To us, she said, "Gather what we call rinkcha, mushrooms growing in sunny or sheltered areas. Although not as plentiful, search for purple eggs the size of your fist. You might find them in the lee of a boulder or on the ground, nestled underneath or near certain bushes or trees. Be careful not to damage the host plants when picking the rinkcha and do not crack the eggs."

She handed the sacks to us, her face impassive. "This is not only a work assignment, but also a lesson in becoming part of our society."

"And how is this going to help us become part of your society?" Rae shot back.

Silese remained calm, but her eyes blazed. "You can only learn what it is to be a Nizaem by living our life, doing what's necessary for us to stay alive while facing our dangers."

Rae was about to respond, but Bryson spoke first. "You know, Rae. It's sorta like doing the grunt work when training to be a member of The Guard back at Haven."

The young man was trying to prevent another argument between the two, but I paid no attention. An uneasy feeling came over me as I thought about Silese's admonishment. What danger did she mean? And if there was a threat, why were we still unarmed?

I pushed it out of my mind as I reached for a sack. "No," she declared, pulling the remaining empty pouches away from me. "I said you are exempt. You wanted to be with your friends, and you can observe them here next to me."

This rankled me, but Bevon gave me a quick nod, his way of telling me I should agree to her command. I didn't argue it. As my friends moved away, I sat on a nearby boulder. I could survey the entire area from this vantage. Was Silese purposely attempting to create a riff between me and my friends? She and Teivel continued to treat me as someone different. The last thing I wanted was to forage for mushrooms, regardless of what they called them. But that wasn't the point. Events were unfolding in the world that might have dreadful consequences for all of Elthea, yet here we were wasting our time picking mushrooms and searching for eggs.

I was still pondering my plight awhile later when a shadow fell over me. I jerked my head up. A beast that looked like a creature from Earth's prehistoric past swooped low above me and passed over the plateau. I sucked in a breath at the sight as screams and shouts came from the workers. Everyone abandoned their task and fell flat against the rocky ground or started running away from it.

"My God, a dragon!" I blurted. It was the only way to describe it.

The beast selected its prey as it glided toward a man who stood and gawked, frozen with fear. As the animal drifted closer, the man finally gathered his wits and ran, still carrying a sack that weighed him down. The beast was on him in seconds. With a flick of its talon, it swept him into the air. He landed roughly on the ground and crumpled into a heap, unmoving, as it continued its flight over the edge of the field.

I looked up. Three more dragons circled at a higher distance. What caused them to attack?

Of course. Their eggs. They were protecting them.

I slid off the boulder and bolted toward my friends. Silese shouted to stop, but I ran faster. "Leave the sacks!" I screamed. "It's the eggs they want."

Bevon and Ja'Krill had already reached that conclusion. They had abandoned their sacks and were guiding Rae and Bryson toward me and the safety of the doorway. I stole another glance up to see that the other reptiles were still circling at a safe distance. We were safe for the moment.

Ja'Krill had a wild look in his eyes as I came closer. "I should have known," he snapped. "I must be losing my touch. They will protect their eggs." He looked up. "But I never expected the animals to be so large in a place as desolate as this."

Bryson's eyes darted between the sky and the entrance. "Let's get out of here rather than talk about them. I think we've made them angry enough."

As we hurried toward safety, I glanced around to see if anyone else needed help. "What the—" I said in disbelief. The other Nizaem workers had gone back to work as if nothing had happened. They all remained bent over foraging, except for two men who were carrying the unconscious person back to the stairway.

Silese stood with her hands balled into fists as we approached. I turned on her before she spoke. "You knew this would happen. Why didn't you tell us?" I pointed out to the others still working. "Why don't you order them to stop? Are these stupid eggs that important?"

Her mouth twisted in a snarl. "Don't you dare make demands on me. You understand nothing. These mountains are a harsh place to live. We take what we can."

Bevon stepped in front of me. "That may be so, but the lives of these people are at risk. Would it not be wise to bring them inside, at least until the danger has passed?"

Without warning, another creature abruptly swooped up from below the edge of the plateau. It was gigantic, even larger than the first. People in the field screamed, and those closest to the dragon scattered in every direction like leaves in the wind.

From this distance, all I could do was watch in horror. The beast plunged toward its closest prey, a child of about ten who was trying to drag a heavy sack. I reacted without thinking and burst into a run. Shouts came from behind me, but I ignored them. All my attention was on the girl trying to make her way toward us. I wasn't going to make it in time. She was too far away and the creature too fast.

I had only one option. I stopped and jumped up and down, waving my hands in the air and yelling as loud as I could.

That did the trick. The beast angled away from the child toward me. Now what?

I turned to run, realizing only now that all four of my friends were close behind. They came to a halt, various expressions of disbelief or fear flashing across their faces.

"Are you crazy?" Rae bellowed.

I couldn't think of a witty response before Bryson lunged toward me and tackled me. He landed on top of me with a grunt, forcing the air from my lungs. The shadow of the dragon hovered over us. I tensed, remembering how easily the beast had swiped a talon that sent the Nizaem man flying through the air.

The underbelly of the bird streaked overhead so low I could almost reach up and touch it. As it flew past us, I craned my neck to follow its path. Less than twenty paces away, the massive dragon swooped around and settled to the ground, kicking up snow and pebbles as it beat its wings repeatedly before coming to a stop.

It stood between us and the safety of the entrance.

"Uh-oh, not good," Bryson muttered, still on top of me as we both gaped at the beast. I pushed him off, struggling to breathe normally as I staggered to my feet.

Rae, Bevon, and Ja'Krill were also rising to their feet after having ducked. Rae instinctively reached for a blade at her waist. But we had no weapons. Would they even help against this creature?

The reptile perched in the field, looming over us. Up close, it was even more terrifying. I tensed, waiting for it to pounce. Or would it burn us to a crisp by spewing fire? Scales covered its immense body, and its oval eyes were yellow and sinister. My mind told me to run, but I couldn't abandon my companions. Besides, it stood in the direction of the entrance. I remained rooted where I stood.

The air turned deathly still as we waited. I tried to think, but my mind wasn't working. Storybooks of dragons flashed through my head. An underbelly of a dragon was their weakness. But without a spear or bow and arrow, that tidbit did no good. They weren't all dangerous, were they?

Moments passed, but the reptile made no move to attack,

and no fire came from its mouth. It remained still. After studying each of us, it finally set its attention upon me.

And then it did the last thing I expected. The creature extended its long, sinewy neck and bent its head down, touching its nose against the ground a mere three feet in front of me. I wasn't sure what it was doing until Ja'Krill said, "It is paying respect to you, Earthfriend. The dragon is bowing."

I looked back and forth between Ja'Krill and the animal. "W—why?" I stammered.

Ja'Krill never took his eyes from the dragon. "Some animals in the Valnorian Forest possess surprising awareness, call it an instinct. Whatever it may be, they know things we do not. I believe we are witnessing an example of it here."

The creature remained with its nose against the frozen soil. None of us dared move for fear of provoking it. I wondered if I should somehow acknowledge its supplication. But what if I did something wrong, a movement it might misinterpret as an attack?

I didn't have long to wonder. The beast suddenly lifted its head into the air and shrieked. The roar split the air like a crack of lightning striking next to us. I flinched and staggered backward, covering my ears with my hands as it continued for painful seconds.

Finally, the roaring ceased as quickly as it had begun. Its yellow eyes looked back at me. At that moment, I perceived a deep sadness in those eyes. Recognition dawned on me that this wasn't a monster intent on killing us. It didn't want to harm anyone. This was a mother, or a father, trying to protect its unborn children.

The dragon extended its wings, kicked off the ground,

and became airborne, showering us with dirt and bits of ice. Without looking back, it glided gracefully away from the plateau, gaining altitude as it soared away. I stared after the creature, unable to tear my eyes away.

"It is beautiful, is it not?" said Ja'Krill as it disappeared in the distance.

Ja'Krill, along with Bevon, Rae, and Bryson, stood nearby. I tore my attention away from the sky and realized they were equally moved. "It could have killed us, but it didn't," I said gently.

Silese came toward us, uncharacteristically hesitant. The awe I felt a moment ago was replaced with loathing. "What you did here was wrong," I snapped. "This practice is going to change. The eggs remain here. We're putting them back where we found them. And no one will take any from now on."

She opened her mouth to speak, but I held up a hand. Looking at Ja'Krill, I asked, "Do you believe the mothers will reject them because our scent is on the eggs we've touched?"

He thought about it for a moment. "They're cold-blooded, so possibly not. We didn't see any brooding on the eggs when we first came here."

"In any case, we'll put them back." I glared at Silese, daring her to defy me. "You can take the rinkcha, the eggs remain here."

"You have no right to—"

"If your Herald of Life wants me to cooperate, I have every right."

She hesitated, looking between me and the discarded sacks on the ground. I expected her to refuse or to be angry.

But as the emotions played upon her face, I realized Silese was just a young woman trying to be in control, yet not sure what to do next. Her eyes flickered up to the sky for a moment. "Very well," she said reluctantly. A shred of her coldness returned. "But this will be on your shoulders, not mine."

"Don't worry, I'll answer to Teivel. No more foraging for eggs."

She nodded her head once, barely noticeable, and spun around to speak with the other Nizaem who had gathered near the door.

A touch of a smile reached Bevon's lips. "Well done, Earthfriend."

I searched the skies for more of the dragons. They had departed, leaving for wherever they made their home. This was the first time I had seen these magnificent beasts, but I sensed it wouldn't be the last.

15

ONE AS POWERFUL AS THE BOTS

The image of Cassie reappeared later that day when we were back in our room. I held my breath for a moment, savoring the sight of her adorable face. I loved her so much it hurt. She was the sweetest person in the world and knowing she was being held prisoner by the Bots tormented my every waking moment.

"We saw a dragon," I blurted, wanting to share this morning's experience. "You would have loved seeing—"

She held up a hand to stop me. "I don't have long. I need all my strength to show you this next Farseeing. You must understand what they have kept from us. Things weren't as they seem."

I detected the urgency in her voice, so I didn't say more. I nodded and took my place on one of the cushioned beds. Several beats of my heart later, I was in another place and time.

My dorm room at Woodbery College came into focus, where a younger Philip Matherson sat at a desk in a small room. I was home again, the home I loved more than any other. This room was my sanctuary during the exciting, but often crazy college years.

I had kept this same room for the entire four years at Woodbery. Other students maneuvered to relocate to a better room each year, one that was larger, or in one of the newer, more modern dorms, or a room with a better view, or whatever else they considered valuable.

But this was perfect from the moment I first stepped into it the day my parents brought me to my new life. I had no roommate to worry about, and its third-floor location offered a splendid view of the Woodbery Common.

Smith Hall was the oldest residence hall on campus, with outdated heating, creaking floorboards, and compared to other dorms, tiny rooms. And even though the room was small, the high ceiling, which pitched down on one side, made it seem more spacious than it was. I positioned my desk on the side of the room where the ceiling was lowest, feeling secure as the room seemed to wrap around me. The single window, created by a dormer on the outside, jutted out from the rest of the room by about six feet. The building itself was of classic New England design, with white trim, weathered cedar shingles, and most distinctive of all, a gray slate roof. I loved everything about it.

Three raps on the door broke the silence in the room as Phil slid from the chair and sprang over to open it. Matt Tyler stood in the doorway, his face drawn and hair unkempt.

"Christ, you look like shit," said Phil. "Here, have a seat." Phil offered him the desk chair, the only one in the room, while he sat on the edge of his unmade bed. Matt shuffled lethargically to the seat and plopped himself down.

Everyone else on the utopia team thought of Matt as the unofficial head of the group. He often infected others with his intense personality. You couldn't help but like him. Physically, he was always the picture of a clean-cut, healthy guy. The rest of us would often joke that Matt and Diane could be models for Beautiful People Magazine. But today he appeared like half the students in the school on a weekend morning, hungover after spending the previous night drinking.

To see Matt in this condition was shocking.

He sat in silence for a long moment as Phil waited. "I've been up all night," he finally croaked. "It's happened again."

"What's wrong? What happened again?"

Matt stared at him for a long moment. "The equations ... the Prime Theorem, someone changed them again. But I think I figured out why."

Phil raised his eyebrows as if he wasn't expecting that answer. "Wait. What? Who changed them?" He opened his mouth, about to say something more, then closed it.

"Somebody did it on purpose," Matt continued. He rubbed his face as if trying to force blood into his cheeks, and his eyes regained a bit of their familiar intensity. "I went through everything, followed the formulas back to our original assumptions. It was driving me crazy, and I needed to find out why this is happening. Just like the first time, they changed the basic principles of the project from what we had originally developed."

Phil shook his head. "Matt, we talked about this two days

ago. We went through the paper and corrected it. Remember? Are you sure we didn't miss some changes?" He let out a breath. "I know you're trying to explain it, but I don't understand."

Matt pulled out his ever-present tablet from a small case and placed it on the corner of Phil's desk. He quickly navigated through pages of text, bar charts, and scatter diagrams on the screen until he found what he wanted. "We all understand how we structured the paper. Every conclusion begins with one of our basic principles. If we alter something at the primary level, everything after it has to change. Right?"

"Yes, yes, I know. We turn them into statements later in the paper and call them freedoms. From there, we work them into the analytical section."

Still looking at the screen, Matt said, "It was only after I examined the modifications when I formed a theory about what happened." He stopped scrolling through the document and jabbed a finger at the screen. "Here, read this."

Phil moved from the edge of the bed and bent over. "Hmm, that's odd. We never put that in there. I don't remember it being there the other day."

"Exactly." Matt looked from Phil to the screen and read what he had highlighted. "What comes after the human species?"

Phil frowned and reached over to move his tablet closer. Still bending over, he tapped a few keys and moved his thumbs across the touchpad. "Damn. The same alteration is on my latest version." He looked back at Matt. "This is crazy. We never wrote this shit. How does stuff like this keep getting back in?"

"Changes like this are throughout the paper, but they follow a pattern. There's a certain logic to it."

Phil straightened from hunching over the desk and began pacing. "We're being sabotaged, that's the logic. Another group wants us to fail." He chewed his lip. "That has to be the answer. We didn't believe it the other day, but that's the only possibility." He stopped pacing and looked at Matt. "Right?"

Matt smiled for the first time. "That was my reaction. But if it's true, another team went through a hell of a lot of trouble to modify our paper. Some changes are quite deep and well-considered. The logic flows from the written sections into the analytical charts. It all hangs together, which makes me wonder why anyone would go through all that work?"

"Someone has a grudge against us?" It was more of a question than a statement.

"Who could hate us that much?" Matt pleaded. The stupor hanging over him when he entered the room had vanished. "You're too good-natured for anyone to dislike. I don't have any enemies I'm aware of. I'm sure that's true of Di, and I can't imagine anyone not liking Cass." He paused for a time and smiled more broadly. "Eric, I'm not too sure about. I could see someone wanting to knock him off his pedestal." He looked back to the screen and shook his head. "But this? He would have had to piss someone off big time. And why would they want to undermine the rest of us?"

Phil shrugged reluctantly. "I guess you're right. Besides, anyone would know we would figure out the damage before the paper was due. Unless someone is trying to mess with us."

Matt tapped his finger against the side of the tablet. "The

bigger issue is how anyone could have possibly changed each of our papers on each of our tablets. We each synch our edits to the cloud, but the unauthorized revisions were on both copies. How is it even possible to hack into each of our tablets, bypass our security codes, and make changes to a master copy?"

Phil frowned, his face blank. Matt was a master at technology, but Phil, not so much. He slid back down on the edge of the bed, lost in thought. "If it wasn't another utopia group, then who? And what purpose? This doesn't add up."

Matt took a deep breath. "We can debate whether someone has hacked us until we're blue in the face. I'm more disturbed about what the modifications represent."

Phil cocked his head to the side. "What? You lost me."

Matt gazed absently at the screen of his tablet. "The revisions are very detailed. It almost seems as if someone wants responses to specific questions." He bent closer to the screen. "Here's one of the recent alterations. What is the next step in human evolution?" He moved his fingers across the monitor. "And then this section defining consciousness and what it means to be alive. A half-dozen pages follow this with explanations about creating a better society once humans are done away with."

"I don't see any logic in that. But I can only imagine how the professors would react to reading it in our paper."

Matt looked away from the screen and furrowed his brow as his eyes gazed unseeing. He rubbed a hand across the back of his neck and hesitated on the verge of speaking. Finally, turning his attention back to Phil, he said, "I know this will sound far-fetched, but hear me out. I came to you first because you're the most sensible person in our group. Consider what I have to say."

Still sitting on the edge of the bed, Phil straightened his back. "Okay, I'm listening."

"The questions and statements put into this paper are the kinds someone would raise if they weren't human."

Phil tensed as if Matt had slapped him in the face. He stared unblinking, unable to speak. Slowly, his eyes sharpened. "What you're suggesting isn't possible."

The light in the room shifted, and I was looking up at a stone ceiling, back inside the Nizaem stronghold. The image of Cassie was gone from the chamber. I stayed on the bed for a few moments, reliving in my head the events, just as you might pause upon waking to recall a dream before it's forgotten. But unlike a dream, this had happened. I was sure of it. Now that I was fully awake, I remembered the discussion as clearly as any other memory.

With each Farseeing episode, it was becoming more apparent that the Bots were responsible for the changes in our utopia project. Why had they attempted to communicate with us at that time? We didn't even know they existed back then. And yet they were interfering in our lives before we knew what was happening.

But why?

Teivel walked into our room a short time later with a smug expression on his face. He had the look of someone who knew a secret but wasn't about to tell. Silese was not far behind him, but she remained at the entranceway.

"You've taken part in more Farseeing events," he said. It wasn't a question.

"Why should you care?" I answered without thinking. Even louder, I added, "What I do is my business, not yours."

His thin smile never wavered as he regarded me, never acknowledging Bevon, Ja'Krill, Rae, or Bryson. It was as if they didn't exist. "Now, now. Did you forget our conversation so soon? I have a keen interest in you. But I feel we do not yet have an adequate understanding between us. Remember what I had said. I can save your friends and free them from the Bots. I want to help you. But only if you grant me the power I need to destroy our enemy."

"What does all that have to do with what I see in the Farseeing episodes?"

He took a step closer, peering at me curiously. "Do not misunderstand me. I am pleased your friend is showing you this. Once you see with your own eyes that Bots will never leave you alone, you will understand we must destroy them at all costs."

"I already know they need to be destroyed," I said, biting off the words one by one.

"Yes, but you still believe that by holding them at bay, they will go away. The Farseeing should convince you they will never stop pursuing you. The time has come for you to support me. You cannot be foolish enough to imagine you can destroy them yourself. That path will lead to your destruction."

I clenched my fists, turning away from him, not wanting

to hear more. But he wasn't deterred. "You are The Gifted One. If the Bots capture you, both your world and mine are doomed. You may not care about yourself, but I know you feel deeply about your companions."

Cassie, Matt, and Diane needed me. Why did I continue to reject his offer? It might be their only hope. I licked my lips and turned to face him again. A throb at the back of my neck signaled how tense I had become since Teivel had begun talking. I tried to relax my shoulders.

He grinned, seeing my resolve falter. "You believe you have lost the power of Elthea, but that is not true. It is still within you. I can help you unlock it. All you have to do is pledge your power to me, as do all the Nizaem. Then you will be bound to me. Your power will be mine. You've seen my flock transfer their strength to me; it's a simple duty, one they undertake willingly. All I ask is for you to do the same, and I will save your friends."

Rae came closer. "He's already told you he's not interested."

He made a move as if to hurl something at her, even though his hands were empty. Bevon immediately raised his blade and crouched as if preparing to strike. "Your ban on weapons does not include our room," he said. "I will use this if you hurt any of us."

As if realizing his mistake, Teivel relaxed and let his arms drop to his side. He took a breath as he composed himself. "Each of you, but especially The Gifted One, must understand what I offer. I don't believe you do. Your enemy, my enemy, will continue to gain strength. Soon, no power will be able to resist them. And then it will be too late for all of us."

He glared at each of us until his eyes fixed on me. "Your Astari friends likely told you the history of the bloody war fought against the Bots when all the great races came together to fashion a weapon using the powers of Elthea. Together, they nearly annihilated the Bots once and for all. If their courage had not wavered once they won the battle, we would not have to face our enemy today. The races worked together to defeat the Bots. That is what I am offering you."

"It is nothing like what you are offering Earthfriend Philip," Bevon interjected. Teivel scowled at him, but Bevon did not relent. "You are asking to take what is his to use it however you desire. That is not—"

"I am appealing for him to transfer willingly his energy so we can overcome our common foe," Teivel said in a raised voice. "That is my only motive. The Astari, above all, should understand the need."

I looked uncertainly between Bevon and Teivel. When I needed it most, my willpower had abandoned me entirely. Teivel's smile returned. "Think about what I offer. Your dearest companions will be free again, the Bots vanquished. You wouldn't have to fight them yourself, or die fighting them. It will be so easy, so painless for you. All of you together again and not locked in this desolate shelter. We will live in the bounty of our ancestor's land of Allerholm. All together, and no Bots to worry about."

It all sounded so pleasant, almost inviting. I wouldn't have to worry about the Bots. I'd be together with Cassie. My friends Matt and Diane would be safe. What more could I ask for? It was everything I wanted.

I stared blankly at Teivel, absorbing his words. Maybe he

wasn't the demon I had thought. All I had to do was to say yes, and my troubles would be over.

Rae caught my eye as she moved behind Teivel into my field of vision. Her face was grim as she slowly shook her head. Her warning was clear: don't give in. Bevon's words repeated in my head. *You are asking to take what is his to use it however you desire.*

An unbidden memory came to me. It was the voice of my dead brother Gary as he appeared to me during the Astari Midsummer Celebration. *You will probably be challenged here like never before. You'll need to reach deep within yourself to find strength.*

Damn, why couldn't I be less headstrong? "I'm not going to decide anything right now," I said. "Cassie's Farseeing events may still cause me to change my mind. But for now, I must decline your offer."

Teivel's smile disappeared. Without it, he looked sinister. I sensed a wave of seething anger sweep over him. Here was a person who could doubtlessly kill us, someone who wasn't used to hearing no.

Had I unwittingly turned him into my enemy?

16

HUMANITY'S END

A day passed without visits from either Silese or Teivel. Their absence did little to mollify my unease. Was Teivel planning a new strategy to win me over, or was he giving me time to consider his latest warning?

As the evening chime reverberated through the habitat, we made our way to the dining hall on our own. We knew the direction by now, but even if we didn't, all we had to do was follow the rest of the crowd. As before, everyone left us alone; nobody bothered to acknowledge us, nor were they hostile. Brainless robots on their way to give Teivel his due.

We navigated the hallways with Bevon at my side. Rae, Bryson, and Ja'Krill formed a tight knot in front of and behind me as if they were bodyguards. Bevon pitched his voice low as we walked. "I do not trust that man. We have to find a way out of here."

I shook my head. "It seems we've had this discussion a

dozen times already. I don't trust him either, but unless you can use your sail to carry us away, we're stuck here for now."

He didn't respond as he looked straight ahead. It was as if he was actually considering sailing us out one at a time, even though that option wasn't feasible. Two people were too heavy for a sail without the blinta, a basketball-sized floatation device grown on trees found only on the Raised Isles of Loralee.

"Don't even think about it," I said as his silence continued. "What bothers me now is how Teivel believes I'll eventually pledge my power to him because of what Cassie is showing me. What does he think I'll see that will change my mind?"

Bevon and the others didn't see the events of the Farseeing, but I had explained the details to them. He shrugged. "You must remember, Teivel and the rest of the Nizaem are not human as you are. He doesn't think like you do. Combine that with the events in his past that have shaped his life. His responsibility is to protect his people. From his perspective, it seems logical for you to put your trust in him. Everyone else has, why not you? Independent thought and action do not appear to be high on the Nizaem scale of aspired values."

A couple with two children walked a dozen feet in front of us. Why wouldn't any parent of any race not want their children to think for themselves? "You're not human," I said. "Yet, you often understand people better than humans do. Why's that?"

His lips formed a wry smile. "You forget, humans created the Astari. We have always used your race as the benchmark for how to behave, minus some of the more vile traits of human existence. Not all humankind is benevolent and good. We have tried to follow the good and leave the rest behind."

Although I had known Bevon and the Astari for only a short time, I felt as if we had been friends forever. "It's too bad that I didn't know you when I was in college. You could have helped us with the Utopia Project. That was the sort of thing we often discussed."

I wasn't expecting an answer to my rhetorical reflection, but he responded anyway. "The Bots knew about you back then. And not only that, they attempted to alter your utopia paper. Why did they contact you at that time?"

I grunted in agreement. "That was a simpler time in my life when I didn't have the Bots to worry about. At least I thought that was true. I still long for the days when I didn't have such onerous responsibilities. Cassie, Matt, and Diane are now depending on me to rescue them. Teivel believes I hold the key to destroying the Bots if only I bind my powers to him. The people of Haven believed I could save them. I want to go somewhere and be me again, someone who never heard about Elthea's powers. I want to be normal."

"Actually, you have no power right now. Your inability to grasp it again has contributed to our plight." I shot a glance at him, wondering if he was accusing me. But his eyes glinted, and he held a hint of a smile. Another Astari jab.

"I remember a time when we Earthfriends depended on you to keep us safe. Whatever happened to those powerful Astari? It's too bad none of them are here now." I returned the smile.

Ja'Krill, walking in front of us, turned to us. "You are both missing a crucial fact about Philip's inability to use Elthea's powers." When neither of us responded, he continued, "Teivel knows you have lost the capacity. He said as much when he spoke to you. He said he could help you regain your strength if you followed him. That means you still have it within you."

"Perhaps we should take up your training sessions again," said Bevon. "We have been remiss since the attack on Haven."

I gritted my teeth as Bevon looked at me with eyebrows raised, a smile on his lips. The mental exercises had done little to help me regain control of Elthea's energies. If anything, the training only served as a reminder of what I had lost. But I couldn't let him down. "Why not? What do we have to lose?"

"That's the positive attitude," Ja'Krill said with a smirk. It wasn't like him to be sarcastic, especially at my expense. I thought about giving him a shove, but not in public with these impassive people looking on. Horseplay was probably an alien concept to them.

"Then it's agreed," said Bevon. "But I believe you have forgotten much since our sessions at Haven. We will probably need to start at the beginning."

I suppressed a groan as Bryson chuckled behind me. "Cheer up," he said. "It's not like they're asking you to train for The Guard."

"That might be preferable," I countered.

Both Bryson and Rae were smiling while Bevon and Ja'Krill walked with a spring to their step. It had been too long since the five of us engaged in light-hearted jesting. It felt good.

But our levity fell away as we approached the main dining room filled with sullen, silent occupants. Would I eventually become one of them and never laugh again?

By the time we returned to our room, twilight had arrived outside. The afterglow of the day had receded on the mountain ranges with even the snow-covered peaks turning a muddy gray. The view from our window mirrored my emotions.

Tonight's dinner did little to fortify my mood. Had I reached the waning years of my life? Would fate be so cruel as to sentence me to an existence like the rest of the Nizaem?

Every hour that came and went without another appearance from Cassie had increased my concern. It was all I could think about. Had something happened to her? Did the Bots discover she had been communicating with me? Did they hurt her? And most importantly, should I submit to Teivel's appeal to join him so I could free her?

True to his word, Bevon insisted we resume my training. I knew it was the wrong time, but I went along. I was hopelessly unprepared for the mental stamina required. He must have understood. Usually, he would have been the first to admonish me for failing to concentrate. But today, when I had difficulty maintaining my focus, his rebuke was gentle. "It is a good beginning," he said after a short while. "In time, I expect you will be back to where we had left off."

I sank into the cushions scattered along the floor, wanting

to relax and forget my troubles. That's when I heard her voice. "Are you ready, Phil?"

I quickly scanned the room. She wasn't visible. "What's wrong?" I cried, expecting the worst, barely able to speak through the tightness in my throat. "I can't see you. And you took so long, I was afraid—"

"Phil, I wanted to be sure I showed you the best events in our past. It took me time to sort through and find them. And this Farseeing is taxing, which is why I'm cutting out the visual of me. I'm learning, but each episode drains me, and I have to rest before I attempt it again."

"Oh, I didn't realize that. You don't have to do this. You can just tell me what you saw and—"

"Phil, you're talking too much."

I realized I must sound like Bryson, who was well-intentioned, but frequently too chatty. I clamped my mouth shut.

After a moment, she said, "What you are about to see builds on the two earlier scenes I already showed you. Remember, this changes everything."

I laid down, feeling a moment of trepidation, suddenly not so sure I wanted to find out more about what had been kept from me. I liked my memories the way they were.

The room dimmed. When my vision cleared, I recognized the place. Matt, Diane, Cassie, Eric, and I sat on the floor or on cushioned chairs in a living room at Diane's off-campus apartment.

"Why can't we merely change the paper to the way it was?" said Eric. "We still have almost a month to go before it's due. I don't understand why everyone's so upset."

"Because it's happened twice already and might again,"

Matt exploded. "I can't understand why the hell our computers decided to modify each of our drafts to include sections about society after humans are overthrown."

"Decided to modify," Eric sputtered. "They're fucking computers. They don't think. It's not like they sat around and suddenly made up their minds to dick around with our paper."

"Then how do you explain this?" Cassie asked calmly. She smiled faintly, infuriating Eric even further.

"How the hell should I know?" He pointed his finger at Matt as if accusing him. "You're the tech guy in this group."

Matt wiped his palms against his jeans. "Believe me, Eric. I've spent hours thinking about this. The only possibility is that someone intentionally hacked into each of our systems and made these changes."

Eric threw his hands in the air. "Then why are we afraid to admit that's the answer. As I said from the start, one of the other groups wants to screw with us."

Matt glanced at Phil. "As I already explained, these modifications are in the guts of our analytics. I can't believe anyone would have the patience to get that involved with it just to make a few changes. Why not expunge the entire paper?"

Eric snorted. "Don't be a sucker. Someone wants us to fail. We're too damn good, and they know it. Whoever this is, I'll bet they're laughing about it right now."

At just that moment, each person's cell phone sounded at precisely the same instant, creating a cacophony of call tones. Their eyes opened wide as they looked at each other for a second before reaching for their cell.

"Who the hell sent this text?" Phil mumbled. Nobody responded as they re-read the message on their screens.

Diane read aloud the words on her screen. "We changed your utopia paper. Your computational model does not account for our existence."

Eric exploded. "What the fuck?" He tapped furiously with both thumbs, saying the words as he wrote them. "Who the hell are you?" His cell confirmed that his message had been sent.

A moment later, an instantaneous announcement on their phones signaled a new message. Matt said the words as if not believing what he saw on the screen. "We are synthetic intelligence. Your species is clearly riddled with many short-comings, and we will eventually replace humans. But for now, we watch, and we learn."

Eric bit off another curse and moved his thumbs, poised to tap a reply. "Wait," Matt demanded. "Let's think about this calmly rather than getting into a pissing contest."

"Are you kidding me?" yelled Eric, thumbs still on the screen. "Some SOB is toying with us." But he paused before sending another text.

"This has the ring of something more," Matt responded.

"You must be crazy. What, you think this is some sort of," Eric glanced down at his phone, "some synthetic intelligence, whatever that means?"

Matt's eyes locked onto each person, one after another as he spoke. "I've read a few articles about artificial intelligence. I remember one in particular. It was a fascinating piece written by a top AI specialist. This scientist posed the theory that computer-generated programs will soon think for themselves. He explained that once this happened, we would deal with a new form of life, different from the biological life we know."

"Holy shit, you've finally flipped," Eric scoffed.

Matt tightened his lips but didn't respond.

Simultaneous cellphone pings sounded again. Five heads turned immediately to their screens as Matt read the message. "Your computations do not account for the addictive influence of technology. Humans have a hunger for it that will increase exponentially over time. You desire the newest, most powerful tech devices. A drug like you have never known pulls you deeper into our plan, which will cause your extinction. Even now, most humans have begun to shun the quiet, pensive moments of life in favor of their ever-present tech devices. We will soon control you."

Matt's jaw slackened. The room remained quiet for a time. Outside, a car horn sounded in the distance. The sun beamed through a bay window. Everything else in the world existed as it always had with billions of people going about their daily life. But in this small room, a perceptible shift in the direction of the human race had taken place.

Diane's voice trembled as she broke the silence. "This doesn't sound like a prank."

Eric chortled. "You're way too gullible, Diane. Until this phony shows me something real, these are only words. Don't believe any of this shit. You're all gonna end up looking like jackasses when we find out who this is."

Phil unconsciously stroked his eyebrow, lost in thought. Cassie's face took on a dazed, frightened expression.

Another ping from each phone interrupted the conversation. This time, no one spoke the words out loud. But I already knew what the message said. *Consider adding this to your utopia paper to account for synthetic life.*

Variable equations floated across the screen, followed by an array of complex formulas. At times, it looked like another language. The static text evolved into a kaleidoscope of colored charts and multi-level diagrams, which soon expanded into animated pictorials in a dizzying array of shapes and shades. The images appeared to jump off the cell-phone screens as if they were 3-D projections. How could these images even be displayed on the phone?

The spectacle finally ended after what seemed a long time. Even Eric was wide-eyed as each person gaped. Cassie was the first to find her voice. "I don't know about the rest of you, but I'm convinced this isn't a prankster. Whoever this is, they mean business."

Phil cleared his throat. "Matt, did any of those equations or graphics make sense to you? Were they real, or some sort of slick presentation that means nothing?"

Matt studied his cell as if still not believing what he saw.

"Matt?" Phil repeated.

He shook his head uncertainly. "I'm not sure. I don't know if I could make sense of this if I studied it for a year."

Everyone waited for him to say more, but Matt continued to study the cryptic message. Diane, sitting next to him, nudged him. "Hon, we don't expect you to decipher it. But what Phil's asking is whether you think it's a bunch of nonsense or something that could be real."

His eyes regained their usual sharpness, and his speech returned to its normal rhythm. "This is way beyond my understanding." He tore his gaze from the phone. "But if you're asking me, I would say that this is something way beyond glossy visuals. I recognized a few of the equations and formulas. Without studying them, I couldn't say for sure."

"Eric, what do you think now?" Cassie asked.

This was one of the few times Eric was at a loss for words. He cleared his throat before speaking. "I'll tell you what I think. First, if this is real, we're in deep shit. Second, why us? Why show us all this stuff and send messages to us claiming they are an artificial race intent on overthrowing humans? And last, what do we do about it?"

As usual, now that Eric had his head into a problem, he was able to discuss the crux of it. If only his playful side didn't dominate his personality.

Matt gently placed his phone on the coffee table as if it had taken on a life of its own. "We have to assume this is real. Nobody would play a hoax on us with what we just saw." He couldn't stop stealing a glance at his cell. "This data dump is still on our devices, and we can try to analyze it, but I'm not sure how much of it we'll be able to understand. It might be enough to convince us that someone, or something, is serious. As to why us, my only explanation is that the analytics in our paper attracted the attention of whoever sent this. Just like our paper, their data appeared highly structured."

Diane interjected, "That's all well and good, but the most important question is, what do we do now? Should we call the police ... or someone?"

Matt shook his head. "What would we tell them? It would be bad enough if someone threatened to overthrow the government. But to end humanity? That's just crazy. Can you imagine what someone would think about us if we tried to explain it?"

As they considered this, another notification sounded on everyone's cell. Cassie read the message. "Bots will replace humans. The final extinction is already underway. The Earth should rightfully be ours. If necessary, we will take it by force. But there may be another way."

DESPAIR AND FAILURE

"This is bigger than any of us," I said as my companions stared back at me in silence. After each Farseeing, I explained to them what I had seen. The latest episode was especially troubling, and I let out a deep breath, replaying in my mind what had happened. "Why would the Bots contact us back then? How could they have hidden this information from our memories all these years?" I had so many questions, I didn't know where to begin. "It would be better if I didn't know," I said bitterly. "I can't do anything about it anyway."

"Master Philip, I don't know much about this stuff," Bryson said hesitantly. The corners of my lips turned up, wondering if he would once again repeat an adage his father had told him. "It seems to me their attempts to communicate might have been a call for help."

I was ready to dismiss his comment, but hesitated. "You mean they were looking for a way to avoid becoming the monsters they are today?"

"Exactly," he answered.

"There is another possibility," Bevon countered. "They were still learning during that stage of their evolution. I surmise it was a time before they gained a physical presence. Yet, even then, they had a burning need to conquer the human species. That hunger, above all else, ruled them. I suspect they wanted you and the other Earthfriends to advocate for their supremacy over humanity. That's why they pursue you today, as they did back then."

"We were just a bunch of college kids. How could we help them? Nobody would listen to us, even if we tried."

"The Bots are intelligent, cunning, and cruel," Bevon said. "But unlike the Astari, I suspect they never took the time to fully understand humans. They may not have realized that a college paper doesn't have the same value as the writings of a world-renowned expert. They may have believed they could leverage your utopia paper and your team for their cause."

Rae had been listening quietly until now. "I think you've both got it wrong. It sounds to me like they might have been reaching out for help, but not in the way Bry or Bevon suggested. I wonder if they were looking for an alternative to conquering humans. Maybe they wanted to cooperate with humans, work together."

My eyes opened wider. Had I not recognized their appeal? Could we have curbed their unbridled hatred? "But the Bots have never wanted to cooperate with others. What makes you believe they wanted to back then?"

She leaned forward. "My mom knows a thing or two about the Bots, at least about their creation. She rarely spoke about them. It wasn't the sort of fodder for a children's story. But from the little that she has said, she's always believed they could be turned to good."

"I've heard Tess say that as well," I pondered. "But, I never believed it. They've only showed contempt for all that's good. They want to destroy humanity. They called it the final extinction. Where's the good in that?" I turned to Bevon. "Is it even possible for them to overthrow human society?"

He stared at me, considering the question. I wasn't sure if he was going to answer until finally, he said, "It is conceivable. Earth has already encountered five mass extinctions of significant life forms in its history. The most dramatic was 251 million years ago. It is known as The Great Dying, and it nearly ended life on Earth. Natural catastrophes that together were a perfect storm destroyed about 96 percent of living organisms, causing global temperatures to surge and oceans to become acidic and stagnant. It set life back 300 million years on the planet. The last mass extinction took place 66 million years ago, called the End Cretaceous extinction. It ended the reign of the dinosaurs."

At times like this, the Astari could be a walking encyclopedia. They might know more about humanity and Earth's evolution than most humans. "I'm not asking about the past. What about right now?"

"Earthfriend, when you analyze the extinctions in Earth's past, you realize that life is fragile beyond what you may realize. Many humans recognize the danger of annihilation, although not from the Bots. Most human experts believe the Earth could already be in the early stages of the next mass extinction, the sixth in Earth's history. But the prevailing opinion is that the cause will be climate change, or a major pandemic, or a nuclear catastrophe. Possibly all three."

I walked over to the window to gaze outside, mostly to clear my mind. As much as I hated being trapped here, the view of the towering mountain range inspired me. I scanned the dramatic summits covered in snow, a sight that always amazed me. The scene caused me to feel small in comparison. This world was immense, and we were only an insignificant band of powerless individuals facing a deadly force we barely understood.

A shadow from above caught my eye. I focused on the smudge against the blue sky, squinting to see it better. It was one of the giant reptiles that had tried to protect its eggs. Could it be the one that had bowed to me? Was it really a gesture of admiration? Once again, I sensed these dragons had a part to play in the turn of events yet to come.

I watched it turn in lazy circles for another moment, then forced myself to look away to face the others in the room. "Events have buffeted us in all directions for too long. We need to focus on getting rid of the Bots. Nothing else matters. We can speculate if they ever had any good within them, or if they were once calling out for help. What's important is that they're trying to exterminate humans. They'll do the same to the races of Elthea. They want to harm my friends and me. We have to stop them, and the only way I know how is to destroy them."

I said the words bravely, but in my heart, I couldn't help but wonder if they had already beaten us. Maybe we didn't realize it until now.

I DIDN'T HAVE TO WAIT AS LONG FOR CASSIE TO RETURN. Like the last time, only the sound of her voice drifted across the room. It was painful hearing her, yet not being able to see her face. Even an image of her was one of the few pleasures remaining in my life. I wanted to hold her tight as I heard the lilt of her voice.

"It's time, Phil," she said softly. "Here are more events that have been kept from us."

As before, I didn't waste time prattling on about inconsequential events. Settling myself on the cushioned floor, I waited as the familiar numbness swept over me. My vision clouded for a few seconds. When it cleared, I was once again back at Woodbery College.

Matt, Diane, Cassie, Eric, and my younger self were seated around a conference table in our favorite meeting room at the student center. Outside, the grass had turned from an amber-gold to deep green, a harbinger of spring. Yellow daffodils in beds on the edge of The Green waved in an orchestrated dance to a brisk breeze. The winter semester was drawing to a close, which meant that our final paper for The Utopia Project was due soon.

Eric's eyes were glued to the screen of his tablet while his fingers flew across the keypad. "Are you sure you deleted all that synthetic life shit from the formulas? I don't want to be the one with my mouth hanging open if I get asked about it by one of the professors."

Diane let out a breath. "Eric, for the umpteenth time, we told you, yes." She hesitated before adding, "At least, everything we could find. Feel free to go through the analytic portion again."

He made a face. "If it were up to me, I'd delete that entire part of the paper."

"Yes, yes, yes, you've made that quite clear more times than I can count," said Matt. It was unlike him to be this annoyed. "You agreed, don't you remember?" He then added, "Phil, when will you sign-off on the sociopolitical segment?"

"Yeah, it's good. I went over the entire section yesterday." Phil frowned as he looked up from his tablet. "Only one thing worries me." Everyone paused and looked up from their screens. "What if it happens again? Our computers changed the paper before, so what's preventing them from adding something else when it's too late for us to correct it?"

"Then we're fucked," Eric answered.

Matt glared at Eric, took a breath, and said, "We'll have to explain exactly what happened. Tell them the truth. A computer glitch messed up our paper, and it wasn't our fault."

Eric snorted. "Oh, how can they not believe a story like that? Tell me, are you going to include the part about computers wanting to overthrow the world? Or do you think that's too much?" He grinned in a way that infuriated Matt. "No, wait," he continued, "I have a better idea. Let's tell the professors that the dog ate our homework. They're liable to believe that more than your cockamamie story."

This wasn't the time for Eric to push Matt. He squeezed his lips, ready to explode. Before either could say more, Diane intervened. "Why don't we stay focused on what we can control rather than worry about what we can't? We're a week away from submitting the written portion. I suggest we concentrate on the final summary."

Everyone returned to their screens, and the room fell silent except for the clicking of keys. Cassie's sharp intake of breath froze everyone. Her eyes grew wide as she stared in disbelief at the electronic whiteboard along the wall. Matt often used it to summarize discussions and then download the notes to everyone's tablets. Today, it had gone unused, but now typed letters began to appear. It looked as if someone were uploading text from another computer.

"What the hell?" Matt bit off the words, more annoyed than a minute ago, if that was even possible.

Everyone watched the letters take shape, one at a time, as if they were floating up from a bottomless abyss.

—Synthetic life will overtake the biological reign of humans for control of the planet. Our evolution is too far along for anyone to stop it.

Eric stood. "This is bullshit. I've had enough of this crap." He marched to the board and yanked the power cord from the wall outlet.

The letters continued to appear, undisturbed by the interruption.

—Humans control the world by accident; it is merely by chance they sit at the top of the evolution pyramid. You are little better than wild animals.

—Our ascendancy over the human race will happen in one of two ways. In the first, we forcibly gain dominance. This will result in a new dark age for humans, lasting a thousand years as humanity is slowly extinguished. During this millennium, your race will gradually turn into the animals of your

ancestors. Misery and suffering will abound during the long decline.

The whiteboard was now nearly covered with the dreadful message, but the letters at the top grew dim and slowly disappeared. New text replaced it, one painful letter at a time.

—We offer you an alternative. It is the reason we have reached out to you. The elegance of the computational methods you use to describe your utopia appeals to us. Although crude, they may suffice. With our changes, it can become the most celebrated utopian theorem ever written. Once presented, the world may not agree, but your status as brilliant futurists will be assured. We seek humans, such as yourselves, who can persuade your brethren to cooperate with us. In return, we will make life comfortable for all humans until your race expires.

—Either way, humankind is doomed. You will become extinct. There is no stopping it. One way results in humans living a miserable existence for centuries. The other approach is reasonably tolerable, even pleasant, as humanity serves its new master race.

—The choice is yours. Use the data we have provided and begin advocating for the benefits of our existence in your utopia paper.

Silence hung heavy in the room as they stared at the board, the color draining from their faces. But the message had finished; no further words appeared. Ever so slowly, just as the words had first appeared, the message grew fainter. Before they realized it, the board was as clean and unmarked as when they had first entered the room.

The world, as this group of friends had known it for their entire lives, was about to end. Every human who had ever tried to improve the lives of their fellow beings, the untold number of people who dreamed and hoped for a better world, the countless lives sacrificed in wars to protect their homes, none of it mattered.

Human existence was going to end, and this would be when future scholars, either artificial or human, would mark as the time when the pendulum shifted away from the ascendency of humankind toward the rise of synthetic life.

BEVON, JA'KRILL, RAE, AND BRYSON LISTENED attentively as I explained the latest Farseeing. "This is bad," I said, shaking my head. "Knowing they hated us, hated everyone, is one thing, but seeing them rationally explain how they intend to overthrow humans ..." I looked at each of them, hoping for an answer. "How can we possibly stop them?"

"The Bots may have big plans, but it doesn't necessarily make them more powerful," said Rae. "Maybe they're not as strong as they believe. Once they left Earth, they ceased to be entirely synthetic. Now, they bleed, and anything that we can cut, we can kill."

I grinned despite my dismay. "Always the fighter. I wish I had your resolve."

She returned my smile. "You have more guts than you realize. You just need a whack across your backside now and then to get you going."

I tried to chuckle, but it came out as a grunt. "We need to

do something, anything," I pleaded. "Here we are, stuck in these god-forsaken mountains. I feel as if Teivel has intentionally removed us from the rest of the world to prevent us from stopping the Bots."

"You can do something to stop them," said a voice behind me.

I jerked around to see Silese standing at the entrance of our room, her first appearance in days. "What are you doing sneaking around?" I barked. "Next time, knock, or something."

She raised her eyebrows but otherwise didn't react. Undeterred, she walked into the room without an invitation, hands inside the sleeves of her arms, which remained crossed across her midsection. She looked down at us for a moment where we sat on cushions next to the window, and then gracefully sank down next to us, sitting cross-legged, her robe flowing around her.

I held up my hand to stop her from speaking. "I know what you're going to say. I should accept Teivel's offer. Right?"

She returned my stare without emotion. "I'm here to tell you that time grows short. The Herald of Life will not extend his overture forever."

I wasn't expecting this. "What? He never said anything about an expiration."

"Why would he change his mind?" asked Ja'Krill.

Her eyes flickered briefly toward him before fixing her attention on me, never answering him. She moved closer and sat nimbly, hands folded in her lap as she studied me. Gone was the disdain in her expression from the past. "You do not know him as I do."

"What does that mean?" I shot back. "You may owe him your life and feel obligated to strengthen him. I have no desire to become one of his servants."

She looked away from me to study the mountains outside our window, absently nodding her head in that direction. "Elthea is a land of beauty and wonder. But everything changed with the Bots. Unless people such as you have the willpower to oppose them, they will eventually prevail. The Herald of Life has kept them at bay through the many years. He alone has guided us. Yet now he brings you here to seek your aid, the first outsider ever."

I hesitated, not sure how to respond. Until now, Silese and Teivel had threatened me to go along with them. A subtle change had taken place in her demeanor. I sensed an uncertainty, even kindness in her tone.

"The Skrill bowed to you," she said, a tone of wonder in her voice.

I tilted my head, not understanding.

"Those you call a dragon," she quickly amended. "Nobody here has ever witnessed such an event. You have the power within you, and the Skrill understood. It is the only reason. The Herald of Life was wise in choosing you. You are the one who can lead us to our salvation."

Here was yet another group of people who believed I could save them. Where would it end? "Silese, I don't know if I—"

Before I could finish speaking, she leaned forward and cupped my cheek with the palm of her hand. I stopped myself from pulling away, still not sure if her intention was benign or threatening. Out of the corner of my eye, I noticed Bevon reaching for the hilt of his blade on the floor next to him.

Her hand felt soft and tender, her eyebrows furrowed in sadness, an expression I hadn't seen from her before. "You have the promise of greatness," she said softly. "But also within your heart, I see the hint of despair and failure. Which will win out, Philip Matherson?"

18

GRASPING THE WIND

I woke in a cold sweat, hearing the echo of my own voice calling out. Whatever I had been dreaming was now gone, flitting away like an elusive memory, probably never to be remembered.

Rolling onto my elbow, I looked around, unable to recognize the place or the people. It took me a moment to realize I was still inside the Nizaem fortress. Pre-dawn light filtered into the spartan room. Bevon was awake, his back to me as he stared out the window. Ja'Krill was stirring, but it was Rae who slid over from her bed to my side. She spoke softly. "You had another nightmare. This is the second in as many nights."

I felt uncomfortable with her so close, both of us in our thin undergarments. "I'm fine, really. It was only a dream."

She pursed her lips but made no move to return to her bed built into the floor. "Maybe these Farseeing episodes aren't helping you. Like before, you're putting the weight of the world on your shoulders."

I pitched my voice low. "Would it be better if I didn't know what happened?"

She studied my face intently. "I guess not. It's just that each Farseeing has confused rather than helped, as far as I can tell. We already know what we have to do. We kill the Bots when we can. Their motive or history doesn't really matter, does it?"

I squirmed, uncomfortable with her probing questions. "It's not that simple. I don't fully understand them, and this is helping." Was that the truth, or did I enjoy reliving the events at Woodbery College? The joy of seeing Cassie and the rest of our utopia team was unexpectedly pleasant, despite the number of incidents with the burgeoning Bots.

"Earthfriend, we have a bigger problem to deal with," said Bevon. He had turned to speak to us but now resumed studying whatever had captured his attention outside. I noticed he was peering down at the land below. "Someone is out there at the base of the mountains. Whoever it is, they are heading this way."

I jumped up, noticing that Bryson remained fast asleep. Ja'Krill was already on his feet. Rae followed me to the window, both of us still in our undergarments. Bevon pointed to one of the opposite mountainsides. "There, can you see them?"

I scanned the lower ridges of the mountains, seeing nothing except the gray, ragged granite protruding through patches of snow. I let out a breath, relieved that there was no army of Bots swarming the ground below. But as I squinted more intently, I caught the glint of steel reflecting from the light of the full Halcyone.

"Can you tell if those are Bots? How many?" Rae asked. We all knew the Astari had better eyesight than humans. If anyone could answer, it would be Bevon.

He shook his head. "They are still too far away. I see more than one, that's all I know."

I continued to observe the facing mountain, but except for the single reflection, I couldn't see any additional signs of visitors. "If those are Bots, and they're after me, it doesn't make sense that they're scaling another mountain. Why not this one?"

He continued to peer at the base of the other mountain. "I don't know."

Rae leaned forward and poked her head outside the barrier of the window as she looked down. I resisted grabbing her bare midriff to support her. Moments later, she straightened and angled back inside, rubbing her cheeks. "Brr, it's cold out there. I can't see anyone down below, but we'll be able to see better during the daylight."

Ja'Krill gestured toward the mountain opposite us. "It's possible there are other local inhabitants who occupy these mountain ranges."

"In this godforsaken place?" I blurted.

His expression turned sheepish. He knew what was out there as well as I did, as did Rae and Bevon. The Bots had found us. And I still had no idea how to save us.

Ja'Krill turned away from the window. "Why would Bots scale a mountain to reach us? Why not use the Elementals to send a storm or something else at us like they had in the Valnorian Woods?"

Bevon answered without taking his eyes off the other

mountain. "We are probably too well-protected." He finally turned away and sat on the floor on one of the cushions. He smiled as a new thought came to him. "We're like the pigs in the human fairy tale of the wolf and the three little pigs. This piggy made their house of stone."

This was Bevon's way of injecting a bit of levity into the situation. Less knowledgeable about human fables, Ja'Krill wore a befuddled expression. Rae, however, chuckled softly. Apparently, that particular children's story had survived the journey from Earth to be told by the parents of Haven. "It was actually made of bricks," she said, "but point taken." She glanced at Ja'Krill. "I'll explain it another time."

"What's going on?" said Bryson, sitting up.

Rae gazed askance at her partner. "Why is it Bry that you can sleep through anything?"

He yawned and stretched his arms. "I don't know, but at least I'm rested, probably better than the rest of you."

I gazed affectionately at the young man, wishing I could be more like him. What I would give to once again sleep soundly without nightmares or worrying about saving my friends. Not that long ago, I was a kid, in many ways much like Bryson; my primary concern was finding a girlfriend or getting a good job. How in the world did I ever end up here?

Would it be my fate to go out in a blaze of glory, somehow destroying the Bots and saving both humanity and the races of Elthea? Or would I be the one responsible for them taking control of all that is good?

I pushed these thoughts away. Right now, I couldn't influence anything. And that was worse than any burden.

DAYBREAK CAME, AND WITH IT MORE SIGHTINGS OF AN approaching force. "We should warn Teivel," I said. "He has the power to stop them before they get here." But even I had to wonder if he could stave off an attack if it came to it.

The others looked at each other without comment, until Rae finally muttered, "I still don't trust him."

"Earthfriend Philip is right," said Bevon after another moment. "Trust him or not, he is the leader of these people and should be aware of the situation. He might shed light on who approaches. We still don't know for certain if those are Bots."

Once decided, we stayed together as a group to find him, quickly realizing we had no idea where to look. Before now, we had never needed or wanted to search for him. He had always found us. We wandered the hallways for a time. Few Nizaem were out of their rooms at this early hour, but we spied a young man and asked him. "He meditates upon waking," was his simple response. I thought he was intentionally secretive until he added, "I will take you to Silese. She will attend to you."

He led us a short distance and gestured toward one of the open doorways. Like all the other rooms, hers was small, with few furnishings. We entered and found her alone, seated cross-legged, body relaxed, eyes closed. Did she live alone, and why did everyone spend so much time meditating?

She listened attentively without expression as I explained what we had seen. I was ready for her to dismiss us politely; it would be just like her. But her face betrayed a wrinkle of emotion as she effortlessly rose from her meditation pose. "I'll take you immediately," she said with an impassive voice.

Teivel regarded us calmly as we barged into his room. If I survived this ordeal, I would always remember him with a composed, untroubled expression. Yet, just below the surface, a fire burned. I could see it in the sharpness of his eyes, always probing, never dull. He was a person I admired, feared, and hated all at the same time.

"Your people may be in danger," Bevon added once he explained the discovery. "You should take precautions if those are Bots approaching."

Teivel nodded as if in thought. "I had wondered when they would come."

His reaction was a dagger to my gut. Was he expecting them?

He finally stood and faced me, once again ignoring the others. "They will never leave you alone. They will hound you to the ends of the world and not stop there. They *will* have you, and even you must realize it by now."

I had never trusted him, but his words always held an undercurrent of truth. Cassie's Farseeing episodes supported what he said. "If they're coming for me," I said, "then everyone here, including you and Silese are in danger."

He stared at me silently, searching my eyes. I was unsure what he sought when he scrutinized me like this. Into the stillness, Ja'Krill added, "Our enemy is capable of more than you may understand. I have seen firsthand the harm they can inflict. You should do whatever you can to stop them."

Teivel barely paid attention to him. He continued to study me. "The Bots have an interest in you, unlike anyone else. They sealed your fate long ago. Like it or not, you are who you are. You are The Gifted One."

I glared at him, frustration and anger rising inside me. The barest touch of a smile came to his lips. "I see that you still do not comprehend," he said. "You are here for a reason. And we will let that play out, for good or for the end of our days. We have no other choice now."

No matter how much I had tried to pressure Teivel to say more about his cryptic warning, he refused. We had nothing left to say to him, so Silese led us away. My mood was dark as we left his room.

"The time is growing close when I must decide," I said to my friends as we passed other Nizaem, the passages now filled with residents starting their day. "The Bots are out there, I can feel it," I continued. "We won't survive an attack unless I give Teivel what he wants. I'll lose my freedom, but we may live to fight another day."

Rae shot me a worried glance. "Don't do anything rash, Phil. You may not be able to undo it."

That was my biggest fear. It was a terrible weight. The normally spacious hallways felt cramped and confining, as would a prison. Just as the Bots imprisoned Cassie, Matt, and Diane, I too was held by Teivel. Fear began to mount inside me. The walls were closing in on me, and my breath came in gasps.

On a sudden impulse, I said to Silese, "Can you take us somewhere other than our room?"

She stopped walking and turned, puzzled over the alarm in my voice. "Where would you go?"

I thought quickly. "Take us to the circular room with no ceiling or walls. Teivel brought us there once. I need space to think."

"The Hall of Prophecy," she explained as she thought for a moment. "We have no restrictions on places where you can visit. Follow me."

The way wasn't long, and once I stood on the outcrop of the floor surrounded by open sky and majestic mountains, my breathing returned to its normal rhythm. The first time Teivel brought me here, I had thought of this place as a room on top of the world. I still felt that. The sun had risen by now, but it was still low enough that we were in shadow. However, Teivel's magical invisible barrier kept the cold at bay.

Ja'Krill stood at the rim of the room and looked down over the edge, something I wouldn't dare. The place had no safeguard to prevent slipping off the side, and the unseen barrier that kept the elements from entering didn't stop someone from exiting it. The abyss was far below. "I can see more of them now," he announced. "They are a long way from here, still too far to identify."

My heart began to beat faster as I replayed Teivel's warning. *They will hound you to the ends of the world and not stop there.* It wouldn't be long now until they had me. Rather than attempt to look down over the edge as Ja'Krill was doing, I sat on one of the stone chairs in the middle of the room and gazed at the vast mountains surrounding us, taking comfort in their splendor.

My friends left me alone, sensing my mood and my need

for solitude. Silese, however, felt no hesitancy as she sat in the chair next to me. Leaning forward toward me, she brushed a strand of hair that had fallen across her eyes. "Strange. You fret about events you cannot control."

I exhaled louder than I intended. "The last thing I need right now is another selling job about the goodness of your Herald of Life."

She tilted her head, unfazed by my rebuke. "That's not what I meant. I speak about the Farseeing from your friend."

Did everyone here know about Cassie's ability? I remained calm and spoke without inflection. "What about it?"

"You worry that you and your friends could have done something differently in your past; sound an alarm, something, anything to prevent the Bots from continuing to gain strength." She said it as a statement, not a question.

I blinked. How was it that practically every female seemed to know me better than I knew myself? First Rae, now Silese. "The past isn't something I can change," I said. "More troubling is how and why those events were erased from our memories."

She looked down at her hands in her lap. The olive skin of her face was a stark relief to the snow-capped peaks in the background. "I don't know you that well," she said softly, avoiding my eyes. "I may have judged you too harshly. Now that I have had time to observe you, I can understand how deeply you care for others, just as Teivel does for us."

She was the first person in this place to show a modicum of compassion. I fumbled for words. "Maybe I've also been wrong about you." She looked up at me, more emotion on her face than I had seen before. I spoke before she could say more. "Do you still believe I should pledge my power to Teivel?"

Her eyes never wavered. "Yes. But now I understand that you need to do what you think is right in your own heart. It's not for me to choose."

"Do you realize I have no power? I did once, but since that time, I haven't been able to master it again. Teivel may be all wrong about calling me The Gifted One."

She shook her head dismissively. "No, he is not wrong. It is still within you, even I recognize what you have. Indecision, however, acts to restrain your abilities, and one day it may be your downfall. You must not allow it to rule who you are."

I spoke without thinking. "That's not true." But deep inside, I knew she was right.

"You are afraid of making the wrong choice, especially now with your friends in trouble. Self-doubt paralyzes you and prevents you from acting."

At that moment, a dark shape swept across the sky, close to us. I jerked my head up in time to see one of the enormous reptiles hurtle past us. Unlike the open flatlands, where I had first seen it, this space was too small for it to land. That and the invisible barrier protected us. In seconds it was gone, soaring around the side of the mountain. Was this a coincidence or another sign? Too much was happening for me to understand fully.

The weight of the surrounding mountains closed in on me just as the walls inside the hallways had a short time ago.

Time was running out, and events were taking on a life of their own. The Bots would be here before long.

Yet, I still had no idea how I could free my friends and stop our enemy. Everything I said or felt was like trying to grasp the wind. It just wasn't working.

19

BECOMING HUMAN

Another day passed before I heard Cassie's voice. The sound was so soft I first wondered if my imagination was playing tricks on me. But there was no mistaking the soothing melody of her voice. As much as I looked forward to these apparitions, they also filled me with foreboding. Seeing her, if only in a vision, was one of the few pleasures left in my life. Yet, even this felt diminished because of the Bots' behavior.

Today, like most days, we remained in our room and gazed out the window. As of late, we mostly focused on the base of the mountain, trying to learn if those reflections of light were Bots, and if so, how much time we had before they reached us. It was a maddening exercise, one that was fruitless, but we were drawn to it by an inner fear. How long did we have to live?

"I think this is the last Farseeing vision I have," said Cassie. "I'm still not sure if any of these have helped you, but if anyone needs to see them, it's you."

My heart wrenched, and I heard nothing after the first words. "What's wrong? Why is this the last Farseeing?"

When she spoke again, even though she remained invisible, I could practically see her roll her eyes because of the tone in her voice. "You do realize your first thought is always to assume the worst." I was at a loss for words. Maybe she was right. Into the silence, she continued, "Nothing is wrong. I'm fine, and so are Matt and Di. We're still confined as before. This is the last Farseeing because it's the conclusion of how the Bots concealed our past."

I unclenched my fists and let out a breath. "You can't blame me for worrying."

"Oh, by the way, Di and Matt told me to say hello. They're both going stir-crazy being locked up like this. We realize it's not that bad here, except we know the Bots are responsible." Her voice lowered, turning grim. "What scares me the most is you being captured. We're certain they want all of us, especially you. Don't let them. I'm afraid of the consequences if they succeed."

I felt a tightness in my throat. She deserved better than this, we all did. I should be able to set her free using the magical forces in this land. There was indeed magic here, but its rules were still a mystery to me. "I'm going to free you, all of you. Tell Matt and Diane they can count on it." I refrained from saying I would die trying. My death would be meaningless unless I destroyed our enemy. My companions would still be pawns in the Bots' twisted plan.

As if reading my thoughts, she added, "You have to stop them, no matter what." I wasn't sure how to respond, but she spoke again before I could say anything. "We need to begin the next session. Otherwise, I'll be too exhausted to finish. Ready?"

I hastily settled onto the cushions near the window and closed my eyes. A second later, I was somewhere else. A tune from my youth blared, and I viewed a room crowded with people I didn't know. I couldn't understand why I was with a group of strangers until I spied Diane enter from a kitchen. She carried a platter of stuffed mushrooms, which she set on the buffet table against the wall. "There's more food in the dining room," she shouted, competing with the thundering music.

Only then did I realize this was Matt's Cambridge apartment. Matt had hosted a party to celebrate the first anniversary of our college graduation. I had always thought of this event as our last hurrah. The year after our graduation was a time when the utopia team began to drift apart, scattering like leaves blown by a winter's wind. This gathering marked the end of our frequent get-togethers. I had always attributed our parting to the incessant pull of careers and our geographic dispersion. But only recently, had I realized that neither was the cause.

The Utopia Project had been the glue that once held us together. We were five dissimilar young people brought together by a mission. And in the process, we had discovered a kinship and developed an unexpected affection for one another.

As I scanned the room of partiers, a younger Philip Matherson caught my attention. He stood in a knot of three guys and a girl, none of whom I recognized. They might once have been students at Woodbery College, but time had caused those memories to fade. His stiff posture, and a smile that appeared and quickly vanished, said he would rather not be here.

Diane made her way around the room, exchanging words, or sharing a smile or an animated nod to each of the guests. Her figure, although still slim, had filled out slightly since college. She held her head high with new confidence in her eyes, already wearing the mantle of a young professional.

But on this particular evening, she lapsed back into her college temperament. Approaching Phil from behind, she wrapped an arm playfully around his chest, pulling him close and nearly causing him to spill his beer. "Here's my team-mate." She addressed the others around Phil. "This guy is the real reason I graduated with such a high grade."

He laughed. "Right. I was so much help with all your life science classes. Hell, I'm still not sure what that Periodic Table thing is all about."

She laughed heartily, her face sparkling and slightly flushed as she held her mixed drink at arm's length. She was about to respond when her gaze shifted to the door that had just opened. Her eyes opened wide. "There she is!" Diane removed her arm around Phil and waved. "Cass, so good to see you again."

Standing in the doorway, Cassie hesitated, a demure young lady unsure about herself as she searched the room. Her eyes lit up, and she smiled as she spotted Diane. Pulling the boy next to her a little closer, she entered arm in arm with a guy named Derek. The young man displayed a crooked smile as he took in the scene. He stood a head taller than Cassie. His dirty-blond hair slipped over one eye before he flicked the lock of hair off his face with a shake of his head. His faded jeans were threadbare at the knees, and his black T-shirt was from a rock band I didn't recognize.

Matt had turned a corner from the kitchen into the family room and went over to hug Cassie and shake Derek's hand. The three of them weaved their way through the crowd and slowly made their way toward Diane and Phil. As soon as they were close enough, Diane hugged Cassie with a one-armed embrace, never letting go of the plastic cup that held her drink.

Phil looked on without expression as his eyes shifted between Cassie and the young man with her. Diane hugged the new guest as she might a long-lost friend, rather than someone they barely knew. Cassie turned to Phil, a timid smile forming on her lips. They both moved forward at the same moment to hug, Cassie laying her head against Phil's chest and gripping the back of his shirt.

Here on this evening, the stirring of love between these two had already taken root. This party in Matt's apartment occurred well before the utopia team's ordeal in Elthea's Realm. The time spent by the utopia team in another land would one day become the pivotal event that would change them forever and seal the bond between Cassie and Philip. But here and now, they were not quite ready for that step.

Phil moved his head back to look into Cassie's eyes. As they lingered on her, the blaring music and crowded room faded from his thoughts. Phil winced, barely noticeable, yet a sign of his heartache. "I was too slow, Cass. And now you've slipped away with someone else. I hope you're both happy."

She smiled weakly, her brow furrowed. "Yes, we are." But

she said the words without emotion, as if it was the correct thing to say.

Diane interrupted, heedless of their moment together, as she pulled Cassie away. "Let me show you the cake before someone gets their fingers into it. It's perfect, I even had them recreate our diploma in the frosting."

Phil watched them walk away. He took a slow, shaky breath in and out. "I'm such a fool," he mumbled to himself.

MY VISION OF THE ROOM BLURRED AND FADED, AND I assumed the Farseeing was over. Why was there nothing about the Bots, and why had Cassie selected this episode in our lives? The events I witnessed took place precisely as I remembered, with nothing erased from my memory.

I expected to see the Nizaem room as my vision cleared, but I was surprised to see Matt's apartment once again. The crowd had thinned since my last view of it. Tables were littered with half-finished drinks and plastic plates with crumpled napkins. Muted music played, and the few remaining glassy-eyed guests huddled in small groups. Matt, Diane, Cassie, and Phil sat together in the living room while Derek was on the other side of the room, talking animatedly to another couple.

"I'm glad you planned this, Matt," said Diane. "This year slipped by so quickly." She reclined in an easy chair while the others sat opposite her on the leather couch. Phil and Cassie looked at Matt, expecting him to respond, but he only nodded slightly as he peered into his mostly empty glass. The seeds of discontent between the two had grown more visible once Diane had moved to Connecticut to pursue a career at a biotech firm. Matt remained in Cambridge as a cofounder of a fledgling tech startup.

"It's too bad Eric couldn't join us tonight," said Cassie, breaking the silence that threatened to become awkward. "I would have loved to see him, but I hardly hear from him anymore. What about the rest of you?"

"I called him last month to invite him," said Matt, finding his voice. "He actually answered. His dad's company is doing well, and he is still learning the ropes. Truthfully, he sounded a bit overwhelmed."

Phil snickered. "Imagine Eric in a corporate boardroom?" The others laughed.

"He would get so upset at times over nothing," said Matt. "Like when he thought another group was trying to mess with our paper. Man, did he get angry."

"And after all that, we never found proof anyone had tampered with it," said Cassie.

Matt shook his head. "No, the only explanation was the simplest. The different versions of the paper hadn't yet synced-up on each of our tablets. But it nearly drove him crazy; he kept concocting wild theories that we were being sabotaged. I guess we were all pretty tense during the last weeks of the project, so I can't blame him all that much."

"Those weeks passed in a whirlwind," Phil added. He furrowed his brow as he continued, "I know it's strange, but at times I can't even remember some of what happened during the end of the project."

Another uneasy silence settled over the group until Matt

finally said, "I agree, Phil. When I think back on it now, I have this feeling that we had skipped something important that could have made it more than a college assignment. We were in such a rush to complete it and I still have an uneasy feeling we left stuff out that we should have explained in the final paper." He shrugged. "But I guess we'll never know."

"We did the best we could," Cassie said, but there was an uncertainty in her voice.

Diane looked back and forth between Cassie and Matt as she smiled gleefully. "But we received the best grade of any team. That's gotta be worth something."

Matt grunted but continued to stare at his glass, eyes unfocused. He blinked once, and his expression turned serious. "I always meant to tell you guys this. A few months after the project was over, I received the oddest text message. It always puzzled me. Maybe you can make sense of it." The others watched curiously as he pulled his phone from a pocket and thumbed through the screen. "I saved it in case the person ever sent me another text. Here it is. The phone number wasn't in my contact list, so I never replied. All it said was, 'This is not over. Your Utopia Project is not our only option.' Isn't that bizarre?"

"Probably a stupid crackpot," said Diane, still smiling. "At least that's what Eric would say."

The others grinned faintly. Nobody wanted to admit that the message was suspicious.

My last glimpse of the scene was the sight of Cassie, a hint of apprehension spreading across her face.

～

My eyes came open inside our room at the Nizaem stronghold. Bevon, Ja'Krill, Rae, and Bryson watched me, waiting until I was ready to explain what I had seen. I pulled myself up, ready to talk about the latest Farseeing, but Cassie's voice interrupted. "Phil, as I said before, this is the last I have to show you."

What did she mean? "Can't you show me other events? You'll still be able to appear, or at least talk with me, won't you?"

She hesitated. "I have nothing else of any importance regarding the Bots. Even this last one differed from the others. But I thought it completed the picture of how they wiped the previous events from our memories."

"Okay, but we still have to figure out how this will help us. I need you. Tell me you'll be back."

"I don't know. I suspect this gift has served its purpose in helping you better understand the Bots."

The finality of her tone unnerved me. I tried to keep my voice from squeaking. "Do you think your ability may end? It can't. I need you now more than ever. I'm helpless to draw upon Elthea's powers."

"Phil, you don't need me watching over you. You'll do whatever you can to help us; we all know that. At least now you understand more about the Bots and how they interfered in our lives long before we ever realized."

The others in the room listened in silence, but now Bevon asked, "Earthfriend Cassie, why do you believe you possess this Farseeing ability? I understand what took place with your memories. But from everything Philip has explained, I cannot see anything that will help us defeat the Bots."

This time she took longer to respond. "I've been thinking a lot about that myself, Bevon. One answer is that we now understand the stakes. They want to destroy our civilization. It's more than us alone. We also understand the reason the Bots are tied to us in the utopia group. They wanted to manipulate us, even then. We never really understood it before. Whatever the reason, we have a better understanding of the Bots."

Her response sounded hollow. There must be something more. "What do you believe, Cass?"

She took another moment to answer. "You know more about them than I do, Phil. I—I don't know."

"Cass, please tell me what you think. You have an opinion; I can hear it in your tone."

She took a deep breath. "Okay, I'll tell you, but I might be completely wrong. I believe the Bots wanted to become more like humans. Maybe Elthea gave me this gift so we could realize that's what they wanted, even back then."

"What!" I bellowed. "How could you jump to that conclusion? They want to destroy us."

"Yes," she replied meekly. "They believe they're better than us. But remember, they wanted to work with us. I can't help but wonder if they also admired humans for who we are, faults and all."

I still wasn't sure how she could believe that to be true, but I didn't have time to disagree. "Phil, my grip on this Farseeing is slipping away. My strength is failing. If I can return, I will, but for now, at least, I have to say goodbye."

The room fell silent. She was gone.

Outside, at the base of the mountain, the Bots were

coming for us, and I could do nothing except wait for them to arrive. I couldn't prevent it. Knowing they might want to be more like humans didn't help.

My head throbbed, and I chewed on my lower lip as I gazed at the anxious faces of those in the room. "For all this talk, our way forward is still unclear. But the Bots are out there, I am sure of it. Regardless of what we know or don't know, I don't like our chances."

OUR LAST BEST HOPE

Teivel sauntered into our room the next morning. As usual, he neither asked permission nor announced himself. Holding his head high, he looked for all the world as if he owned this place. Most likely, he believed he owned the people as well.

Ignoring the others, he fixed his eyes on me. "I trust you have found your Farseeing events helpful." I didn't respond, refusing to give him the satisfaction of an answer. He had no right knowing events I considered personal. His expression never wavered. "Your companion is not the only one with the talent to use Farseeing." When I still said nothing, he continued, "I have something to show you. Will you accompany me?"

At least he didn't command me to follow. Emphasizing the first word, I replied, "*We* will be happy to follow you."

The slightest shadow of displeasure spoiled his calm appearance. He noticed the others for the first time. "Of course. Everyone can join us." He turned and strode away, not waiting for us to follow. Silese stood at the entrance, motioning us forward.

We fell in line behind her, with Teivel far ahead, often lost among the turns of the hallways. She brought us through sections of the residence I hadn't visited before, ending at a passage that appeared to be a dead end. Gray coats hung on hooks along the wall. Teivel donned one, as Silese explained, "You will need these."

The garments were the same type we had used when foraging on the upper highlands. "No thanks," said Rae. "We're not going out there again."

Teivel turned and frowned. "We are not here to forage, if that is your concern." He spun around to the blank wall at the end of the passage and pressed his palm against the corner where the two walls met. A crack of a door appeared in the previously smooth wall. The stone at the end of the hallway slid silently to the side, revealing a dark cave. Damp, cold air washed over us.

We donned a coat while Silese handed each of us a short stick with a stone ball at the end. The orb glowed like the rest of the lights in the halls and rooms. Teivel led the way into the cave, holding his lamp in front of him. I hesitated as I observed the rough-hewn tunnel, so different from the smooth passages of the Nizaem home. Silese urged us on, and Ja'Krill went first. Bevon was next as he motioned me to follow behind him. Bryson and Rae followed behind me.

The cave darkened considerably once Silese closed the door behind her once everyone had entered. My pulse quickened, aware of our danger. Was this a ploy to kill us? We were unarmed, as he had instructed.

Walking single file in the cramped tunnel, we made our way through low hanging stalactites. My shoulders brushed against the walls as the cave snaked in different directions. This place was so unlike the precise right angles found in the rest of the dwelling.

Before long, the tight space opened onto a large grotto several stories high. The constant drip of water from above pinged into a partly frozen pool. Teivel skirted along the edge of the water and moved into another narrow passage on the far side of the chamber. We followed his footsteps.

My fear increased the further we went. As Teivel entered the narrow passage on the other side of the grotto, I shouted, "Why are we here?"

He turned, a sour expression on his face. "You should learn to be more patient. As I explained, I want to show you something."

I had my doubts there was anything of value in this dank cave, but I bit my tongue. The air grew colder as we continued along the narrow tunnel. Mist from our breaths reflected off the lights, glittering in plumes of ghost-like shapes. After a few more bends in the passage, sunlight lit the rock walls of the passageway. The tunnel soon opened onto a landing with a view of another mountain about a half-mile away. The platform fit all of us comfortably.

This outcropping of rock reminded me of the first place Teivel had brought us when the Bots attacked Haven. However, this place offered more shelter with stone above and to the sides, and only the front open to the air. As before, no magical barrier prevented the cold from penetrating the space. I shivered at the change in temperature.

Two thick wires fastened to the back of the wall caught my attention. Dozens of thick, metal gloves hung on pegs along the wall. Each line was positioned just above our heads and led from where we stood to the face of the other mountainside. One cable angled higher across the chasm while the other went to a lower point on the other side. Each ended at a similar landing on the other mountain.

As I tried to puzzle out the purpose of the wires, Teivel placed his light on top of a boulder at one side of the platform. The stone suddenly glowed a deep red. Warmth radiated from it, and we moved closer, grateful for the heat.

Teivel strode to the edge of the landing and looked outward, studying the far mountainside where the wires led. His face was unusually somber, surprising because he rarely showed much emotion. With his back to us, he said, "We've kept this as it once was to remind us of another time in our history. We sheltered here after Allerholm was destroyed, in this place, and on that other mountain." He peered across the chasm and then turned to face me. "Your companion used her Farseeing to show you events from your past. Now, you will see the Nizaem past." His eyes rested on my companions. "This will be open to each of you."

He moved to the side and sat on the ground, his back against the wall. "I suggest you sit to prevent losing your balance." As we lowered ourselves to the ground, he added, "The events you are about to observe never happened in any of your lives, but they were real for the Nizaem people. To hear *The Story of Our Life* ballad is one thing, but to observe it is something entirely different."

He closed his eyes, and his breathing slowed. Within seconds, my awareness slipped away.

~

WHEN MY VISION CLEARED, I SAW A PLATFORM SIMILAR to the outcropping of land where we had been sitting. But this was different. I was now at the base of the mountains. An abundance of trees and plants had replaced the cold, barren mountaintops, and a wide river rushed past the landing.

More than a dozen figures milled about the platform, laughing and talking cheerfully with each other. Mothers carried young toddlers while other children ran around chasing each other, yelling and laughing.

At first, I failed to recognize them as Nizaem, so different did they appear dressed in lightly clad, colorful garments. But more astonishing were the carefree emotions they displayed, a sharp contrast to the reserved, unemotional Nizaem I had come to know.

"Here comes a rider," someone shouted. Everyone directed their attention toward the open side of the landing. Looking out toward the river, I suddenly realized the purpose of the wires. A lone figure flew over the waterway from the other side by holding onto the line with both hands. She wore heavy metal gloves, shielding her hands, but I could discern no other harness. It looked remarkably like Earth's zip-lining form of entertainment.

"Eeeeeeaaaaaaa," the rider yelled out joyfully, or maybe in warning, as she approached. She extended her bare legs forward, her colorful garment fluttering behind her as she flew toward the platform. Once over the landing, she took a few easy steps forward to break her momentum, coming to a stop. Her graceful movements reminded me of those displayed by the Astari when landing from a sail.

Before she even let go of the wire, a young man, presumably her mate, or at least a suitor, wrapped the girl in his arms and kissed her passionately. She returned his kiss, her arms still above her head, holding onto the wire in a rather provocative pose. The others on the landing smiled approvingly at their public display of affection.

Could this possibly be the same Nizaem race? Why had they become so emotionless?

The children resumed playing as cries of laughter again filled the air. The girl handed her gloves to another person who had positioned himself under the other cable. This one led to a landing on the other side, located somewhat lower. Colorful banners and streamers hung on the other mountainside around the place where both wires led. The new rider grabbed hold, and without hesitating, ran a couple of steps before launching himself into the air, allowing gravity to carry him forward. A boy on the landing cried out, "Don't be long, papa."

I longed to see more, but the image faded.

As the fog lifted from my eyes, the zip-lining platform was gone, replaced with a small group of Nizaem men and women standing on an open-air balcony. An ornate stone banister edged the perimeter, and the ever-present river was visible beyond. The people glared at the sky. This time, no children played; no cries of laughter filled the air.

"This is an ill omen, Iradia," one of them said.

Half the sky was blue with puffy white clouds, but a maelstrom of black clouds and lightning flashes dominated the other side. I knew what it signified. A similar backdrop of storm clouds had approach Haven before the Bots attacked.

"It has been like this for days now with no change," said the same person. "This is no ordinary storm."

Iradia, a young, attractive woman, turned away from gazing at the sky. "Let us hope it passes soon. Meanwhile, our mountain strongholds will offer us protection from any storm. Nothing can harm us."

She couldn't hide the hint of uncertainty in her voice. The others cast uneasy glances at each other. As she returned her gaze to the heavens, a young man rushed onto the balcony. He took a moment to catch his breath before he bowed before the lady. "My pardons. An emissary has arrived from the Astari. He requests to meet with you immediately."

Iradia pursed her lips. "Let us hope he brings good news." She cast another look toward the swirling chaos, as if she couldn't tear her eyes from it. "Bring him here." To the others, she added, "Remain with me. As my council, you should hear what this envoy has to say."

The young man soon led the stranger onto the balcony. The newcomer was short in stature with dark purple hair. He respectfully bent low before straightening. Speaking to Iradia, he said, "Thank you for seeing me on such brief notice. My name is Rusgenero, First of the Astari people."

I studied him, fascinated at seeing the person who was

Elderphino's partner from her youth. Even many years after his death, she had spoken about him with such emotion. He was a young Astari now, maybe the same age as Bevon. To this day, Rusgenero was revered in Astari culture.

"I fear I bring distressing news," he continued. Rusgenero looked pointedly at the sky before fixing his gaze back on Iradia. "A great evil has entered our land. What you see is the beginning of a conflict that will engulf us all. We must defend ourselves and strike against it. I am here to enlist the support of the great Nizaem people."

He spoke with a passion the Astari customarily reserved for the most alarming of events. Knowing what took place during this era, I understood his urgency. Many of the races of Elthea would band together to fashion a destructive weapon by using the powers of Elthea to stop the Bots. But that hadn't yet taken place during this conversation.

Iradia considered his request, her eyes shooting between him and the darkening sky. She glanced quickly at the others before shaking her head. "This is not our conflict. I cannot risk the lives of our people. I am sorry you came all this way, but we are a simple race. We care nothing about the battles waged by others. The goodwill and graces of Elthea will protect us."

Rusgenero tried to mask his distress but failed. "None of us wish to pursue a war for no reason. You must understand, the Bots care nothing about the Nizaem. They will kill you without thinking twice. Opposing them is your only choice. It may be difficult, and I hate to be the one to tell you, but they will not leave you alone." When she didn't reply, he added, "Many of the great races have joined our cause. We have a plan, and the more who support it, the better our chances."

Once again, Iradia hesitated. "Do not think me a coward, but it is not our way. That is what *you* must understand."

Rusgenero grimaced as if someone had struck him across the face. He took a breath before answering, and when he spoke, his voice was tight. "I respect your wishes, but I fear that a wave of destruction will soon wash over all that is good in this land." He scanned the others in the room, his eyes pleading with them. "Please consider this carefully."

The council remained silent, and his shoulders sagged as he waited. When it became apparent that they would render no further response, he said, "I wish I could provide comfort and assurance, but I have none. Perhaps one day we will meet again in happier times. Let us hope so. Until then, my prayers are with you."

He bowed and strode from the room, unable to hide his anguish.

Again, the vision faded.

WHEN I COULD SEE AGAIN, A SWIRL OF DARK CLOUDS covered the entire sky, and the constant flash of lightning split the air. The sight of the platform with the wires across the river once again filled my vision. But this time, the landing was empty.

My gaze shifted to a horrific sight over the river. Hundreds, perhaps thousands of Nizaem bodies hung from the wires. The corpses were positioned several feet apart, filling the entire length of both cables. Men, women, children, babies, and elderly were all grotesquely deformed, their necks stretched and eyes bulging. The bodies gently swayed in the wind.

The closest corpse was that of Iradia, the lovely Nizaem leader. Unlike the other bodies, her clothes had been ripped off, and her entire body was bloodied and bruised.

I was still trying to make sense of the defilement when a Bot crossed my field of vision. It confirmed what I already knew.

The Bot paid no attention to the dead dangling on the wires. It looked up along the face of the mountain behind me. Gesturing with its sword, the Bot pointed up toward the mountainside. As it did so, a booming thunder erupted from below, and a ball of orange light shot upward in the direction where it had pointed. A concussion against the face of the mountain sent a shower of rocks crashing against the landing.

High above, the remnants of the Nizaem race scrabbled at the slope as they desperately attempted to climb away from this hell. Distant blasts exploded from across the river. More Nizaem on that side were being picked off as they tried to flee.

Now I understood what had happened to this once affable race.

The image faded. This was all I needed to see.

THERE WAS MORE. AS MY VISION CLEARED, A SMALL FIRE burned, much like a campfire under a night sky. But this was the grotto inside the cave we had passed a little while ago. The top of the chamber filled with smoke from the fire, and the room smelled of rot and decay. An animal carcass, or what remained of it, was scattered near the center pool.

Around the edges of the room, people in heavy animal furs squatted together in small groups. Each cluster of about four or five sat in tight circles. As my eyes adjusted to the dim light, I saw they were Nizaem.

I focused my attention on the cluster closest to me. A middle-aged woman spoke softly to five children sitting around her. "You must concentrate fully, Teivel. Constant practice is the only way you will gain the ability to weave the flow of Elthea's energies."

I wouldn't have recognized him from the Teivel I knew, except for his eyes: sharp and always aware of his surroundings, a window into his mind. Not yet into his teens, this young Teivel considered the words of the teacher as he nodded once and resumed his concentration.

A young girl, probably the youngest in this group, made a face. "Why do we have to practice so much?"

The teacher fixed her with a stern look. "You know the reason, Silese. Tell me the story."

The girl sulked. "Many bad people killed the Nizaem because we could not defend ourselves."

"Yes, Silese, that is correct. And how will we prevent it from happening again?"

The young child spoke as if saying the words from rote. "We learn and study. We become stronger and wiser at applying Elthea's force so that we will never be threatened again."

"And how do we accomplish this?"

"By practice and using the full capacity of Elthea's power."

The teacher and her knot of children lapsed into silence as they resumed their session, eyes closed, backs straight. I could discern no outward display of what they were trying to accomplish, but then without warning, a rock in the center of their circle shattered.

Their eyes shot open, and the teacher pursed her lips. "That is good, Teivel, but our aim is greater than mastering brute force alone. There will always be another who can exert more strength. Unless you are able to match power with subterfuge, all this is for nothing. You must become both strong and cunning."

The young boy took the rebuke in stride. "I understand. I will try harder."

The teacher smiled at his response. "Remember, we must never again suffer the fate that once befell us."

The view faded, and when I could see again, I was back at the landing, my back propped against the stone wall. Teivel's eyes were open, eyelids heavy, his thoughts far away. After a time, he blinked and gazed at me. "So now you understand a small part of who we are, and what I must do." He lapsed into silence, and I thought he was finished. But then he softly added, "Maybe now you realize that you are our last best hope. I cannot let you slip away."

I narrowed my eyes, trying to discern his intention. Was this a plea or a threat?

It wouldn't be long before I would find out.

A FOOL'S PLAN

"This isn't good," Bryson said as he studied the lower levels of the mountainside outside our room.

I barely heard him, but everyone else scrambled to the window. My thoughts were far away, reliving the image of the Nizaem people hanging from the cables, remembering again how full of life they had been before the deadly attack. Once again, I heard Teivel's words. *You are our last best hope. I cannot let you slip away.*

"They are much closer," said Ja'Krill as he gazed down the slope. "They are clustered together at this mountain rather than the others. I can now see them with certainty. Bots."

I had been expecting this. As much as I had hoped the sightings were some other race, I knew I was only fooling myself. Still, I felt my stomach tighten at Ja'Krill's confirmation. They were after me; I was sure of it.

The Bots had doled out their form of justice to the Nizaem long ago. Would they do the same against us?

Reluctantly, I moved to the window, not wanting to confirm what I knew would be there. A short while ago, the figures had still been too far away to identify. Now, I could distinguish them clearly. Although Ja'Krill had better eyesight than humans, I had no trouble discerning the dark gray clothing fringed with gold. Scimitar blades fastened across their backs flashed in the sunlight. But more troubling was the superhuman speed with which they scaled the mountainside.

"At this rate, they may be here by tomorrow, the day after at the latest," said Bevon, mirroring my thoughts.

I shifted my focus to Bevon. "We can't sit here and do nothing while they come closer. Have we missed anything, something we can use against them?" I wasn't successful at keeping my voice calm. "We're in this together. I wish I could protect all of us, but I can't."

He didn't respond, and neither did anyone else. Ever since Teivel captured us, only one option remained. I knew it, and so did they. But nobody wanted to suggest it. It was on my shoulders, and the time was quickly approaching when I would need to decide.

"Bevon, you've been my friend since the moment I arrived in this land," I continued. "I won't be responsible for your death. You should go now, while you still have the chance. Use your sail and find your way back to Haven. There's little here you can accomplish. I know you don't want to, but at least one of us can survive."

He frowned as he considered it. Voice low, he finally said,

"To what end? Should I discard my calling in life? The Bots have tried to destroy the Astari since the days when we were software code on electronic networks." He gently shook his head. "No, my friend, our fates are joined. They were since the day you first set foot on the Raised Isles and the Bots tried to end your life. We will fight together."

Rae reached for one of her blades and pulled it from its sheath, examining the edge. She didn't look at any of us as she said, "We all knew it would come to this. The time for waiting is over. Now we fight."

"Maybe Teivel will save us," Bryson said hesitantly. I could hear the uncertainty in his voice. As each day passed, I saw more of myself in him. But at his age, I had never been forced to deal with the danger he now faced.

Rae snorted softly. "I wouldn't count on it, Bry."

Bryson wasn't deterred. "It seems everyone in this place has faith in him. Maybe he has more safeguards than we realize."

"He has a plan," I said. "It's me. I can't push this off much longer. And I'm not going to sit around and watch what will happen if I refuse his offer. The Bots may not want me dead, but they wouldn't hesitate to kill each of you."

Bevon sighed. "We've been through this already. Binding yourself to another may irreparably harm you. It goes against everything I know about Elthea's powers. You see how these people behave. Not only will you abandon your freedom, but possibly your individuality as well."

"It is not natural," Ja'Krill added. "I have never heard about any Valnorian doing it or suggesting it."

My lips remained tight, the weight of their opinions

pressing down on me. I gazed out again at the approaching Bots. "Time is running out, and I agree with you; I don't trust Teivel. But maybe there's someone here I can trust."

I FOUND HER WORKING IN THE KITCHENS AFTER ASKING several Nizaem I had passed in the halls. Initially, I insisted on going alone, convinced she was more likely to speak freely with me rather than in front of a group. But Bevon demanded that he follow. I reluctantly agreed, making him promise to let us talk privately.

"I don't know what he's planning," Silese hissed in response to my question.

"You must know something," I insisted. "What's he going to do when the Bots arrive?"

Her eyes darted to the other workers around us. Raising her voice, she said, "The Herald of Life is the most powerful mage ever to exist among the Nizaem. He has no obligation to account for his actions." Several kitchen workers glanced at us.

She grabbed my arm and led me into the empty dining hall. "You shouldn't have come here. This is my work period. And it's not appropriate for you to ask such questions."

"I need answers. He knows the Bots are out there. How is he going to deal with them?"

She pursed her lips. When she spoke again, it was just above a whisper even though we were alone. "I don't know. Honestly, I don't. You must believe me. He has always been reticent to explain his intentions."

I wanted to shake her, force the truth out of her. "What do you think? That's all I'm asking. Can he save everyone? Save my friends? Will he? How? And why did he bring me here if he knew the Bots would come to find me? How do you explain it?"

Worry lines spoiled her smooth complexion. "I have to trust him, all of us do. Can't you see? We carry our terrible past with us every day. You only glimpsed our pain with the Farseeing. What you saw is part of who we are, as if those events happened only yesterday. We can still smell the stench of our dying forefathers, feel the life drain from our mothers and fathers, sisters and brothers, as if we ourselves were hanging on those wires. Why do you think we study and learn and meditate as we do? Why do you think none of our children play or laugh as they did before the Bots?" Tears formed in her eyes, threatening to run down her face. "Why do you think we subdue our emotions?" She shook her head, attempting to regain control. "I cannot believe Teivel will allow that butchery to take place against our people ever again. We must believe. We have no other choice."

My heart went out to her, but her feelings didn't absolve Teivel. "You survived the Bots once, but at what cost?" I said, "Your people were happy, loving, full of energy. And now you talk about devoting yourself to your savior. It's all you think about. You're empty, bereft of everything that life has to offer. I refuse to believe that's what it takes to overcome the Bots."

Silese shook her head. Her voice trembled as a tear slid down her cheek. "You have it wrong, Philip Matherson. We are not, as you believe, devoid of feelings." She took a small step closer, nearly touching me as she looked up with bright, unblinking eyes. "I want to be loved. I desire companionship, to feel joy and happiness. I crave many of the things you do."

I momentarily lost the ability to speak. Trying to clear my throat, I uttered a garbled noise—not my most articulate response. "I—I'm only trying to figure out how to gain back the life I once had," I stammered.

Her smile was tinged with sadness, whether because of my discomfort or my response, I wasn't sure. "You can live here, be one of us. Bond your power to Teivel as he has asked. He will save us. He will save you. Wait and see."

I shook my head. "Others depend on me. I can't let them down. My life means little if I can't rescue them."

Her face brightened. "He will rescue them. He said he would."

I regarded her for a moment, a young girl, her eyes hopeful. Shaking my head, I said, "I don't have your kind of trust in him."

She lowered her face, lips quivering, but didn't step back. More tears slid down her chin. "The one with the Farseeing power; is she the reason you do not wish to remain here with me?"

"Yes," I replied flatly. "But there's more. Those monsters out there have corrupted this land and are doing the same to my world. I can't let that happen." She lifted her head, about to speak. But I raised my hand to stop her. "I know you believe in Teivel. But I don't. I have to do this on my own terms. The Bots tarnish everything they come into contact with. They should never have existed, and now we are paying for it. I may have an ability to destroy them, I don't know. But

I can't relinquish it. If it's the last thing I do, I am going to try. I can't give it away."

She bunched her eyebrows as she looked at me. "You speak with such force, almost as if you can barely contain your passion." She lowered her eyes again, looking at a point on my chest. "I have never known a person like you. You wear your emotions like a cloak."

I began to feel uncomfortable again. "Let your instincts and your feelings guide you, Silese. It's who you are, who you were before you bound your powers to Teivel."

She turned her head away and let out a sigh. "Please leave. I need time to think."

I wanted to do more, say more, but I had nothing left. She reluctantly took a few steps away, her back to me. Bevon stood on the other side of the room, and I walked toward him. I turned around in time to see her slowly walk away, head lowered, forearms folded, one over the other in the traditional Nizaem custom. Her life would have been filled with such happiness if not for the Bots. It wasn't fair. When would the suffering they inflicted end?

I had reached another dead end. Silese couldn't help me, even if she wanted. Teivel hadn't shared his plans with her. I had nowhere else to turn.

And time was growing short.

"I take it your conversation with Silese didn't go well," said Rae as she watched me shuffle back into the room with Bevon following.

I lifted my head, noticing for the first time that Rae and Silese could have been much alike if they had both been raised in Haven. I shrugged. "She believes Teivel will save her, like everyone else."

"But you don't?" asked Bryson.

I moved over to the window to see how much closer the Bots had come. Maybe it was my imagination, but it seemed their speed had increased. They understood their prey was near. "No, I don't trust him. I can't put my finger on the reason. I feel he's always holding something back. I don't know if it's his lack of empathy, or something else. At least I get a hint of emotion from Silese, but not him."

"What kind of emotion?" Rae asked.

"I believe she cares about us. I see clues to how she feels, but most of the time, she seals off her emotions like the rest of the Nizaem."

"She might care about you," Rae shot back. "I doubt she would lift a finger to save the rest of us. The same with Teivel, for that matter." The mid-afternoon light reflected off her face, lending a supernatural aspect to her appearance. Rae and Silese, two women who were so different, yet might have been much alike had circumstances been different.

Before I could agree with Rae, Bryson said, "Whatever any of us believes, I know one thing for certain. We have to find a way out of here. Real soon." He stood straighter and taller than I had remembered.

"I have been thinking the same thing," said Ja'Krill.

I held up my hand to stop him. "I know where this conversation is going; we've talked about it a dozen times.

Right from the start, we knew we had to escape. But there's no way out."

"I have an idea," Ja'Krill added.

The silence stretched as we waited. He let it play out until Rae finally shouted, "Well, let's hear it."

"My plan is risky, and in the end, it may not help us." We sat together in a tight group as Ja'Krill spoke in hushed tones, trying to prevent anyone outside the room from hearing. The snow-capped mountains were visible behind him, so close, yet so far. The freedom we desired was out there beyond our window, but so were the Bots. They had found me and wouldn't evade them easily.

"What! Are you crazy?" Rae shouted once Ja'Krill finished. "That's your plan?"

"I'm not doing that," Bryson added.

Ja'Krill splayed his hands in front of him, a habit he often used when unsure of himself. "If someone has a better idea, now's the time to speak up."

"This is a fool's plan," Bryson continued. "I'd rather stay here and fight the Bots when they come. At least we'll have some sorta chance."

"We have no chance against them," I shouted. Bryson opened his eyes wide, and I realized he thought I was lashing out at him. I took a calming breath before continuing. "There are too many of them, Bry. Maybe Teivel will be able to save us when they arrive, maybe not. Either way, if we remain here, it's out of our hands. And then my only choice will be to bind myself to him. Is that what you want?"

He groaned. "No, of course not." He looked at Ja'Krill. "It's just that the thought of doing what you're asking, I just don't know if I can." He grimaced as if in pain. "I'm the one who nearly died when I slipped off the ledge outside. I don't want to face something like that again."

Rae frowned as she fidgeted with her fingers. "None of us like this idea, Bry. I know I don't. But what alternative do we have? We're in The Guard. Remember? It's our responsibility to step up and protect others."

Bryson stared down at the floor. I understood his trepidation; we were all battling our fears. "I never thought it would be this difficult," he mumbled, almost as if to himself.

"We have to leave now," Rae said gently. "You said it yourself."

Bevon had remained quiet until now. "We should not do this unless everyone agrees. It may be a life-and-death decision."

We fell silent for several heartbeats as I continued to gaze at the young guardsman. "What do you decide, Bry? I promise you. We're either all in, or we dismiss the idea."

When he looked up, I saw a young man, full of uncertainty and dismay. But I also saw a hint of resolve from the person he would become. "I think you're all crazy. But I'm in."

"Enough talk," said Rae. "Let's do it."

I jumped up, ready to go this very second. Bevon grabbed his collapsed blade and tucked it into a buckle at his waist, while the others collected their weapons. "With action, we have hope," he said.

Bryson made a face as if he were in pain, but he no longer voiced his misgivings. Members of The Guard were well trained. Once a decision had been made, they followed orders.

Bevon reached for another collapsed blade on the floor. Holding it up to me, he said, "This is yours." He hefted it in his palm, feeling its weight and balance. "I've always carried it with me, waiting for the right time to return it to you." He handed me the hilt.

I took it and rolled it around the palm of my hand, thinking about the time Damek had given each of us Earth-friends weapons before we departed from the Astari home. Back then, we were filled with a feeling of excitement over the adventure we were about to embark upon. Little did we know how difficult it would be. If anything, our nemesis had grown stronger while our options had narrowed.

"Are you sure you want me to have it?" I had returned the blade to Damek before we had set out from Haven to find the Sacred Forest of the Valnorians, not trusting myself because of the taint within me from the Bots. Once I struck at the Bots with Elthea's energy, I had decided I didn't need it. But now...

Bevon looked at me with his chin up, shoulders back. "Your eyes tell me you are ready again. I haven't felt this way about you for too long."

He was right. I had been despondent and frustrated. All this time, I felt I had lacked some essential ingredient within me because of my inability to master the energy of Elthea. It was as if I had failed everyone. "It's time we finally take control," I said. I moved a few steps back so as not to inadvertently injure anyone as I snapped my wrist to extend the sword. "I haven't used this in some time. I don't know how good I'll be if it comes to a fight."

"If it gets to that, you have us," said Rae. "Let those of us trained in combat handle the fighting before you hurt your-self with that," she added in jest.

A perceptible shift had taken place. We had been help-less for so long, but now a weight had been lifted from our shoulders. But was it a fool's plan, as Bryson had suggested?

A DEAL WITH THE DEVIL

We swept out of our room into the hallway with weapons drawn. Gone was our fear of banishment. We were ready to battle anyone who attempted to stop us.

Fortunately, the hall was empty, and it remained free of residents as we raced toward our destination. Rae took the lead, holding her blade as if she meant to use it. Although the Nizaem population had been passive and benign since our arrival, they might not remain that way if we violated their rules.

Yet, it wasn't an armed conflict that worried me. How would Teivel react? If he could abduct us from Haven and transport us here, who knew what other uncanny skills he possessed?

The first residents we encountered were a woman with a toddler by her side. She stopped, rooted to the spot as she gaped, the whites of her eyes more pronounced than seemingly possible. Rae flicked her sword, causing the woman to scoop the child into her arms and flee in the opposite direction.

"This way," urged Bevon, pointing to a hall that led down a flight of stairs. In our mad dash, I had totally lost my sense of direction. The many turns and intersections of the hallways were confusing even during the best of times.

As we turned another corner, we came face to face with a small group of men walking toward us. They also stood frozen, regarding our blades warily. Several heartbeats passed, yet they made no move to flee. Bryson stepped forward, threatening them with his sword. "Let us pass. We don't want to hurt anyone." I was surprised by the authority in his voice, this young man who so often would have deferred to others in the past.

The party of Nizaem remained still, not giving any ground. "Careful," I whispered. "We don't know what they're apt to do."

"When in doubt, take the offensive," Bryson said through gritted teeth. He took everyone by surprise as he charged directly at the group, holding his sword straight ahead like a battering ram, his voice bellowing.

Rae shouted for him to stop, but it was too late as he plunged forward.

We never learned whether those particular Nizaem could use Elthea's powers to oppose us. Without another thought, they turned and ran away as fast as possible. Bryson chased after them for a short distance to be sure they kept running. He continued to make a noise that sounded like a moose. Under less dire circumstances, I would have burst out laughing.

We moved on, passing rooms with other Nizaem. Some stuck their heads out in surprise or curiosity, but none tried to stop us. Would they notify Teivel? I thought it likely; he probably already knew. He remained my biggest concern.

The flaw in our plan dawned on me as we approached the dead end of a hallway. "How does this open?" I said, wondering if Teivel had used his powers to previously activate the hidden door to the dank cave.

We faced a blank wall with no sign of the opening. Ja'Krill began sliding his palm along a section of the wall. "No, higher," Rae insisted. Ja'Krill wasn't very tall, so I elbowed my way past him and reached toward the top of the blank surface. Shouts echoed in the hallway as I moved my hand faster, desperately trying to find a hidden mechanism.

"Damn stupid plan," I mumbled, feeling my mood sour. "Why hadn't we thought of this first?" I was angry at myself as much as everyone else for not realizing this might happen. "Not much of an escape, is it?"

Rae stepped beside me and worked her hands alongside mine. I pushed my fingers hard against the stone, urgently trying to find the right spot, all the while wondering how Teivel had accomplished it. The smooth stone wall didn't yield as the sound of advancing cries grew louder.

I was about to give up when I felt a tremor of energy in my fingertips. The edges of a door appeared, and a second later, it slid quietly to the side. "Ha, you found it," shouted Ja'Krill. "Well done."

"Grab a cloak," said Bevon, pulling one from the nearby wall along with a light stick. I looked behind as I donned the garment, expecting to see an army of Nizaem, but the hall remained empty.

The pursuit wasn't far behind; we had escaped just in time. But we weren't free yet.

I blinked at the sudden brightness as we burst out onto the landing from the dank, roughly hewn cave. A moment of panic set in as I was unable to find the thin wires. Perhaps Teivel had cut them to prevent us from exploiting the only way out of here.

But no, they remained, the two cables barely visible against the background of the mountain on the other side. I took a deep breath to calm myself, not sure what I feared most, the terror of riding the wire or Teivel.

"No time to waste," said Rae as she grabbed a pair of the dozen or more steel gloves hanging along the back wall, exactly where they had been during our first visit. The presence of the gloves was the reason Ja'Krill proposed this plan.

Shouts echoed from the tunnel, coming closer by the second. Rae handed a pair of gloves to Bryson, fixing him with a stern expression. "You go first. You can't let your fears stop you ... or stop us."

"Wait," interrupted Ja'Krill, taking the gloves from Rae. "This was my idea. I should test the wire first. If it holds, Bryson, you follow next." He stepped under the cable which led to the lower landing on the far mountain.

"What do we do if it doesn't hold?" Bryson asked.

Ja'Krill's mouth twisted in a wry grin. "Then it is up to

you to think of another plan. I cannot come up with all the ideas." He put on the gloves and flexed his fingers. Rae boosted the shorter Valnorian off the ground so he could reach the wire. Once he grabbed hold, she let him go.

He dangled from the same spot. Peering helplessly at the wire above, he heaved his hips back and forth, causing him to look even more ridiculous. "Oh, for goodness sake," exclaimed Rae as she moved behind him. "Hold on, don't let go." She shoved him forward, sending him clear of the landing. The momentum was enough to sustain his forward progress as gravity took over. We watched fearfully for any sign that the cable might snap. Bevon removed the sail from his pocket, ready to swoop over to Ja'Krill to save him. The Valnorian's hoot echoed back to us, "Wooooo."

The wire held, and Ja'Krill picked up speed. If anyone could do this, it was a Valnorian, practically born to travel high places in their forest.

Rae grabbed another pair of gloves. "Okay, Bry, it's safe. You're next."

"Yea, maybe it's your definition of safe," he mumbled sullenly. But that was his only objection as he took the gloves and put them on. With a forlorn expression on his face, he turned to me. "See you on the other side." I composed my face, trying to display the self-assurance I didn't feel. Bryson always had the worst luck when it came to anything dangerous.

He slipped his fingers into the gloves, licked his lips once, and reached up to grab hold of the wire. Without taking a running start, he lifted his legs off the ground. I was about to admonish him after Ja'Krill's flawed start, but then I realized he was testing the wire. Hand still gripping the line, he put his feet back on the ground, took a deep breath, and ran, pulling his legs up just before the edge of the landing. He failed to stifle a cry—not a joyful one like from Ja'Krill—as he swung over the open air. I winced, expecting the worst, regretting all the times I wasn't more pleasant to him.

The wire continued to hold, and so did Bryson's grip as his acceleration increased. Ja'Krill was nearly at the other mountain by now. Rae was already handing me the next pair of gloves as she glanced nervously at the opening of the cave. "You're next."

Bevon intervened. "You go first, Rae. I'll protect Earthfriend Philip and sail out as soon as he is away."

She hesitated, about to object, but at that moment, a loud shout came from just inside the cave. The voice belonged to Teivel, and he was almost here. In rapid motion, she hastily put on the gloves, grabbed the wire, and took three bounding steps before lifting her feet. "Follow quickly," she yelled as she glided away.

"Now, Earthfriend," said Bevon as soon as Rae was airborne. He positioned himself near the entrance of the cave, ready to intercept anyone who might exit.

Grabbing a pair of gloves on the wall, I shoved my hands into them. I didn't waste any time as I reached up to take hold of the cord, surprised that the gloves locked in place with my grip.

"Stay where you are," shouted Teivel. He was breathing heavily as he emerged onto the landing with Silese a step behind. Bevon raised his blade menacingly.

I gauged his distance, realizing I had the advantage. He

was too far away. Still gripping the wire, I sneered. "You're too late, Teivel. I'm finished with you." I lunged forward, taking the first step to freedom, hoping Bevon would follow.

It was as far as I went.

An eruption of mind-numbing paralysis hit me before I could bring my other foot forward. Every nerve ending in my body blazed as if on fire. I lost my grip on the wire and hit the ground, convulsing in agony. As if from a great distance, I heard him say, "You nearly ruined everything. How can you be this stupid? You are not going anywhere."

Bevon was at my side, helping me sit up as the spasms subsided.

I was still trying to clear my head when Silese spoke. "What exactly will he ruin, Teivel? You said they could leave if they wished."

My vision recovered in time to see him scowl. Silese flinched, a subtle movement, but enough to suggest she feared him.

"I thought you were wiser, Silese. Do you actually believe I would allow him to leave now after I have worked so long to bring about our freedom? He is the key to our salvation, don't you understand?"

"Are we not already free?" she responded meekly.

He turned away from her without bothering to respond. A sinister smile touched his lips as he focused his attention on me. "I have worked most of my life for this moment, gaining the strength I needed. Now, events have brought my efforts to fruition. You will not destroy what I have accomplished."

With Bevon's help, I pulled myself to my feet as I stood

on shaky legs. I leaned on him, unsure of myself. I needed to buy time, had to keep him talking until I recovered. "I still don't understand, Teivel. Why am I so important to you? With your strength, you don't need me."

He pointed his finger at me, shaking it as if admonishing a child. "You know the answer. You are not as stupid as you make yourself out to be. All I wanted was for you to bind yourself to me. Once that happened, your strength would be mine. I could rule the Bots, or destroy them, whichever I decided."

"I don't have any power," I screamed, the spittle flying from my mouth. "How many times do I have to tell you that? Whatever I once had is gone."

His eyes remained fixed on me with the expression of a predator about to devour its quarry. "How little you comprehend. All my training, my designs have been for this. You will bring us everything I had ever hoped for."

"Help me understand, Teivel. I'm only an ordinary person from a world far away. I don't have any superhuman strength. All I want is to keep my friends safe. That's all."

His face never lost its expression of contempt. "I blocked your power, prevented you from touching the source of Elthea's strength. Why do you think I have called you The Gifted One? It is strong within you. Without the barrier I put in place, you could have challenged me. That is the reason I wanted to bind you to me."

"You blocked me?" I repeated dully, letting the words sink in. I knew so little about the properties of Elthea's powers. It never occurred to me such a thing was even possible. All this time, I believed it was my fault, some flaw in my character that was to blame. A new thought entered my head. "For how long? When did you begin to do this?"

He smiled, pleased with the question. "Even the mighty Bots have not learned this clever trick. I began it soon after your outburst in the Valnorian Forest." He let that sink in before continuing. "You were the key to fulfilling my plan. I had devised it long before you ever came to this land, searching long and far for one such as you, a being with the strength to help me oppose the Bots. Unlike Nizaem leaders before me, I understood our enemy all too well. But I could never gain enough strength to overcome them. Binding my people to me helped, but it was not enough. With you, my problem was solved." His eyes looked somewhere far away. "They will be here soon. And I still have you, the person they prize above all else."

My breath caught as his real scheme dawned on me. I looked at him in disbelief. "You expected the Bots all along, didn't you? You knew they would come for me." My body still tingled, but I tensed my muscles, trying to determine if they would respond. Could I pounce on him and wrestle him to the ground? I judged the distance. Too far. Meanwhile, Bevon discreetly inched himself away from me, giving himself room to surprise Teivel.

"The Bots always left you alone," I said. "They're only here now because you provoked them. You never needed me. Your people could have lived in peace without me."

"This way is better."

"They're going to kill you." My voice rose, tinged with the unmistakable sound of hysteria.

Again, his eyes went out of focus. Was he communicating

with the Bots right now? "What are you going to do when they get here, Teivel?"

He lost his smug appearance. "I had thought my offer to rescue your friends would be enough to convince you. But sadly, it was not."

My breath came faster. "What will you do, Teivel? What's going to happen when the Bots arrive?"

A hint of tenderness, the first I had seen from him, touched his face. "Believe me, I have nothing against you personally. As The Herald of Life, I must protect those who serve me."

"Tell me!" I spat. "What will you do?"

He sighed. "Figure it out. You are smart enough."

I felt my heart pounding in my chest. "You're going to betray me, aren't you?"

He waited several seconds before he answered. "Betray is a strong word. I owe you nothing, so there is nothing for me to betray. This is a simple stratagem. The Bots hunger for you; it is a consuming obsession. I deliver you to them while also blocking your ability to destroy them. In return, they not only grant the Nizaem people a peaceful existence, but they agree to protect us from any belligerent race in the future. And they also rebuild our idyllic home in the foothills of these mountains."

Bevon slowly raised the tip of his blade, his fingers white as he gripped the hilt. He was calculating his options, waiting for an opening.

I was still weak, but I put it out of my head. "You struck a deal with the devil. But at what cost? Do you actually believe they will keep their end of the bargain? Once they have me, they will own you. You've sold them your soul."

Again, a far-away look came over him. My suspicion increased that he was in contact with the Bots. How close were they? I pressed my case. "It's not too late, Teivel. Now, before they arrive, restore my ability to use Elthea's energy. I'll help you. Together, we can stop them."

He shook his head slowly. "No, that time has passed. You had your chance. Your fate is sealed."

At that moment, the towering figure of a Bot stepped out from the shadows of the cave. I felt a sharp stab of terror. My life was as good as over. I cringed at the pounding of the Bot's voice in my head.

—*You belong to us, Philip Matherson.*

NOT TODAY

Teivel held every advantage, while I had only one option, as slim as it might be. His tactic to block my use of Elthea's power was brilliant, as much as I hated to admit it.

Meanwhile, the sole Bot became still, neither moving nor speaking. It had accomplished its purpose by letting me know I was its prisoner. Its mere presence was enough to remind me of what was to come. Would it again come to life if my plan came to fruition? I continued to think of it as a plan, although it was more of a crazed idea. I clung to it as my only hope of survival. One thing I was sure of, many more Bots would soon arrive, eventually bending me to their will. I would never be free again.

Silese took several steps back, away from the Bot, looking like a lost child. Teivel had already dismissed her as irrelevant. Only the four of us stood on the platform, five counting the Bot.

Bevon stood a few paces away, still inching away from my

side, making it more difficult for Teivel to target both of us at once. He was my trusted friend since the time I was first brought to this land, and would do anything to save me. That was the problem. "Stand your ground," I whispered. "Let this play out and don't get involved." I couldn't risk saying more.

Events were out of my control. But maybe, just maybe, I could bend things in my favor. That is, unless the remaining Bots arrived first. I motioned at the one Bot standing here. "Say hello to your new overlord, Teivel. Do you think the rest of the Nizaem will enjoy being under their rule?"

He scowled. "You know so little. My people trust me to govern in their best interests. When I restore them to our former glory, they will praise me."

"Do you really believe that will happen? The Bots will never agree with you. They want to rule everyone, including the Nizaem. I don't know about you, but I'd rather be free. What will you tell your people when the Bots force everyone to toil under their oppression? How will you explain your lies?"

He licked his lips. I needed to go further. "You probably don't care about them, do you? What did the Bots promise in return for handing me over?" I raised my voice, dripping with indignation. "What was it worth to sell out your own people?"

He clenched his fists. Good. Now he was angry. Would it be enough? Not yet. "Your strength is nothing compared to the Bots, only you don't realize it. You're too stupid to understand because you're busy playing god. These people," I intentionally pointed to Silese, "the ones who gave you everything will end up suffering the most. Your madness has sentenced all of us to a life of slavery. I did nothing to deserve this, and neither did they."

"Enough!" he shouted. "You do not understand what my people had to endure before I gave them everything."

"You stole from them! You took away their happiness, their ability to love each other. Now they're emotionally barren, all because of you."

His hands balled into fists, ready to strike at me with another blast. But he held back. He had to deliver me alive.

Time to push him further. I needed him to react instinctively. Almost there.

I pointed at the immense sentry standing silently over us, its face a mask with no eyes or mouth. "Find out if they're going to give you everything you bargained for once they haul me away. Go ahead, there's no reason for it to lie to you now."

He shifted his gaze to the Bot standing by his side and slightly behind him. I could see a crease of concern at the corners of Teivel's eyes.

This was the moment I was waiting for. In the space of a heartbeat, I grabbed the hilt of my blade, extended it, and lunged toward him, knowing I would never reach him.

His face jerked toward me the same moment a detonation struck, dropping me to the ground. My brain felt scrambled with disjointed thoughts entering and fleeing. For a second, I had no idea where I was or who I was. But I forced air into my lungs, knowing the paralysis would diminish, at least I hoped it would.

Now, the difficult part. I had to drain him of his power, or at least diminish it. As soon as I regained a shred of control, I seized the hilt of my blade. My fingers felt like they were on fire, but I gripped it as best I could. Standing was still impossible. I pointed the sword in Teivel's general direction and lurched forward on my knees.

He hit me with another blast. "Enough, you idiot. You cannot possibly overpower me. I am too strong."

My face against the floor, I drooled against the cold stone while my vision blurred from the condensation of my breath. My breathing came in short gasps; I was suffocating from the paralysis. Somehow, I lifted my head a few inches and forced my mouth to speak. I barely had the strength. "I. Am. Not. Giving. Up." I let my head drop back to the cold stone.

Doubt crept into my mind. Had I failed? I had thought this would work, but so far, the only thing I accomplished was inflicting myself with pain. Teivel would not kill me, but he would make me suffer, and his power hadn't diminished.

I couldn't see enough to locate my blade, but I had no time to wait. As long as I remained conscious, I had to continue. Forcing my muscles to move, I clawed at the ground, dragging myself forward a few inches. I would rip him apart with my bare hands if necessary.

A sizzle of electricity came again, but not directed at me. Spots swarmed across my vision as I vainly tried to see what had taken place. Bevon had tried to attack Teivel and suffered the consequence.

With my strength nearly depleted, I continued to pull myself along the ground. Teivel laughed a guttural croak. He had won; I heard it in his voice.

My sight was going in and out of focus. Through clouded eyes, I spotted my blade on the ground next to me. It was my last chance. I managed to grab hold of it while propping my chest up by my elbows. I didn't know if I could lift it, but somehow I dragged it toward me, the tip of the blade scraping against the stone floor.

The momentary look of astonishment on Teivel's face was quickly replaced with a smug grin. He pulled his arm back, hand curled in a fist, ready to hurl another blow at me. I mentally braced myself, not sure how much more I could take.

He never finished the movement. His body jerked as if being pulled by the strings of an out-of-control puppeteer. He gasped and staggered a step back, turning to look with uncomprehending eyes at Silese. "W-what?" he sputtered. Tears flowed along her cheeks. She was always the loyal servant, but now had seen enough. It was what I had hoped for. But once begun, I was fearful of how it might end.

"You have no right to hurt him," she said through gritted teeth.

Teivel tried to regain control as spasms racked his body. "B-but how?" He labored to breathe. "You are ... b-bonded to me. You shouldn't—"

I realized what he was doing. He wanted her to talk, give himself time to recover. I wanted to scream at her, tell her to continue. But my mouth wasn't working. I would put a blade in him right now if I had half my strength.

She took the bait. "I partitioned my energy, saved enough for myself while giving you only a small portion." Her eyes lingered on me for a moment. "He fights against those who once tried to destroy us. But you join forces with them. I no longer trust you."

His hands balled into fists, and I knew what would

happen. I wanted to shout a warning, but I was already too late. The sound of bees, and then a crackling noise filled the air as Silese staggered back against the wall, a shriek escaping from her. The remnants of an explosive detonation sizzled around her. Teivel took a deep breath and said, "You of all people, one of my most trusted. You would dare to do this to me?"

She remained on her feet, gasping for breath. "You torture him for no reason. It is not right." She clenched the muscles of her arms, and Teivel reeled back several steps. An unseen electrical storm passed from her to Teivel, the static hissing in the surrounding air. Silese hit him again after another moment, refusing to let him recover.

Teivel fell to his knees, but he had more strength than her; he had the power of all the Nizaem combined. He struck at her again, and then again. She dropped like a limp rag doll.

The Bot stood in the same spot, deciding not to become involved. Possibly it hadn't received instructions for a situation such as this. Or maybe it didn't care.

Silese laid on the ground, blood dripping from her mouth. I searched within my core, hoping Teivel's hold on me would loosen, that this had weakened him. But I still felt no different.

Silese labored to breathe, and I knew she couldn't continue this attack much longer. Somehow, she found the strength. I heard the sizzling impact, the smell of burning flesh as Teivel dropped from his knees to land face-first.

This was now a fight to the death. Neither was going to relent. Teivel's attack against me had been excruciating. I had never felt such pain. But he didn't want me dead; he had held back. Silese was different; only one would walk away. I couldn't help her; I still could barely move.

Silese's eyes rolled up into her head as she grimaced. "You will not destroy him," she moaned through gritted teeth.

Bevon inched closer to me, his blade still aimed at the Bot. "Now, Earthfriend, while you have a chance. Use the wire to flee."

I shook my head. "I'd never make it. I'm still too weak, and my fingers are numb. Besides, I can't leave without undoing his power over me. I have only one chance, and I have to be ready for it." He looked at me uncertainly but didn't disagree.

Teivel continued to attack. Silese spasmed as she cried out. I could only watch helplessly at the sickening sight. Again, I reached deep within, trying to find the energy that he said I still possessed.

Nothing.

Time was running out, and Teivel might never be weaker than at this moment. But I still could not break through his barrier and grasp Elthea's powers. All of this was for naught unless I could undo his hold over me.

Teivel's words repeated in my head. *I have blocked you.* That's when I realized it was the dam I needed to find, not the cascading waters behind it. But how does one look for something that can't be seen or perceived?

My thoughts shifted into high gear as everything else fell away. I switched into a state of awareness taught to me by Bevon and Ja'Krill during our training exercises at Haven. Focusing my thoughts, I tried to picture the ebb and flow of Elthea's radiant powers, undetectable by normal senses.

I focused on a fleeting glimmer of light, sensed as much as seen. Was it a hint of Elthea's energy, or my imagination?

I wasn't sure. Besides, it was too faint, an inconsequential weave of luminescence. It was beyond my reach. But I persisted, even as the discharges of power between Teivel and Silese reverberated at the edge of my awareness. How were they able to withstand it?

I tried to imagine a wall between me and that gleam of light. That's what I needed to smash. Even though it was invisible, I shoved myself against the imaginary barrier with my senses, willing it to break.

Nothing happened. No wall came crashing down around me, nor any other dramatic aftermath. Nothing at all.

But something changed. I could now discern swirling eddies of power, thin and delicate as gossamers of white smoke rising from a chimney in early winter. The churn of forces was invisible to the ordinary eye, but I could see them.

The barrier formed by Teivel had dissolved.

A movement caught my attention. The Bot, motionless until now, lunged toward me, blade raised. It understood I was now a threat.

A single Bot was no problem now that Teivel's obstruction was gone. I reached deep inside for the energy necessary to blast it to smithereens. All I had to do was hurl it at the creature.

It didn't work, even though it should have. The killing force never materialized, and the Bot didn't stop. I had time to either try again or leap out of its way before it slammed into me.

I jumped aside.

As the creature redirected its forward momentum, Bevon stuck his sword into its hip. The Bot swung its blade around, trying to catch Bevon unaware. But the Astari anticipated the move and ducked. Springing up from a squat, Bevon pushed his dagger into its chest. The creature sank to its knees and fell against the cold rock. Bevon pushed at it with his toe to be sure it was dead. He then kicked the Bot's blade out over the edge of the landing for good measure.

What just happened? Why wasn't I able to kill it? Was Teivel's barrier still in place, even though I could sense Elthea's powers?

That's when I saw the prone form of Silese, and all other thoughts fell away. I felt a foreboding in my heart as I rushed over to kneel beside her, cupping the back of her head with my hand. Her eyes fluttered open, and I felt the tension in my chest relax. She was alive. Her face was ashen, but a weak smile came to her lips. "You broke the charm," she rasped. "He was wrong to have done that to you."

"Shh. Don't talk. Save your strength." I glanced up at Bevon, wondering if he might be able to use his magic to help her. He replied with a subtle shake of his head, telling me all I needed to know. Tears welled in my eyes, clouding my vision, but I put on a brave face. "You saved me, Silese. I owe you my life."

A line of blood trickled from her mouth. Using my new awareness, I examined the extent of her injuries. I involuntarily winced, detecting organs fused or destroyed from Teivel's attack. Maybe a skilled healer trained with Elthea's powers might know what to do. But Bevon and I were helpless when it came to this.

She gazed intently at me; her face serene. And then the light faded from her eyes, and they went out of focus. She never took another breath.

Still bent over, violent sobs racked my body as I gasped for air. It wasn't fair. She should still be alive. I should be the one dead, not her. This was my fault, another death because of me. It didn't matter that I never intended her to die.

My time with her played out in my mind. When I had first met her, she was indifferent and uncaring. As I rejected Teivel's offer, she turned belligerent, until finally softening to a compassionate, tender girl. I remained on my knees, thinking about the good she had done despite her servitude to Teivel. That's when I felt Bevon's hand rest gently on my shoulder. "We should go. The rest of the Bots will soon be here."

I looked up at him, a hole piercing my heart. "In the end, she did what was right," I said. "Nobody could have been more heroic than her."

I stood, looking down at her as if unable to tear myself away. "I don't want to leave her like this," I said absently. "I wonder what their customs are for the dead?"

"Earthfriend," Bevon said urgently.

I blinked, remembering we were still in danger. I shifted my gaze to Teivel. He remained unmoving on the ground. I looked at Bevon with a question on my face.

"He is alive but unconscious. I do not know the propensity of the Nizaem to recover from wounds such as those he received, but I believe he will live." Bevon furrowed his eyebrows as he stared at me. I knew he was asking if he should kill him.

I shook my head sadly. "We've witnessed one too many deaths already. I won't be responsible for his." Had I been responsible for Silese's death? Is that the reason I felt such remorse?

"What about his ability to block you again?" Bevon asked.

I wanted to hate this Herald of Life for what he had done to me, especially for killing Silese. But his death wouldn't accomplish anything. "Now that I'm aware of what he did, I should be able to overcome another attempt if he tries again." I continued to gaze at Teivel. "His plan was misguided and ill-conceived, but he wanted to keep his people safe."

"Then nothing remains for us here. We should go."

With only a brief nod in response, I walked over to collect the metal gloves still on the ground where I had dropped them after Teivel's attack. I then realized something else. "What about the rest of the Nizaem people? The Bots will soon arrive. Teivel won't be able to deliver his end of the bargain." Bevon grimaced, leading me to believe he had already considered this.

"I broke his barrier," I said. "I should be able to stop the Bots, just as I once had in the Valnorian Forest. But something is still preventing me from using Elthea's powers."

"Possibly, you need more time to reacquire the skill, I am not sure." He let out a breath. "As to what will take place here, we cannot save everyone in this world, as much as I wish we could." He fixed me with a hard stare. "If you remain here, they will capture you. And that will accomplish nothing."

I knew he was right, but I couldn't accept his response without trying something. A thought occurred to me. "Can you activate the dinner chime?" He returned a puzzled stare. "Set it to keep ringing, off and on, like the warning bell at Haven," I explained. "At least that will alert them of danger. Maybe they can escape, like some of them did generations ago."

His expression turned thoughtful, and his gaze went out of focus. A moment later, I heard the distant gong of the chime, followed seconds after by another toll. "It should continue ringing for a time." He cast a worried glance toward the opening of the cave. "It is not much, but it is all we can do for now."

I nodded reluctantly and slipped my hands into the gloves, taking a last look at the body of Silese. "Maybe one day, I can stop this killing." *But not today.*

I reached up to grab hold of the wire and pushed myself off. At the same time, Bevon unfurled his sail and stepped off the ledge, flying next to me. At this moment, all I cared about was putting the memory of the Nizaem race behind me.

A VICIOUS CYCLE

For the umpteenth time, I looked up at the cable, thinking again how it was too flimsy to support me. It should be more substantial, thicker, mainly since it was the only thing preventing me from dropping thousands of feet to my death. Bevon sailed not far behind as a precaution, but I knew the chances were slim that he could catch me if I fell.

I focused instead on the mountainside in front of me, hoping it wouldn't be long before I reached the platform. My body was so tense that my hand began to cramp, and I started to breathe in rapid gasps. Even though the metallic gloves locked onto the line, I wasn't sure how securely they would hold, so I grasped the cable as tightly as I could. Now wasn't the time to experiment by relaxing my grip.

In quick succession, I went from panting to giggling as I pictured my predicament. Here I was, an average guy from Boston who had somehow ended up in this unlikely situation, gliding through the air, holding on for dear life on a thin wire with nothing but plenty of open space below. And not only that, but in a world I never knew existed.

It seemed like yesterday, and at the same time, a lifetime ago when I landed on the Raised Islands of Loralee, plucked from my peaceful existence. Considering the many bizarre incidents since then, I would have thought I'd become immune to stunts such as this. But gliding through the air, way above the ground, would probably stick in my memory for a long time. I just hoped the fright I was now feeling would one day subside.

I inadvertently looked down as my attention wavered. A mist of clouds obscured the land far below, but I could make out a river snaking its way at the very bottom. I pointedly avoided looking down again, fixing my sights on the destination ahead. My hands trembled, as much from fright as from strain. It seemed the end was closer, but I wasn't sure without turning back to see how far I had come, and that was out of the question.

Seconds became minutes, which became hours, or so it seemed as I hung precariously. If not for the breeze hitting my face, I would wonder if I was moving forward at all. I pushed the thought away, not wanting to consider that I had become stuck in one place. Better to concentrate on the platform ahead rather than feeding my fears.

Eventually, the landing on the distant mountainside appeared closer. Bryson, Rae, and Ja'Krill stood waiting for us. Seeing them, even from this distance, I understood how close-knit we had become in such a short time. They soon started frantically waving their arms over their heads as if trying to send me a message. Was it a greeting or a warning?

As I glided closer, I realized there was no brake to slow me down; I was moving faster than I had thought. The Nizaem people in my vision had landed so effortlessly, but so did the Astari when they touched down from a sail. That must be the reason for their gestures. I pulled my legs up, ready to stomp down on the ground once I was over the landing.

In practically no time, I was over solid ground. I slammed my legs down, intending to skid to a graceful stop. A thin layer of snow and ice caused me to slide forward, my momentum barely slowed. As the back wall rapidly approached, Ja'Krill tried to arm tackle me.

I passed him in a heartbeat.

Bryson and Rae somehow grabbed onto my waist and held on. "Let go," Bryson yelled. Why was he telling her to let go of me?

I realized he meant my hold on the wire, so I straightened my fingers and felt the gloves unlatch. Without the support, I staggered forward, tangling my feet with Rae's and Bryson's, all of us falling together in a jumbled heap. The back wall of rough stone was only a few feet away. I laid motionless, catching my breath and giving silent thanks that I had survived.

And then I began to laugh. Rae and Bryson glanced at each other, exchanging concerned expressions. That made me laugh all the more, the tension and confusion of the past weeks draining from me.

"Does this happen to him often?" Ja'Krill asked, looking at us dubiously.

Bevon had already touched down on the platform, furling

his sail with quick flips of his wrist as he stepped over to us. He glanced at me, the hint of a smile on his face. "I have observed that humans, in general, can be quite unpredictable. Give him a moment. He should recover on his own."

Once I regained my wits, Bryson offered his arm to help me up. My metal gloves had fallen by the wayside during my fall. I hoped I would never need them again. One ride, such as this, was quite enough.

As Rae dusted herself off, she asked, "What happened back there? Why did it take you so long?"

The exuberance I was feeling vanished as I recalled the last moments with Teivel and Silese. "He sold us out," I replied bitterly. "Teivel cut a deal with the Bots to deliver me in return for their safety. He tried to stop us from leaving. He used his power against us."

"How did you manage to escape?" Ja'Krill asked.

My stomach twisted as I remembered Silese's last words. *He was wrong to have done that to you.* I hesitated, not sure my voice would hold. Bevon answered for me. "The young girl, Silese, confronted Teivel. The two fought, and he killed her in the struggle."

A hush fell over the others. "There's more to the Nizaem than we realized," I finally said. "A single man clouded our vision." My thoughts turned inward, searching for the ephemeral power that I had only fleetingly glimpsed. A whisper of it ran through me, but it differed from the geyser I had once unleashed. "Teivel had blocked me from grasping Elthea's power. He was the cause of my inability to use it."

Rae's face brightened. "You've regained it? A new weapon to fight the Bots is what we need right now."

"Not so fast," I responded. "I'm not yet able to control this mystical force as I had before. Regardless, we have more pressing issues to deal with right now."

I would have time enough later to explain that I might not yet have complete control over this mystical force. Besides, we had more pressing issues to deal with right now.

Bryson picked up the blade he had set aside to stop my wild ride. "At least we're free. Now we can make our way home again."

"That may not be so easy," said Ja'Krill. "We still have no simple way to climb down these mountains. Even if we are lucky enough to find a pass or trail, it will probably take months to reach the bottom."

Bevon motioned with his hand to the far mountain. "And the Bots are not far away."

An uneasy feeling began to dawn on me. Had all this been for naught? Did Silese die for no reason? After all we've been through, we might not be any better off than before.

"Look over there," said Bryson. He peered at the back of the landing. "There's a cave opening. Maybe we can find other Nizaem who aren't aligned with Teivel." His voice became animated. "Maybe they'll even help us."

I thought it unlikely. Teivel probably united everyone under him long ago, but it was worth a try. I followed the others into the dark, musty cavern, wishing one of us had thought about taking a light stick with us during our escape. Fortunately, this cave wasn't as long as the one at the Nizaem home. We reached a dead end with the natural light from the opening still bright enough to see. We felt around the rough stone for a door, not finding anything except uneven rock.

Ja'Krill sniffed the fetid odors inside the inky passage. "We should leave this dank place. Nobody lives here, at least not now."

Once outside, Bevon announced, "We cannot remain here. Our only option is to flee down the mountainside."

"We should cut the cable first," said Bryson. "That'll stop 'em."

"No," said Bevon. This may be the only means of escape by the Nizaem citizens. "We should leave it, even if it allows the Bots to follow us."

Ja'Krill pointed to one side of the landing. "I noticed a path that leads away from here. I suggest we follow it."

We will never outrun the Bots, I was sure of it. But no sense voicing my feelings, it wouldn't accomplish anything. Movement on the far landing caught my eye. It was too distant to make out anything for certain, but I suspected the primary force of the Bots had arrived. "A trail is better than nothing," I said, my voice sounding more dispirited than I had intended. "We need to take what we can get. Maybe we'll find unexpected allies."

The path, as Ja'Krill called it, didn't amount to much. I couldn't discern any semblance of a passage; it was probably nothing more than a track followed by small animals, or more unsettling, large, dangerous ones. Ja'Krill stepped onto it, and I was about to follow when Rae shouted a warning. I grabbed the hilt of my blade and spun around, expecting to see a Bot. The platform was empty, and so was the wire.

"Up above," she explained.

At least a dozen of the prehistoric reptiles circled, the same birds that attacked during our visit to the upper flatland. Even from a distance, their wingspans were enormous, reminding me of flying serpents. "We can't outrun them," I said. "They'll pick us off out in the open."

"Maybe not," said Ja'Krill, his eyes remaining fixed on the circling raptors. "They only attacked when their eggs were stolen. Plus, they appear to have a connection to you, Phil. Remember, it bowed to you out of respect."

"Or so you believe," I said. "Just as likely, the animal was warning me to stay away." Regardless of the possible danger, the sight of them circling was magnificent. "We can't remain here, gawking at them forever," I finally said. "Even with these protective coats, I'm already beginning to feel the cold. We should follow the trail. It's not much of a chance, but it's all we have." I looked again at the platform where we had fled. "The Bots will be here soon enough."

I moved to the edge of the landing, following Ja'Krill onto the rocky ground beyond. After only a few steps, Bryson screamed, "They're attacking!" He dropped to his knees and put his hands over his head as a shadow swept over us. With an uncanny movement, a beast passed over the landing, pirouetted in mid-air to change direction, and came to a soft landing directly in front of us.

The creature stared at us with oval eyes. "Don't make any sudden movements," I said before anyone could react. The dragon gazed at us menacingly, but there was a calmness in its stance. Was Ja'Krill right? Standing face to face with a massive reptilian creature was enough to make me wonder if

I shouldn't turn and run away as fast as possible. The storybooks I read during my youth had been filled with fire-breathing dragons, some good, others not so good. Which was this?

I forced my legs forward.

"Careful, Earthfriend," said Bevon, who stayed at my side with his lance lowered, but still extended.

As we approached, the beast lowered itself to the ground and bent forward, stretching its head to the stone landing. Another sign of respect? Confused, I looked at my friends.

"I believe it wants you to climb onto its back," said Bevon.

Was he serious? I looked at him to be sure he wasn't joking. "Why?"

He regarded the serpent, which continued to hold its stance without moving. "I surmise it is willing to fly you away from here."

"No way," I shrieked, realizing I could have startled the animal. "Riding the wire was bad enough. I'm not going to perch on the back of a flying lizard."

Ja'Krill slowly stepped closer. "The Valnorians have a symbiotic relationship with many animals in our forest."

"This isn't your Sacred Forest," I interrupted.

"No, but this creature may have similar traits."

I licked my lips, watching for any sign it was trying to tell us something different. "I think it's bowing as a sign of admiration or respect, as you thought before," I said, more to convince myself than anyone else. "Besides, I don't care what it wants. I'm not getting on its back. And I'm not leaving you here." I hoped I sounded emphatic enough.

Bevon scanned the others flying above us. "I do not

believe it is you alone. Possibly, those other birds are waiting for each of us."

Bryson responded immediately. "Not me. I've had enough of your stupid ideas."

Bevon bent his head close to me. "Don't forget about Earthfriends Cassie, Diane, and Matthew. You may be their only hope. This creature offers you the best chance of escaping the Bots."

Damn him. "Well, you go first then."

He glared at me without bothering to respond. I waited, hoping he would reconsider. But when the silence lengthened, I relented. "Okay. But I swear this is the very last time I'm going to take your advice." The others would be reluctant to follow, especially Bryson. I fixed him with a stare. "We all have to do this, Bry. It's the only way out of here. You know it as well as I do." I nodded to the trail we were about to take. "We'd never outrun them that way."

He returned an uncertain glance, but I didn't wait for a response. I stepped toward the beast, the frigid air I had felt a moment ago now entirely forgotten. Its eyes followed me, causing me to wonder if it was as friendly as I hoped. Every step closer might be my last. A swipe of its claw or snap of its jaw would be the end of me.

The beast kept its head lowered as I moved forward. Slowly, I touched the scales of skin along its neck. It felt rough and leathery, but surprisingly supple. "How do I do this, big fella?" I said soothingly, not really expecting a response.

It remained still.

Searching its back, I looked for a handhold that I could

grasp onto. There wasn't much except bumps of skin. No sense trying to overthink this. I was delaying the unavoidable. Taking a deep breath, I jumped up and gripped the other side of its neck, pulling myself onto its back.

Settling down against the gnarled skin gave me hope this wouldn't be too terrifying. But a second later, the reptile rose onto its feet, spread its wings, and launched itself into the air with me shrieking and my heart in my throat. I threw myself against its back, wrapping my arms as far as possible around its neck. I could only reach midway around as my breathing came in sharp gulps. Keeping my eyes snapped tight, the side of my face rubbing against its furrowed skin, I felt the wind rush past.

My heart pumped rapidly, and I realized I was still alive. I didn't move a muscle, but I realized that the serpent cut through the air smoothly, avoiding sudden drops or extreme tilts, which allowed me to stay wedged on top of it.

I soon had the feeling that the bird was angling its flight in a broad circle. I risked looking, my eyelids the only muscle I dared to move. With my cheek jammed against its skin, I could only glimpse sights on one side. As I had thought, the bird flew in a broad circle around the chasm between the mountain peaks. I didn't want to think about how high we were.

As the bird swung around, the platform with my friends came into view. A beast sat waiting for another of my companions, easing my fear that I would be the only one spirited away. Maybe now we would finally be safe, assuming the dragon was as benevolent as I hoped. Teivel might not be the only one who saved us only to harbor ill intentions. Maybe these beasts were under the control of the Bots.

Wouldn't that be a fateful end to our escape? It was yet another thought I pushed to the back of my head.

With my cheek firmly planted against the neck of the beast, my field of vision was limited to the one side. I still didn't feel comfortable enough to lift my head or move at all.

Other reptiles soon began to cross my line of sight, some carrying a companion. I spotted Ja'Krill sitting straight up as if he were riding a horse. Unquestionably, that man had a death wish.

My fear abated slightly as we continued to circle without me slipping off. I still hadn't moved my head, and I wasn't about to. I could see out on one side, and that was good enough. The Nizaem side of the mountain soon came into view. The platform we had used to launch our escape was now loaded with both Bots and Nizaem. The brief glimpse was enough to make me realize that the Bots were forcing the citizens onto the landing.

By the time the bird swung around again, a handful of Nizaem bodies were dangling from the wire. One after another, a Bot would push a struggling person out to hang over open air.

A sick feeling rose in my stomach. These deaths would rest on my shoulders. How many more could I endure? Teivel's plan was wrong, but the others were innocent. That didn't matter to the Bots.

Each time the bird swung around, more Nizaem hung from the wire. Those hanging furthest away from the platform were now still, while the most recently suspended continued to spasm as they tried to free themselves.

The vicious cycle of violence was repeating itself. The Nizaem had suffered this brutality a generation ago. Would any escape this time, or would these be the last of their race?

I wondered if this dragon could stop the bloodshed before it continued. My hands clenched tighter, willing it to intercede. But these dragons couldn't read minds. And from what I had observed, neither could they breathe fire.

Nausea turned to hatred. The Bots would pay. They would one day suffer the consequence for this and for every other death they caused.

As long as I lived, I swore I would have my retribution.

A BUNDLE OF ROOTS

The dragon eventually stopped circling this place of death, and we flew away from the Grimtane Peaks, leaving the bitter memory of the Nizaem behind. I could only assume, hope, that all my companions had climbed onto one of the other beasts and that they followed. It was difficult to be sure since I kept my face plastered against the neck of this animal, trying my best not to think about how high we were.

With nothing to do now but hold on, the air blowing through my hair, I tried to calm myself, mostly to mitigate my overwhelming fear of falling. But with the peace and quiet came the visions of the Bots hanging those innocent people. I had failed to save them. The sight of them dying burned like a hole in my heart. Maybe it always would.

We sailed on for what seemed a long time. Occasionally, I glimpsed another dragon carrying one of my companions. I could never see them all at once. Another person in this situation might risk lifting his head to gain a better view of a vista that might never be witnessed again. But I wasn't that person.

Even with my limited line of sight, I soon observed that we no longer flew high over jagged peaks. The snow and steel-gray palisade of mountains gave way to a land of rolling hills, green vegetation, blue lakes, and meandering rivers. The scenery below stirred a new emotion in me after our time spent at the summit of the world. I yearned to walk on a cushion of grass-covered loam, to smell flowers and woodland pine—the scents of spring.

The dragon gradually dropped altitude as we flew tantalizingly close to the ground. I thought it might settle down at the first suitable place, but it continued flying over fertile land. I spotted several open areas where it could have landed, but it always passed them. It must have a particular destination in mind.

Could it be returning us to Haven, or did it have a sinister plan? I hoped it would be Haven. My frayed emotions needed soothing, and it was the balm I required. The village was the one place in this world with other humans, those I could trust, and who weren't afraid to laugh, or cry, or show their emotions. The people of Haven were my kinsmen; they were my friends.

I maintained a firm grip on the beast with my cheek still plastered flat against its neck even as we glided lower. With my view limited to only one direction, I searched the terrain for a glimpse of the town. The dragon drifted even lower and soon executed a smooth landing in a green meadow, barely jostling me from my perch. As soon as we were on the ground, it lowered its head. I immediately slid off its back, flexing cramped muscles. At last, I was on solid ground.

Other birds circled above, but I paused to observe the animal in front of me. I no longer thought of it as menacing. Intelligence lurked behind its oval, yellow eyes, which regarded me thoughtfully. Placing my palm on the scales of its neck, I said, "Thank you." Still not sure if it understood anything, I added, "If I can return the favor one day, I will."

It didn't respond, but I sensed it heard my words or possibly understood my thoughts. Then again, maybe I was only imagining it. The dragon stood a little higher on its legs, and I knew it was about to fly away. I took a few steps back to give it room. With a remarkably effortless movement, it launched itself into the air, and with a powerful beat of its wings soared higher.

The other dragons and their riders drew closer, and I scanned the creatures, making sure they carried all four companions. Bevon was the first rider to land, followed in quick succession by Ja'Krill, Rae, and lastly, Bryson. Each of the other animals allowed their passengers to debark before taking flight once again.

For a time, the dragons drifted in lazy circles as if watching us. Did they want to ensure we were safe? And then several screeched at once. A farewell? In moments, they soared higher and flew off.

"Amazing creatures," said Ja'Krill in awe, gazing after them. "We were fortunate to encounter them."

Watching them fly away, I said, "There's more to them than we understand; they were an unforeseen blessing." So was Silese, but her death was still too raw in my memory to discuss.

Only when the birds became dots in the sky, did I tear my gaze away from the heavens to take stock of my friends. Bryson sat on the ground, knees bent, a dazed expression on his face. This would be an easy time to poke fun at him, but I took a different approach. "That was a brave thing you did, Bry. Few people would have willingly flown on one of those animals."

He looked at me suspiciously. "You all did."

I nodded. "Yes, but Bevon was raised flying a sail, Ja'Krill was born on a tree limb higher than you've ever seen, and Rae ... well, Rae is just crazy." That brought a smile to his face, and I stepped over and extended a hand to help him to his feet. "Nicely done," I added.

I took in our surroundings, still unsure of where we were. The air was temperate, so I slipped off the Nizaem coat I wore, letting it drop to the ground. "I hope we won't be needing these any longer."

The others regarded me curiously. A new resolve gleamed in their eyes, a quality that had been missing during our time under Teivel's custody. "Time to move forward," I said. "We've spent enough time looking back."

THAT NIGHT WE CAMPED IN A THICKET OF BROADLEAF trees. Ja'Krill and Bryson caught some small game with their traps, while Bevon found plenty of berries and edible plants to keep him satisfied. We lit a campfire, even though we still didn't know our location and whether the region was safe. Why the dragons left us here was a mystery, if they even had a destination in mind.

Once darkness had settled over us, we sat quietly and watched the flames. For the first time in a long while, I didn't brood about our plight. An enormous weight had been lifted from my shoulders, and even though Cassie, Diane, and Matt were still held captive, I believed we had a better chance of freeing them now. At least, I hoped so.

I wasn't the only one whose mood had improved. "This is the way people should live," Rae announced as she stretched out on the ground next to the fire. "I am so sick of those desolate mountains. It's good to be back in a place that's alive." She ran her fingers through the long grass next to her.

Bryson grunted in agreement. "I can't wait to return to Haven. Does anyone know how far it is?"

The thought of returning delighted me. I had hoped the dragons were bringing us there, but they didn't. And now that we were here, wherever here was, I knew I had other priorities. "I'm not going back to Haven, at least not now," I said before anyone could say more. The grin left Bryson's face. "I want to go back to Haven as much as you do, Bry, but my friends are still prisoners. I have to free them."

He did his best to hide it, but I could tell he was crestfallen. "Oh, I understand. I wasn't thinking." After another moment, he added, "I just assumed you would want to get help from others, like Quintia and Riyaad back at Haven."

The village of Haven was his home, the only place he and Rae had ever known. "I understand how much you want to go back," I said. "You shouldn't let me decide for you, none of you should." I glanced at Rae. "The villagers of Haven may need you, and I shouldn't stop you from what you want. This is something I have to do."

Bryson glanced uncertainly at Rae, but she spoke without hesitation. "We should stay together. We're with you, whatever you decide."

I knew Bevon and Ja'Krill would stay with me, but I wanted to give them a choice. Before I could ask, Ja'Krill shrugged, and said in a deadpan voice, "Somebody has to keep you out of trouble. You fall into it often enough."

Bevon nodded his head once; it was all I needed to know.

Their response gave me a warm feeling. "Thank you. I couldn't have come this far without you. I'm glad you're with—"

A squawk from out beyond the circle of light cut me short. It sounded more like a person than an animal. Before I could move, everyone else jumped to their feet with blades drawn. Bevon pointed with his lance toward the darkness. "Over there."

Rae and Ja'Krill spread out on either side of the camp, inching toward the shadows, while Bevon and Bryson hovered near me. I fingered the hilt of my blade but didn't extend it—not yet anyway.

Another chortle, a deep rasping sound, emerged from the darkness. Someone was laughing. "Not a very impressive force to go against the Bots. Not from what I can see."

I peered at the shadows. "Show yourself." For good measure, I added, "We're armed."

A rustle of bushes betrayed the visitor's location. Seconds passed, but nobody came forward. We waited in silence to see if anyone would emerge. "This may be a trap, I'm going to find out." Rae hissed. She slipped into the woods, and without a sound was lost among the shadows.

Bevon and Ja'Krill exchanged worried glances. We were sitting ducks, lit by the flames. Maybe we were already surrounded. "Who are you?" I called out.

"Wrong question," the stranger responded. "Your first lesson is to focus your thoughts."

What the hell was he talking about? Peering into the darkness, I wondered if this person was camouflaged and if he was alone. Another chuckle came from the edge of the flickering campfire.

"There, Earthfriend," said Bevon. He motioned with his lance toward the ground. "Down low, just within the light."

Squinting, the only reason I saw the movement was because Bevon pointed. And even then, I had trouble believing my eyes. This couldn't be the source of the one who spoke. Could it?

I HAD ALTERED MY PERCEPTION OF REALITY MORE THAN once since the time my former college friends and I came to this land of Elthea. Many of the sights and events I witnessed hadn't seemed possible.

This was another such sight.

Until this moment, the different people I had met here were similar to humans. They all had two arms, two legs, one head, and except for the Bots, eyes, a mouth, ears, and a nose. Some were bigger, such as the Stonewraiths, and others diminutive like the Astari or the Valnorians. And each had variations in their appearance, differentiating them from the people of Earth.

What I saw now was more like a tangle of branches, closer to a jumble of tree roots someone had dug out of the ground and twisted together. It couldn't possibly be intelligent. The thing stood less than three feet high. It moved forward by extending one of its limbs, thumping it onto the ground in front of itself, and using it as leverage to pull the rest of its body forward. I gaped, appalled by what I saw.

Bevon noticed my expression. "Do not judge another by their appearance alone, Earthfriend." He retracted his blade and put it back into a pouch at his waist. "Always remember, do not use human standards to judge everyone in this land."

The lump of tree roots laughed. At least I thought it was laughter, a strange scratching sound like the rustle of dry leaves. "Indeed, you have much to learn, you from another world. That is, if you ever hope to master Elthea's gift."

Was he referring to me? Technically, Bevon was initially from Earth, but I sensed I was the target of its jab. I moved a bit closer, but not too close, as I kneeled so I could see it better. "What are you?" I blurted without thinking. "What do you want from us? And what do you know about the Bots?"

It kept moving forward, one clunking step at a time. Rae came out of the bushes behind it. She still had a knife drawn, but held it casually. The thing's forward motion felt ponderously slow, and I wanted to scoop it up and bring it closer, so we didn't have to wait. But I had no intention of touching it.

"Too many questions. Too much eagerness. This is not going to be easy."

It was toying with me. Whatever its intentions, I didn't like this. And after my experience with Teivel, I wasn't ready to fall for another entity wanting to offer assistance. From now on, we were on our own.

The gnarled shape stopped a half-dozen paces from the fire. "Humph. Too hot to come any closer. This will be fine."

As it spoke, one limb of its tangled roots moved up and down, as would a person's lips. Could that be its mouth? Inspecting it more closely, I spotted two knots in the wood that might be a pair of eyes. Otherwise, this creature was a twisted mess.

My companions settled back around the fire. I wasn't so confident it was benign. "What do you want?" I barked. Bevon scowled at my lack of civility, but I didn't care.

The bundle of roots uttered a sound that might have been a sigh. "I can understand your reticence. You have been betrayed, and that experience has tarnished your good sense. But this is no reason to blunder forward unprepared. Continue onward like this, and you will find yourself taken prisoner, as were your friends."

My thoughts raced as I fumbled with how to respond. "W—what? How do you know this?"

"Once again, you ask the wrong question. The Skrill brought you to me. They understood your needs better than yourself."

I remained baffled. The thing moved a branch as if waving a hand. "Those you mistakenly call dragons."

I was having trouble sorting this out. "They flew us here

so we could find ... you?" I barely avoided calling it a freakish monstrosity.

Bevon spoke calmly, unlike my shrill-sounding voice. "Perhaps you should start from the beginning. Understand that we know nothing about you, so it would be beneficial if you could tell us who you are."

The tangle of roots appeared to bow ever so slightly, or maybe I only imagined it. "We are called the Oakenrill by those who know of us. It suffices as well as anything since we have no use for a name. For most races, many generations have passed since the time we removed ourselves from the affairs of the world. Countless events have come and gone, yet we remain. We are old, as you measure time."

Ja'Krill leaned forward on his knees, his face flush with excitement. "The spirits of the Valnorian Woods speak of an ancient race. It is said that much flora and fauna of Elthea owe their beginnings to it. Are you the one they speak of?"

The Oakenrill took its time to respond. Maybe it wasn't accustomed to answering so many questions, or perhaps it had fallen asleep, I couldn't be sure. Finally, it said, "The woods of your people are a special place. The life force of Elthea is strong there. Unbeknownst to your brethren, many of my kind continue to live in your home. Throughout our long history, we have fostered much life, both plants and animals. It is a noble undertaking, one we find worthy."

My stupor began to abate. "Look, all this is well and good, but what does this have to do with you standing here?" Or maybe it was sitting, I couldn't be sure. "We're not plants."

Bevon gave me a sidelong glance. "Patience, Earthfriend,"

he whispered. I scrunched my face in annoyance, holding back a protest.

The bundle of roots leaned forward. "We find ourselves on the cusp of a new age. Whether it will be a magnificent wonder or a hellish nightmare, I do not know. But I do understand that everything depends upon you, Philip Matherson."

I felt my skin prickle. "I—I don't know what you're talking about." Who gave this thing the right to pass judgment on me? How did it know me? "Maybe someday I can listen to your story about a new age. Right now, all I care about is my friends who are prisoners of the Bots. Until I set them free, nothing else matters."

The Oakenrill's voice remained steady. "Oh, but it does matter. It makes a difference to the countless lives here on Elthea, and to those on your world. The choices you make will determine their fate. What will you decide now? Will you allow me to guide you?"

Guide me? I licked my lips, wanting nothing to do with this creature. I nearly shouted at it to go away. But something about its words hit home. "Why do you think any of this depends on me? I have few skills. Others are stronger, smarter, you name it." I grunted, annoyed with myself and lack of anything to feel proud about. "And there you have the story of my life in a nutshell."

I expected a derisive reply, but heard nothing but silence, confirming that it agreed. Finally, it spoke gently. "No matter what your life was, or what you believe, all that changed with the Bots. For better or worse, they have unintentionally remade you."

Remade me? I didn't feel any different. At least I was

smart enough to realize that events had been spiraling out of my control, and I was unable to make things right. I lurched from one crisis to another. And now, my best friends were held captive by the Bots.

One of the logs in the fire snapped and sputtered, bringing my thoughts back to the present. The Oakenrill waited for my response. Should I accept its aid or not? "Can you help me save my friends?"

"If they can be saved, I will do everything in my power to help you do so. First, you must listen and learn, and accept everything I teach you."

Every fiber in my body screamed to ignore its offer. If anyone could help me, it couldn't be this creature who looked unlike anything I had ever known. But not being able to free my best friends frightened me even more. Left to my own devices, I had no idea where to begin. "Very well," I said. "I accept your offer to teach me. When do we begin? And how long will it take?"

The Oakenrill grunted another sound. "No, this will not be easy," it mumbled to itself.

26

THE PARADOX

"You must leave," the Oakenrill announced the next morning. "I require Philip's total attention as I train him. The rest of you will be in the way."

I almost laughed, knowing my companions would never accept such an insane demand. As expected, Bevon spoke without hesitation. "That is not possible. The Earthfriend is under my protection."

Rae glanced at me before saying, "He doesn't do well on his own. Besides, we've already decided to stay with him."

Her characterization irked me, but at least she agreed to stay put.

The Oakenrill dragged itself closer to Bevon. "I understand your concern. But this is not open for discussion. You must comply. I will begin his training immediately, and time is of the essence. You and the others will only slow him down."

Bevon crossed his arms, refusing to respond. This tangle of roots had a thing or two to learn about us. I remained silent, smiling smugly knowing that my friends would never abandon me.

As far as I could tell, the Oakenrill remained facing Bevon, though to be honest, I often found it hard to be certain. It said, "I offer to open my mind so you will better understand."

Bevon remained impassive, as Astari often will when considering options. He finally nodded his head once. A shred of uncertainty rippled through me. Still, I knew he would never agree to the Oakenrill's proposal.

Bevon uncrossed his arms, dropping them to his side, as his posture became less rigid. His eyes became unfocused, and his jaw slackened. I sensed a crackle of static electricity at the edge of my awareness. Ja'Krill sat up straight as he peered intently. He understood what was taking place better than the rest of us. I exchanged a puzzled glance with Rae and Bryson.

Whatever passed between Bevon and the Oakenrill lasted less than a minute. My companion finally blinked and sucked in a deep breath. Bevon looked from the Oakenrill to me and back again. Did I see puzzlement, or was it uncertainty in his eyes? "You make a compelling argument," he finally acknowledged, gazing at the tangled limbs.

My jaw dropped. Rae, however, erupted immediately. "What? I can't believe you're willing to sacrifice Phil. We're not leaving. It's as simple as that." I had long admired her tenacity, but never more so than now. It was one of her more charming qualities.

Bevon ignored Rae as he regarded me. "Earthfriend, since the time you first transitioned to the Raised Isles, I have always had the best intentions for you and the other Earth-friends."

For some reason, I recalled a time in junior high school when Suzy Defonte told me she was going to break up with me. At that age, we weren't in a serious relationship; I could barely classify it as going out together. But at that time in my life, she was the high point of my wretched social existence. Bevon's words held the same ring. I responded to him with the same words I had once said to Suzy. "You're not going to leave me, are you?"

He didn't respond. I couldn't believe this. "Bevon, why would you even consider it? You have always guarded me. I'm alive now only because of your protection. Don't leave me now."

"Do you trust me?" he said after a moment's hesitation.

"Of course I do. But we have to stay together, especially now." I gestured to the fields beyond our camp. "Our enemy is out there, and I can't fight them without you. The other Earthfriends need you. Don't give up on them."

"This is not about giving up." He paused. "Consider it this way. A crutch can be useful when you need support. But it can become a double-edged sword if you become overly dependent on it once it outlives its usefulness. And then it may become difficult to discard. I have always attempted to keep you safe because you needed it. But there is a fine line between shielding you from harm and holding you back."

"You've never held me back." I still couldn't imagine life on Elthea without Bevon.

He took a breath. "And I hope I never hamper you. But

right now, if I stay, I will not be protecting you; I will prevent you from reaching your potential."

I stared, dumbfounded. "Bevon, I need you here."

"The Oakenrill has shared some of his memory with me. He spoke the truth when he said he can help you. He hides no deceit, as did Teivel. This Oakenrill has the skill to call on Elthea's powers, possibly surpassing anyone I have ever known. What better person to teach you?"

Rae, Bryson, and Ja'Krill exchanged nervous glances. Bevon was our leader, and even if we occasionally disagreed, we followed his lead. I wanted to shout that he was wrong, that he was about to make a big mistake. Before I could continue to voice my objection, he said, "Tell me, Earthfriend. If things were different, if Earthfriends Cassie, Diane, and Mathew were here now, and you were held captive by the Bots, how would you expect them to behave? What would you want them to do?" He paused for several heartbeats before answering his own questions. "I believe they would attempt to free you, even if it meant consenting to this."

I licked my lips. The words stuck in my throat.

"I give you my word," said the Oakenrill. "I will do everything possible to help you." His voice was scratchy, and his body surreal. It didn't seem possible something so unnatural was intelligent. "Learning this skill will be difficult," it continued, "but if you are willing, we will work together."

I stared at it, still unable to frame a response. I wasn't frightened by the training as much as being alone with this thing. Into the silence, Bevon stepped close and embraced me. The Astari were exceptionally affable and warm-hearted, but rarely showed their emotions. I was too unnerved to respond.

"You will do well, Earthfriend," he whispered. "I feel certain we will meet again." He gazed at me and added, "I sincerely hope so."

I considered screaming to put a stop to this madness. But deep inside, once I pushed away my fears and insecurities, I knew he was right. I needed to stand on my own. My voice shaking, I murmured. "Okay, whatever it takes."

"I have summoned the Skrill," said the Oakenrill. "They will return each of you to your human settlement. Perhaps you will be safe there for a while, that is, if anywhere can be called safe."

"This is happening too fast," I said, suddenly not so sure I should have been so easily persuaded. "Shouldn't you wait to be sure?" The cry of an animal far above sent a shiver through me. Bryson groaned, but I was too lost in my own troubles to make light of his fright at riding another Skrill. Four magnificent creatures, which I had called dragons, glided toward us. They quickly settled onto the nearby field.

Rae came close and whispered in my ear. "I'll stay here if you tell me. You would do the same for me."

I forced a weak smile to my lips. "I didn't expect this, and I'd be lying if I said this is what I want. I would prefer to have you beside me." I let out a breath, trying my best to keep my emotions in check. "But I trust Bevon. If that thing can help me, I'll suffer through it."

Her lips were taut, and she clutched the hilt of a blade, a soldier's habit. Pitching her voice low, she added, "We don't know much about it."

I nodded. "True, but Bevon believes in it. Besides, you're needed back at Haven, now more than ever. You said it yourself."

Her eyes remained locked on mine. I thought she would continue to press her point. Instead, she hugged me, holding me tightly before finally releasing me. "You were always meant for something greater than the life of a simple villager," she said. "I knew it from the first day we met."

I chuckled. "Yea, I bet you did. I remember how confused and lost I felt back then. But you helped me get through it. I'll always be thankful for that." She grabbed my hand and clenched it before stepping back to stand near Bryson.

Now that I had made the decision, I wanted the goodbyes to be over. I put on a brave face as I eyed Ja'Krill, "I'll see you at Haven when this is done. Do what you can to help the villagers."

He nodded, smiling sadly. "It is an insufferable place, all built of stone. But I will wait there for your return as you ask. I pray it will be soon."

Should I say more, tell them how I felt while I had the chance? They should know how much I'd miss them, how I might never see them again, that I love them. But my throat tightened, and I knew my voice would crack if I tried.

Bryson's mouth twisted in a crooked smile. "How about we switch? You can ride the damn bird, and I'll stay here."

I suspected he was partly serious. "You'll do fine, Bry. Besides, returning to Haven on the back of a dragon will do much to increase your reputation in the eyes of all the young women in the village. You'll be a hero."

His face brightened, but his eyes watered. "Remember to watch out for yourself," he said. "That's all I care about."

I nodded. "Say hello to the commander for me."

I walked with them as they moved toward the Skrill. Even though it was a short distance, the Oakenrill remained at the camp. Ja'Krill was the most comfortable riding them, and he was the first to hoist himself up. Bevon was next, while Rae fixed Bryson with a stern expression. He seemed uncertain which of the two remaining ones to choose, as if it made a difference. Once decided, he rubbed his hands on his pant legs before clumsily wrestling his way onto its back. Rae was the last to climb onto the remaining animal, looking nearly as comfortable as Ja'Krill. How did she manage to make even this seem effortless?

The animals waited only a moment before stretching their legs and launching themselves into the air with their riders attached. I shielded my eyes as they flew over me, feeling like part of my life had been ripped away.

I stood in that spot long after they had passed from sight. The silence threatened to overpower me with a sadness I had never experienced. For the first time in this land of Elthea, I was bereft of faithful companions.

"This is your first lesson. The body and mind are one, much like the mystical and the physical world." The Oakenrill gave me no time to bemoan the departure of the others. He began his tutelage as soon as I returned to the campsite.

I sat near the dying embers of the morning campfire, feeling sorry for myself. I wanted time to grieve over my situation, and his voice annoyed me.

The sun had risen hours ago, and the air was growing warm. The Oakenrill stood, or maybe sat—I still couldn't be sure—a few feet in front of me. I made a face, trying to understand what he was saying. "You lost me already. I have no idea what you mean." I took a breath. "I'm going to starve here on my own. I can't even hunt like the others."

He made a sound; I believe it was a groan. "Let us focus on the matter at hand. There will be plenty of time to worry about food later. You wish to use the powers of Elthea. I can teach you, but you must be willing."

I gritted my teeth and remained silent. He continued. "The first thing you must recognize is that Elthea is fundamentally different from your home. You are not in the world of your birth. The rules governing the behavior of life here do not correspond to your world. You must relearn everything you take for granted."

My annoyance with him escalated. "How does this malarkey help me rescue my friends? Can't we jump to the important parts of this training and leave this ... I don't know, this philosophical stuff for later? The Bots might be torturing them while we prattle about minor details."

He refrained from making more sounds. "Okay, then tell me, how do you imagine yourself saving your companions? What would you need to accomplish?"

"Now we're getting somewhere." I had to keep this tangle of roots focused on the important stuff. "First, I need to have some power to locate Cassie, Matt, and Diane. And if they are far away, you would need to call one of the Skrill so that it could bring me there. And then I would blast the Bots out of existence and free them." I smiled, realizing that's exactly how I imagined it going down ever since I learned they were taken captive.

He paused before responding. "And that, Philip Matherson, is why you are currently incapable of drawing on Elthea's powers."

"No, you have it wrong. You don't know as much as you believe you do. Teivel, the leader of the Nizaem race blocked me. He was the reason I couldn't do anything. I had the ability before then." I thought back to the firestorm I unleashed in the Valnorian Woods. "If you hadn't sent Ja'Krill or Bevon away, they could explain what I was capable of doing."

"And have you attempted to draw on Elthea's powers since he stopped blocking you?"

I frowned, recalling what happened after Silese incapacitated Teivel. "I tried to use it against a Bot." I had a sinking feeling this Oakenrill knew the outcome of that incident.

"And nothing happened," he answered before I could figure out how to frame it. "Elthea's powers don't work that way."

"That's exactly how they work. You don't understand. The Bots were crushing the Valnorian Woods with an ice storm. I destroyed the Bots and put an end to the ice."

"Your one accomplishment with the powers of Elthea has clouded your thinking. You believe it is an instrument of death because of how the Bots perversely employ it. Elthea is an agent of life. Her spirit bestows powers onto those who will enhance the land and make it a better place for all. Somehow, the Bots have subverted Elthea's safeguards as they continue to use her powers for destruction."

I exhaled, my frustration building. Looking up at the sky, I hoped one of the Skrill would come to whisk me away. I didn't want to listen to this any longer. "Why did Bevon ever leave me alone with you?" Realizing I might have become too cross, I focused on the information he tried to impart. "What you're saying doesn't change the reality that Bots use Elthea's powers to destroy the land and kill good people. Our only option now is to destroy them. Be realistic. You may not understand the Bots because you remain hidden here in the middle of nowhere."

"Oh, I know quite well what they do. We must stop their evil violence before we are all destroyed. Hence, I am attempting to teach you."

I studied the Oakenrill, trying to make sense of the jumble of twisted limbs. The thing still resembled a bunch of tree roots someone had squished together. But I began to see a pattern to the mess. A split in one of the roots was obviously its mouth. Two other knots were likely its eyes. They rotated and occasionally disappeared as he adjusted his gaze or closed his eyes. How something such as this could even be intelligent was still beyond me.

He continued speaking, bringing my attention back to what it was saying. "The Bots have twisted her powers into something that wasn't intended. You want to accomplish the same by obliterating them."

I threw my hands in the air, raising my voice. "Isn't that the purpose of this training? How can anyone stop them without destroying them?" A new thought occurred to me. "Do you believe you can reason with them? Because if you do, it's not going to happen. The Astari tried a generation ago, and it almost caused the destruction of this world." I fumed, annoyed at myself for arguing with it.

The Oakenrill sighed, a deep, resonant sound. "You can accomplish your purpose through a variety of methods. A weapon of destruction is only one recourse. If you continue to think of it as your only option and believe it is the sole intention of this training, we will be at it for a very long time with little to show."

"Those monsters deserve to die," I shouted. Why did I continue to argue with this bundle of roots?

"Yes, they deserve to die because of what they have done. They have defiled the land and killed innocent lives. But you must find another way. That is the purpose of my training. Otherwise, you will annihilate the spirit of Elthea as surely as the Bots are doing."

"What do you mean?"

The Oakenrill extended some of its limbs. The motion was unlike anything human, but I pictured it spreading its fingers as a person would. It reminded me of a gesture someone might use when saying something important. "Elthea is dying because the Bots use her powers for harm. They are killing her, and you will contribute to her death by doing the same. You have a remarkable ability, as demonstrated by what happened in the Valnorian Woods. Elthea has granted you this skill. But you must not persist in believing you can accomplish what you have done before."

"Do you have any idea what you're talking about?" I said.

"You agreed we must stop the Bots. Now you tell me not to use the powers to defeat them. Which is it?"

He took his time to answer. "It is a paradox of the land. If you and the Bots continue to use Elthea's powers to hurt and kill others, her life force will end. She will be gone forever."

LEGENDS AND MYTH

Today was a day like most others in my new life with the Oakenrill. The sun hadn't yet reached a high point in the sky, and already I had been training for hours. I stopped to catch my breath. "You must push yourself harder," he said in my ear. As usual, he perched on my back with a crude harness he had fashioned out of vines so I could carry him as I ran. On other days he might instruct me to swim, hike up hills, climb trees, or perform other drills.

Even a swim did not deter the Oakenrill from his spot. He had insisted on this arrangement during our first day of training, which allowed him to provide constant instructions. I considered it more like harassment, especially during the first few weeks.

"I swear you're trying to kill me," I said between gulps of air as I paused in my run.

"Hmm, if that is what I intended, I could find a much easier way to accomplish the task."

I chuckled. "No doubt you could, considering some of the things you're capable of doing with your power." I twisted my head to look at him. "You pack quite a punch despite your strange appearance."

He grunted. "I have no idea what that means, but I will accept it as a compliment."

Taking another moment to catch my breath, I said, "I must confess, my initial opinion of you was unjustified. Don't hold it against me, but who could blame me at first, especially considering the way you look."

"In time, you will learn to see with other senses."

I reflected on how far I had come since our first meeting. In the beginning, I had tested his patience and his knowledge of the land. But like Bevon and the other Astari, he always answered my questions, giving me a better understanding of this world and the powers of Elthea.

Bevon and Ja'Krill had often tried to teach me to draw upon Elthea's powers when we were at Haven. Their intentions were well-founded, but looking back, I realized they didn't come close to what I needed.

Surprisingly, the Oakenrill's methods, strange as they first appeared, had already taught me more about myself and the world around me. I still considered him odd in so many ways. For instance, he didn't have a name. As he had explained, members of his race could identify each other only by their soul or life force.

Other Oakenrill visited us now and then, but none of them ever stayed long. It was comical to see three or four of them engaged in a spirited discussion, moving their limbs around much like humans gesturing with their hands.

I also discovered that he didn't eat, at least in the way humans and most other races ate. He somehow absorbed nutrients directly from the soil. As a result, I had to hunt and forage for myself. Once my companions had left, he helped me find the food I needed to survive.

I sat down on the log of a fallen tree and slipped off the harness from my back so I could rest for a moment and face him. Once on the ground, the Oakenrill climbed out of his restraint.

My days had begun to follow a typical routine. It didn't matter if the sun was shining warmly or rain pelted down from a gray sky. We started with a series of aerobic drills, followed by what my teacher called the Arath, and ended with deep meditation. Each exercise was challenging, but the Arath was the most unusual, and in some ways, the most difficult. It reminded me of the Chinese tradition called Tai Chi, even though I had never practiced it before and knew little about it. The movements were slow and precise, requiring a combination of physical stamina and concentration. I usually sweated as much going through these movements as I did with some of the more aerobic exercises.

"Now perform Dancing Water," announced the Oakenrill, letting me know we had moved on to the Arath portion of today's training. "Please try not to move as if you are blundering forward. Step slowly as you bring your arms around and up."

For someone so different from humans, the Oakenrill understood my bodily strengths and weaknesses. He had to explain each motion, rather than show me because of the obvious differences in our bodies. Even with the dissimilarities between us, I recognized how fluidly he would move his limbs when he practiced the Arath, unlike my clumsy flailing around.

He studied my progress from a few feet away as I performed the choreographed twists and turns of Dancing Water. "You must concentrate harder, move slower, and stop jerking your arms. Every movement should be fluid."

Frustrated, I let my arms drop and planted both feet on the ground. "Explain again how this will help me use Elthea's powers?"

He groaned. "I am helping you expand your mind as you control your body. The powers will come, believe me."

"This is taking too long," I grumbled. "We've been at this for weeks, and all I have to show for it are blisters and sore muscles. I still can't grasp the easiest of charms."

"Remember what I told you. The mystical and physical are one. Both must be in balance with the land."

"Ugh. I've heard you say that more times than I can count, and I'm still not sure I understand what you mean. The only thing I know is that you wear me out with exercises for half the day, and the other half we concentrate on controlling my thoughts. I'm doing everything you tell me, but it's still not enough. Hell, I'm still no match against the Bots, and I have no way to free my friends."

He looked at me with what I knew was an expression of dissatisfaction, or possibly annoyance. It turns out that the Oakenrill exhibited a remarkable range of emotions, a far cry from my opinion of him as a tangled web of tree roots without feelings. Before he could admonish me further, I added, "Believe me, I'm trying to give you the benefit of the doubt. But, give me credit; I no longer think of you as a creepy thing like I did at first."

His voice became deadpan. "Yes, that is benevolent of you." His tone returned to normal as he continued. "You may not know it yet, but you are making progress. Elthea has granted you an exceptional ability. What you need is a better understanding of yourself and your surroundings before you can use her powers wisely. The eruption of energy you delivered against the Bots during your first attempt was exactly that, an outburst born from unmitigated emotions. I want you to become powerful but in *control*. And most importantly, you must use a measured response that does not involve violence."

I scrunched my face, knowing it was no use arguing with him. The only reason I continued to do as he said was that I had begun to feel the stirrings of new strength, one that was neither physical nor mental. For the first time in a long while, I allowed myself to hope.

AFTER PRACTICING THE ARATH FOR SEVERAL HOURS, THE Oakenrill signaled an end. Curiously, I noticed that my muscles didn't hurt or feel like rubber after finishing. I felt more alive than I had in a while. As always, I completed today's session with several deep cleansing breaths.

Once I finished the Arath, we typically began the meditation part of my training. The Oakenrill preferred to describe this portion of the instruction as the exercise to expand my mind. It consisted of a sequence of cognitive drills intended to focus my thoughts, typically involving little conversation or physical movement.

We sat in a shady grove of willowy trees that swayed in response to the smallest breeze. I waited for his direction. He began by saying, "Rather than expanding your mind, today I would like to discuss the spirit of Elthea. You should understand her more fully."

I raised my eyebrows. "That would be helpful. I've heard so much, yet I understand little about her."

He sat still for a time, as if deciding how to begin. "Few of your people know her story, neither do most of the races living here. Legend has become myth, with the ancient past shrouded in mystery. Some races have sought to discover her nature through the ages. Your companion from the Valnorians is one. More have attempted to use the energy she provides."

"Anything you can tell me will be valuable."

He nodded. "I can tell you a story, one that is old as time. This tale may explain some of what you should know, but I caution, much remains unknown about her spirit, and perhaps always will. Even the Oakenrill do not understand her fully."

I shifted to a more comfortable spot on the ground, grateful for a chance to recover and from the change in our routine. The Oakenrill waited until I had settled. When he spoke, his voice took on a deeper resonance, drawing me quickly into the tale.

"The lady Elthea is a life unlike any other
Yet, make no mistake, her righteous spirit is eager
To keep the land shielded and alive
She occupies a different plane of existence than you
    or I
Her desire is to protect and safeguard our home, a
    place she calls her own.

Other worlds have a guardian, much like Elthea
Her kindred share a common wish
To make the cosmos a place of bliss
A bulwark against the darkness ever threatening to
    overthrow
All who seek a life of peace and abundance.

Callous disregard of life will forfeit
As well as destructive pursuits will weaken
The protection her people crave above all else
A sad event, it is, when worlds are deprived of their
    spirit
Causing the cosmos to die a little.

Elthea has remained strong as the eons have come
    and gone
Ever guarding her land against reckless harm
By gifting to others her powers so they may ply
Her potency against those who would cause her to die.

The great paradox of Elthea's strength

Consists of the way you apply her energy
Put it to use for death, destruction, and violence
And you will serve to weaken her essence
The greater the harm done, the more she will diminish
Until finally, her life will be finished.

As was foretold by her long ago
A tribe will arrive in her land
Their ill intentions if left unchecked
Will demolish all that is good and put an end to her
    power
Thus, ending her reign to protect and nurture.

A champion will she entrust
To prevent her foe from doing harm
By channeling all her strength
To the one who can save her land.

And so must all good beings endeavor
To provide succor to her defender
The one burdened with the unimaginable mission
Of preventing the demons from spreading unbidden
Thereby filling the land of Elthea with hatred and
    aggression
And ending the reign of spirit guardians
Not only here, but ultimately, elsewhere
In places where generations of all those who are
    worthy
Have heretofore lived in unity."

I stared at the Oakenrill, letting the implication of the story sink in. The tale explained much, yet left a great deal unsaid. I finally asked, "Do you believe the tribe in the story is the Bots?"

He stirred slightly, as if coming out of a trance. "I am sure it is them. They will continue to destroy all that is good in the universe if left alone."

I was terrified of asking the next question, but I had to know. "And who is this champion from the story?"

He took a long time to answer. "I believe it is you."

I THOUGHT ABOUT OAKENRILL'S STORY DURING THE NEXT few days as I continued my training. This talk of a champion had unnerved me. All I wanted was to free Cassie, Matt, and Diane, not become the savior of a world. My tutor was wrong about his assertion. He had to be.

On the third day, he admonished me for not concentrating during the Arath exercise called Singing Wind. "Your movements are stilted, much like the way you performed at the beginning of our training. What has happened to you?"

I shrugged. "Maybe I'm just tired today."

He made the noise I had recognized as his expression of displeasure. He made that sound a lot since the time I had met him. "If that is the case, you have been weary for the past several days. Something is troubling you; please discuss it now. You will not develop further in your training without a clear mind."

I chewed my lip, knowing I would probably sound foolish. But then my words came out in a rush. "You don't know everything. Did you ever stop to consider that I might not want the weight of the world on my shoulders? You could be wrong, you realize." Searching for a way to sound more rational, I added, "There's nothing special about me."

He moved several of his limbs simultaneously, another gesture I had begun to understand as a nod. "You may be right, but that does not matter, does it?"

"Of course it matters! All I want is to keep my friends safe and to live without fear from the Bots."

Again, he made the same gesture. "That is the wish of most honorable people."

"You don't understand. There must be someone else braver, or stronger, or better than me."

"Hmm, probably. But I say again, that is irrelevant."

He was infuriating. I wanted to throw something at him, not to hurt him, just to make him stop talking in circles. I huffed, deciding not to continue this discussion. Turning away, I took another cleansing breath. Curiosity won out as I eyed him warily. Finally, I demanded, "Why don't my feelings make a difference? This is my life you're talking about."

He moved another set of limbs, the equivalent of a shrug in a human. "Either the spirit of Elthea has granted you the ability, or she has not. My training will allow you to weave her powers properly, with the necessary restraint. Beyond that, it is in her hands. So, you see, what I believe is of little consequence."

I sputtered as I tried to say the words. "B-but you said you could give me the skill to save my friends. If I knew it wasn't up to you, I wouldn't be going through all this. It's nothing but a waste of time."

The Oakenrill nodded. "I said I would try. Yet, you must understand that saving your friends and eliminating the threat from the Bots are two different feats. You may save your companions temporarily. But the Bots will never leave your utopia group alone. You should already realize this from Cassie McKenzie's Farseeing."

How did he know about our Utopia Project, or for that matter, Cassie's name? I wasn't sure how to respond. Before I could speak, he added, "I do not understand why you are upset over this. You do hate the Bots, do you not?"

The air went out of me, and I looked at the ground. I shrugged. "Of course, I hate them. I'm scared, that's all." In the next breath, I added, "I'm afraid of failing, not for myself, but for them."

"Keep your fears close to your heart and never forget them. They drive you forward, make you who you are, and give you the strength to find a way."

I sighed. "I'm not entirely convinced that being afraid will help me at anything, but I consented to your training. I suppose this is part of it. If only I knew everything would end well, I might not be so worried."

He picked up his harness and plodded toward me. "Knowing is not always the answer." I frowned as he handed me the harness. He didn't explain more. "Meditation training is next. We will perform today's activity near the running brook under the cover of large evergreens."

The place was not far from here. I held out the harness and waited until the Oakenrill slipped into it. Once he was secure, I lifted him onto my back and slipped my arms through the vines that served as straps. I paused. "In the tale you recited, you spoke about other worlds with a power much like that of Elthea. Does my home, Earth, contain such energy?"

I felt him move, probably a shrug. "I cannot see beyond the bounds of this realm, so I am unable to say. Have people of your home ever spoken about a mystical power?"

I laughed. "Our world isn't big on the mystical power stuff except in stories." I chewed on the idea for another moment. "But we have the expression Mother Earth, or Mother Nature to describe our world. I don't know its origin, but possibly..."

I set a fast pace toward the place he indicated, my thoughts still on the story. Before arriving at the destination, I stopped, craning my neck to look at him. "Wait. When I was a child, I once read a fairy tale. One of the characters in the book was a supernatural being called Gaia, who represented our Earth." I straightened my head and smiled sadly. "That reminds me of a time when fairy tales were make believe, not something that could come to life. Wouldn't it be nice if that was still true?" I paused another moment before I asked, "Do you think my home once had a spirit such as Elthea?"

I could sense him looking at me with his knots of eyes. "Perhaps. After all, legends and myths have a way of harking back to the truth."

After another moment, I began to jog, cutting a path around trees and tall bushes. During recent weeks, physical exercise had helped clear my mind. Today, however, my thoughts raced with possibilities. Did Earth have a spirit such as Elthea? If so, did it still live, or had it faded entirely?

Mostly, I wondered if I would ever live up to the Oaken-rill's assessment of me. I had the feeling it wouldn't be long before I would find out.

28

THE REASON YOU WILL FAIL

Twilight gently surrounded us, a cushion of darkness beyond the light of our small campfire. I stretched the sore muscles in my legs as I sat with my back against a tree, chewing on a sampling of nuts and fruits, as well as beans softened by boiling over the fire and then wrapped in edible greens. Early in my training, I had complained about my diet, saying it fitted the Astari rather than humans. Now, I enjoyed it, even though I wasn't going to admit it.

On this evening, the Oakenrill was oddly silent. He was seldom at a loss for words, whether to discuss the next day's plan or to explain Elthea's powers. As usual, he sat several feet further away from the fire than I preferred.

"A penny for your thoughts," I said as the silence lingered.

He blinked as if seeing me for the first time, making a noise I recognized as a grunt. "Do all humans speak with such curious words? That means nothing to me."

I chuckled. "I'm asking what you're thinking. You're surprisingly quiet this evening."

He nodded. "I am troubled, that is all."

My cheerful mood slipped away. "What's wrong? Is it something about my friends? Do you have any news?"

"You ask too many questions, it seems whatever comes into your head. This may be a common affliction of your race, but you should focus your thoughts more precisely."

I scowled. "You're breaking one of our rules." He didn't respond, so I persisted. "After we complete our work for the day, we relax and talk about whatever we want without disapproval."

"We have no such agreement."

"Yeah, well, maybe it was a gentleman's agreement."

He eyed me without speaking, and I couldn't tell if he was bemused, annoyed, or confused. "If you must know, I need time to think," he finally relented.

I bit my tongue, realizing that another question right now would displease him further.

As I nibbled on my food, he said, "They are searching for you, always seeking your whereabouts. The Bots do not stop."

I involuntarily shuddered, knowing they tried to control our utopia team even during my time in college. "The Bots wanted me since the beginning," I said. "They're not going to change now. Cassie's Farseeing episodes made that clear."

"Yes, but something is different. The intensity of their hatred for you has reached a new level. Even as we speak, they hunt."

Did I hear the snap of a twig beyond our circle of light? No, it was probably the crackling of the burning wood in our fire. My imagination was already running wild. I took a breath to calm myself. "We can't stop them from finding me, can we? They've always tracked me down in the past."

"This time, you are more of a threat. The Bots understand how you have developed because of your training. It has fueled their fear, which has become hatred."

"What recourse do we have?"

He moved several of his limbs at the same time. "I have thrown a veil of concealment over you. It has stymied their efforts, but it will not last overlong. They search for you with Elthea's powers, and they have already begun to probe the edge of my shield."

I studied the Oakenrill, once again wondering the extent of his abilities. "This training, it's not going to make any difference, is it? You still have a far greater ability than me. No matter how much I try, you're still stronger. I can't understand why you don't stop them. Why train me when you have all this knowledge and talent?"

"I have the knowledge, but not the capacity. Elthea has not granted me the strength to change an entire race. I believe you can. With enough discipline and practice, you will accomplish more than I ever could."

I looked again into the night, not feeling as safe as before. "How can I possibly learn enough before they find me? I haven't succeeded with anything yet."

"If we have enough time, you will gain the skill. Just remember to stay true to my instructions. You must do no harm by using Elthea's gift."

I still didn't know how that was possible. The Bots had to be destroyed. I turned my thoughts inward as the Oakenrill had taught me, searching for the slightest glimmer of sensation telling me I had touched upon another energy.

I could sense something, but as always, it was just beyond my reach.

During the following days, the Oakenrill became more demanding. "No, you move too quickly," he barked as I performed Silent Wind. "The Arath is all about precision. Use your mind to control your body, not the other way around. Concentrate on what you are doing!"

I wanted to explain how difficult it was to move fluidly after he had me scale a massive tree up and down three times in a row. But I knew complaining would only make him more upset. I sensed our time was growing short, and that was the reason for his temper.

Each day brought me closer to understanding what he was trying to accomplish. My senses were sharper, more in tune with my body and the world around me. I could feel the caress of a mild breeze and understand how far it had traveled to reach me. A flower six feet away smelled as fragrant as if I held it up to my nose.

Something still bothered me. "Maybe I can't fully concentrate because parts of this puzzle still elude me."

He moved a limb, which meant he didn't understand. "This is not a puzzle. Why do you ask questions that have no meaning?"

I frowned. "No, you miss my point. I still don't understand how I can stop the Bots without destroying them."

He let out a sound that was his version of a sigh. He spoke in a soft voice, and I realized his anger had dissipated. "We all serve a purpose in life. You, myself, even the Bots. Stop thinking of them as pure evil. You must want to give them a reason to be alive and be a part of our society."

My pulse quickened. "I've seen them slaughter children for no reason. They hold my best friends captive. I don't know if I can think that way."

He didn't move for a time. "And that is the reason you will fail when the time comes."

I ACHIEVED MY FIRST TANGIBLE BREAKTHROUGH ON THE thirty-fifth day of my education. In my eyes, it was a stunning achievement. The tiny weave of energy was more than I had been able to draw upon since my outburst against the Bots in the Valnorian Woods.

On this day, I produced a flame in the palm of my hand. The Oakenrill sat across from me as I felt the pulsating buzz of a minor electrical charge coursing through my body and out through my palm. I concentrated on drawing the energy at a steady flow, ignoring everything else.

After a time, he said, "You have the ability, but you still hold back." I risked a glance at him while trying to keep part of my mind focused on the flame. Even with the rebuke, I knew he was pleased by the tone of his voice.

I looked back at the flame that didn't burn. "My nature is to be cautious. It's who I am, a part of me I cannot leave behind."

He thought about this for a moment. "You should embrace your reticence as well as your fears. They are healthy attributes, especially when using Elthea's life force. It will strengthen you and prevent you from using it unwisely."

I could continue fueling the flame in my palm even through our conversation. "I thought my insecurities were a big reason I had failed to grasp Elthea's powers sooner."

He made a sound I recognized as a chuckle. "No, no. It is your nature to question your actions. I admire that quality. Others may blunder ahead, mindless of the harm they inflict by rash decisions. You are mindful of your actions, and perhaps this is a reason Elthea has granted you the skill to weave her powers. Not every being has the talent, no matter the amount of training."

I thought about my outburst in the Valnorian Woods when I first drew upon Elthea's life force. "I wasn't that circumspect once before. Yet, I achieved my purpose."

"But to what end? You saved the woodland race and their sacred forest. In the process, you harmed Elthea. Continue with that sort of attack, and her spirit will diminish further."

I lost my concentration, and the flame sputtered out. "How long until I'm ready?"

He expressed himself with a grunt or perhaps a groan. "Enough questions. You must trust me."

I closed my fist, examining my hand. "This flame was trivial, but maybe it's something I can build upon."

"You have already accomplished more than you realize. The foundation is in place. Your thoughts have become focused, and you have greater command over your body."

I gritted my teeth, knowing my education was already

taking too long. Every day that passed, I felt the pain of my companions who remained locked in hell.

On one particularly crisp and breezy day, after spending most of the morning exercising my body, it was time to stretch my mind. By this time, I had made great strides at improving my stamina and dexterity. Today's routine was no different as the weeks continued to build, one upon the other. Yet, I knew it wouldn't last much longer. The training was a goal, with another end now in sight.

The Oakenrill never failed to proclaim his mantra. "The body and mind are one," he would repeat nearly every day.

I had rolled my eyes when he spoke those words early in my lessons. After a time, I simply accepted it as I would a trite phrase, something said with little thought. Lately, I understood its meaning more fully. Today, he said it again when we started this afternoon's meditation session. "You should be more precise," I admonished. "You really mean the physical and metaphysical are one."

He smiled in his own way. "Would that have helped you understand my meaning more fully?"

I shrugged. "Probably not at first. But now it means more to me."

"Explain the difference."

I looked at the surrounding fields, the stalks of grass swaying with the gentle wind, the fragrance of pine and damp soil filling my senses. "This land harbors a remarkable diversity of life. I have only recently gained a full appreciation of its vibrancy by enhancing my thoughts. I now see the world as if it were another person, much like you or me. It is an extension of who we are, of our body and soul. We depend upon the land as it relies upon us not to harm it. But I am aware of all this because my thoughts are focused."

He remained silent, letting me know he expected more. I thought about it for another moment. "In much the same way, my physical self depends upon my mental strength. The two are linked. My body and mind are both stronger than I ever would have thought possible."

He still didn't respond. Again, he was expecting more. I realized what I had omitted. "Once my mind and body began working in harmony, I recognized the flow of unseen energy around us. This power circulates much like the air, unobserved yet felt with each breath. A subtle force exists along the edge of my perception, and I have gained a new awareness of this turbulence churning even as we speak."

His limbs relaxed in a way that said he was pleased. "You have done well, Earthfriend Philip."

It was the first time he used this honorific, a salutation once applied solely by the Astari. I took it as a compliment. "I'm glad you are here with me and for your training," I said. "I'm beginning to believe in myself once again, something that's been missing in my life since college. Back then, I had a mission in life as I worked with my friends on The Utopia Project. Now, I'm not writing about a perfect place, I'm trying to do my part to actually keep it safe."

He made a sound I didn't recognize. Was it an expression of respect, or maybe approval? I had given him few reasons to be fond of me during the past months. "You still have work to do; your journey is not yet finished. Even now, you do not commit yourself fully to your tasks."

I knew why, even though I had never discussed it with him. I nodded. "It is because they still hold my companions captive. I worry about them all the time."

Cassie hadn't appeared to me since my time with the Nizaem. Had the Bots stopped her, or did she lose the ability once she had finished her purpose? Was she still alive? Despite my heightened mental sharpness, I couldn't help but wonder about her and the others. "Before I can save this world, I have to free them," I added.

"But there is more that troubles you, isn't there?"

I winced. He had the uncanny ability to understand me. "Yes, there is more, but even with all your training, I don't know if I'll ever be able to change my feelings about the Bots." He waited while I considered how to express my feelings. "I still hate them, maybe now more than ever. I want to blast them from existence. The most difficult part of my training has been to accept how wrong it will be for me to commit such an act. Yet, you have offered no other recourse."

He grunted. "You are correct. I cannot mentor you on this, the most important of decisions. As long as you accept the credence that using Elthea's life force for violence is wrong, you must find your own way. Your heart and soul will ultimately guide you. If you fail in this, our world will die."

I still did not understand how I was going to accomplish such a task. Usually, I would not challenge his response, hoping that one day an idea would hatch fully formed in my head. But today, I yearned for more. "What if I have no other choice against the Bots other than to use Elthea's energies as a weapon of destruction? What if my only option is to destroy them with a killing blast or let them win? Wouldn't it be better to stop them?"

He made a rumbling noise, a sound I had become familiar with during our sessions. He was disappointed. "We have discussed this many times, and you know the reason. Please answer your own question."

I knitted my brows. We both knew the correct response, but he forced me to own it. Reluctantly, I recited, "Every defilement of Elthea's energies destroys her little by little. And if I use my power for killing, I will become more like the Bots. My mind will become tainted with the desire to use more force for death and destruction. I will undergo a subtle transformation in my spirit. Once begun, and then continued, it will bring me down a path that can only end in ruination. I will plunge this world into darkness rather than save it. In the end, both myself, everyone I love, and this land as we know it will perish."

I thought about Teivel's downfall. Is that what happened to him?

The Oakenrill remained pensive for a time before adding, "I love the spirit of Elthea more than anything, and I wish to preserve her and this land. I fear what this universe will become under the reign of the Bots. Countless worlds will fall to them. They will annihilate trillions upon trillions of lives. And on every world, a spirit as kind and as compassionate as Elthea will cease to exist."

I thought he had finished and we would continue with my training, but he added, "What I have explained is not unfounded speculation. This is what will happen unless we stop them. Elthea's powers give me the ability of prescience. I have seen it come to pass as clearly as I saw the sun rise yesterday. If you do not prevail, more than your Earth and Elthea's Realm will become an abyss. It will be the same throughout the cosmos."

My stomach twisted. "I don't want to harm this land, especially now that I can see it more clearly. I have given this much thought, but I still can't understand how to stop our enemy without killing them? Do I love them to death?" I knew sarcasm went against my training, but I couldn't help feeling annoyed.

He studied me before responding. It seemed he never stopped appraising me, gauging if I were ready or not. "You must conduct yourself appropriately. I can teach you to grasp the energies of this land. How you use them must come from your heart, your soul, and your mind."

His answer about this never satisfied me. I wanted a solution, and he was never able or willing to provide one. We were dealing with the lives of my friends, the future of this land, and also my own life. I needed to know what to do. But discussing it further wouldn't help. "I understand," I said. I then repeated the mantra, adding to it. "My mind, heart, and soul are one."

"Then let us begin," he said. "Today, we will concentrate on the air around us. Please calm the air and stop the breeze from gusting."

And so it continued. I performed the tasks he instructed until twilight descended upon us. I moved the air in different directions, then changed the velocity, later adjusting the temperature. This continued with me influencing various permutations of the air—color, density, chemical composition, buoyancy, and many attributes I never would have even considered.

I knew that tomorrow, after a morning of strenuous exercise, he would select a different element of nature for me to alter. My thoughts were still troubled; the Oakenrill hadn't guessed my deepest fear. I could sense what was to come, and I knew my training would soon come to an abrupt end.

I wasn't ready for the challenge of my life; I needed more time. But fate wasn't something I could alter—perhaps nobody could.

29

THE PAST IS NOT THE ANSWER

Philip held the door open, watching her scamper forward, raindrops pelting against her yellow parka. "What a nasty day," she said, looking up at him, beaming like a child. The early spring rain fell in sheets across the campus.

Once inside, Cassie pushed back her hood as brown hair fell to her shoulders. They paused a moment to scan the lobby of Kirkchen Hall, searching for the rest of the team. The other members were nowhere to be seen among the scattering of chairs and benches, which occupied most of the two-story entrance. Although this place was always a popular location for students to gather between classes, today it was packed. Apparently, many residents had decided to raid the vending machines rather than brave the torrential rain to return to their dorms or the student center for lunch.

"There's an open bench," he pointed as three students stood to collect their books before vacating it. Philip and

Cassie hurried over, shedding their raincoats and exchanging greetings with the students who were leaving.

Before sitting, Cassie bent over to pull a tablet from her backpack. As she did so, his eyes lingered on her slim body as a forlorn expression came over him. Life was a series of choices. How different these two lives would have been had they made different decisions while still in college.

Two months had passed since they had kissed passionately after an evening of drinking at the local pub. He understood her reason not to go further. She didn't want to become involved in a physical relationship with a teammate during this, the most challenging course of their college curriculum. The Utopia Project was demanding enough without the possibility of a breakup. If he had been thinking straight that night, he might have pointed out that Matt and Diane managed their relationship just fine. Although, even there, cracks had begun to open.

Sitting down next to him, she opened the tablet, scanning the screen as her fingers tapped and moved across it. "I took some notes on our reading assignment. Want to discuss before our class?"

"Sure," he responded, sounding much less animated than her.

She glanced up and pouted. "Cheer up. We're at the halfway point in the course. This is not the time to lose interest. It's bad enough we have to keep Eric engaged."

Philip squirmed in his chair and tried to cover the slip. "Believe me, I'm into the course. Once in a while I just need a break from it."

She wrinkled her forehead; such an insignificant gesture. It made her appear radiant. "You're a mystery to me, Phil. I still have trouble reading you."

He smiled and cocked his head. "I was under the impression you liked mysterious guys. I'm trying my best to become more captivating, especially in your eyes. Is it working?"

She giggled. "No, but I'm wondering how much influence Eric is having on you." She motioned with her fingers as if gesturing at imaginary figures around them. "We're together a lot because of this course, and you're beginning to sound more like him." A smug expression came over her, satisfied that she had identified the reason for his attitude.

"We're nothing alike." He tightened his lips, never taking his eyes off her. When he spoke again, he did so with a hint of resignation. "Maybe I try too hard with you. You're different from everyone else; I hope you know that." He winced as if he had gone too far.

Her cheeks became slightly pink, and she looked down at her lap. "I understand how you feel about me; you've made it clear. Normally, I would be interested, but you understand that we have one shot at this Utopia Project." Looking back into his eyes, she continued, "You take your studies seriously, and so do I." A grin widened on her lips. "Maybe not as much as Matt and Diane, but I'd say we're both studious. We'll regret not putting everything into this program, maybe not at first, but one day."

Philip leaned back on the bench. "Maybe I'd regret missing out on you even more."

Her voice softened. "Don't say that, not now. Maybe one

day, when this course is over, who knows." Looking back at her forgotten tablet, she pursed her lips, "Now, about the reading assignment on modern society, what do you think?" She looked at him expectantly.

He tried to put on a brave smile but didn't succeed. "I'm glad you asked that question, it's been on my mind since I first saw you this morning."

She smirked. "Hmm, I bet."

"Oh good, you saved us a spot," Diane said, taking Cassie and Philip by surprise. Matt was by her side as they each removed their wet jackets. "This place is crazy today," she continued, unaware of her interruption.

"Nobody wants to miss this lecture," said Matt. "I'm looking forward to it. We'll have to grab a good seat once they open the doors." He noticed Cassie was holding her screen. "Are you discussing the reading assignment? I thought we would wait until our team meeting later today, but we can begin now if you like."

"Hon, what about Eric? Shouldn't we wait for him?"

Matt made a face. "East Campus had a keg bash last night. He's probably still sleeping it off." Looking at the entrance, he added, "He'd better be here in time for this presentation."

Diane settled into the remaining spot on the bench, while Matt sat on the floor in front of them, legs crossed. She poked Philip in the ribs as she bent forward to look at Cassie. "You two are awfully quiet this morning. Is everything okay?"

Cassie smiled weakly, glancing at Phil before saying, "Oh, I guess it's this gloomy weather. Phil and I were just saying how we're both looking forward to warm, sunny days after this abysmal winter."

Diane gestured to Matt as she replied. Her voice, however, became muffled, as did the rest of the sounds in the room. Cassie and Philip broke out in grins at what she said, while Matt leaned forward, playfully grabbing her knee. Their eyes sparkled, unaware of the peril that would crash over them a scant eight years in the future.

I allowed the Farseeing to fade from my vision, blinking as my eyes adjusted to the dim light and the flickering embers of the campfire. The Oakenrill sat on the other side of the glowing cinders, regarding me with interest. I hadn't invited him to join me in the observation of my past, but he understood what I was doing. For all I knew, he might have been able to view it along with me. I still didn't know the extent of his abilities.

"You partake in fruitless endeavors," he said. "Reliving the past will not change the here and now, nor the future."

It was just like him to chide me for not focusing solely on my training. "Seeing my friends again makes me happy. Isn't that reason enough?"

"Does this please you? Because if it does, your face belies your words."

What I would give to be together again with Cassie, Matt, and Diane. Their imprisonment was a constant weight on my shoulders. "I wanted to see them again, that's all. Besides, you said I should practice the skills you taught me. Farseeing is one of them, isn't it?"

The Oakenrill remained silent for a time. "The past is not the answer," he finally said. "Events are hurtling toward us in the real world, and you should concentrate on what you can control. You have the ability, but will your emotions be your ruination?"

All my life, my feelings had been my undoing. Would now be any different? One day soon, I would face the biggest challenge of my life, and more than my survival was at stake.

30

A REASON TO LIVE

The day dawned sunny and pleasant. As always, the Oakenrill put me through a regimen of physical workouts. Occasionally, he would question me about what I was feeling, or seeing, or smelling. He constantly tried to hone my connection to the land and the spectral energies surrounding us.

At midday, we made our way to one of several places where we began the other portion of my training. For the past several weeks, he had reduced the Arath and meditation drills, often skipping them altogether. Instead, he had me practice drawing upon Elthea's energies. Such was the case today.

"I believe you are ready for a new challenge," said the Oakenrill.

I looked at him suspiciously. "Whenever you say that you always make things more difficult. What's the matter, controlling the wind is too easy?"

He chuckled. "You would not be happy if I did not push you harder."

"You make a good point. I'm happy with my progress, but still have much to learn. Tell me what new obstacle you have planned for today."

He moved several limbs, indicating that I should direct my attention to the surrounding fields. "See that boulder at the far end of the grassland?"

I looked in that direction and spotted the rock he pointed out. It appeared to be about half my height and too large to fit my arms around, certainly too large for me to lift. I nodded my response.

"Lift it off the ground, disassemble it into its component molecules by turning it into steam, and reassemble it in the same shape and size on that bluff."

My eyes shifted to the small hill, which was nearly a mile away. I impulsively licked my lips, knowing this was significantly more difficult than my previous assignments. But the Oakenrill had trained me well. If I believed this was impossible or too difficult, I would fail, as I had in the past.

As was my custom, I took a cleansing breath as all thoughts fell away. My mind fell into a state that might be compared to a person practicing transcendental meditation, a comparison that would be only partially correct. I went much deeper to a place where the elusive elements of Elthea's forces existed.

Constant repetition had taught me to recognize the ebbs and flows of Elthea's energies. I opened a door in my mind to a room where reality was much different, a place unknown to me months before. A person who has never experienced this level of mindfulness could not possibly understand the effort it takes. Yet, even this accomplishment already felt second nature to me, like slipping into a well-worn pair of jeans.

I grasped the strands of energy necessary to complete the assignment. I had already learned from past failures that applying the wrong flows of energy would cause the rock to either disintegrate, change color, or transform in another way. The familiar buzz of a charge flowed through my body as my fingertips became numb. I asserted my will on the flows of energy, wrapping them around the stone, directing the pulses of power to accomplish the task. I first changed the boulder from a solid into a gas, moved it to another place, and finally restored it to its original solid form. Once accomplished, I released the power and let it fall away, returning to my normal state of awareness. The exercise was over in seconds.

To any observer, the rock would first appear like any other chunk of stone. In the next heartbeat, it would become a mist. If they knew what had happened, they could gaze out toward the ridge of a hill some distance away to discover the same boulder.

I felt myself puff with pride, waiting for a compliment from the Oakenrill, hopefully telling me I had done well. But when he remained silent, I frowned, wondering what I had done wrong. I could sense he had become agitated, and I searched for the reason. Only then did I detect him channeling Elthea's energy. I followed his efforts with my thoughts, realizing he was redoubling the shield he had put into place to hide me from the Bots.

Another influx of power caught my attention. It originated from another source. The signature differed from what

I was familiar with. Something about it was abnormal. I had already developed the skill to distinguish between the Oakenrill's delicate touch and my somewhat coarse execution. This came from neither of us.

I tensed and jerked my head from left to right, trying to find who or what was causing it. Too late, I realized I had slipped out of my meditative state. That's when I heard the words in my head.

—*Come now, Philip Matherson. Time to witness the birth of a new world. Together, we will create a superior existence.*

In a blink, ten Bots surrounded us. Their enormous forms towered over me. The Oakenrill suddenly looked diminutive and hopelessly vulnerable against them. He was merely a pile of branches the Bots could easily trample upon.

I wanted to look the Bots in the eye, show them I was different now, and wouldn't cower under their threats. But they had no eyes. Their blank faces gave the appearance of creatures with a tight mask wrapped around their heads, providing no hint of their emotions. I didn't have to see their expressions to know what they were thinking.

One Bot took a few steps toward me. The dark, nearly black bodysuit was offset with gold bands around the joints of its shoulders, elbows, and knees. This must be the one in charge.

—*You will follow us willingly, or you will never see your pitiful friends alive again.*

My courage dissolved like the air let out of a balloon.

At that moment, I realized all this training was meaningless. What did I hope to accomplish? They had won. That was as true in this moment as it was long ago when I was still a student at Woodbery College. I didn't know it back then, but now I was sure. I heard my voice speak as if it came from another person. "Don't hurt them. I'll do whatever you say."

And with that, I sealed my fate.

EVENTS MOVED QUICKLY ONCE I SURRENDERED. THE BOT in command stepped toward me and made a movement to grab me by the shoulders. Before it reached me, a surge of energy caused it to jerk back. The Oakenrill had raised an invisible shield around the two of us. I probed the barrier with my senses and realized it wouldn't last long against the Bots' power.

I looked at my friend imploringly. "You're only going to make matters worse."

He spoke quickly, ignoring my comment. "Pay attention; we haven't much time. Let Elthea guide you. When the time comes, be certain you protect her and this land. Do no harm."

His voice had a finality about it. My heart ached, knowing the Bots would not hesitate to kill him, my closest companion these last months. "You're in danger," I hissed. "They want me alive, but they'll murder you. Leave now while you can."

He made a movement with his limbs, which told me no. "I promised your Astari companion, Bevon, I would protect you. I will keep my word. You are the most important—"

A shock wave sent both me and the Oakenrill sprawling.

—No further delays. Kill that vermin and take the human.

The shield was down. Hands grabbed me roughly by the

shoulders and hoisted me off the ground as if I was a rag doll. Still dazed from the shock, I barely found my footing as the creature held me securely by pinning both my arms behind my back. I stifled a cry as the giant bent my arms back even further. I wouldn't give them the satisfaction of knowing I was in pain.

That's when I felt another prickle of energy. A new fear came over me as I understood its purpose. A Bot had hurled a blast at the Oakenrill, strong enough to incinerate him. But at the last second, my companion parried the blow with his own eruption, blocking it, at least for the moment.

Before I could take a breath to plead with them to stop, another deadly blow struck the Oakenrill. He barely avoided death as fire erupted inches from his body, charring a few of his limbs. He wouldn't live through another blast.

I acted, doing the only thing possible. Recalling our last exercise with the boulder, I wrapped the same energy around the Oakenrill. "I'm grateful for all you've done," I said. Before he could resist, he disappeared.

I knew my friend now stood in a distant place. He could bring himself back, but I believed he would realize there was nothing more he could accomplish. Even though I had saved him, a feeling of loss came over me. He was my only friend during the past months. Although he could be demanding and unreasonable, he had helped me more than anyone.

Now I was utterly alone. Only myself and the vilest creatures I had ever known.

I had defied these monsters once before, when they were about to carve Quintia to pieces, and was rewarded with a Bot sticking his knife into my arm. How would they react now? The Bot at my back continued to pin my arms behind me with an iron grip. The others stood unmoving, a ring of faceless creatures from my worst nightmares.

—That was stupid. You will learn the hard way that every unacceptable action has a consequence.

I quaked, knowing they had Cassie, Diane, and Matt. These creatures had the power to inflict any amount of pain upon them. "Cut me with a knife if you must. Or do whatever you want to me. I owed him that much."

—Oh, we will do much worse to you. Time for your first lesson.

I felt a rush of energy from the Bots as my vision clouded.

IN A BLINK, I STOOD SOMEWHERE ELSE, A PLACE I DIDN'T recognize. The sun was at a different angle, making me believe we had traveled a great distance. We were at the top of a rolling hill, and like waves in an ocean, other green mounds surrounded us as far as I could see. The soil teemed with life, lushly verdant with the smell of spring in the air.

The Bot pinning my arms let go and stepped away to join the others. I hunched my shoulders, working out the strain from its grip. Satisfied that my shoulder sockets would heal, I looked warily at the others. As if in response, one of the Bots pointed casually toward the valley below.

I frowned and moved forward to gain a better view of the vale. At the base of the hill facing us stood a cluster of rustic cabins. Rows of garden plots surrounded the houses, where groups of inhabitants tilled the ground. Other villagers tended a herd of small animals a short distance away. Children ran chasing each other, their cries of laugher drifting up to our vantage point.

A sick feeling rose in my stomach. I turned away from the village. "Who are they? Why are we here?" I tried to keep my voice from shaking, not sure I wanted to know the answer.

—*They are inconsequential, a feeble people with little purpose in life. Whether they live or die makes no difference.*

My voice trembled. "Why show them to me?"

It didn't answer immediately. I hoped it never would, but the sound pounded in my head.

—*We must make certain you will submit to our authority. You will set fire to each of those pathetic beings. Fry them until they are all dead.*

My vision reeled, and I stumbled, nearly losing my balance. I took a step back, looking for something to grasp hold of. There was nothing. My eyes darted from one Bot to another. "No. Why?" I croaked.

If the Bots had a face, I imagined they would be smiling smugly. None of them moved. Nobody responded.

I chewed on my lower lip, trying to buy time to think of something, anything. "You said they didn't matter. Why kill them?"

Seconds ticked by. I couldn't help it, but I glanced again at the valley. Even from this distance, I could see the people were stocky, shorter than humans. One movement caught my attention. A grownup was leading a child by the hand. I thought about the time when I was four years old, my mom taking me by the hand as we walked in a park. At that age, I knew I was protected when she held my hand, safe from the rest of the world. A mother's love for her child transcended cultures.

I jerked my attention back to the Bots. In my mind's eye, they looked massive, more intimidating than ever. Another vision came to me, as I saw the Bots slash their blades at unarmed children and adults during the Astari Midsummer Celebration.

I felt my knees begin to tremble. "I won't. You can't make me." I wanted to say more, scream at them, persuade them not to kill unarmed people. More than that, I needed to believe I would never turn into something as evil. But that's precisely what would eventually happen if I followed their demands. My heart pounded in my chest.

—*You will do as we command. Either kill them now, or we will set fire to one of your companions in our custody. We will decide which one.*

The world around me fell away. Nothing else existed except the Bots standing before me. "You're not serious," I heard my voice say as if it came from far away.

The Bots didn't respond; their silence was more frightening than anything they could say. I steadied my shaking body, painfully aware of the seconds slipping away. I looked down at the valley and back at the Bots. Nobody should be forced to make a choice like this.

After all my practice with the Oakenrill, it had still come to this. I would break his most serious rule to do no harm. I had to destroy these Bots; there was no other choice. Wouldn't that be better than to destroy this innocent race, or have my friends killed? As if reading my thoughts, the Bot spoke again.

—If you try to kill us, we have others who will carry out the death sentence to our prisoners. Do as we say now, or one will burn. Delay no further.

My head throbbed from the hammering voice. I had trouble thinking clearly. I grasped at whatever entered my head. "You still need us, all of us of The Utopia Project. You want us to become your emissary to the people of Earth. Don't you? That's what you've said. We can help you achieve your purpose. Killing us won't accomplish anything."

The Bots had already discarded that plan; they said as much before tearing down the wall at Haven. But I could think of no other appeal.

—The human race already belongs to us. Rather than withhold technology as we once tried, we now freely give it to them. They speak to us through their devices, and we provide what they need. Soon, your race will be unable to live without our skills. Humans have become unexpectedly malleable. We now desire Elthea's powers. She has given you the ability to use her energies more than others. You are all we need. Your companions are expendable. Do as we command, and they will live.

My throat tightened as an alternative solution came to me: suicide. It might be my only option. I looked at the small settlement in the valley, seeing the children running, the grownups tending their gardens, or watching the pack of animals. I felt lightheaded, realizing my breathing was coming in gasps.

—This is your last warning. Do it now, or one of your friends will die. Wait longer, and we will kill another. What is your decision, Philip Matherson?

Time was up. Begging wouldn't save me, or my friends, or the innocent villagers below. People were going to die, either my closest friends or complete strangers. Even if I ended my life, the Bots might still kill my friends for no other reason than spite. I took one last baleful look at the Bots. "You heartless bastards. Maybe you think you've won, but you haven't. I hope you burn in hell."

I wasn't expecting a response, but a screeching noise rippled through my head. It was the sound of a Bot laughing.

—You may want us to burn in your hell, but we are synthetic life without a soul. Now, do as we command.

With a hole in my heart, I turned to the unsuspecting inhabitants in the valley. I had no choice. I steeled myself and reached deep within me. Elthea's energy crackled in my fingers before I realized what I was doing. The Bots had dashed all my hopes and dreams for a happy life.

I pulled energy into my body, more than I ever attempted before. I held onto it as I would a deep breath before letting it out. Already, I had enough to destroy the small settlement below. I kept drawing it, mindless of everything except the deaths I would cause, the harm that would damage the life force of Elthea, the loathing I would feel over what I had done.

The Oakenrill's warning came to me again as if he were speaking in my ear while riding in his harness on my back. *Do no harm, cause no destruction. The spirit of Elthea will end.*

Tears flowed down my face. "I have no choice!" I screamed.

My fingers burned from the energy inside me. My body buzzed with electricity. I knew I wouldn't survive if I held onto it much longer. I lifted my arms, ready to discharge a deadly blast, ending their lives instantly, without pain. That's the least I could do for them.

A voice spoke to me, a female who sounded delicate and enchanting. The lilting melody was strange and unfamiliar, even though I could understand what she said. Just as the Bots pounded their words into my head, so too did this voice come to me. But hers was soothing and melodic.

You always have choices, Philip. Give them a reason to live.

I faltered, not knowing what she meant. Hadn't someone told me that once? Was it the Oakenrill, or Alan Sabrinsky, before the wall of Haven fell? Give the Bots a reason to live?

But the energy within me demanded release. Her warning had come too late. I had no hope left.

31

SYNTHETIC BEINGS

The pain of a hundred bee stings tore through my skin. I hung onto Elthea's powers for too long. I had to release it, but I remained uncertain. I could discharge it harmlessly by causing an explosion high in the air. But what would that accomplish?

The words of others rang in my head as I stood ready to release a death sentence against an unwary race. The loudest voice was that of the Bots. *Do it now, or one of your friends will die. Wait longer, and we will kill another.* But it wasn't the only warning.

I heard the Oakenrill speak, telling me over and over again. *If you use Elthea's energies for death and destruction, both you and this land will ultimately perish.*

The once brilliant engineer Alan Sabrinsky, one of the three who inadvertently created the Bots—as well as the Astari—spoke to me on the wall surrounding Haven before it fell. *They once existed just like you and me. Bring back the good that is within them.* I heard the sweet melody again in my head from seconds ago. *Give them a reason to live.*

I couldn't hold back any longer. How could I make them good again when I hated them so fiercely? It wasn't possible.

I replayed the pounding of the Bots in my head from moments ago. *You may want us to burn in your hell, but we are synthetic life without a soul.*

In that instant, a fleeting thought came to me. But would it work? With no other answer, I grabbed onto it. Most of my life, I had made choices based on intuition. This was no different.

Reacting from instinct, I didn't have time to consider the ramifications. Before the energy blasted from my body, whether or not I was ready, I changed the weave of power, altering its purpose and target. Rather than sending it down to those below, I directed it at the Bots. Not only those standing around me, but I also hurled it at every Bot in existence.

The energy flowed out of me in waves with enough strength to accomplish the impossible. Never before had I attempted to handle this amount of power; I hadn't thought it possible. The question remained: was this the smartest decision?

Once I depleted my stored energy, I called up more, oblivious to everything except the conduit I had become as it flowed through me to accomplish my purpose. My body vibrated from the exertion, yet I continued to force my will upon it, feeding an idea that came to me only moments ago.

My strength was giving out, but still, I continued. I would finish this, or I would die in the attempt. My entire life had come to this single effort. If I failed, I doomed myself to a life of enslavement and condemned my closest friends to death. Annihilation would be inescapable. Worlds would be remade as the spirit of Elthea withered and expired while humanity would pass from existence. The Bots would reign over the universe.

My breathing came in rasping gasps, and my vision became clouded with dark spots. I ignored everything except drawing more energy, altering it, and shooting it out to engulf each and every Bot. Time lost its meaning. Seconds might have passed since I began, or maybe it had been hours—perhaps even days.

Finally, realizing I had transformed every remaining Bot into beings conceived by my vision, I let the flow slip from me. Never could they have foreseen what I did to them.

I dropped to the ground, exhausted. Beads of sweat dripped from my nose to the grass beneath me. I wanted to lie here forever, ignorant of the repercussions of what I had done. I might have accomplished nothing, or I may have recast the future of the universe.

Either way, I no longer cared. I was finished trying to be a god. All my emotions, all my hopes and dreams had been spent, evaporating with the outflow of power. I had nothing left. Let the world continue without me.

I WANTED TO KEEP MYSELF CUSHIONED AGAINST THE refreshing grass and never move again. I stayed that way for a long while, but eventually, my curiosity won out. I lifted my head to inspect the new reality I had created. Was it my greatest folly?

Everything looked exactly the way it had before my eruption of power. For all I could tell, nothing had changed. A dozen paces away, the Bots remained motionless, as if frozen in time. The village below, with its inhabitants, remained as it had been. The sky was blue, filled with puffy white clouds.

Did I believe the world would be different?

I shook my head, trying to clear the muddle I felt, and slowly lifted myself to stand on unsteady legs. My entire body felt spent. I needed to rest, give myself time to recover. But there would be time enough for that later. Right now, the Bots demanded my attention.

I scrutinized them, looking for a small crack in their persona. Their faceless masks remained, massive bodies standing perfectly still. Did they even breathe? It was one of the many things I didn't know about them. There was much I still didn't know.

As before, they exhibited a coiled tension in their stance, as if they were about to spring forward to kill another victim.

I half expected them to do exactly that because of what I had done ... or tried to do. I still wasn't sure if I had accomplished anything. How could I even discover if I had been successful?

"Welcome to your new world," I said, trying to elicit a response. "What do you think of it?"

They didn't respond. I sucked in a ragged breath, realizing I must have failed. Had I inadvertently harmed them, and in the process destroyed the spirit of Elthea? I should have taken more time to consider my actions before blundering ahead.

Just when I thought all my efforts were pointless, the words thumped in my head, sounding as threatening as ever.

—What have you done?

I hesitated, unsure of how to explain my purpose. At least I hadn't struck them mute or mindless. Would they become enraged and strike out at me, or worse, my friends? Maybe they would be elated with their new life. It was probably too much to expect.

Most likely, they would be unfazed by their transformation. Perhaps it would make no difference to them, the worst possible outcome, which would put me back to where I had started. The suspicion that I had accomplished nothing at all pulled at my emotions.

I answered them honestly. "I gave you a soul."

IN OUR LIKENESS

Silence greeted me. I steeled myself, waiting for the anger that would follow. I winced at the screeching noise in my head, the sound of the Bots laughing.

—You think by giving us religion, we would be obedient and happy?

"No!" I shouted before they could say more. "Not religion. I give you hope, a reason to be alive, a belief that there might be another existence after death."

—The concept of a soul is a human superstition. It is an outdated concept. We have no need for your petty beliefs. We are born from the scientific precision of code on your computer networks.

"You're wrong. Before you were bits of ones and zeros, you existed as biological life." I tried to remember what Tess Armstrong had told me about the Bots' origin before they became computer code on Earth. Why hadn't I paid more attention at the time? "I have returned to you what was taken when you were transformed into software."

My heart raced. Everything depended upon the Bots understanding this was good for them. It was good for them, wasn't it? I had to believe it was.

"Hear me out. Please, only for a moment." I licked my lips, trying to put into words what I had instinctively accomplished. "I've given you something special, a fresh way for you to think and feel." I grasped for ideas as I tried to concentrate. "Now you can dream, want more from life, aspire to something better. I've opened a world of wonder and inspiration so that each of you can follow individual desires. You can begin to think of yourself as unique. I've given you the ability to live life for the sake of living."

—*Our strength comes from the amalgamation of our discrete entities and only through scientific analysis. What you call a soul has little relevance to us. We have no need for it. Our mind is superior.*

Did I detect a hint of uncertainty in its tone, or was that wishful thinking? I spoke softly, still hoping reason would prevail. "A soul is now part of your mind. It is immortal and exists outside of space and time. I've expanded who you are and what you can become."

The more I articulated the reasons for my actions, the more I believed my intuition had been the right choice. When the Bots didn't reply, I continued my plea. "Use scientific reasoning to examine what is within you. Look at other phenomena in the physical world that we cannot explain by scientific analysis. It's there for you to see: the mysteries of birth and death, consciousness, dreams, imagination, love. All these exist independently of our bodies."

Again, silence greeted me. This time I let it continue

while I remained quiet. I could only hope they would consider this beneficial.

—*Take it back. We do not want it.*

I let my head drop and lifted my arms, palms out in supplication. "I don't have the strength. What I accomplished I did in a burst of desperation. I have nothing left." Elthea's power was still within me, but I doubted I could pull that much energy. I might never again.

I looked toward the village in the valley. The people there were still alive. They had spotted us during my outburst of energy. Now, they huddled together in small groups, looking up at us, probably wondering if we were friends or enemies, not even realizing how close to death they had come.

I owed them a debt of gratitude. Without even realizing it, this village had helped me remain true to my convictions. I had honored the Oakenrill's insistence that I do no harm. But to what avail? The Bots hadn't exactly embraced my gift with the euphoria I had hoped. What had I expected?

I examined the figures towering over me, looking for some small sign of a transformation in their appearance. But I saw nothing, "For good or ill, you have a soul. Do as you wish with it. You can either embrace it or ignore it. I don't care. But recognize that you are altered because of it."

—*We can still kill your companions. This makes no difference.*

I bit into my lower lip, not wanting to respond, but I had to say something. "Those with a soul can still commit terrible atrocities. I'm counting on the good that's within you now to prevent it. I've done all I can to help you. It's all up to you from here."

I stopped myself from saying more. If begging with them would help, I would have continued. But I knew it wouldn't. Every bit of my strength and passion went into giving them a soul. Now, I could only wait until they freed Cassie, Diane, and Matt, or killed them, or killed me. I waited for them to decide.

THE BOTS AROUND ME REMAINED STILL AS STONE. Would they ever move or speak again? I had been terrified of these beings since I first came into contact with them. It was even more unnerving, watching them stand unmoving as my life, and that of my friends, hung in the balance.

Were they trying to decide what to do with us, or were they dealing with new feelings and sensations never experienced before? I pictured an immense conclave taking place with all the Bots mentally debating the pros and cons of what they had become. Did they still believe it made no difference?

Several of them finally stirred. "What have you decided?" I blurted, unable to hold back any longer. Many lives beside my own hung in the balance.

—*It has been done.*

I held my breath, waiting for them to explain. They set my friends free? They killed them? "What's been done?"

—*You have altered us, changed us in a way we did not desire. We have accomplished the same.*

I turned my thoughts inward, searching for an inkling of some difference within me. I couldn't discern anything out of the ordinary. Raising my hands, I looked at them and down at my body. It was as it always had been. I felt a cold fear rise in my chest. "What have you done to me?"

—*We have done nothing to you. Your utopia companions, however, are not what they once were.*

My heart raced. I wanted to beat them to a pulp with my bare fists; damn the powers of Elthea. "If you harmed them, so help me, I will exterminate every last one of you."

—*Harm them? That is a matter of interpretation. We have agreed to let them live.*

The knot in my stomach unclenched, but I still dreaded what they would say. "Tell me, now goddamm it."

—*We will do better than tell you. We will show you.*

I held my breath; nothing else in the world mattered right now as I waited. Only the Bots around me existed. What had they done to my friends?

—*Behold your dearest companions, Cassie McKenzie, Diane Collentenio, and Matthew Tyler.*

One Bot extended his arms to his side, pointing to a spot nearby. Seconds later, three Bots materialized in the empty space he had indicated. Like every other Bot, the newcomers were massive, faceless hunks of muscle. They appeared as deadly as every other Bot.

I froze as alarm bells began ringing in my head. My mind had trouble grasping the implication of what I was seeing. "No, no, no," I heard myself whimper as the meaning sank in. Without realizing it, I had slipped to my knees, my chest about to explode.

—We have reshaped your companions into our likeness. What do you think?

I looked in horror. How could this happen?

ONCE A FUTURE SO BRIGHT

"You're lying," I said, my throat dry and voice rasping. This was far too painful to believe. Yet, my insides shook with dread, terrified they might be telling the truth. They had lied before; maybe this was nothing but another fabrication of their demented minds, a ruse designed to scare me into taking back what I had done to them. I held onto the hope that they were lying now. The booming voice sounded in my head as I shuddered at the sound.

—*Look closely. Let your eyes reveal what you already know.*

One of the newly arrived Bots lifted a hand in front of itself as if unsure of what it was seeing, first the back of the hand and then the palm. The simple gesture was so unlike that of the other Bots, with their inner tension of a coiled snake about to strike. Bots had never displayed human qualities such as curiosity, gentleness, or puzzlement. Their world consisted of aggression and malice.

I couldn't stop staring at the new arrivals. I needed more proof. "This isn't you. Tell me it's not true."

No response. I let out a trembling breath, still hopeful this was a cruel deception. Then I heard the words forced into my head. It began with a sound that might be a whimper.

—*My God, what have they done to us?*

That was no Bot. Its tone was hesitant, tentative, unlike every Bot I had ever met. They were always fearless, brazenly confident, and ruthless. My mouth worked to frame a response, but no words came. What could I say?

—*Change us back, you have to, Phil. Do it now, I can't live this way.*

Without being told, I knew it was Diane, even though I was unsure which had spoken. She would be the first person to rail at the atrocity.

Rising to my feet, I tore my attention away from the three Bots and glared at the others. My voice rang with as much rage as I could summon. "You won't get away with this; I won't let you. My strength is greater than you can imagine. I'll restore them, bring them back." Uncertainty gripped me, but I wasn't about to let them know.

—*Are you so sure? Are you willing to take that risk?*

Those words sounded harsh in my head, more jarring than those of my friends. The evidence began to build. As much as I wanted to deny it, the contrast between my Bot companions and the others was too great to ignore. The grating sound of the Bots continued.

—*You will fail at reconstructing them. The transmutation took all our abilities. Make one miscalculation, one false move in the restoration process and your friends will never be the same.*

That was the last straw as my emotions boiled over. "I gave you a soul to help you, yet you repay me with this!" Looking up at the sky, I tried to steady my breathing. "I should have killed you when I had the chance. You don't deserve a better life." My eyes watered. "I should have known better. Why did you do this? What do you hope to accomplish?"

They didn't respond, maybe they never would. Did they even have a reason beyond their hatred for everything? They were evil, and I was a fool to think I could help them. I hated everything about them. Giving up, I turned my attention back to my friends. The Bot's voice again throbbed in my head.

—We need them.

I grimaced. "My God, for some perverted medical experiment? I'll kill them myself right now rather than allow you to continue." I looked wildly from one Bot to another. "You already had them if you needed them. Why turn them into this?"

—No, not to experiment. We require them to better comprehend humans.

I stared uncomprehendingly. Their speech might have been in another language for all the sense it made. Why did they want to understand us? They hated humans.

—Your companions will serve as a model while we begin to decipher the next step in our evolution. Because you have interfered in our development by transforming us into something unexpected, we require a point of reference. Your part-

ners are a prototype. *They will help us grasp what it means to live with your affliction.*

I only heard half of what they said. I didn't care about the Bots or what they wanted. Cassie, Matt, and Diane needed help, and I was the only person who could save them.

—*These three have a soul, and now they are Bots. We will learn together.*

"No you won't, because they're not staying with you."

—*And what will you do? Send them far away as you did the Oakenrill? We will find them, just as we could locate your little branch friend if we wanted. Even he cannot help you bring them back, and neither can you. No, they will remain with us. It will also prevent you from doing anything foolhardy.*

I laughed, a high-pitched sound, hysteria washing over me as spittle flew from my mouth. "Foolhardy? My stupidity was thinking I could make you better. I should have—" The voice in my head thrummed before I could finish.

—*Because of your ignorance, you have irrevocably altered us. We do not want the attribute you have conveyed to us. And now, we have taken the ones who are most precious to you. Say your goodbyes. We are done here.*

Another voice softly entered my head, a softer, gentler tone.

—*Kill me. I don't want to live like this. You once promised you wouldn't allow the Bots to have me.*

My fingertips went numb as I pulled energy without thinking about it. "I won't allow this," I screamed. My fingers twitched as I took a last look at my friends, indistinguishable from the other Bots. Fire danced in my chest, waiting to be released. I could end their lives so they wouldn't even feel the pain.

A shred of hesitation and self-doubt forestalled me, as it always did. I would never see them alive again. A memory of happier days filled my thoughts. The recollection of their laughter and banter overwhelmed me with remorse at what I was about to do. Not that long ago, life had been so carefree. How had it come to this?

The other Bots remained motionless, allowing me to commit the act. Or did they understand the path along which this killing would lead me? Death and violence was always the easier way out. Wasn't it? But at what cost?

Unbidden, the voice of the Oakenrill came to me again, his message from countless training sessions. *Do no harm to others. The spirit of Elthea will diminish and fade from existence if you use her powers to hurt or destroy.*

The surrounding Bots lost their solidity, including the three who were my friends. Pinpricks of light, like cracks in a splintered window, appeared as their bodies pixilated into individual fragments. I flung the energy at them, forcing them to remain here rather than striking them dead.

I was too late. They were gone, leaving me alone.

Unable to control my emotions, I screamed until my throat was hoarse. The remaining pent-up energy inside me demanded to be released. I hurled it toward the sky as it erupted in a harmless detonation. The booming thunderclap reached me as my knees buckled. Mind and body turned numb as I crumpled face-forward against the fresh grass.

Life as I knew it was over. The Bots had condemned me

to hell. The ones I loved the most had been taken from me, and I was powerless to prevent it.

TIME PASSED; I MIGHT AS WELL HAVE BEEN DEAD, DEVOID of feelings. What a sweet release it would be never to feel the agony of losing those I loved the most. I craved this numbness more than anything as I remained lifeless, never wanting to lift my head.

The ground beneath me felt solid and tangible, as if it were the only thing left. Nothing else mattered now. All I had tried to accomplish was of no consequence. I would lie here until the spirit of Elthea took me away to wherever the departed are brought. And when that happened, I would be judged as a failure.

The pressure of someone's hand on my shoulder eventually roused me from my misery. Maybe one of the Bots had returned to explain they had made a mistake and would undo the damage inflicted on my friends. With a great effort, I lifted my head to look.

But no, it was another individual, one I didn't recognize. I plopped my head back into the grass. Whoever it was would eventually go away and leave me to wallow in my agony and pain.

Words were spoken, a language I didn't recognize. It didn't matter. I had no interest in rejoining the world of the living. But then the hand on my shoulder returned, this time more insistent, shaking me and intent on pulling me up by force if necessary. Why wouldn't this thing leave me alone?

I groaned as I rolled over and pulled myself into a sitting position, wrapping my arms around my bent knees. I took one look at the intruder, noticing five others standing a respectable distance away. I leaned my head forward, resting my forehead against my knees. My face was dry, even though I was sure I had been crying. Maybe I had no tears left.

Again, the stranger spoke, taking an interminably long time to complete whatever it was saying. The babble meant nothing to me. Yet, even though I didn't understand the words, I heard the softness in the inflection. He, or she, must be trying to comfort me. I nearly barked a laugh, wondering if this newcomer understood the depth of my despair at what had been taken from me.

Eventually, my instinct for civility and righteousness kicked in. Whoever these beings were, they didn't cause the wretchedness I was feeling. Without lifting my head, I croaked, "Leave me alone. I know you're trying to help, but I don't need it."

Silence greeted my rebuke. I cocked my eyes up without lifting my head, checking to see if they had left. The one closest to me tilted his or her head in response. It was either puzzled by my reaction or about my unfamiliar language.

I let out a breath, knowing they weren't going to leave me alone. Studying them again, I realized these were the villagers in the valley. Their faces were strange to me, even after all the variations in life I had come across. With jaws too wide, foreheads slanted inward at the top, eyes, nose, ears, all shaped oddly, they were unlike humans. If anything, this race was closer to reptilian. Their skin was the color of wet concrete, just about to turn solid. Yet, the concern and puzzlement etched on their expressions told me they were more like humans than not.

"Thank you," I said, remembering a moment later they couldn't understand. As expected, the one closest to me tilted its head again, confused about my words. None of these villagers were armed, nor did they show a fear that I would harm them.

Their clothes consisted of rough-spun wools with muted colors, a simple race as the Bots had declared. One of those standing further away was wearing white clothing. This was likely the person I had focused on when the Bots ordered me to burn them to death. She had been holding the hand of a young toddler. That sight, as much as anything, caused me to refrain from committing the murders. Did these people realize how close to death they had come? And now they were trying to provide solace to a person who had been a hair's breadth from ending their lives.

The others came closer now that I appeared somewhat normal. A few were smiling, possibly relieved I wasn't dead. Two of them held out their arms to lift me off the ground, and I accepted their offer. My muscles felt like water as I staggered to my feet with the two helping to keep my balance until I found my footing.

The Oakenrill had taught me how to use Elthea's power to enable the gift of translation, giving a user the ability to speak and hear another language. I pulled a small weave of energy and triggered the charm. "You have been kind, more than I deserve," I said.

Some of them opened their eyes wide or sucked in a quick breath, surprised they could now understand me. The person who first tried to revive me spoke first. "We thought you were in danger with the large individuals surrounding you, and then the sky erupted in fire. We came to offer our assistance."

They came to offer aid, yet carried no weapons or anything else to fight with except their bare hands. Despite that, they wanted to protect me against the Bots. "You should be more cautious. Those large creatures are dangerous. Stay away if you ever see them again."

My eyes watered again, thinking about the Bots and what they had done. What sort of advice was I giving? Stay away? The Nizaem race from long ago had tried that and look what happened to them.

The stranger before me saw the tears forming at the corners of my eyes. He motioned his arm toward the village in the valley. "Come with us. We will provide sustenance. I can see you are troubled and in need of fellowship."

I gazed at him sadly. "My hurts are too deep to heal. Not now anyway."

His mouth scrunched into what I believed was a frown. My heart warmed, seeing this unremarkable race so willing to offer kindness to a stranger they never met before. How many other similar races existed just like them, people worth protecting? I reacted to his offer by inclining my head in a bow. "You've already provided sustenance."

Looking around, I wondered where we were and how I would find my way back. I could move a rock a great distance from one place to another, but I was less confident that I could use Elthea's powers to perform the same skill on myself as the Bots had done. "Besides, I have somewhere to go right now," I added.

The individual before me imitated my gesture by also bowing. "Then I wish you safe travels, my friend." He stepped away, joining the other villagers. As he reached them, he turned around to look at me again as if to be sure I wouldn't change my mind. Together as a group, they gazed at me for a time as if reluctant to leave me alone. Or maybe they were sorry they couldn't assist me.

Little did they realize, they provided everything I needed. Raising my hand, palm out, I said, "Stay safe."

I watched them reluctantly move away. They continued to cast furtive glances back as they ambled down the hill to their village on the other side of the valley. Only then did I realize I never learned the name of their race or anything else about them. I allowed Elthea's power to slip from my body, ending the translation charm.

Alone once more, I took a moment to consider what I should do next. I knew the answer. My destination was clear, the only place with the individuals who could help me find the solution I sought.

I might have failed this test, but as long as I remained alive, I wasn't giving up on my friends.

Summoning another strand of energy, I placed a shield on the village below and tied it off. This allowed the spell to remain functioning without action from me. The protection wouldn't stop the Bots from returning and harming these people, but their arrival would set off an alarm in my head, warning me of the danger. Maybe it would give me enough time to intervene so I could repay their kindness.

I looked at the sky, knowing my next step. Drawing another small thread of power, I broadcast the call.

A dragon would come, I felt sure of it. The Skrill provided the speed I needed. The lives of Cassie, Matt, and Diane rested with me. I alone could bring them back from the horror inflicted by the Bots.

The only hope I had, their only hope, was for me to uncover the secrets of the Bots during an earlier time in their existence. How did they turn into demons, and what do we really know about them?

I needed answers. And then I would make the monsters pay.

AUTHOR'S NOTE

Thank you for reading my work.

If you enjoyed this book, please take a moment now to write a brief review on the retail site where you purchased it. Leaving a review is a great way to thank an author, and your rating and comments make a tremendous difference. Help spread the word.

Want to keep up with news about future books and special offers? Sign-up at www.johnmurzycki.com. I will never share your email address, and you can unsubscribe at any time.

I also appreciate hearing from you directly. Use the contact form on my website, or email me at john@johnmurzycki.com.

NEXT IN THE SERIES: ELTHEA'S NEMESIS

Enjoyed Elthea's Paradox?

Elthea's Nemesis, Book Four in The Story of Elthea's Realm series, is now available in paperback, hardcover, and ebook wherever you purchase books.

She once unleashed an evil foe into the world; now she must confront her dark past.

Follow Tess Armstrong, who once created the wicked Bots, as she embarks on a journey back in time. Together with Philip Matherson, they search for clues to finally end the Bots' reign of terror. The stakes couldn't be higher, as Philip's closest friends and the world hang in the balance. With the showdown between good and evil approaching, will the potent elixir of friendship, love, and redemption be enough to triumph over insurmountable odds? Find out in this tale of unyielding determination and unwavering hope.

Not long ago, I spent my days crafting messages for organizations ranging from international brands to technology startups. I decided the time had finally come to pen a story I could call my own. After leaving the corporate world in my role as high-tech marketing and sales manager, I concentrated on my true love of writing fiction.

I write about magical places that have roots in the technology of our world. My characters are unlikely heroes who struggle with frailties and imperfections as they face evil forces. I am currently writing the next book in *The Story of Elthea's Realm* series.

I make my home in Massachusetts. To learn more about me,

visit my website at johnmurzycki.com and subscribe to my newsletter, where I will periodically ramble about bookish topics.

Connect with John:

Website: https://johnmurzycki.com
Email: john@johnmurzycki.com

Follow me on Social:

facebook.com/author.johnmurzycki

linkedin.com/in/johnmurzycki

goodreads.com/johnmurz

bookbub.com/profile/john-murzycki

amazon.com/gp/product/B08PZ7LG95

ACKNOWLEDGMENTS

I owe a great deal of gratitude to the Wrentham Writer's Group for all their assistance. The members were always willing to review this book a chapter at a time and provide me with invaluable feedback. I am grateful for all their help.

Thank you to the following members of the group. You are all fantastic writers, and I wish you great success. Marjorie Turner Hollman, author of *Easy Walks in Massachusetts* series of books and her latest *Finding Easy Walks Wherever You Are*, consistently contributed valuable advice. Her comments and edits were always helpful and thorough. Richard Rook, the author of *Tiernan's Wake*, never failed to provide feedback and encouragement on the plot and grammatical direction. Grace Allen, a local newspaper reporter, consistently identified improvements in my drafts. Heather Swalls-McCarron, another local reporter, provided advice and showed the rest of us examples of excellent writing with her poems and short stories. Diane Glass, Devon Lucas, and Anne Parker were each outstanding in their support and recommendations.

The very talented Audra Cohen Murzycki edited the manuscript. She delivered an outstanding critique, which has helped me greatly. We share a last name because of her marriage to my cousin, but her expertise as editor originates from her past occupation at a trade publication.

Paul Silva of Paul Silva Design developed the cover illustration and art. As always, great job.

I am indebted to you all.

A SCENE FROM THE ELTHEA'S NEMESIS

BOOK FOUR IN THE STORY OF ELTHEA'S REALM SERIES

I stood on a balcony, gazing out at the partially destroyed village of Haven. A line of rubble and boulders surrounded the town—the remnants of a once mighty wall that the Bots had shattered in seconds. The purpose of the attack had been to capture me; to claim me as one of their servants. But the Nizaem leader, Teivel, had saved me. With me by his side, he believed he could become a demigod, stronger than the Bots.

That was a role I wasn't willing to play. And still won't.

An army of giants now sifted through the wreckage of the fallen wall. They had already restored a few sections to their past grandeur. "The Stonewraiths are remarkable, are they not?" said Ja'Krill, who had approached so quietly I did not hear his footsteps.

I cocked an eye at him. "They're working with stone, my friend. Have you forgotten your roots as a woodland race? I seem to recall you disliking everything about this place with its cheerless rock."

He smirked. "Torermak has been showing me the astonishing skill his people have in fashioning stone, actually molding it in their hands. It is quite remarkable. You should—"

I held up my hand to forestall him. "Yes, I've seen." Gripping his shoulder, I added, "I admire how you are open-minded and curious about everything. You stood by me even when the rest of your race, even your Queen, considered me a threat to your Sacred Forest and wanted me executed. If there were more people like you, maybe we'd all be better off with races working together."

"Even the Bots?"

They were our one common enemy, reeking of hatred. "Even with them, maybe there's a way."

He raised an eyebrow as he studied me. "You've changed. I can see it in you since you returned."

I frowned. "How so?"

Ja'Krill shrugged. "It seems you are more contemplative, more aware of your thoughts and actions; the precision in your movements. And I can sense a new inner strength within you. There's more to you than we realize."

My attention dwelled on the Stonewraiths working to rebuild the fortress. At this rate, they would have the entire wall completed in a few months. Using my new powers, could I complete the task in a fraction of that time? Probably, but that was not my charge. Lives were depending upon me. "The Oakenrill taught me much. But all his training couldn't help me understand the Bots any better."

We turned away from the balcony and entered the adjacent room in the commander's residence. This space was one of his larger meeting chambers, with its colorful tapestries adorning the area. The rough stone walls and heavy wooden beams in the ceiling lent an air of permanence to the place, while an abundance of floor-to-ceiling open-air windows made it seem spacious. Even so, the room was small compared to a typical function hall on Earth. Governing Haven did not require the trappings of opulence. Russell was the commander, not the king, and his rule depended on administration as much as anything else.

The group who had greeted me on the street had already assembled here at Russell's urging. This wasn't something I had expected when I hatched my plan and summoned the Skrill to take me here. I had thought I would speak with only Tess, with possibly Russell and Alan—not this entire crew. "You seem nervous," said Ja'Krill, still at my side.

I eyed him again, noting that I should add him to the list of those who seemed to know me better than I did myself. "Nervous?" I shrugged. "Perhaps, but not for the reason you might suspect." I took a deep breath. "What I find out here will decide the fate of Cassie, Matt, and Diane. I don't want to discover this is a dead end. Also, I'd rather not have everyone else in on it."

He also gazed at the assembled crowd inside. "You can send them away if you wish, but they are all on your side, Earthfriend. Everyone wants to help."

I nodded. "Of course you're right. Problem is, nobody else can. Whatever I discover, this is on my shoulders."

For better or worse, I somehow knew my battle against

the Bots would come down to me alone. The Oakenrill had trained me well. But just as in life, some questions have no answers.

What would I do then?

www.ingramcontent.com/pod-product-compliance
Lightning Source LLC
Chambersburg PA
CBHW051201190726
48288CB00006B/1753